I had no idea where I was going. Primal instincts had taken over. Thoughts clamoured for attention but I kept them at bay because I knew they would only make the picture blacker and I was committed to the only route open. . .

A spasm doubled me over the wheel. Through the snow a battery of blue and yellow and white lights were spinning. In the first petrified moment I assumed it was a road block and jammed my foot on the brake, not realising how powerful they were, locking the wheels in the slush. The truck drifted sideways and for a suspension of time I was sure I had lost it. . .

Now I could see the obstruction and it wasn't a road block . . . A policeman in a fluorescent waistcoat was directing traffic around the crash . . . I stopped. I couldn't help it. If the Skoda was one of the vehicles, my nightmare would be over.

'I think I know who was in the other car.'

'Pull in over there. I'll send someone to take a statement.'

I skirted the pile-up, weighing up the odds of justice falling on my side, but there were too many indeterminates for me to establish which way the scales would tilt. Any evidence linking the thugs to the murder had almost certainly been destroyed, while I was driving along with a whole case of prosecutor's exhibits. In the mirror I saw the policeman with his back to me. The lights were falling away. I was past and my last chance had gone. A great sense of detachment came over me.

I was on the highroad to hell.

Windsor Chorlton was born in the north of England and worked for an international publisher before taking up full-time writing. He is the author of two previous acclaimed thrillers and lives in Dorset.

By the same author

Rites of Sacrifice
Canceleer

BLIND JUNCTION

Windsor Chorlton

ORION

To Deborah

An Orion paperback
First published in Great Britain by Orion in 1994
This paperback edition published in 1996 by Orion Books Ltd,
Orion House, 5 Upper St Martin's Lane, London WC2H 9EA

Second impression 1996

A CIP catalogue record for this book is available from the
British Library.

ISBN 0 75280 080 9

Typeset by Deltatype Ltd, Ellesmere Port, Cheshire
Printed and bound in Great Britain by
Clays Ltd, St Ives plc

I

It was New Year's Eve and the country was shutting down.

From behind the service station's plated windows I watched the motorway traffic performing its low trajectory over the bridge. The procession moved sluggishly, more like a refugee army than a holiday exodus. The sky beyond was the colour of old tyres, and it had been that way for weeks – a perpetual overcast that had lasted so long that by now it seemed permanent, a climatic manifestation of the national pysche. But change was on the way. At intervals an announcer interrupted the sense-depriving music to bring warnings of blizzard conditions by midnight.

It was a bad night to be travelling, I knew that. It was a night for the fireside and Auld Lang Syne, a night to bid good riddance to the miseries of the past year and raise a glass to tomorrow. It was a night, I thought, looking again at the photograph, to be with the woman of your dreams.

I'd promised to call her at four, and it was already twenty-past. In the lobby the gaming machines flickered restlessly to themselves. The row of phone booths was vacant. I paced outside them, rehearsing what to say. 'It's Matthew Reason. I'm on my way. I thought I'd better call in case you wondered if . . .'

I whirled in frustration. What pulled me back was the fundamental issue of self-recognition. I didn't believe in

Matthew Reason, and neither would she. I was inhabiting an identity that was no longer plausible.

I found myself in the empty washroom, peering into the mirror for guidance. 'Tall, dark and athletically built,' is how I'd described myself, which is true so far as it goes. I'm over six feet tall, fairly slim but with rower's shoulders and a high-bridged nose that was broken by my sister when she was six and I was ten. I'm grateful for that childhood fracture; it redeems my face from . . . not weakness, exactly, but a certain emotional susceptibility. In the unconsoling light I looked much alone.

I glanced again at the photo, then tentatively, as if trying to touch an apparition, I put a hand to my face. 'I'm Hugh Travers,' I whispered, and this time the silence absorbed the claim.

Before doubts could rout me again, I returned to the booth, fumbled change from my coat and shoved it into the machine. Waiting for the connection, I watched the traffic crawl west in the leaden twilight. On the wall a severe weather warning urged motorists to stay at home unless their journey was necessary. My nerves shuddered.

The phone went live. I shut my eyes. 'I'm Matthew Reason,' I said, my voice barely audible.

'I was hoping it might be you.' The quiet gravity of her voice matching my own.

There was rapport there, a vibrant intimacy that made me tingle. I cleared my throat. 'I'm sorry I didn't call earlier. My business in London took longer than I expected.'

'How did it go?'

'Very well.'

'Dealing in rare maps sounds fascinating. I look forward to hearing all about it.'

I was sure she must be able to hear the pounding of my heart. 'Does that mean tomorrow's still on?'

'I can't deny I'm nervous,' she admitted, 'but if you can face it . . . ' her voice grew firm ' . . .then yes, I still want to meet you.'

I felt as if I'd driven fast over a steep crest. 'I'm calling from a service station on the other side of the river. I thought I'd drive down tonight and beat the weather.'

'Take care. The forecast's atrocious. I was supposed to see the New Year in with friends, but I've decided that I'm not moving from in front of the fire.'

I pictured her in firelight, curled like a cat. I didn't have her address. All I knew was that she lived what she called a life of 'contemplative obscurity' alone in a cottage somewhere on the Gower.

'Can I ask you something?'

'Please.'

'Did you receive many replies?'

She laughed, a little embarrassed. 'More than I expected. I was surprised.'

'I'm not.' I thought my chest would burst. 'Why did you choose me?'

'Oh God,' she said, and drew breath. 'Well, the others seemed to have either very complicated or very boring lives – or, in some cases, wives. I don't know – you sounded interesting. Also, I have to admit it, you looked attractive.' Another breathy laugh. 'Your turn.'

The sense of her was so intense that I trembled. 'I . . . I . . . . can't put it into words. When I read your letter, I knew we were made for each other.'

'Matthew, please. Don't get carried away.'

'I'm quaking. I've never done this kind of thing before.'

'Nor me. Isn't it awful? I mean, getting together through a computer. It's such an admission of failure.'

'No it isn't. It's the first positive step I've taken in years.' I hesitated. I wanted us to meet where we could be alone, where we could talk without interference, but I couldn't expect her to take risks with a stranger. 'I was going to suggest we meet for a drink or lunch tomorrow and then go for a walk, but . . . '

'Lunch will do for a start. If our illusions survive that, we can try the walk next time.'

'Yes,' I said on a surge of elation. 'Yes, we can.'

We arranged the time and place and closed on formal farewells. 'Oh, by the way,' I added, 'I've shaved my beard since I sent that photo.'

'I'm sure I'll recognise you.' She laughed. 'You'll be my first foot – my tall dark stranger.' She hesitated. 'Matthew?'

My heart kicked.

'Yes?'

'It's been such a grisly year. I do hope the New Year will bring something good our way.'

Navigation lights pulsed on the bridge. 'It will,' I said, my heart brimming. 'Of that I'm sure.'

For a long time after I put the phone down I remained in the booth, drained by the enormity of my deception. The lies were painful, but necessary, and they had done the trick. Tomorrow we would be together. In less than twenty-four hours the circle would close.

I left the booth and present reality struck. At this critical juncture in my life, all I had was fifty pounds, the clothes I stood up in and the contents of an antique hide suitcase sporting BOAC and Cunard stickers. I could have used the money for coach fare, but I needed every penny for tomorrow. I would just have to try my luck on the open road.

Twilight had thickened into dark gusty night, and now I could smell the bitter threat of snow. Long coat flapping, I headed towards the stick figures silhouetted against the

4

blowsy lights of the fuel bays. On my left the lorry park was dead space under a sodium haze. My breath clouded. The cold penetrated. I loitered in the reek of petrol, assessing each vehicle and its occupants in turn. A husband with a reindeer motif on his sweater came out of the office clutching a couple of free tumblers. I gave him a miss.

An old Beetle decorated with life-affirming stickers drew up, crewed by a student couple. I waited until they had paid for their gallons of unleaded and were climbing back in before I approached.

'Excuse me, I'm trying to get to Swansea.'

'Can't help,' the girl said, without looking at me.

I'd noticed the Aberystwyth University sticker. 'Don't worry,' I assured them, 'I'm harmless. In fact, I used to be a lecturer at your university.'

The youth hesitated, half-in, half-out of the old banger, then turned to his girlfriend, who vetoed the proposition with a tiny but definitive shake of the head.

'Actually,' the boy said, shamefacedly backing into his seat, 'we're turning off at the next junction.'

Adopt a Whale, said the sticker on their departing rear screen.

Three more drivers gave me the brush-off with varying degrees of offhandedness. Another car pulled in. This one said that the occupants had seen the lions of Longleat, experienced the thrills of Alton Towers and supported the good works of the National Heart Foundation. I knew that their charity wouldn't extend to night-time travellers. They had the unassailable air of the British nuclear family; they made me think of tamper-proof supermarket goods.

After filling up, Mum and Dad and the two kids went into the office. I saw the keys dangling in the ignition and a rogue impulse flashed. One dash and I could be behind the wheel and away. Crazy, I told myself. There were tolls to pass. I wouldn't get a mile before they caught up with me. And yet the ultimate possibility of committing some outlaw act persisted, producing a shiver that had nothing to do with the cold.

God, but it was cold! I trudged towards the exit lane, the place of last resort. I eyed my thumb with distaste, then cocked it – a gesture which in my youth had been an affirmation of freedom, but which now marked me down as the lowest form of deadbeat.

Nobody was disposed to help me on my way. Several drivers shook their heads in what seemed more like warning than rejection. Frankly, I couldn't blame them. Only a pervert or someone afflicted with terminal loneliness would risk picking up a total stranger on New Year's Eve. I stood there, my suitcase at my feet, my teeth chattering. I jumped up and down on the spot and swung my arms against my chest.

By now I had charted every oil stain and crisp wrapper and cigarette butt within a twenty-foot radius. This forlorn spot had become the centre and compass of my world. Infirm of purpose I watched a fresh set of lights approach. As they slowed I offered my thumb, then abruptly withdrew it.

Two police officers – one male, one female – climbed out of the Range Rover.

'Good evening, sir,' the policeman said. 'Not having much luck, are we?'

'Disastrous.'

'Where are you making for?' he asked, his voice still pitched at the level of polite interrogation.

'Swansea. It's okay. Someone will take pity on me.'

'Oh yes?' he said, as if I had offered him a dazzling line of enquiry. He eyed my old suitcase.

The policewoman was skirting around me as if I was a

suspect packet. 'I wonder if we could see some identity.'

'I don't see why that should be necessary,' I said, friendly but firm.

'If you wouldn't mind,' she insisted, folding her arms.

'I do mind rather.'

She looked along her nose at me and gently punched one gloved palm with her fist. 'We've had complaints from the public.'

Too cold and demoralised to resist, I produced my driving licence. The policeman barely glanced at it before handing it to his colleague, who took it to the Range Rover. The radio began to squawk. They were running me through the computer.

The policewoman leaned out, her lips compressed, and called her partner over. I didn't have a criminal record, and yet I could feel the shadow from my past reaching over me. The letter and the photo were burning a hole in my pocket. The officers weren't looking. Stomach churning, I crammed the documents into the torn lining of my coat. The policeman turned and noticed the guilt staring out of my face. His eyes narrowed. 'Open your bag.'

'You have absolutely no right.'

He squared up to me. 'Come on, Mr Reason, make it easy on yourself.'

I stood back while he ransacked my case. The radio exchange had stopped. The policewoman was coming back.

'What's this?' the policeman demanded, lifting a cardboard tube.

'Be careful,' I said, starting forward. 'It's a map. It's very rare.'

He unrolled it and held it towards the light. 'It's nearly blank.' His frown intensified. 'Hey, this is Russian writing!'

'Because it's a Russian map.'

'Where did you get it?'

'A dealer. Pfizner's in Charing Cross.'

'How do you spell that?'

'P for policeman, F for fascist . . . Look, this is a waste of time.'

'What are you doing with it?'

'I deal in rare maps.'

'Oh yes,' the policeman said, smiling as if I had given him the breakthrough he was looking for. 'Business address?'

'I work from home.'

'And where would that be?'

Suddenly I couldn't muster the energy to keep up the pretence. What was the point? Guilt was written all over me –the guilt of poverty, the sour whiff of the DHSS office. I turned my head away.

'Where did you spend last night?' the policewoman demanded.

'Salisbury. With a friend.'

'Address?'

'I've forgotten.'

'And tonight?'

I hesitated. I hadn't got a clue where I would lay my head. 'Also with a friend.'

'Can you remember where *they* live?'

'Offhand, no.'

'Do you spend every night with friends?'

'At the moment,' I admitted, 'my existence is rather unsettled.'

'Empty your pockets.'

'What for?'

'Empty your fucking pockets.'

Their search was cursory, intimate in an impersonal way that set the seal on my humiliation. But at least they didn't find the letter and photo. The policewoman shoved my case towards me with her toe, then walked away to the Range

Rover. Dazed with shame, I repacked my belongings.

'On your way,' the policeman ordered.

With nothing left to lose, I resorted to beggary. 'Any chance of a lift, officer?'

He came right up to me, breathing hard. 'See out there?' he said, gesturing at the motorway. 'There'll be carnage tonight, and we're the poor sods who'll have to clean it up.' He prodded me in the chest. 'When we get back, I want you gone. Understand?'

'How?'

'I don't care,' he said, and pointed at the bridge. 'Once you're across the river, you're someone else's problem.'

I tramped the swaying footwalk suspended over the night. Lights whizzed past like atomic particles. Occasionally a motorist acknowledged me with a derisive hoot. The wind scourged me. On and on I walked, the river black beneath and the cables moaning above.

It took an hour to cross the river. Swansea 70 miles, the sign said. Right, I vowed, I'll walk it.

I kept going, no longer offering my thumb, my eyes on the hard shoulder, the landscape invisible. Someone hooted and blearily I looked up to see a car stopped ahead, hazard lights flashing. I gazed at it as a desert traveller contemplates a mirage, fearful that it would vanish at the first unconsidered move, and then I broke into a run.

The driver was leaning out of the window when I came panting up – a florid middle-income type who'd started his New Year binge back at the office.

'You bloody fool!' he shouted. 'What do you think you're doing? Get off the motorway before you cause an accident.'

My mouth went cottony with anger, but before I could even muster a response, his window shot up and he accelerated away, darting back into the stream. When I could no longer see his rear lights, I wiped the snail tracks from my eyes. 'You'll be sorry when you see my little red shoes,' I murmured.

Utterly beaten, I sat down where I was. The traffic pounded me with shock waves. I no longer saw it as humanly propelled. The drivers had lost control. They were mind-locked into the flow and couldn't stop even if they wanted to. In France, a motorist who had climbed out of his broken-down car had been run over in the fast lane, and no one had stopped. The cars had just kept coming, the thump-bang of the first collisions moderating to compliant tremors as the tyres reduced him to a smear of tissue and a hank of hair.

So it's come to this, I thought. No fixed abode, no job, no money, no place left to turn. And yet in a way, it was fitting that in this moment I should plumb the very bottom of my fortunes. I had suffered, and suffering had purged my conscience, and now fate had rewarded me and was turning the wheel upwards. I took out the photo again and gazed on her smiling face. All things eternal come round in a circle.

But first I had to reach her. Up ahead there was an emergency telephone. Woodenly I climbed to my feet and made for it. I picked up the phone and an operator asked which service I required. When I said motorway rescue, she wanted to know my membership number. I told her I'd lost my card. She checked and told me no one of my name was registered. I promised to join up if she sent help. She asked for vehicle type and registration. I admitted I had none.

'Then what is your request?'

'It's me. It's me who needs rescuing. I'm freezing to death.'

I heard her mutter something to a colleague, and when she addressed me again, her tone was dark with warning. 'You have no right to be there. There are genuine motorists in need of assistance. Please leave the motorway at once.'

'I can't. I'm stranded.'

'I'm passing this information on to the police. We know precisely where you are. Be assured of that.'

Brakes squealed behind me. I whirled to see a truck pulling in, pulling in right beside me. Airbrakes hissed. On the cab it said ARGONAUT HAULAGE, and above the sign was an illuminated Christmas tree.

'Trouble?' a serene Welsh voice said.

'Stuck. Any chance of a lift?'

The driver shook his head. 'Sorry, mate. I'm not insured for passengers.'

Desperation forced the lie. I gesticulated down the motorway. 'My car broke down.'

The driver craned round, frowning.

'About two miles back. The last telephone was out of order. Look, I've got to get to Swansea by nine.'

He hesitated, not entirely convinced, then swung open the door. 'Come on then.'

2

'I'm breaking at the next services,' the driver said after hearing my improvised tale of mechanical failure. 'They'll send a rescue truck.'

'No,' I said with too much emphasis. 'My own garage will pick it up.'

'By the time they get there, the police will have impounded it.'

'I'll have to risk it. I've got an important date with my girlfriend.' From the crease in the driver's brow, I saw that he wasn't comfortable with my story. I gave a sheepish laugh. 'Actually, it's our first date. I can't miss it.'

The driver wasn't impressed. 'I'm turning off at Port Talbot,' he said with finality. 'You'll soon pick up another ride.'

Fat chance. But for the next hour or so my life was taken care of, and at least I was heading in the right direction. Already the cold was a memory. I fought my way out of my coat and stowed it at my feet. I glanced at my saviour, wondering if he expected conversation. He was about my age and height, but black-bearded and much heavier, built like an ox. He was engrossed by the road, his eyes constantly monitoring the traffic for signs of danger. In his competent presence I was restored to solidarity with mankind. Now that I was part of the procession, I even shed my prejudices about driving. From our commanding height I admired the rearlights of our fellow travellers snaking into the distant darkness.

The driver programmed the radio to a local station. A disc jockey-cum-newscaster was rattling off a litany of the world's woes – religious riots in India, famine in China, the economy of the Pacific rim in a tailspin, a sex scandal in the Vatican. All over the world, systems were coming unstuck. Everything was negotiable.

'Where's it going to end?' the driver murmured.

'Weather?' the newscaster announced. 'Naaas-ty. Three above zero and dropping down, down, down. Snow before midnight, people, so take good care on the roads all you revellers. And remember,' he added, his voice assuming the gravity of a minister asking his flock to remember the fallen of both World Wars, 'if you're thinkin' of drinkin' . . . '

With a grunt the driver flicked him off. We drove on. The silence expanded, a vacuum demanding to be filled. I surveyed the cab. It was comprehensively equipped, boasting a bunk, mobile phone, television – even a sandwich toaster. 'All the home comforts,' I said. 'You could live in here.'

'I practically do,' the driver blurted, touched on the quick. He swung out intimidatingly close to a dawdling minibus. 'Listen, officially I'm on holiday. I only got back from a long haul yesterday. Swansea, Plymouth, Roscoff, Paris, Freiburg, Basle, Turin – 3,000 miles in ten days. This afternoon I'm still sleeping it off when someone starts banging on my door and I go down and there's Vaughan on the step, tearing his hair out. "Hello Vaughan," I say, "I thought you were off on holiday." "Not if I can't find a driver," he says. "There's a bloody priority load in the Bristol depot and every bugger's gone down with the flu." '

'Who's Vaughan?' I asked, stumbling to catch up.

'Fleet manager. He's all packed for two weeks in Jamaica.

His flight's leaving in six hours, but I'm the only driver fit for the road and the job can't wait because the day after tomorrow the Spanish fishermen are blockading the ports.'

'You're going to Spain?' For a moment, I wondered if I'd accidentally crossed the motorway and was heading in the wrong direction.

' "It's only Zaragoza," Vaughan says. "It's not as if it's the end of the earth." "Listen, boyo," I tell him, "while you were tucking into turkey and mince pies I was making do with a cheese roll in the truck park at Aosta. Now you expect me to spend New Year in transit while you swan off to the West Indies." '

I made a sympathetic murmur.

'And the thing is, look you,' the driver said, working himself up another notch, 'it's not as if it's a load of perishables, it it? No, it's only furniture.' He turned to me. 'What's so special about household effects that they can't wait until after the holiday?'

'I don't know.'

'Victor Style,' the driver declared. 'That's what.' He shot a glance at me, as if I was expected to know the name.

'He sounds,' I said cautiously, 'like a hairdresser.'

'Vic the Style? Jesus Christ and all his bloody angels, boyo.' With one hand the driver began to count off Victor Style's commercial attainments. 'Sportstyle, the chain of bookies. Leisurestyle, the time-share village at Mumbles. Lifestyle, that bloody great hypermarket on the Bridgend ring-road. That's who Vic Style is.'

I erased my mental picture of Vic Style the bouffant-haired Welsh lizard and substituted the image of a flabby Rotarian who wore camel-hair coats and drove a Jaguar XJ-S with a body-styling kit.

'One of Vic's top men is relocating to Spain and his wife refuses to budge unless all her knick-knacks are sent in advance. I ask you. Call Pickford's, I tell Vaughan. Call an independent. But he's raving on about it being a prestige job, and how if we do it right, Mr Style is going to put more work our way. I'm in no state to drive, I tell him. I'd be a menace to the public. The office is closed down. How can I do a European run without back-up? But Vaughan keeps on at me. "It's not as if you're married, is it? You haven't got a bloody family making demands on you." ' The driver's indignation mounted again. 'Just because I don't have a wife and kids doesn't mean I don't have a life of my own.'

'Completely unjust.'

'Vaughan puts me under the cosh. "Take the run," he says, "or you needn't bother showing your face after the break." He means it, too, but I know he's not going to find another driver at two hours' notice, and I know that if he has to cancel his holiday, his wife will bloody murder him. "Tell you what," I say, "special delivery, special rates – triple time and a couple of hundred spending money." Like a flash he's on the phone to Style, and he's back so quick I know I could have asked for as much again. "Here's the deal," he says. "A thousand quid, cash-in-hand, out of Style's own pocket, and you can stay on in Spain for a week, have some fun in the sun." ' The driver opened his palms. 'What could I say?'

'You got yourself a good deal.' A thousand pounds for a few days' work! For the last nine months I'd been trying to survive on less than forty quid a week.

The driver rummaged in his door pocket. 'I've got to pick up some paperwork from Style's house.' He pulled out an Ordinance Survey sheet and passed it to me. 'Look up Penygraig, will you? It's off Junction 41, on the B4287 about two miles out of Port Talbot.'

It took only a few seconds. 'Got it.'

'A mile outside there should be an unclassified road on the left.'

'Hang on. Yes.'

'Now follow that past a couple of farms, fork left and Style's place is at the end, down a private road.'

I couldn't pinpoint the house itself, but the directions made sense. 'It's a bit out of the way.'

'If I get lost, Style can guide me in.' The driver tapped a black box fixed to the roof. 'VLD,' he said, 'Vehicle Location Device. Supposed to be able to track me to within fifty yards. Brand new, too. One of Style's men asked for it to be fitted special.'

'He's gone to a lot of trouble.'

The driver eyed the unit as if its presence vexed him. 'Yeah, I thought it was a bit funny, too.'

Sleet splattered against the windows. 'Here it comes,' the driver said, setting the wipers in motion. 'At this rate, I'll be lucky to make the ferry.'

Liquid ice streamed across the windscreen and I thanked God I was safe from the elements.

'I take it Style's self-made.'

The driver shook his head in baffled admiration. 'There's enterprise, look you. His family were gyppos, lived in a railway carriage behind the steelworks. Danny his da was a horse dealer and scrappie, always in trouble with the police. His mam died when he was a baby. Vic never saw the inside of a school. All he knew was horses – used to ride in the gypsy races for Hywel Moses, a bookie who owned a lot of property down by the docks. Old Hywel sort of adopted Victor, took him on as a collector, and when the cancer got him, he left the lot to the kid. Vic wasn't more than eighteen, could hardly write his name, but by the time he was twenty he knew all about the betting and property game. Now they reckon he's worth twenty million.'

Once again I was forced to revise my image of Style. He was beginning to intrigue me. The man was a shifting target, always sliding out of range when I thought I'd got my sights on him. 'That doesn't sound like honest money,' I said.

The sleet packed against the wipers. 'I expect he trod on a few toes,' the driver said, peering forward. He mused for a moment, then uttered a short laugh. 'There was another bookie – Dewi John – owned a casino, the Ace of Clubs. A right evil bastard Dewi was – loaned you money at a thousand per cent and broke your hands if you didn't keep up the payments.'

The driver set the wipers to fast. 'So when Dewi heard a kid was taking over Hywel's business, he reckoned, right, I'll have that off him, no bother. He offered to buy Vic out for peanuts, and when Vic told him what to do with his money, he sent his boys to burn down one of Vic's betting shops. The next Saturday, three men walk into the Ace of Clubs carrying shotguns. Two of them grab hold of Dewi and the third pulls out a razor and cuts his face – not slash and run, look you.' The driver took one hand off the wheel and wrote a big V in the air. 'Victor couldn't write, but he knew how his name was spelt.'

'Good lord!'

'Gypsies, you see. No one knows who they are, no one knows where they live. Victor brought them in special.' The driver blinked his lights at an overtaking coach. 'Never cross the travelling people, my friend.'

'How to get ahead in business.'

'Hey, Dewi was filth. Vic was looking after his interests, same as I would have, and after Dewi was out of the way there was no more rough stuff. He tarted up Hywel's slum properties, turned them into a dockland village. Same with the betting shops. He put decent skirts in them and coffee machines, installed satellite telly for the big events. He bought a caravan park and added amenities – swimming pool, go-kart track, kiddie centre. Other people were doing the same, but Vic always went that bit better.' The driver turned to me. 'He knows what people want, you see.'

'The golden touch.'

'In the end, Wales wasn't big enough for him. He went to America – Miami. He was away ten years, got into the time-share business, married an American girl. They came back only a couple of years ago.'

'Why?'

'Well, it wasn't for the rugby, was it?' The squall had passed over and the wipers squeaked on the glass. The driver switched them off. 'No, he'd picked up a few ideas and I suppose he wanted to try them out over here. Take his new supermarket. It's got the lot – restaurants, gym, beauty salon. An integrated entertainment experience, the adverts call it. Also, I reckon he got homesick. That's the gypsy in him, look you. He still sees the travellers, you know. Goes to the horse fairs.'

I felt humbled by such conspicuous achievement. 'He sounds like an interesting man.'

'He is that,' the driver said, distracted by the erratic lane discipline of the vehicle ahead. 'I'm looking forward to meeting him.'

'Oh,' I said, 'I thought you knew him.'

'Only by reputation. This is the first job he's put Argonaut's way.' The driver suddenly turned on me. 'You,' he said. 'What do you do for a living?'

I contorted in my seat. 'I deal in maps.'

The driver edged a smile. 'Maps, is it? Well, no chance of *you* getting lost.'

3

Lulled by the engine note, I drifted into a half-doze. We were bypassing Cardiff and the traffic was bunched, the pattern so static that I had the sensation that all forward motion had ceased. We seemed to be linked in common purpose, yet the faces behind the headlights were blank with solitude, capsuled in their own thoughts. Drifting souls.

Now the space on each side of the road was dark and empty. A wild impulse entered my mind. I stole a look at the driver. In the light of the dials he was only a shadow. I didn't even know his name, and in half an hour we would go our separate ways.

'Something extraordinary has happened to me.'

The driver grew still and didn't speak.

'Do you believe in coincidence?' I asked. 'Fate?'

He shrugged. 'I've seen some pretty funny things on the road.'

'I used to think the world was just a haphazard arrangement of atoms, but now . . .' My breath shuddered. 'My name is Reason. It isn't the name I was born with. Until four years ago I was Hugh Travers.'

'Oh yes?' the driver said indifferently.

'I changed my name to cut myself off from the past.' Calmly I watched the road. 'Four years ago my life fell apart.'

The driver's doubts about me crystallised into accusation. 'Listen, before you go giving me any old sob story, what about this car you say broke down on you? That was a load of bollocks, wasn't it?' With one up-and-down glance he stripped away my pretensions. 'You're on the rocks, boyo.'

'Yes,' I admitted. 'She cost me the lot.'

'*She?*'

'A woman. One of my students.'

The driver took both eyes off the road to appraise me. 'Student, is it? There's fancy.'

Now that sex had hooked his attention, I didn't know where to start. I wasn't going to inflict my life story on him, but even though my background was unremarkable, my ruination could only be understood in the wider context. My parents were – still are – solid, conservative working class. I was the first Travers to go to university, and they were enormously proud when I was awarded a junior lectureship. They were just as thrilled when I married Angela, and part of their delight stemmed from the fact that Angela was a couple of rungs up the social ladder – a solicitor's daughter. So you can imagine my parents' shock, my father's unforgiving devastation, when my career and marriage collapsed in disgrace.

'What about this student?'

I took a breath and began.

'Until four years ago I was a history lecturer in the Classics department at Aberystwyth. My wife taught there, too – business studies. I'd met Angela at university and we got married a month after we graduated. Neither of us had much experience of the world. We both had a lot of growing up to do.'

The driver grunted.

'We were happy enough in a passive way – content that we always knew what tomorrow would bring.'

A connection side-tracked me. Epicurus, one of the philosophers I had studied, used the metaphor of the garden as a refuge from the anxieties of the world. Thinking about it now, I realised that our marriage had been like that – an orderly plot in the thorny jungle of human relations.

'But I suppose we both felt something was lacking.'

'Sex life not so hot, eh?'

'When Angela got pregnant, it brought us close in a way we'd never been before. I think we hoped the baby would give our relationship the excitement we didn't get from each other.' I overrode a pang. 'It was a girl and she was born with a fatal heart condition. She lived for only two days. We put a brave face on it. Life resumed, and on the surface nothing had changed. We never talked about the baby. We hadn't named her, you see. We'd decided not to know the sex of the baby, so we hadn't settled on a name, and then when we learnt that . . . well, I suppose we thought that by not acknowledging her as a person, it would make it more bearable if she didn't survive. That was a bad mistake.'

My voice trailed off. You can't talk about someone who doesn't have a name, but the baby existed all right – a dark core of silence that grew and grew until. . . Oh, what does it matter? Our marriage had become a place of weeds and gravestones.

'You got married too young,' the driver said.

I sat straight. 'Yes. There we were. Twenty-four years old, no longer in love, and the rest of our lives stretching in front of us.'

The driver sent me a shrewd look. 'And then you met this student.'

I'd never told anyone else and the prospect made me thick-tongued. 'Her name was Eleanor Barry and she was a second-year politics student. She was about four years younger than me.'

The driver pursed his lips. 'Welsh girl, was she?'

'To the point of caricature. Eleanor was a coal miner's daughter from Tredegar, and she was radical from her spiky hair to her unvarnished fingertips.' My tongue had loosened up. 'You name it – Class War, Sons of Glendower, Animal Liberation Movement – she was a paid-up activist.'

'Lesbian?' the driver said, sharp and to the point.

'No,' I said, taken aback. 'That was about the only thing she wasn't.'

The driver gave the steering wheel an unnecessary turn. 'Doesn't sound like your type.'

'That was part of the attraction.' It was hard to put into words. 'Eleanor Barry represented a world I'd never known –a world where emotion is the main currency.'

'Hot and sexy, you mean.'

'I found her very attractive.'

Even to myself I couldn't describe the effect Eleanor Barry had on me. When I thought about her, when I imagined being with her, it was . . . as if my heart was being wrenched in two.

'I was obsessed with her, infatuated to the point of insanity.' I hesitated, then made the next admission in a rush. 'I mean, I really did do crazy things. Once I followed her home and stood for an hour in the dark, staring up at her window.'

The driver looked at me obliquely. 'You could get into trouble for that.'

'I know.'

'Why didn't you just ask her out?'

I made a feeble gesture with my hands. 'I was married. I didn't want to betray Angela.'

'Christ, boyo, when did that stop anybody?'

'Well, in the event I never got the chance.'

Sensing the moment of revelation was close, the driver stayed quiet.

'Eleanor had submitted an essay. It was weeks late and I expected it to be terrible – full of the half-baked radical opinions she used to trot out in tutorials.' I blinked in surprise. 'But it was excellent. I was so pleased I sent her a note asking her to see me.' I turned to the driver. 'Believe me, I had no ulterior motive.'

The driver snorted.

Under the weight of memory, I closed my eyes. 'It was a very hot evening in early June. A thunderstorm was building up. Eleanor Barry came to my office wearing a tee-shirt with some political slogan on it . . .'

I checked myself, realising that the only significance of the tee-shirt was the fact that she'd been wearing nothing underneath and I could see the small thrust of her nipples. Every detail remained imprinted – the delicate features under the jagged crop of hair, the mocking hazel eyes, the film of sweat on her temples. Sitting beside her was like being trapped in a dangerous electric field. The essay had been on the influence of stoicism on Roman political thought, and the more I rambled on, the more confused and inarticulate I became.

I shuddered – a convulsive reflex of the moment when my hand had brushed Eleanor Barry's.

'Yeah?' the driver said.

'Our hands touched. When I dared look at her, she was smiling and frowning at the same time. We kissed.' I stared into the headlights of an approaching car. 'The next thing we were on the floor. We made love.'

The driver laughed coarsely. 'And then your wife walked in.'

I rubbed the glare from my eyes. 'Two days later Eleanor Barry went to the police.'

With infinite deliberation, and after many glances, the driver said: 'You raped her.'

'No,' I cried, stung into unintended passion, 'I didn't. That's what she alleged, but the police decided there wasn't enough evidence to make a case.'

The driver sucked air through his teeth. 'You were bloody lucky, boyo. Bloody lucky.'

My fingers were locked on the dash. 'There were inconsistencies in her story. She had bruises on her face and neck which she claimed I'd inflicted, but friends who'd seen her later that evening said her face had been unmarked and that . . . ' I stared at my clenched knuckles ' . . . she didn't appear upset.'

'So why did she point the finger at you?'

'I don't know. I honestly don't know. I'd give anything to find out.'

'Face it,' the driver said with sudden anger: 'I'm only hearing your side of the story.'

I wasn't trying to prove my innocence. This wasn't a plea or a justification. 'Well, I didn't get off. When word of what happened spread, the students organised a campus-wide protest. My lectures were boycotted and my office was picketed and sprayed with threatening slogans. They were determined to have my blood.'

'And did they get it?'

'Oh yes. My position at the university was impossible. The chancellor interviewed me, asked if I had sex with Eleanor Barry, and when I admitted it, demanded my resignation or face dismissal for sexually harassing one of my students.'

'That's the way it goes.'

'Angela . . . my wife . . . ' My stomach contracted around the memory of her hysterics, her even more frightening silence. 'She took it very badly. Rape or no rape, I'd been unfaithful and every soul at the university knew. Imagine how that made her feel. She left me and went back to her parents. Next day, her father phoned to say she was starting divorce proceedings. Although I tried for some kind of reconciliation, she's never seen me or spoken to me from that day to this.'

'You both sound well out of it.'

'The last I heard, she was running a successful business. As for me . . . ' I laughed, still capable of astonishment at the speed with which my foundations had crumbled. 'My academic career was finished. No university would employ a teacher who couldn't keep his hands off his students. I looked elsewhere for work, but jobs weren't forthcoming.'

'Come on – an educated bloke like you?'

'An imperfect knowledge of Roman thought isn't a particularly marketable commodity. The recession was beginning to bite, and after the umpteenth rejection, I decided to start my own business – dealing in rare maps. I'd been an amateur collector for years. At an auction I met a charming Hungarian who offered to introduce me to one of his German clients. We arranged to meet in the client's hotel suite.' I shrugged. 'You can guess the rest. I went to the bathroom. I was only out of the room for a minute, but when I came back, the Hungarian and the German had gone, together with my collection.' I smiled. 'I told you I had a lot of growing up to do.'

The engine note hardened as the driver accelerated. He wasn't sure where the narrative line was leading. Maybe he thought I was after money.

'So it was back to the drawing board,' I continued. 'The divorce settlement had wiped me out. A job was a necessity, but I had to set my sights low. To date, the high point of my work experience has been eighteen months teaching the rudiments of literacy to prisoners in Salisbury Jail. I must say, that broadened my horizons considerably. The post was cut nine months ago and I've been unemployed since.' I sensed that we were getting close to the dropping-off point. 'So that's it,' I concluded. 'The decline, fall and extinction of Hugh Travers.'

'You know your trouble?' the driver said. 'You live in the past. You've got to look forward.'

'You're right. That's what I'm doing. That's why it's so important that I don't miss my date in Swansea.'

The driver settled into a period of reflection. I took out the photograph and the letter. I could only read odd lines by the fleeting headlights. *Since losing my job, I have struggled to find my identity; I'm angry with myself for . . .*

'That her?' the driver asked.

'She's a television researcher. Ex-television researcher. Another casualty of the recession. Actually,' I admitted, 'it's a blind date. We met through a graduates' contact club.'

The driver took a squint at the photo. 'Tidy. You can never tell, though. This mate of mine met a bird through one of them telephone dating lines. Gruesome, it was. The lady was definitely mental and she had something wrong with her leg. False, my mate reckoned.'

'Oh, this woman's all in one piece and the computer has established our compatibility beyond scientific doubt. We've corresponded. We've spoken on the phone.'

'Don't be soft. It's like when you advertise a car. Immaculate, you say, perfect condition – even though you know it's a complete lemon.'

'She's been candid about herself. She's lost her job, been disappointed over a man, feels isolated.' I glanced again at the letter. *For the moment my dreams have failed me.*

The driver sent me a dark look. 'But does *she* know what she's letting herself in for? Like, I bet you haven't told her about that business with the student.'

'There's no point in hiding anything.'

The driver smiled thinly. 'An unemployed rapist. That

should go down nicely.' He flicked on the turn indicator. A sign warned that the services were coming up.

Heart beating, I turned to the last page of the letter. The compulsion to share my secret was overwhelming. 'Look,' I said. 'The signature.'

But the driver was busy checking the mirror to see that nothing was trapped in his blind spot. No, I decided, it was better if he didn't know. The truck canted on to the sliproad and I braced myself against the door. Light slid over the handwriting and there it was – a coincidence so perfect I could only interpret it as destiny.

Sincerely looking forward to your call,
Eleanor Barry.

4

Pressure bled off the brakes with a pneumatic sigh. I breathed out with it, then stayed facing ahead across the lorry park. Cold auras hung around the sodium lamps. The driver yawned.

Reluctantly I reached for the door handle. 'Thanks for your kindness.'

'It helped pass the time.' The driver took a leather jacket and an executive briefcase from the bunk, pushed open his door, then hesitated, coming to a decision. 'All right, I suppose I can take you as far as the turn-off.' He climbed down and looked up at me. 'I'll be about half an hour. The rig's alarmed, so don't try getting out.' He gestured at the bunk. 'Watch a video if you want.' He winked. 'It'll put you in the mood.'

Limp with gratitude, I watched him saunter across the tarmac. Not much milk of human kindness had come my way these last few months.

I settled back. No other vehicles were in the lorry park. Against the distant lights of the service station, people moved like figures on a television screen. I wished myself far away, back by the river that ran through the country of my childhood. At night, lying half-awake, listening to the river's drowsy murmur, I would plot its downstream course, pool by pool until the current slid between a dark arch of trees. It was there that my real journey began, for beyond the wood I didn't know the way except from maps. And when even they ran out, imagination took over, carrying me down into the sea of sleep.

It was the river that gave me my passion for maps. I have no wish to scale lofty peaks or cross wild horizons. For me, the landscape of infinite possibilities exists only on paper.

A yawn cut through my reverie. It had been an exhausting day and I still didn't know where I'd be spending the night. Wearily I pulled myself into the bunk and stretched out on my back.

At this precise moment, Eleanor Barry was no more than twenty miles away. Flesh and blood. She would be looking into the fire, perhaps conjuring my image in the flames. She would be wondering what to wear, practising her conversation, editing her life. She would be excited, and she would be apprehensive.

'A life of contemplative obscurity'. That was a phrase she'd picked up from one of my lectures. And yet she hadn't recognised me from my photograph. With a little jolt, I realised she'd forgotten my existence. After what I'd gone through, that was a bitter pill to swallow. But I got it down. She *had* to erase my memory; it was the only way she could live with her lie.

Practical problems jarred. As soon as it dawned on her who the computer had picked as her ideal partner, she'd scream or run, imagining that I'd sought her out for revenge. But retribution wasn't in my mind. Oh, I admit that in the aftermath of my humiliation, all kinds of violent thoughts had swirled through me. But I had lived through that, and though I was still plagued by the question of why she'd revoked her consent, it was love that drove me.

Fate had given me a second chance, and I was determined not to miss it. I was sure that for Eleanor, too, our extraordinary reunion would mark the start of a new fulfilment. Life hadn't gone all her way since she left university. 'My dreams have failed me,' I repeated, and then, torn by tenderness, I placed her photograph to my lips.

In the first dislocated moment of waking I thought that the beeping phone was the burglar alarm. I lay rigid, like an intruder caught in the act, until it stopped. With ponderous effort I lifted my wrist to eye level and saw that I'd been asleep for twenty minutes.

The lorry park was still empty. Larval shapes moved in the remote glow of the services. A few flakes of snow spun down like wood ash.

A cone of light wavered across the park. A car had appeared on the far side, following the perimeter. As its single functioning headlight groped towards me, I shrank back, thinking that it might be an unmarked patrol car. Slowly it came past, definitely prowling, its exhaust note deep and uneven. But it wasn't a police car. It was a downmarket East European import and it had a red plastic nose on its front that made it look like an unpleasant joke. In the sodium light its colour was anyone's guess, the matt paintwork absorbing the light and giving none back, so that the car was a leaden absence of colour, like a piece of darkness given form. And the menacing impression was heightened by smoked windows that made it look as though there was no one behind the wheel.

Joyriders, I told myself, as the car began another circuit –though for tearaways they were driving with remarkable restraint. I glanced at the far-off services, not exactly worried, but conscious that a cry for help would go unheard. The car was heading towards me again. Mild unease tightened into concern as it glided to a halt twenty yards from the truck. Its light dimmed and now I could make out behind the semi-opaque screen two faces, two white smears.

Nothing happened for several seconds, then both doors opened simultaneously and two men got out. They were bundled up against the cold and I could only infer that they were young, working-class and of a violent disposition. I twitched the curtain shut, but not before I saw that one of them was walking straight towards the cab while the other had detoured around the back. I heard a series of thumps as he slapped the side, then another bang right at the rear. A moment later the other man tried the driver's door and the cab tilted as he jumped on to the step. I could feel him peering in.

My mouth had gone dry. If I'd known at the start that they were planning to break in, I would have shown myself, scared them off, but now that they were right on top of me I was as paralysed as a rabbit cornered by a stoat.

The cab rebounded, relieved of the intruder's weight. I braced myself for the crash of breaking glass. Instead I heard muffled voices followed by the slamming of doors and the engine starting up. The burbling exhaust grew fainter. Light planed across the cab. Parting the curtains I saw a fuel tanker in stainless steel articulating towards me, shadows sliding over its flanks. The car was on its way out of the park, its brake lights brightening as it slowed at the exit.

The tanker backed alongside like a friendly dinosaur. My first impulse was to go in search of my driver, and then I remembered that I couldn't open the doors without setting off the alarm. Leave it, I told myself. No damage had been done. They were just opportunist thieves who'd been scared off.

My eyes grew heavy again.

Next thing I knew, the driver was storming into the cab, shivering and beating at his jacket. Groggily I saw that it was

31

snowing. Real snow, this time, slanting and whirling in the headlights. The driver seemed to have forgotten I was there. He stripped off his jacket, tossed it behind him, fired up the engine and released the clutch with a jerk. Seeing he wasn't in any mood for distraction, I kept quiet, and by the time we were back on the motorway, there didn't seem any point in mentioning the visitors.

'Someone called while you were away,' I told him.

He grunted, his attention on the road. Although the carriageway had been freshly gritted and was still clear, the verges were already white.

'Style must be worried that you won't be able to reach the house. Some of those minor roads were pretty steep.'

'I never asked for this run, did I?' the driver snapped, angry with himself for letting the weather catch him out. 'Only a lunatic would send a load out on a night like this.'

The snow was blowing straight at us and it was like driving into a white vortex. Visibility couldn't have been more than fifty yards. I held on to the edge of the bunk, apprehensive about the prospect of running into the back of another vehicle. But the minutes went by and gradually my fear of collision was replaced by dreary anticipation of the moment when I would be deposited back on the roadside.

'What do you think of my video collection?'

'Oh, I didn't see . . . I fell asleep.'

'Pity. You missed something special.'

The snow showed no sign of letting up. I was wondering how I was going to complete my journey. 'How far to the turn-off?'

'Fifteen minutes.'

'And how far from there to Swansea?'

'Five, six miles. Come on, get out of there.'

It took a moment to realise the driver didn't mean me.

'Some fool using me as a snow plough,' he explained.

'Silly bugger's right up my arse.' He shook his head at the other driver's lack of road sense. 'Some of the things you see. Incredible.' He opened his window and waved to show it was safe to pass. The icy slipstream fluttered the curtains.

I craned to look in the mirror, but the glass was dark.

'Probably pissed,' the driver said. He tooted his horn.

'Who is it?' I asked, a bad feeling starting inside me.

'A one-eyed joker,' the driver said, and dabbed on the brake. He laughed. 'That's shifted him.'

A glare filled the offside mirror. A black shape nosed out of the snow.

'Skoda special,' the driver said in derision. 'I bet they're from up Ogmore way. I tell you, those boys have got webbed feet.'

The Skoda didn't draw away. The nearside window opened and a hand stuck out, jabbing towards the rear of the truck. The driver peered into the rearview. 'Must be a flat.' He gave the wheel an experimental turn. 'Funny – feels okay.' He heaved a sigh and applied the brakes.

'I don't think you should stop.' Even though I'd left it too late, I had to warn him.

The driver shot me a look.

'They were hanging around at the services. I think they were planning to break in.' I drew back from admitting that they'd been climbing all over his rig.

Although the driver didn't say anything, the atmosphere in the cab thickened and I knew that he regretted picking me up and was already blaming me for whatever was going to happen.

For several seconds, the Skoda maintained an even speed alongside us, the hand languidly pointing at the rear wheels, then abruptly it was withdrawn and the car accelerated and angled sharply in. Slush obscured its registration plate.

The driver shifted down. He flashed his lights. 'Don't be

silly,' he said, his voice quiet with concern. 'What are you playing at?'

'Maybe they're after the load.'

'A pile of furniture? A couple of wardrobes and a three-piece suite? No, they're cowboys, been out on the beer, thinking carving up trucks is . . . Christ!'

I was nearly thrown out of the bunk as the driver stood on his brakes. His composure snapped. 'God, they wouldn't try that if I was in my Powerliner.' And he ran through the Powerliner's technical specifications as if reciting an incantation. 'Flagship of the fleet. Thirty-eight tonnes, sixteen-gear electronic split-shift. Pulls five hundred horses and puts out more than a thousand pound-foot of torque.' He pressed the heel of his hand on the horn. 'I could annihilate them.'

'You're still a lot bigger than they are.'

The driver dropped another gear. We were crawling, our cab overhanging the rear of the Skoda. *Honk if you had it last night*, I read on the screen.

'How many?' the driver asked, his manner gone dangerously quiet.

'Two. Not very pleasant-looking.'

'Right,' he said, groping under the dash. I saw him slip something metallic into his right hand. 'They're going to wish they'd stayed at home watching Jimmy Shand.'

We stopped with a lurch, bumper to bumper. The snow closed in on us and the lights made a stage in the middle of nowhere. I could smell the driver's sweat through his aftershave – a dangerously unrestrained smell.

'Do you want me to come with you?' I asked. Physical confrontation was the last thing I wanted.

'Keep out of it,' the driver ordered, flat-handing his door open. He was swinging down, leaving the lights on and the engine running and the wipers switching back and forth.

What happened next took place in the full glare of the headlights. The driver had taken no more than four musclebound strides when the doors burst open and the two men erupted. There was no taking up of fighting positions, no aggressive posturing. They simply flew at him, and he barely had time to get on his back foot before the first blow landed. Under the next impact he went down. They were all over him, kicking with big laced boots, but he managed to get hold of a foot and twisted its owner down and then with a roar that I heard in the cab he was straddling him, rolling over and driving metal into his face, while the other one danced around them, yelling something.

The driver was merciless. The sound of his blows was sickening. 'No!' I shouted.

And in the same moment the other man stabbed down. The driver reared and turned and the knife flashed again, and this time the driver raised a hand and seemed to stare imploringly at me before the next blow fell and he tried to get away, back towards the cab, crawling and stumbling with the knifeman following, frenziedly slashing and jabbing and the snow blowing around them in wild turns and eddies, so that the killing took on the horrific aspect of a primitive hunt in some glacial era of the past.

And I just looked on, frozen against the back of the cab. I saw everything that was done, yet I just couldn't believe it was happening. I couldn't believe that so much violence could come out of nowhere.

Then it was over. The driver lay still not fifteen feet from me and his killer was helping his accomplice to his feet. They held each other for support, the face of one of them dripping black in the lights. They looked dazedly in my direction before they bent and took the driver by the arms. They began dragging him away, up the embankment, into the snow and out of sight.

Sense rushed back. I had to get into the driving seat, ram the car, stop them getting away. But before the thought was even finished, one of them came slithering back down the slope, half-falling, travelling so fast that I knew I wouldn't be able to get the truck going before he was inside. He ran for the cab and I could hear his dragging breaths. He bobbed beneath the windscreen and then his face appeared at the door, demented with fright and adrenalin. He reached to pull himself up and in his bloody hand was the knife. He saw the briefcase lying on the passenger seat and grabbed for it, and as he made contact he half-turned and saw me.

With spastic effort, too exhausted for co-ordinated movement, he lunged forward, and in the moment he was off-balance I kicked out with all my rower's weight and muscle, using the bulkhead for leverage, catching him full in the face with both feet, catapulting him across the cab. The knife clattered against the screen and landed on the passenger seat. Without thought now, I hauled myself forward and kicked out again, making only glancing contact but forcing him to drop the briefcase and driving him half out of the door. The other one had seen me and his mouth was gaping in a blood-filled shout. Another kick and the knifeman was out of the door, lurching towards his accomplice, who was screaming and gesturing, desperate to get away. I jumped out, lost my balance, and by the time I was on my feet the killers were throwing themselves into their car. With a desperate effort I got my fingers around the top of the door and nearly had them torn off as the Skoda fishtailed away, leaving me spreadeagled on the road.

By the time I pushed myself to my feet, the snow had swallowed them. Breath sobbing, I stumbled up the slope, slipping in my city shoes. The driver was lying face-down over the brow. He was outside the radius of light and I couldn't see his injuries, but he wasn't moving. I felt his limp wrist for a pulse. I couldn't find it.

Lights rifled out of the snowstorm. I ran down the slope, flailing for balance while trying to signal the car to stop. It was a big Mercedes and it went past like a targeting missile.

Cursing, I hauled myself into the cab. The briefcase was lying against the pedals. The knife was still on the seat. I flung it into the footwell and knelt on the seat to get at the first-aid box, which was stowed above the bunk. Then I ransacked the glove box, finding a torch. I grabbed my coat to use for a blanket and staggered back up the embankment. Another vehicle came past without stopping.

The driver was exactly as I'd left him. I turned him over and felt sticky warmth on my hands. I shone the torch on his face and it was cold, pallid and still. He's dead, a voice said inside me. I laid my coat over him and crouched down, willing my mind into useful thought.

The phone! Back down to the cab, more in control now. I collapsed into the driving seat and grabbed for the phone. I saw the knife glinting at my feet.

'Emergency,' a calm voice said. 'Which service, please?'

'Police and Ambulance. There's been a murder. Hurry.'

'Your name, please.'

My hands were gory. Mangled warning signals flashed across my brain – hitchhiker, police, driver, knife. I stared at myself in the mirror and across my eyes I saw all my terrors paraded. The driver was dead, knifed to death, and the man he'd given a lift to – a penniless vagrant – was sitting in his cab with the murder weapon, the victim's blood on his hands.

'Your name, please.'

I slammed down the phone and clawed at my hair. Seconds is all it had taken. In a matter of seconds, events which I had merely spectated had tied me in a knot of bloody circumstances so neat and sound that I might have murdered the driver myself.

But I didn't murder him!

I dismissed this plea immediately. At Salisbury Jail I'd met prisoners convicted on flimsier evidence than I could see stacked against me. The police who'd stopped me at the bridge had presumed guilt before they even knew who I was.

Eleanor! That consideration went through me like a knife. Even if the police believed me, they'd detain me for questioning. They would want to know why I was going to Swansea. I would have to tell them about Eleanor Barry. They would check with her. They'd find out that I'd concealed my identity to set up a meeting with a woman who'd accused me of rape. Christ!

No, I couldn't go to the police. Not now. Not with so much to lose.

All the time, the truck's engine had been running. Sudden consciousness of it stampeded me into a decision. There was nothing I could do for the driver, and beyond a description of his murderers and their car, there was little I could tell the police. I'd phone them anonymously, from Swansea. I'd have to take the truck because the motorway was a no-go zone for pedestrians. I seized the wheel, shifted the briefcase on to the bunk, dipped the clutch and took hold of the gear stick. And then I remembered my coat. With a moan I leapt out, almost into the path of a car. Several vehicles had gone by, but the men in the Skoda had picked their spot well, knowing what I had already learnt that night. The motoring public stops for nothing.

Brake lights veered on to the hard shoulder. Then came the whine of the engine in reverse. In horror I watched the car back right up to me.

The driver leapt out, grinning. 'Need a hand?'

'Er, no. It's fixed, thanks.'

'Puncture?' he enquired cheerfully, taking in my wet, stained clothes and grazed hands. 'You picked a right old night.'

'I certainly did,' I said, my smile aching. One glance to his right and he'd see the trails ploughed up the embankment.

'Thought I'd better stop just in case.'

'Not many would.'

He began to walk away. 'Do the same for me some time.' He waved. 'See you then.'

As I toiled back up I knew that the Good Samaritan was the type who would be tuned into police appeals for witnesses. Everything was conspiring to sink me deeper.

Snow had drifted against the driver's corpse. If the blizzard kept up, he would be completely buried by dawn. The forecast was for more foul weather. Days might pass before he was found, and by then I'd be long gone, the witness's memory a blur.

I snatched my coat and turned to run at the same instant, but some other impulse prevailed. The driver was dead all right, his face grey, his eyes set into splinters of glass. I couldn't turn my back on him; I couldn't let his killers get away with it. I laid my hand on the icy forehead. 'I'll make sure they pay. One way or the other. I promise.' My voice broke and I spun round and dashed down to the truck as if devils were on my tail.

My nerves were hanging by a shred, but I forced myself to take a quick cast around the truck, and I was glad I did because I found the metal object the driver had armed himself with – an old-fashioned knuckle-duster.

Shock took me when I got into the driving seat. My limbs were useless and the controls meaningless. With both hands I managed to force the gearshift into a slot. The truck jumped forward like a startled dinosaur and stalled with a bang. I'd forgotten the bloody airbrake. I churned the engine back into life and dropped the lever. The cab shuddered as the clutch bit and then the truck was moving, a dragging weight, reluctant to depart. Not daring to change gear, I kept in first, taking the revs up to the red line. I was still on the hard shoulder. I veered into the slow lane and a horn erupted in my ear as a car swerved past.

Sweat soaked me. I snatched a glance at the mirror, but the snow blotted out everything. After a couple of attempts I suceeded in getting out of first and worked up through the gears. I trundled along at thirty miles an hour, my eyes out ahead of me, trying to distinguish the road from the phantoms created by the snow. It had begun to settle on the motorway itself and the carriageway was striped by tyretracks.

I had no idea where I was going. Primal instinct had taken over. Thoughts clamoured for attention but I kept them at bay because I knew they would only make the picture blacker and I was committed to the only route open.

Three or four miles went by. Soon the motorway would run out and I would have to choose a place to leave the truck. Somewhere by the docks, I decided, where it wouldn't attract notice.

A spasm doubled me over the wheel. Through the snow a battery of blue and yellow and white lights were spinning. In the first petrified moment I assumed it was a road block and jammed my foot on the brake, not realising how powerful they were, locking the wheels in the slush. The truck drifted sideways and for a suspension of time I was sure I had lost it, but I made the right moves and everything came into balance again.

Now I could see the obstruction and it wasn't a road block. Emergency vehicles crowded the carriageway – fire engines, ambulances, police cars. Arc lights flooded two cars locked together against the central barrier. I fumbled a change-down and slowed to a crawl. The accident must have happened only minutes before I arrived. Glass and metal fragments littered the clearway. Smoke or vapour was still rising from the wreckage and the stink of burnt oil and rubber filled the cab.

A policeman in a fluorescent waistcoat was directing traffic around the crash. He waved me through without looking, his attention on the fire crew who were cutting into the wreckage of one of the cars. It was unrecognisable. The other one was the Mercedes that had ignored my appeal for help. Ambulancemen were gathered around it. The driver's door hung half open and beneath it protruded a pair of legs stretched out in a thoroughly orderly fashion, as if the driver had suffered a nasty shock and was sitting down to get over it.

I stopped. I couldn't help it. If the Skoda was one of the vehicles, my nightmare would be over.

'Keep moving,' the policeman shouted.

'I think I know who was in the other car.'

He turned, his features distorted by the riotous lighting. 'The burn-out?'

'Burn-out?'

'Can't you fucking see?'

The Skoda's paintwork had been so nondescript that I'd failed to see that it had been incinerated to bare metal. 'You mean the people inside are dead?'

The policeman gave an ugly laugh. 'None of this lot is going to see in the New Year.' With an effort he remembered his duties. 'You say you can identify the people in the Skoda?'

'Not identify, but I was involved in an . . . incident with them a few miles back.'

41

'Pull in over there. I'll send someone to take a statement.'

I skirted the pile-up, weighing up the odds of justice falling on my side, but there were too many indeterminates for me to establish which way the scales would tilt. Any evidence linking the thugs to the murder had almost certainly been destroyed, while I was driving along with a whole case of prosecutor's exhibits. In the mirror I saw the policeman with his back to me. The lights were falling away. I was past and my last chance had gone. A great sense of detachment came over me.

I was on the highroad to hell.

5

Style phoned again, but I ignored him. At least I assumed it was Style, anxious about his overdue load. I was slumped over the wheel in a lay-by off the Port Talbot turning. I had switched off the wipers and the snow had accumulated on the screen, sealing me in a grey gloom. The horrors that I'd tried to keep at bay now assailed me in an unbroken ring. My wild flight had only mired me deeper. The truck was expected at Style's place and when it didn't turn up he would raise the alarm. The police would discover that the driver had disappeared between the service station and Swansea. I checked the time: just after eight. There was enough fuel to keep me running until dawn, but I reckoned I had no more than an hour before they started searching.

More horrors reared. The Good Samaritan had seen me in a dishevelled state at the murder scene and I had shown myself to the patrolman at the crash. If either of them could give even a partial description, it would be recognised by the police who had questioned me at the service station. And they knew who I was.

Still I vacillated. My eye fell on the knife. Whether or not I gave myself up, it made sense to remove the false but damning evidence. I climbed out. The snow was now three or four inches deep and my feet made prints. I wiped the knife and buried it blade down in the verge. It was just the start. My coat was stained with the driver's blood. I couldn't leave it near the knife; I would have to ditch it somewhere else.

I was beginning to think like a murderer – the feverish mental backtracking for the forgotten clue, the fatal oversight. When I returned to the cab, I methodically inspected it. The sight of the briefcase fanned a tiny hope. That's what the knifeman had grabbed, and perhaps its contents would suggest a link with the killers, help eliminate me as a suspect. The driver had left its lock on the correct combination and it sprang open at a touch. Inside there was a passport, a personal organiser and a thick folder. I opened the passport. The driver's name was James Vernon Griffith, thirty-one years old, no distinguishing features.

The folder contained a sheaf of travel documents, including ferry tickets from Plymouth to Santander and an inventory of the load. I remembered how one of the killers had toured around the truck, slapping the sides, as if taking mental stock. I'd already revised my assumption that they'd been casual thieves. Casual thieves don't follow trucks and hijack them on the public highway. I swivelled, staring towards the back. Whatever they'd been after must be in there. I ran my eye down the list but couldn't pick out anything worth killing for. As the driver had said, the truck was ferrying domestic belongings to Spain. The consignee was a man called Hutchinson, a name that meant nothing to me.

Behind the driver's seat, I found his travel bag. It contained only his spare clothes and a few other blameless items. I turned my attention to his leather jacket. From the inside pocket I took his wallet. Of course! The killers must have known that he was carrying a thousand pounds cash. I shook out the contents – exactly sixty pounds in new notes and two credit cards.

My mind was forced full circle. Perhaps the driver had been right, and robbery hadn't been a motive. Perhaps the killers had been a couple of psychotic drunks out on a New Year spree. Or perhaps they'd been motivated by personal revenge. Maybe the driver had been having an affair with the wife of one of them, or . . .

This speculation was only wasting time. Realisation that my prints would be all over the cab touched off another panic attack. I set about cleaning up – wheel, gearstick, dashboard, screen, instruments, door handles. It was endless. I would never be able to eradicate my presence. All I was doing was tampering with the evidence.

I found myself staring at the small red light above me. Slowly I stiffened. It was the Vehicle Location Device and it had been switched on the whole time. I wasn't sure how it worked, but I imagined that somewhere a computer was recording the truck's movements, plotting and timing every stop and turn. At this very moment Style might have me pinpointed on the screen. Stored in the computer's memory would be the precise location of the driver's body. I reached up to switch the unit off, then sank back. The damage was done.

Maybe Style would know what the killers had been after. He'd ordered the VLD to be fitted especially for this trip, which suggested that the cargo was valuable and at risk. The fact that a man in his position had personally organised the trip proved that it must be out of the ordinary. Perhaps the best thing to do would be to drive to the house and explain everything to Style. He might even have a good idea who the murderers were.

But I stayed sitting in the darkness. Even if Style believed me, he'd have to call in the police. What could I tell them? Justice had already been done without any intervention from me. The killers were dead. Nobody had got away with anything. I had nothing to gain and Eleanor Barry to lose. That prospect was too cruel to accept. There had to be some other way.

My mood congealed into apathy. At some point the phone rang again and wouldn't stop. By now, Style must know that something was wrong. Suspecting an accident, he would have called Griffith's boss to find that the driver had left Bristol on time. No, he wouldn't get through because Griffith's boss was en route to Jamaica and the office was shut for the holiday. Poor Griffith, I thought, lying in his snowy grave with only me to mourn for him. No family, he'd said. If only Style hadn't been expecting him, his disappearance might have gone unnoticed for days.

I sat upright. My throat gave an involuntary swallow as I digested the implication. Griffith had never met Style, and I guessed from what he'd said that they had never even spoken. This was the first time Style had used Argonaut. Almost certainly there would be no one at hand to say that I was not James Vernon Griffith. It was so simple! All I had to do was present myself as the driver, pick up some papers and clear out. It would give me time to organise my defence.

Grotesque, a voice said. Look where your witless actions have landed you already. But no matter how hard I tried to suppress the fantasy, it kept coming back, dangling before me – a lifeline or a noose. On and on the phone rang.

My hand hovered over it, trembling between the knowledge that if I picked it up I would have passed the point of no return, and the conviction that as soon as it stopped ringing, Style would call the police.

I pounced. 'Mr Style?'

'Eeles, actually,' a fastidious English voice snapped. 'Where in hell are you? You were supposed to be here two hours ago.'

46

My mouth was so frozen that I could barely form words. 'I've just turned off the motorway.'

'What's the hold-up?'

'An accident,' I managed to say. 'I was involved in an accident.'

'Are you hurt?'

'No.'

'Is the truck damaged?'

'No.'

'The load, then?'

'The load's fine. There's nothing wrong with the load.'

Silence intervened. 'What kind of accident are we talking about?'

'A crash. Fatal.'

'Griffith, are you all right?'

I shivered under the first touch of the dead man's identity. 'Shocked,' I stammered.

Eeles' tone was incisive. 'I'll come and fetch you. Can the truck stay where it is?'

I stared through the closed screen, picturing myself stumbling across the fields, understanding now why the hunted beast turns and waits for its pursuers even when it is still sound in wind and limb. 'No, I'll come to you.'

On the way up the sky cleared and the snow began to freeze. I drove as if the truck was on tiptoes, but occasionally the steering went weightless as the tyres lost grip. This wasn't the rich man's territory that I'd imagined. Rough pasture sloped up to the skyline; on the other side, impoverished fields and old mine workings fell away to the lights of the coastal strip.

Where the road ran through a dense plantation, I stopped and hid my suitcase, intending to pick it up on my return. Because nothing is certain, however, I hung on to my

47

passport and the precious map. My coat I hurriedly buried in a drainage ditch. When I returned to the cab, I reached for the driver's leather jacket.

I couldn't put it on. I couldn't carry through the deception. It was beyond my capabilities. The man called Eeles would cry impostor the moment he clapped eyes on me.

But why should he? Just as Eleanor Barry believed that I was a successful businessman because that's what she *wanted* to believe, so Style and the man called Eeles would accept me as the driver because a driver is what they were expecting – nothing more. Griffith's was a minor, walk-on part. Drivers aren't people who command centre stage. My accent was neither Welsh nor working-class, but with the economy in flux and the Job-centres teeming with downwardly mobile former merchant bankers, city analysts and disenfranchised television station personnel, a well-spoken truck driver shouldn't arouse suspicion.

All I had to do was act with conviction. I put on the dead man's jacket. It was soft and luxurious and fitted me better than I expected. Then I turned the key. A leap into the dark was better than a drop off the scaffold.

At a parting of the ways I turned left, over the cattle grid and past a sign prohibiting trespass. The drive was newly fenced with post-and-rail. Saplings in plastic tubes had been planted at regular intervals. Lights appeared and the house showed in silhouette, built into the hillside, its long pitch of roof reminiscent of a ski chalet. I drove over another grid through a gateway lit by a converted Victorian street lamp.

Security lights popped on, isolating the front of the house. On the forecourt several luxury cars were drawn up – a Bentley, a Porsche convertible and a Bristol, plus a Range Rover. Fresh trepidation filled me. Style was entertaining guests, and among them might be stalwarts of the local business community and clients of Argonaut Haulage who would ask me questions I couldn't answer. But it was too late to cry off. On a falling tide of confidence I parked in a corner and climbed out. The wind pierced my clothes. My shoes squeaked on virgin snow. The house was a neo-Georgian chalet built nearly a thousand feet up.

Nobody was waiting to greet me, and the glass-panelled door was locked. I peered through and shied back from a still figure in the hallway, but it was only a suit of armour, recycled as a coat rack. I rang a bell, half expecting musical chimes, and the voice of the man called Eeles said: 'Tradesman's entrance, I'm afraid. Round the back and through the garage.'

I went down a driveway lined with fake Greek statuary and fast-growing conifers in mock marble urns. Garage was an understatement. The ground floor was a hangar occupied by Italian classic cars. With faltering step I went in. The garage was cold, lit by a miserly light. I shivered. Almost for comfort I ran my hands over the luxuriant curves of a Ferrari.

'I'd rather you didn't touch.'

I swung round, my eyes as stiff as stones. After a long pause, a pair of doors slid open. 'Second room on the left.'

I stood in the very centre of the lift. As the doors closed, I said goodbye to myself.

6

I expected the man called Eeles to be waiting outside the lift, but the lobby was empty. It was a large hall, floored with parquet and hung with paintings of horses and dogs. Riding gear was strewn on a brass-bound reproduction nautical chest. The hot atmosphere was a cocktail of saddle soap and liniment and polished wood. There wasn't any suggestion of a feminine presence.

Distant voices were raised in discussion. They didn't come from the second room on the left, which proved to be an untenanted study with more parquet flooring and lots of brand-new yew and leather furniture cluttered with equestrian statues and trophies and expensive scale-model automobiles. The single bookcase appeared to have been stocked by the metre.

Imagining an unseen onlooker, I pretended to examine the photos, which showed Victor Style in the American South racing sportscars or playing polo and receiving prizes for these activities. He was handsome enough not to appear out of place among people who looked as though they should be celebrities and who certainly enjoyed a mutually admiring relationship with the camera, but there was an unconforming aspect to his good looks that I couldn't fathom until I remembered his gypsy blood. There was something proto-European about his wide-spaced lumi-nous eyes and the dark hair growing in tight curls down his neck. In the company of the pampered and well-heeled Americans he looked feral – a middle-aged Pan. Many women, I guessed, would find Vic Style attractive – women who were turned on by body hair and gold jewellery, romantic dreamers in fluffy mules who ate chocolates while communing with crooners of the fifties. But this stereotype didn't correspond remotely to the coolly attractive woman who accompanied Style in several of the photos.

I jumped. The study curtains were gliding open, exposing a night-time coastal panorama – strips and grids of light strung out between winking beads. Slow red flames and pillars of steam rose from the steelworks. I could see the curve of the motorway and imagined I could identify the place where Griffith lay. My eyes searched for the static blue fluorescence that would show he'd been found.

'How do you like Mr Style's view?' Eeles' voice said behind me.

I couldn't turn round. Stage fright pinned me fast. 'Impressive.'

'I've visited the seven wonders of the world,' Eeles said in a mocking sing-song, 'but there's nothing I've seen, look you, to beat Swansea Bay by night.'

The room was insanely overheated and I could feel the guilt rising off me. I bit my lip. 'Where's Mr Style?'

'Getting changed for a party.' Eeles' voice came nearer. My elbow was gripped. 'Goodness me, you *have* had a nasty fright.' He turned me round.

At the last moment I had teetered. My defences were threadbare. Better to own up now than juggle an unsustainable lie to its inevitable destruction. If it had been anyone else, I think I would have confessed there and then. Not to Eeles, though.

Something about his smooth exterior rubbed against my grain from the start. Maybe it was his appearance – sleek

51

and podgy, somewhat effete in his over-tailored double-breasted suit and spotted bow tie. But the impression of indulgence stopped short of the eyes. They were small and spiteful, unabashed in their scrutiny, assessing me, weighing me up with almost insulting brevity.

'Perhaps you'd better sit down,' he said. Gently he steered me to a seat, then hoisted himself on to a corner of the desk. His short legs dangled clear of the floor. He brushed imaginary dirt from his knees and stationed his eyes on me. He had dispensed with the smile. 'Well now, you'd better tell me about this accident. I'm afraid your earlier explanation left me none the wiser.'

I braced myself. 'It was a two-car pile-up. Three dead. I arrived just after it happened.'

'After?'

'Yes.'

'How long after?'

'A few minutes.'

'Oh, I assumed you must have been on the spot.'

'No.'

'First on the scene, though.'

'The emergency services were already there.'

'So you didn't help the victims?'

This wasn't going according to the script. I couldn't work out where Eeles' questions were leading and the uncertainty rattled me. 'There was nothing I could do.'

'But you said you were *involved*. Seeing the aftermath of a crash isn't involvement, is it?'

'I arrived as they were cutting the bodies out. They'd been burned alive. That's involvement enough.'

'Nobody you knew, though?'

The thrust flushed a wild response. 'Why should I know them? They were just . . . people I drove past. I only saw them for a second.'

'Statistics,' Eeles suggested.

'That's not how I see them.'

'Clearly not.'

I looked at him in a way calculated to avoid eye contact. His expression betrayed no suggestive glint; in fact, his gaze had wandered to some invisible point behind my head. And yet I knew with foundering hope that the pose was a sham.

'How long have you been a driver?'

All his questions struck as a succession of unpleasant surprises. 'Six years,' I answered, thanking God for having given me the foresight to study Griffith's licence.

'Six years? I'd have thought road accidents would be a pretty common occurrence in your line of work. I'm surprised you're taking it so personally.'

I buried my face in my hands, not entirely acting. 'There are some sights you don't get over.'

Eeles sighed as if he was about to make a supreme concession. 'My problem is, Griffith, you arrive hours late, obviously distressed, in a somewhat . . . ' He ran his eyes over my stained clothes. ' . . . grimy state, and tell me that all this is due to some accident which you happened to drive past. I can't help wondering if you might have caused the crash or been to blame in any way.' He leaned earnestly. 'I'd much rather hear it from you than from the police.'

'I've told you. It was nothing to do with me.'

'If you say so,' Eeles said, his voice leaving doubt in its wake. He crossed his stubby legs, signalling a change of tack. 'How long did this accident hold you up?'

I stole a look through spread fingers. I had expected blame for being late, but not this comprehensive going over. 'I'm not sure,' I muttered. 'About ten minutes, I suppose.'

Eeles inspected his feet – a stagey pause designed to remind me of unseen pitfalls. 'Then obviously you must have stopped elsewhere.'

'Stopped?' His insinuating tone spiked even the simplest of responses with hazards. My fear of him was growing by the moment.

'You left the depot at five. The drive from Bristol shouldn't take more than three hours.'

'I broke for something to eat at Bridgend services.'

'For how long?'

I peered round at an invisible jury. 'Forty minutes, I guess.'

'Forty minutes at the services and ten at the accident.' He frowned at the ceiling. 'That still leaves an hour unaccounted for.'

I ran my hand round the inside of my collar. 'Maybe I spent longer at the services than I thought.'

Eeles tendered a short smile devoid of amusement. 'Please don't insult my intelligence, Griffith.'

Never ask a question to which you don't know the answer – the cardinal rule of cross-examination. But if Eeles knew I wasn't the driver, why didn't he say so? All he had to do was point his finger and the truth would come tumbling out. Why was he hounding me like this?

My fears condensed in an image of the all-seeing eye on the roof of the cab. Eeles must have been following my erratic progress on the VLD. He knew I'd stopped three times after leaving the service station.

'You see my problem?'

I could, and yet if he'd been keeping the truck under surveillance, he didn't need me to confirm my movements. It was as if he was playing a sophisticated game which ruled out direct accusation – as if he was trying to lead me out question by question, until I found that I had trapped myself in a dead end.

'I'm waiting.'

I drew a sharp intake of breath, jarred by an image of the

Skoda nosing into the park. Every second that I hesitated damned me, yet something implicit in that vision wouldn't let me answer. It was like a termite gnawing in a dark recess. The Skoda had entered the services at least twenty minutes after we arrived. The killers couldn't have been tailing the truck, so unless they were scavenging for random targets, which seemed less and less likely, they must have known Griffith was there. I looked at Eeles and suddenly the quality of my fear had drastically altered.

'Yes?' he said, sliding off the desk.

I made my tone sullen. 'I pulled off the motorway a couple of times because visibility was down to zero.'

Eeles had been poised to pounce and his disappointment was obvious. He subsided with a little grunt and peered at me with his head on one side, searching for a way around my screen of lies. 'Why didn't you say so?'

I was still trying to revise my perception of events. It was inconceivable that Eeles had directed the killers to the truck. He must have had the VLD fitted because he *knew* there would be a hijack attempt, and his questioning was hostile because he was certain that my story was a limp effort to evade that fact. But there could be no backtracking now.

'I didn't want to get into trouble.'

Eeles sucked in his cheeks. 'How did you hurt your hands?'

'My hands? I slipped on ice.'

Eeles' mouth puckered in a sphincter of disdain. 'You *have* had a hectic night. No wonder your performance is so unconvincing.'

I faced Eeles square on. 'I don't know what you're insinuating.'

'I'm saying, Griffith, that you bear the unmistakeable hallmark of a man with something to hide.'

I had only myself to blame. Forced on to the back foot

from the start, I'd been defending myself against the presumption of guilt instead of doing what any genuine driver would do and telling this pompous little twerp to bugger off.

'Look, I apologise for turning up so late, but now I'm here, so why don't you drop the third-degree, hand over the papers and let me get back on the road?'

'Why didn't you answer my calls? Why didn't you phone in to explain the delay?'

I opened my mouth confidently enough, but this time my brain refused to cooperate.

'Come one, Griffith. That shouldn't need too much rehearsing.'

Anger gave me my cue. I rose to my feet, taking full advantage of my height. 'Mr Eeles, I don't work for you. I'm employed by Argonaut. I answer the phone as and when I choose.'

Eeles' jawline tightened. 'You answer to the bloody people who are paying your wages.'

'And that's not you.'

Eeles lined me up with a trembling finger. 'One word from me, Griffith, and you're finished with Argonaut.'

'And one more word from you,' I shouted, flinging myself into the role, 'and you can drive the load to Zaragoza yourself.'

He stepped back, blinking rapidly. 'Now look here, Griffith, your boss won't take kindly to one of his drivers losing him a valuable contract.'

'And yours won't be too happy about losing his one and only driver.'

'He's right, Rip.'

Our breath rasped in the sudden silence.

'Oh, Victor,' Eeles said, his face relaxing in a smile, 'nothing to be alarmed about. Griffith was held up by the snow.'

'Why didn't you answer the phone?' Style demanded, before I barely had time to register Eeles' about-face. He appeared older than in his photos – the skin tighter and more leathery, the curls tending towards grey. He was wearing evening clothes and his grim expression was aimed at me.

I wiped my palms on my trousers.

'There was a blizzard,' Eeles explained. 'It was all Griffith could do to stay on the road. He's lucky to have got here at all.' After this astonishing intervention, Eeles shifted delicately, apparently stepping on to sensitive ground. 'No harm done, Victor, but it's given me serious misgivings. Frankly, this job is too important to be left to the mercy of the weather. I really think we should consider the other option.'

'Go and see to the guests,' Style ordered. He went on staring at me – a slightly distracted stare.

A slight irritation ruffled Eeles' composure. 'This will only confirm their doubts. Please, Victor, let's leave it to . . .'

'Now.'

The corners of Eeles' mouth turned down mutinously, but after a moment's hesitation and with a vicious glance at me, he walked out. Style watched him go, a faint speculation troubling his eyes, but before I could do any more wondering on my own account, Style had me back in his sights. 'Vaughan Starling told me you're his most reliable driver.' He appraised me without enthusiasm. 'You'd better not disappoint me.' His husky accent had picked up a faint American intonation.

'You're not seeing me at my best.'

'The best is what I'm paying for.'

I let it go.

'I expected a local man.'

'My family moved away when I was a kid, and then I was in the army.' Gingerly I backed out of this dangerous cul-de-sac. I gestured out of the window. 'That's a tremendous view you have.'

To my relief, Style accepted the diversion. He moved to the window and stared out. 'When I was a boy I used to come up here to ride the travellers' horses. I swore then that one day I'd build a house on this hill.'

I cleared my throat. 'You've come up a long way in the world.'

Half a minute passed without Style speaking. His expression was agonised.

'I was admiring your trophies,' I said, to crack the weight of silence.

Pivoting stiffly, using his whole body, Style turned to contemplate his prizes. 'Do you know anything about polo?'

'Yes. Er, I mean, no.'

'Most people think it's a game for playboys. They forget it was once played for the head of an enemy.' Style began to touch himself – wrists, elbows, ribs, thighs and, finally, his neck. 'I have broken thirty-four bones,' he said, 'some more than once.'

It wasn't a boast and it wasn't a complaint. He was looking in the direction of the room where his guests were assembled, a nasty glitter in his eyes.

He walked over to the desk and it was only then that I became aware that he was of less than average height, shorter than Eeles, but physically a much more formidable proposition. He handed over a fat envelope. 'Sorry to drag you away from your holiday.'

As I riffled the notes, a chink opened at the end of the tunnel. A thousand pounds doesn't go far these days, but it takes you a hell of a lot further than fifty quid.

Style passed me a map of Zaragoza. A circle on the outskirts of town showed me where I was supposed to make the delivery. 'It's a freight yard,' he told me. 'You're expected. When you get there, your job's finished. A local firm will handle the unloading. Pick the wagon up any day after the sixth.'

I nodded, not really taking it in, already anticipating my departure.

But Style's next words yanked me back with a bump. 'Call this number three times a day – eight in the morning, midday, and seven at night. Leave a message on the machine if there's no one at the other end.'

I accepted the directions with a polite grimace. 'On a long haul, it's not always easy to get to a phone at fixed times.'

Style fixed me with his light eyes. 'Mr Griffith, I'm paying you very well. In return, I expect you to do what you're told.'

I shuffled my feet. 'Is it a valuable load?'

'Just furniture.'

'Antiques?'

'How would I know?' Style said, his patience threatened. 'It's all in the inventory.'

'Right,' I said, after a brief but fatal pause.

'Is anything wrong, Mr Griffith?'

'It's such short notice,' I said, extemporising. 'Usually I supervise the loading myself. It saves time and trouble if any problems crop up at Customs. It means I can look them in the eye when they ask me if there's anything to declare.' I gave a short laugh to stress the remoteness of this possibility.

Style frowned into the distance for a considerable time. 'Driving long distance must give you a lot of time to think.'

'I suppose it does.'

Style rounded on me so quickly that I flinched. 'Don't do any of your thinking on my time.'

I shifted awkwardly. 'I'll bear that in mind.'

Style began to head for the door. 'You'll leave at three. Your room's ready.'

'Room? Aren't I leaving now?'

Style wasn't the kind if man who repeated himself. 'Collect your things from the truck, then go and join my guests.'

'We might get snowed in. I could miss the ferry.'

'I never worry about things that aren't in my control,' Style said. He held the door open for me. 'They're expecting you, Mr Griffith.'

7

To my exhausted eyes the room appeared full of shiny, irradiant faces, but that was only the multiplier effect produced by a wall hung with mirrors in a room with too much light. When I had separated the real from its reflection, I found there was only Eeles and two guests – both male, both displaying the tenacious smiles of men whose main reason for being there was myself.

'The driver,' Eeles announced. 'James Griffith.'

A big man with a red face, bald pate and Papa Hemingway beard adjusted his grip on his drink and stuck out his hand. In his softly draped suiting he put me in mind of an American television judge – an impression negated or, for all I knew of these things, bolstered by the diamond stud in his left ear lobe.

'Bless you, fella,' he began, giving my hand an un-reserved squeeze. 'Carl Axnoller,' he declared in a rumbly bass. 'Carl Magnus Axnoller. Helluva name.' He paused as if he had presented me with a prize-winning conversational gambit. 'Norse.'

The heat and the reflections were overpowering. 'Anglo-Saxon, surely,' I heard myself say. 'Ax after the river in Devon and noller from the Old English for "alder" –the alder by the River Ax.'

Axnoller's smile grew quite intense. 'How about that?' he marvelled.

Eeles guffawed. 'So much for your ancestors raping and pillaging across Europe. Grubbing for turnips in the . . . ' His voice dwindled to nothing under the vigour of Axnoller's smile.

'You've already met Rip,' Axnoller said, in a 'so you know what a bozo he is' tone.

'I won't shake hands,' Eeles told me. 'I'm trying to avoid this ghastly flu epidemic.'

'You're safe with me. I've been in a different disease pool.'

While Eeles evaluated this statement, my attention strayed to the tweedy young man seated in the corner. He was another American, I guessed – long in the bone, with jug ears and crimped fair hair parted an inch off-centre and flattened down on his skull. His big idle hands made it look as if he hadn't stopped growing, but despite the demeanour of hillbilly simplicity, there was something controlling about his presence. He didn't introduce himself and I wasn't going to ask.

I turned back to Axnoller. 'Is it one of you who's moving to Spain?'

From the interchange of glances, it seemed that no one was quite sure. Then Eeles said: 'No, Mr Hutchinson is already in Spain.'

'Well *I* don't mind shaking hands,' a woman's voice announced.

A tall brunette with an aerobically nurtured slimness stood in the doorway.

A smile pasted itself on Eeles' face. 'Darling, you look exquisite.'

Everyone was obliged to give her their attention as she catwalked in.

'Camille van Damm,' she declared, offering me her hand palm down, as if she expected me to kiss it. 'It's real kind of you to give up your vacation like this.' She engaged me with eyes of an eerily beautiful green that I had to conclude wasn't natural. 'Can I get you a drink, or will it interfere with your driving?'

'Tonic or lemon. Anything soft.' I was grateful for the offer. My mouth was arid.

In the hiatus I watched her high-heel to the drinks cabinet, which stood against the wall of mirrors. They were many and various, in all shapes and sizes, and the brightness they imparted gave the light an almost audible quality. I'd read somewhere that mirrors played a part in gypsy symbolism. In one of the looking glasses Eeles' reflection was watching me with a dark surmise.

Axnoller gestured at the window, which offered a widescreen version of the view from the study. 'Wild night for travelling.'

I shrugged off the perils of the road with some banal response.

'Driving must be a fascinating job,' Camille van Damm said, handing me my drink. She blinked to signal that I had her complete attention and it was up to me to make the most of it.

So far, the conversational rhythm had been so limping that I didn't feel out of step taking several seconds to prepare a reply. 'Mostly it's traffic jams, industrial estates on the edge of town, customs posts and fast food.'

'Oh,' she said, frowning as if I had demolished a favourite myth, 'what a shame.' Her slim hand lingered on mine. Her candid green gaze targeted my own eyes. For van Damm, I guessed, a varied sex life would be an obligatory adjunct of her lifestyle – like the Porsche Cabriolet and the Versace dress and the Rolex chronograph.

'Well,' she said gaily, raising her drink, 'here's to a real smooth trip.'

Axnoller twiddled his glass. Eeles glanced furiously at his watch. The atmosphere was so stilted I was sure the party must soon break up. The guests were simply killing time until Style finished dressing. All I had to do was keep my teeth parted in a semblance of a smile, speak when spoken to, and wait until they shuffled off.

'How do you plan to spend your free time in Spain?' van Damm asked.

'Oh, I've got nothing definite in mind.'

Eeles started nervously. 'Darling, Griffith will have plenty to occupy him.'

Van Damm gave him a sweet glance. 'Rip and I are going to be in Madrid next week,' she explained. With a conspiratorial smile she began scribbling in an elegant notebook. She tore off the page and placed it in my grasp. 'If you find yourself in the capital, we'd love to entertain you to dinner.'

'I'd love that, too,' I said, purely for the discomfort of Eeles.

He showed his teeth at me. 'You're pretty articulate for a lorry driver.'

'Don't be so snooty, Rip,' van Damm said, making a pretty little pout. She wrinkled her nose at me. 'He's such a snob. He's *so* constipated and English.'

'I mean,' Eeles said, ignoring her, 'you're obviously well-educated. You didn't pick up that accent behind the wheel of a juggernaut.'

What the hell, I thought. 'I was at Oxford.'

'Ha, ha,' Eeles said. 'Very good.'

'Oxford.'

His expression curdled.

'Hey, *la crème de la crème*,' van Damm said. 'Rip, you didn't make it to college, did you?'

His smile was stiff. 'Some of us got where we are by starting at the bottom.'

'And kissing it,' the guest in the corner said in a twangy drawl, and then he laughed at his own wit, snuffling long after I had stifled my own mirth and the insult had been milked of humour.

'Obviously you weren't always a truck driver,' Eeles continued grimly.

'I was an army cartographer,' I said, beginning to feel dangerously careless. 'I designed maps.'

Axnoller examined me from different angles, as if figuring the ins and outs of my past. 'Map-maker to truck driver. That's a damn perverse career move.'

My inhibitions were disappearing. 'After I left the army I worked for the Meteorological Office, but I was made redundant in the spending cuts and I couldn't find another job. My flat was repossessed. My car was repossessed. I got out just before they repossessed me.'

Axnoller pursed one corner of his mouth and shook his head in commiseration. 'Same old story.'

'This happened when?' Eeles enquired.

'Two years ago,' I replied, and in the same instant saw Eeles' eyes narrow. 'Fortunately, I'd got my HGV licence when I was in the army.'

'You poor thing,' van Damm said, clutching my arm. 'How do you cope with that kind of personal downturn?'

'Down only looks that way from above,' I answered, parrying Eeles' stare. 'Once you're there, it's just like anywhere else.'

The young man in the corner gave another of his nerve-jangling guffaws. Nobody but me looked at him. I wondered if the balance of his mind was shaky, and in that same precise moment he stopped laughing and gave me a crafty look. I averted my eyes.

A vein had thickened up in Axnoller's temple. 'Don't

mind us. We've just finished a brain-storming session. It gets pretty primal.'

'You're over on business?'

Axnoller winked. 'Fattening frogs for snakes.'

'Mergers and acquisitions,' van Damm explained.

'International real estate,' Axnoller added. 'I'm looking to acquire some land for a company that plans to expand its operation to Wales.'

'That will be welcome news to local business. What kind of company?'

Axnoller clapped a hand on my shoulder. 'Hey, I can't tell you that, fella.' He gestured at the panorama below. 'There are Japanese out there, Koreans, Germans – a whole world of competition.'

I turned to van Damm. 'You work in property, too?'

She dipped her eyelashes. 'Public relations.'

That left Eeles. 'And you? I take it you're a lawyer.'

'Rip works under Camille,' the man in the corner announced, and snuffled into his drink.

'Actually,' Eeles enunciated, cheekbones burning, 'I'm a company doctor. No, not a medical doctor. I minister to the body corporate.'

I tried to see where this range of activities tied up with Style's businesses. 'What's your cure rate?'

'Pretty good, all things considered. Of course we get the occasional hopeless case.'

'Do you get paid by result?'

'Not exactly, no.'

'So if the patient dies?'

'When did you hear of a doctor giving a refund?'

'When he's guilty of negligence, lard-ass.' This time the man in the corner didn't laugh and everyone except Eeles gave him their attention, though most reluctantly. He rose steadily, poured himself another drink, then went and stood at the window, his back to the company.

Axnoller frowned into the bottom of his glass, as if he had spied a fly. 'I don't like this mess one goddam bit more than you do.' His tone was almost appeasing.

'I ain't gonna hold off any longer,' the man said – a matter-of-fact statement delivered in the drawn-out vowels of some geographically imprecise part of the American South. Louisiana, perhaps, or Arkansas. 'I was sent here to do a good job of work, and dammit, that's what I intend doing.'

Uneasy crosscurrents swirled in the room. Van Damm let her breath go in any edgy laugh. 'We're in a very active phase right now. Anxiety time.'

Style came in.

'Of course,' Axnoller said, 'Rip doesn't only deal with the sick and the lame. Companies, like people, benefit from the occasional check-up, a regime of exercise, a healthier diet.'

Style's hands gripped the chair, bracketing Axnoller's neck. 'Griffith isn't interested.'

Axnoller gave a deep chuckle. 'Sure he is. Business is life. You know, Victor, there was an article in *Time* demonstrating a heavy correlation between executive success and sex drive.'

Style's hands were locked in a stranglehold. 'We're late.' He looked at me. 'Griffith, you know where your room is.'

'Poor Mr Griffith,' van Damm said. 'He looks exhausted before he starts.'

Style led the exodus with his stiff gait, Eeles obediently following and Camille van Damm departing with an off-the-shoulder smile for my benefit. At the door Axnoller paused for a moment, regarded me with a brooding, much less avuncular expression, and then, apparently coming to a decision, he motioned to his compatriot with a gesture that encompassed me.

I turned to find the young American looking out of the window, scratching his ear, building a silence, letting it fill the room from corner to corner.

'Time for bed,' I said, faking a yawn.

'Mister, I don't think you're gonna make it.'

I stole a glance at the door – not wishing to bring my fear to his attention. 'Weather permitting,' I said carefully, 'I don't see why not.'

He knocked back his drink, pushed himself straight and swung round. His long jaw parted in a primitive smile. 'This here says why not.'

Before I could react, he had slapped a packet into my palm. He closed my fingers round it with his oversize hand. 'I'm saying,' he murmured with whisky-scented breath, 'miss the ferry and you're a two-time winner.'

I swallowed. 'But why?'

Close up, his eyes had a clear yellow tinge that made me think of dogs not wholly domesticated. They widened good-humouredly. 'You're carrying an unstable load, that's what.'

'What about Mr Style?'

'With all that bad weather out there, he ain't gonna know the difference.'

I swallowed again. 'What if I don't miss it?'

'You got a hard-on for that van Damm bitch?' He let his tongue dangle. 'Mister, you gotta be in some serious training for what she got in mind. I'm saving you from moral *hurt*.'

'That's got nothing to do with it. Driving's my *job*.'

His clench tightened. Something drained out of his expression and I knew that his good humour operated within extremely tight margins which it would be unwise to overstep.

'Then everyone's a loser,' he murmured. He gave the packet a backhand flick. 'What's it to be, mister?'

I looked into his canine eyes and they didn't move a flicker. I looked at my imprisoned hand holding the envelope stuffed with money. 'I won't be on the ferry.'

He cupped a hand to his ear as if he was hard of hearing.

'I won't be on the ferry.'

He released my hand and the superficial mellowness slid back across his eyes. 'Attaboy.'

'Do you work for Mr Axnoller?' I asked as he was walking towards the door. My fingers smarted from his grip. The doubts that had been festering had hardened in a block. A ghastly new dimension yawned before me.

'From time to time, as the market dictates.' He reached the door, held the frame, and gave me a sliding smile. 'I'm a loss adjuster.'

He laughed, carefree in his calling, and as he went away down the corridor he began to whistle – a virtuoso trilling that lingered on my nerves long after he was gone.

8

Sleep guaranteed nightmares, but sitting up offered no repose either. Style's expensive mail-order décor was as restless as fashion, as jittery as technology. I stood behind the triple-glazed picture window, fidgeting with the twelve hundred pounds the man who called himself a loss adjuster had pressed on me. I had reached that realm of paranoid exhaustion where figures sidled just outside the periphery of vision.

No matter how often I shook the dice, they always fell the same way. The bribe wasn't the first sabotage attempt. Eeles hadn't interrogated me because he doubted my credentials; he was surprised and fearful because he hadn't expected me to reach Style's house. Eeles had directed the Skoda to the service station. Eeles was behind the driver's murder.

But why would he and Axnoller want to prevent a load of furniture going to Spain? The answer was obvious – up to a point. The inventory must be incomplete or false. The truck must be smuggling something abroad, something they didn't want to arrive at Zaragoza. The point where this train of thought broke down came when I tried to work out what that something was – drugs, dirty money . . . My speculations floundered, but I had one foothold. Style had a criminal past. He had stepped on toes. He had carved his initials on a rival's face. And standing at his study window he had given me the impression of a man besieged by calamity.

My breath left me as I realised the full extent of my

predicament. I was in double jeopardy now, a fugitive from the law and beyond its protection. When I recalled the man who called himself a loss adjuster, and how no one cared to meet his eye, I sensed with a spreading chill that the police were the lesser of my perils. What did he mean when he said he wasn't going to hold off any longer? Hold off on *what*? *Why*?

Standing there, I had a premonition of a disaster building up, with me skewered in the middle. The minute hand of the clock was beginning its curve towards midnight. Griffith's bag was lying by the couch and I had the house to myself. In ten minutes I could be lost in the matrix of lights far below. I blacked out the urge. The worst was over. I'd survived Eeles' interrogation, and with the country shut down for the holiday, there was no chance of him ferreting out my identity before Style's return.

I lowered myself on to the couch and sat dry-eyed and rigid, listening for some sound that never came.

Into my mind came a memory from childhood. One of our cats had given birth to a litter in an airing cupboard. When I found her, the newborn kittens were clamped to her teats, and to my great astonishment there was a mouse among them. I could only guess that the mouse had rashly decided to infiltrate the litter for a free meal. As I watched, it began to creep away, but when it had scurried only a few inches, the dozing cat lazily extended one padded paw and, with blind maternal instinct, gently scooped the mouse back into the warm curve of her body.

Next time I visited the cat, the mouse was gone, but whether it had escaped or been eaten, I never did know.

I couldn't stand the silence. I couldn't shake off the feeling that I was under surveillance. My hand strayed to my pocket and found the photo of Eleanor Barry. I couldn't bear to look at it.

My eyes seized on my map. I uncapped the tube and unrolled the yellowed sheet on a glass-topped coffee table.

The map's soothing beauty resided in its blankness. It was drawn to 1:500,000 scale and covered 100,000 square kilometres, but in all that area there were only half a dozen contour lines, a tract of seasonal marsh, and a single-track railway line that ran straight as an arrow and ended fifty kilometres short of the top right-hand corner. It was a late-nineteenth-century map of the Karakum desert in Central Asian Khorasan. My thoughts slowed into a dream of the men who had surveyed that desolation – ants with theodolites, imposing order on unknown space.

A faint whoosh of hydraulics snapped me awake. My heartbeat accelerated and my stomach queased up as I heard the lift doors sigh open. Quick footsteps tapped on the parquet.

A woman wearing a luxurious coat walked in, radiating cold. She stopped still as I clambered to my feet.

'Everyone's gone,' I stammered. 'I'm the driver. Your husband hired me.'

'Hired you for what?' she demanded, scanning the room in case it held more unwelcome surprises. She was another American, another southerner, but from a higher social caste than Axnoller or the loss adjuster.

'To drive a load of furniture to Spain.'

Her frown switched back to me. 'Spain?'

'One of your husband's employees is moving there.'

She had the haughty stare that only the rich and privileged are heir to. Her eyes were poppy-seed blue and around them were the faint but ineradicable lines of encroaching middle age. Her bones were elegant, her mouth wide, her make-up understated. Her shoulder-length hair was heavy and nearly straight, and it would have been mousy except that the sun had lightened it to dark honey tones. I thought she was beautiful.

'How do you know I'm Victor's wife?'

I pointed in the direction of the study. 'I recognised you from the photographs.'

She brushed back her hair with one hand. Her eyes drifted, as if a sound had disturbed her. 'You said everyone had gone. Who's everyone?'

'Someone called Axnoller and a . . . '

'Axnoller!' she cried, drawing back as if I'd confronted her with a sexually transmitted disease. She strode to the door. 'I haven't been here, friend. You haven't seen me.'

'They've gone to a party. They won't be back for at least an hour.'

Her eyes narrowed. 'Who else?'

I told her about Eeles, van Damm and the other man, but they didn't mean anything to her. She sat down, arranged her coat about her and crossed her legs – all in one fluent and economical movement. Under the coat she was wearing a simple tan wool dress that outlined the curve of one thigh. She fumbled in her bag and produced a gold case, pulled out a cigarette and stared at it with vexation. She had a very mobile face and the way her features projected her feelings made me think of the girl she must have been. 'I'm supposed to be giving up the killer weed. It's number three on my list of New Year resolutions. But Christ – Axnoller!' She repeated his name as if she was spitting bone marrow.

I checked my watch. 'It's only ten-to. You still have time for one last cigarette.'

Her grin stripped years from her face. It was unnerving and attractive, her blend of cool sophistication and vivacity. 'I guess I do too,' she said, and lit up. She inhaled deep and grimaced. 'Lousy timing. I fly from Miami to Wales on New Year's Eve, and then I find Axnoller's beaten me to it.' She shivered theatrically. 'Sorry, but that guy gives me the bads.'

'I only just met him.'

She squinted through smoke. 'You know what he does?'

I half shrugged. 'Property, mergers . . . '

'Property, shit! He's boss of the third largest waste management company in the States.'

'By waste management, I take it you mean . . . '

'Garbage disposal. He dumps toxins, waste, stuff that makes your bones glow green.'

'Illegally dumps?'

'Maybe not in the States,' she conceded, 'not anymore. But in Africa, the Philippines, the high seas . . . ' She broke off. 'I didn't come all this way to talk about Axnoller. Listen, Mr . . . '

'Griffith,' I said. 'James Griffith.'

'Do you know how to make an Old-Fashioned, Mr James Griffith?'

'You could teach me,' I said, getting to my feet.

'Hold it. Sit down. I'd better get used to looking after myself. That's resolution number two.' She went to the drinks cabinet. Her walk was less affected than van Damm's, but just as attention-catching. 'Can I fix you something, James?'

'I'd better not. I'll be hitting the road in a couple of hours.' Being addressed intimately by my new name gave me a strange sensation, both scary and arousing. For the first time, it occurred to me that my assumed identity might open up possibilities denied to Matthew Reason.

'One for the road then. Lighten up, James. It's New Year.'

I accepted a whisky and ice.

'Don't tell me you're going that route,' she said, craning over the map. I could smell her perfume and was uncomfortably aware of my sweat and the acetone taste that fear and hunger had left in my mouth.

'No, it's a collector's item.'

She came round and sat beside me. I wished I'd taken a shower. 'It's practically blank,' she said. 'Is it unfinished?'

'No, that's all there is. It's a desert plain in Central Asia.'

'Where does the railroad run?'

'Nowhere. Maybe it was a branch line serving a garrison, or maybe they ran into swamp or dunes.'

'Or maybe they just got scared.' She paused. 'One time, I was staying with friends in Oregon, I decided I wanted to see the Pacific. So I got in a car and drove, but as I got near the ocean I began to feel the heeby-jeebies, and about ten miles from the coast it got so bad I just turned around and hightailed it home.' Her voice slowed. 'It was weird. I felt that if I reached the ocean, all the troubles I'd left behind me, all the baggage I'd dumped, all of that would catch up with me and there would be nowhere left to run.'

'I'm not sure that Russian engineers suffer from existential dread.'

She grinned. 'Sure they do. All Russians do. It's in their blood.' She reclined and eyed me lazily through cigarette smoke. 'Speaking of which, you look kind of Russian and soulful yourself.' She half-smiled. 'Am I safe with you?'

'Of course you are,' I said, startled to feel myself blush. 'Perfectly safe.'

She stood up and took off her coat. Her figure was athletic, soft. 'Good, you can be my witness.'

'To what?'

'New Year's resolution number one.'

'I won't be around to see you break it.'

'But *I'll* know, won't I? And whenever I think of you I'll feel guilty.'

The thought of this woman thinking about me filled me with confusion.

'What time do you have?'

The hands of the clock had nearly converged on midnight. 'Less than a minute to go.'

We passed the time in silence, and as the year ended she took hold of my wrist so she could see the seconds sweep up to the meridian. At the stroke of midnight she shut her eyes like a child granted a wish. Ships' sirens saluted far away. 'This year,' she whispered, 'is going to be different. This year it's going to be my turn. This year is going to be the year of hope.' She opened her eyes and they were shining. 'Eight years ago I gave up hope for style.' She laughed. 'That was my maiden name. Hope. Lisa Hope.'

I raised my glass. 'Here's to hope.'

'Come on, James. A little more conviction.'

'Here's to hope's triumph over reason.'

We drank to optimism.

'Now your turn, James.'

I turned away. 'Wishes only come true if you keep them to yourself.'

'Hey, why so doomy?'

I gave a short laugh. 'It's been a bad year. From beginning to end, a very bad year.'

Lisa took my hand. 'It's over now,' she said softly. 'Done with.'

I bit my lip, thinking of the worse one that had just begun. 'Are you divorcing your husband?'

'Yes,' Lisa said, letting go of my hand. She moved away a little.

'Can I ask why?'

'No you can't.'

Gently I plucked the cigarette from her mouth.

She stared ahead for a while. 'Incompatibility. Profound

76

personal differences.' She smiled into distance. 'I thought he was the most wonderful man I'd ever met. I'd grown up in a world of tame privilege, and suddenly I was confronted with this exotic creature – so fearless and natural.' She glanced at me. 'You know he was a gypsy, never knew his mother, never lived in a house until he was grown up?' Tenderness misted her eyes. 'My wolf-boy, I called him.'

'What went wrong?'

Conflicting emotions rippled across her face. She swigged at her drink and pulled a face as if it was bitter. 'Hey, look at this place! Can you imagine me living here?'

Poor Style, I thought with his carriage lamps and reproduction antiques and uPVC windows. 'You could house-train him; you could educate his tastes.'

She punched my arm, quite hard. 'Hey, did Vic ask you to plead for a reconciliation?'

'I don't think he was expecting you.'

Her mouth made a rueful smile. 'I'm spoiled, James. I'm an American rich kid who had it too easy.' She gave me a pleading look. 'You can't give up what you're used to.'

'Some of us have to.'

She glared. 'It wasn't money if that's what you're thinking.' Her hands were agitated; I couldn't see her staying off the nicotine for long. Words suddenly spilled from her. 'Two years ago Vic had a bad riding accident. He broke his back. The bones healed, but the nerves were permanently damaged and he was in pain a lot of the time. It affected his personality and also it destroyed our . . . ' She reached for the cigarettes and remembered her resolution just in time. She sat there. 'Things were never the same again.'

She could have meant that Style had become violent or depressed, but I sensed a more tender disappointment. Out of the fragments one piece of the picture took shape. Sex, I thought, recalling Style's anguished contemplation of his riding trophies and Axnoller's taunt about libido and success in business. Style's accident had left him impotent.

Like any man who has experienced the occasional flop, I felt some sympathy for Style, but at the level of animal behaviour, his incapacity aroused a primitive quiver, an instinctive whetting of the carnal appetite. Glancing at Lisa Hope, I was struck by the naked intimacy of her neck, and when she turned, frowning because she sensed my scrutiny, I felt a secret swell of power, conscious that under the drug of passion those cool eyes would grow languid, the lips part and redden.

Hastily I rearranged my thoughts. Style's infirmity was not an area open to examination, but it wasn't irrelevant. Axnoller had implied that it had some negative bearing on the company balance sheet. Sex *and* money – the most powerful motives. But motives for what?

'In what way do your husband's interests coincide with Axnoller's?'

'That's something I've never troubled to find out.'

'But you know about Axnoller's operation.'

She compressed her lips. 'Only what I read in the papers.'

I pictured Axnoller, rosy-faced and puffed with greed. 'He implied he was expanding his operation over here.'

Lisa affected a careless laugh. 'Wales is a property-owning democracy. Axnoller dumps his trash in parts of the world where public scrutiny is lacking.'

I didn't smile. 'There are a lot of holes in Wales, and times are hard.' I took the plunge. 'Even for your husband.'

She swung on me, her pupils dilated with anger. 'That's a goddam lie.' Her fury vaulted to another level. 'What business is this to a goddam trucker?' she shouted. 'Just who the hell do you think you are?'

'I'm only the driver.'

'Then what are you doing poking around in my husband's affairs.'

'Axnoller said something about fattening frogs for snakes. He's the snake. He gave the impression that your husband is the frog.'

She shut her eyes. 'Oh God,' she whispered. 'Poor Victor.'

'I think he's pretty desperate. I mean, I think he's capable of doing something desperate.'

She shook her head, stunned.

I resisted the urge to lay my arm around her shoulders. 'Is there no chance of you getting back together?'

Lisa went limp. 'Love isn't something you can re-invent.' Her eyes were brilliant. 'Dammit,' she cried, struggling up. 'I knew I shouldn't have come.'

I was on my feet, helping her into her coat. 'Why did you?'

'To discuss the settlement.' She smoothed her coat and instinctively glanced in a mirror. 'I'd be indebted if you didn't tell anyone I was here.'

'Not even your husband?'

'Not anyone,' she said, and touched my lips. She smiled. 'Promise me.'

I had no defence against that smile. 'My word.'

'I guess you are a gentleman too.' Eyes veiled, she leaned and brushed her lips against my cheek. 'It's gone midnight, and my carriage is waiting, and I'll never know what a prince is doing driving a panel truck.' She touched my hand. 'Too bad.'

Then she was gone, her footsteps tapping on the parquet, her voice calling back: 'Wish me luck.'

'Good luck,' I murmured, stroking my face where she had kissed me, already beginning to replay the encounter from the moment she walked into my life to the moment she walked out.

9

I was stopped at a red light with a rush-hour queue jammed behind for as far as the rearview could see. The lights changed and I put the truck into gear and the engine stalled. I tried again, casting rabbity glances behind. Everyone wanted to get home. Already I was sweating, braced for the first impatient toot, and as the engine churned again, there it came, scattering what senses I had left so that I kept pumping the throttle to the floor, flooding the engine and filling the cabin with the explosive reek of fuel. The traffic had struck up like a crazed orchestra. Can't you see I'm stalled? Doors were slamming all down the line. In the mirror I saw motorists striding towards me with knives in their hands, and at the front were Eeles, Axnoller and the murdered driver.

I jolted upright with a yelp, and even in the first scrambled moment I knew that the nightmare wasn't over. I fumbled for the light. I'd been asleep for only forty minutes. My mouth was parched, my back oily with sweat.

The room was stifling. Outside, the wind sang dreary harmonics around the eaves. I left my bed and tried to open the window, but it was locked.

I went out into the hall. Style had put me in an annexe for his stable hands, who had gone home to Ireland for the holiday. I groped my way by available light. In the bathroom I drank copiously, glanced at my reflection in the dark mirror, and went back into the corridor.

I lost my way. I took a wrong turning and found myself at a dead end.

As I turned to go back, a sound intruded on my consciousness – a rhythmic clicking. At first I thought it must be a branch fretting in the wind, but when I looked in the direction of the disturbance, I saw a grey crack of light further down the corridor. I hesitated, then crept closer. The light was showing through a slightly open door and the metered clicking was coming from inside. It stopped, to be replaced by a faint whirring that accelerated to a subdued whine.

I touched the door without meaning to and it swung open another few inches. A blank but live television screen glowed in the dark. I recognised the noise now. It was a video cassette rewinding. Someone must have programmed the machine to record a late-night programme.

The television popped into life and two figures began walking through the entrance of a supermarket. One of them was Victor Style, smiling in an unpractised way. Apparently the footage was from a local news programme. Beside Style walked a tall, slim, assured-looking man.

It was only when the film halted that I realised someone was in the room, controlling the playback. The person was sitting in a high-backed armchair, invisible from the door, studying the freeze-frame. Knowing that any move I made, however slight, would alert him, I remained as frozen as the figures on the screen, waiting for the tape to restart. A pulse throbbed in my temples. The trembling image stayed constant and the person in the chair made not a sound. I began to fear that he had sensed my presence and was waiting for me to declare himself. I imagined his eyes turn, just his eyes.

With a click the screen blanked out and the video went into fast reverse. I fled, and I did not let my breath go until I was back in my room, the door locked behind me.

I lay in the fevered dark, flinching at each change in the wind. I don't know why, but though I couldn't put a face to the man watching television, I had a vague, floating feeling that it wasn't anyone I'd met in that house. I wondered why he had been studying film of Style, and then it occurred to me that the focus of his attention might have been the other man.

On top of everything else, it was too much. 'Something isn't right,' I whispered. 'Something is very wrong.'

An insistent rapping galvanised me from a slide into stupor.

'Time to go.'

I blundered to the door and unlocked it. Style was still in evening wear. He appraised my condition. 'Take a shower,' he ordered. 'I'll get breakfast started.'

Sleep had unravelled events from their context. Confronted by the blank door of the room where the faceless man had been sitting in the dark watching the video, it was almost possible to believe I'd imagined him. Almost. Under the shower memories bombarded me in random flashback, like dislocated episodes of a vivid dream. Lisa Hope came back as a succession of pangs – her cool republican voice, her expression fleeting between emotions, the way her dress moulded itself to her thigh. Of all my recollections she was the most intense, yet the most elusive.

Except for James Griffith, I realised in guilty after-thought. I was putting on his clothes, picking up the keys to his truck, yet somehow I couldn't quite make the connection between these acts and the fact of his death. Like the Mercedes driver whose legs I had seen sticking out under his door, he had become an abstraction, shocking but remote – as Eeles had said, a road accident statistic glimpsed in passing.

Cooking smells guided me to the kitchen – another

excruciating triumph of money over taste. The room was lined with solid beechwood units piped in red and blue and capped by an equestrian frieze. The hob extractor was hooded by a canopy of planished copper. The tile surrounds featured a motif of shepherdesses picking posies. The rustic beams were fibreglass fakes.

Style had cooked an authentic trucker's fry-up – bacon, sausage, eggs and beans. I was very hungry and felt bad about it. Style watched the clock, fretting to send me on my way, while between mouthfuls I stole looks at him, wondering how he'd react if I told him that I'd felt the touch of his wife's lips here in this house not more than three hours ago. A settlement, she'd said, but Style hadn't been expecting her.

I was still chewing that one over when Style rousted me out.

Night still had hours to run and down below the lights twinkled brighter and harder than ever. The wind had fallen away and it was very cold and clear – jumping cold as the Welsh say. I breathed deep when I saw the truck.

'I'll come with you as far as the motorway.'

'No need for that,' I said, worrying about my miserable possessions stashed in the wood.

But Style was already walking away to the Range Rover.

I pulled myself aboard. The engine fired at a touch and I scanned the instruments, my hands suspended over the wheel like a pianist about to begin a tricky solo. Style gave me an impatient toot. The red eye of the Vehicle Location Device glowed patiently. Deciding to wait until I was well clear before switching it off, I dipped the throttle and eased away.

Until I had negotiated my way off the hillside, I couldn't afford to do any forward planning. The country roads were treacherous with snow over a glaze of ice, and though I drove with delicacy, using the gears instead of brakes, I had a couple of heart-stopping moments when the truck's mass threatened to get away from me on awkward cambers. By the time I reached the motorway my hands were slick and I felt I had already done a day's work.

Style was parked on the sliproad, his face immobile behind the screen. The landscape was white and completely empty. One lane on each carriageway had been ploughed clean, but there were no vehicles moving in either direction. I climbed out into a polar stillness.

'You've got six hours before the ferry sails,' Style said. 'No need to rush it. Call me when you reach Plymouth.'

His voice was muted, his manner low key, but behind the pose I discerned a secret excitement. The certainty of betraying him made me feel rotten as hell. 'The road's pretty bad,' I muttered, 'and conditions will be worse once I'm off the motorway. I can't guarantee I'll make it.'

His breath misted in a sigh. 'I said I never worry about things that aren't under my control.' His eyes panned towards me. 'Don't make me start worrying about you.'

'Right.'

Sobered by the threat, I drove off with one eye on the mirror, not taking my escape for granted. Darkness closed down behind and the motorway stretched ahead, wide and empty, and only then could I accept that I'd come through unscathed and richer by two thousand pounds. This was the moment I'd anticipated. I'd imagined waltzing down the road, pounding the wheel in glee. But the elation didn't come. I felt corrupt, good for nothing.

I began to examine the range of actions open to me. My first impulse was to find a quiet spot where I could tear the truck apart. 'An unstable load,' the loss adjuster had claimed – whatever that meant. If it was drugs or arms, I'd have the evidence that would get me off the hook. And if it was something else, something I hadn't considered? I'd have to balance moral duty against personal risk.

A bridge loomed over my imaginings. I was approaching the spot where James Vernon Griffith lay. I sat forward, tensing for the moment when I saw it again, but in the dark and snow all places were the same. With a concussion of air the bridge was behind me, another one ahead. I tried to reconstruct the place in memeory, only to find that I'd been too shocked and frightened to take any bearings. When the third bridge went by, I knew that I must have passed the body.

I couldn't get a fix on anything. The motorway and the countryside had merged into the same blank whiteness; the black lane was a corridor without reference. Faced with the strange emptiness, my mind took wing, gliding along the illusion that I had slipped through a warp and was travelling in time as well as space, not only reversing my direction but also wiping out the events of New Year's Eve, so that by the time I reached the other side of the river, Griffith would still be alive and I would be back where I had started.

Locked in a dreamy overdrive, I cruised on, the shadowy cab my nightquarters on a trip through the universe. At some distance impossible to gauge, a chaplet of amber lights flickered in a mesmerising sequence – another traveller, a long way off. Slowly we converged, two migrants drawn through space, and it wasn't until I had closed right up that I recognised the vehicle as a giant snow plough, its driver enthroned ten feet above the ground, a godlike silhouette with arm raised in salute.

I massaged my eyes. A junction was signalled one mile ahead. Several turnings had offered themselves, but I kept postponing the moment of decision, wanting to put my getaway beyond doubt. I would have to leave the motorway soon, though, because Cardiff was coming up and I would lose the chance to find a rural backroad where I could search the load without interference.

Distance indicators counted me down – three hundred metres, two hundred . . . My jaw set. I dropped a gear and gripped the wheel as if I was taking off in a plane, but in the moment before I sheered off an inner voice called a warning. This is a very crowded island, it said, and if at dead of night in a country lane someone sees you searching the cargo bay by torchlight, they'll suspect a criminal act. Besides, you don't know what you're looking for. You might not recognise it even if you found it. Wait until daylight. Wait until you can pick your spot.

Keeping my options open – that's how I rationalised my decision. But as I continued down the road, my lack of resolution grated. Looking back, it seemed to me that there must have been some point when I could have avoided all this, some juncture where positive action could have carried me clear with honour. Instead, all my reactions had been short-term, based on aversion to the forseeable consequences. Like a rat feeling its way through an electrified maze, I had avoided the immediate shocks and taken the route of least personal pain and found myself . . .

Out, I reminded myself, and with the cheese too. And if that was more by luck than courage, so what? Luck isn't to be sneezed at.

I drove on, soothed by the empty night, my thoughts gradually sinking inside me.

Half an hour must have passed before consciousness surfaced. I was coasting down a long incline, the engine note bouncing back from the walls of a cutting, when the hairs lifted on the back of my neck and I glanced left, half-expecting to see the figure of Griffith in the passenger seat. It was empty, of course, but the sensation of being in a presence persisted, and before I could help myself, I had twitched the drapes of the bunk apart. There was nothing there.

Only the ghost in the cab – a phenomenon common to tired drivers the world over.

I *was* tired. I'd slept for no more than three hours in the last twenty. The adrenalin that had kept me going had dried up. My mind was growing sluggish and my eyes were like peep-holes peering down an endless tunnel. I ventilated the cab with icy air and switched on the radio, quickening the tempo with foreign music. A time-check revealed I was making surprisingly good progress. At this rate I could have caught the ferry with time to spare. My foot slackened on the accelerator, but the speed crept up again, and since it didn't matter whether I reached my destination early or late, I let the truck set its own pace and went along with it, just a part of the machinery.

IO

Traffic began to appear in dribs and drabs and the towers of the suspension bridge rose against the sky, enveloped in halogen spheres. Once I'd passed the tolls on the far side, all directions would be open to me.

Oncoming cars smeared me with their headlights. Edginess returned. On the motorway I'd been a shadow behind lights, but in the glare of metropolis I felt conspicuous. So far, I hadn't encountered any other commercial vehicle, and it was possible that the police would flag me down to ask what was so important about my New Year mission. Reproaching myself for not thinking of it earlier, I hid my own passport and driving licence in a gap between the VLD and the roof-lining.

Up ahead, toll booths picketed the road. I had the money ready and the window open when a routine glance in the mirror revealed a car that had been tucked behind me for at least a couple of miles. The thought that it had been following me, at first no more than an idle testing of possibilities, took hold and wouldn't let go. Either Style or Axnoller might have decided to keep an eye on me; both parties must have detected a certain ambivalence in my attitude.

Only one of the booths was open and two cars were queueing to go through. I waited my turn, my attention on the mirror. I thought I could see two occupants. A hoot startled me. The toll was clear. In my nervousness I crashed gears and slightly overshot, drawing a quizzical look from the collector. He would remember me, I thought distractedly, watching the car close up behind me again and begin to overtake. Slowly it drew abreast. My stare was met by the vacant glance of a stranger.

There, I thought, switching off the VLD. Now try and find me.

At the next big interchange I peeled off on to the M5, intending to orbit Bristol until I could siphon off into the university district. Time was still on my side. If anything, I was too early; dawn was still a couple of hours off. It would be sensible to lie up until the city went to work.

Work? Today was a public holiday. The commercial area would be shut down. No trucks would be loading or unloading. My inability to think ahead was frightening. Forget the truck, I told myself. Apart from the risk, there might be nothing to find. The truck might be going to Spain to pick something *up*.

Ditch it now, I decided. Ditch it and walk away. Call the police and let them worry about the load.

Freed from that responsibility, my worries fell by the wayside and my mind drifted into a pleasant reverie about Eleanor Barry.

In a way I had never stopped thinking about her, though not thinking of her in particular. Was it really only twelve hours since we'd spoken? Impossible. But unless I had somehow lost a day, it must be so, which meant that there were still six hours to go before we were due to meet. She would still be asleep, her head dark on the pillow.

At last I saw the way ahead open, nothing between me and my goal. My arrangement with Eleanor still held. Eeles, Axnoller, Style – they had been nothing more than a detour off the clearway of my obsession. I had time in hand

and money in my pocket. I could be back in Swansea long before lunchtime. I would travel by train, first-class – or even hire a taxi if necessary. Nothing was going to make me miss my date.

Ten minutes later the phone rang. It was Eeles.

I hailed him blithely. 'Good morning. A happy New Year to you.'

'What's your position?'

'Lost track, have you?' I could afford to bait him. Being someone else was like being invisible. It was better than being invisible because I could take part in the drama without any risk to myself.

'Have you turned off the VLD?'

'You can't be too careful.' Now that I'd put safe distance between us, I almost regretted having to shed Griffith's identity so soon. It would have been fascinating to see how far I could take it.

'I called the police about that crash. What they told me is causing deep concern.'

It was consolation for the ordeal he'd put me through. The mystery of the driver who never was would madden Eeles to his dying day. 'Rip,' I said, 'I promise there'll be a lot more sleepless nights.'

When at last he spoke, he sounded gratifyingly out of sorts. 'All right, Griffith, let's stop this play-acting. The only matter of relevance is the agreement you made last night.'

Only one decision counted, and that one I was determined to keep to through thick and thin. 'Which agreement would that be?'

'Griffith, listen very carefully. When you accepted the money, you made a binding contract. I must impress that on you.' He paused for the impression to make itself felt. 'To do otherwise would be in your own worst interests.'

'I thought it was Victor Style's interests you were paid to protect.'

'Precisely.'

'In sickness and in health, eh?'

'Damn you, Griffith. Just tell me that you won't catch the ferry.'

I was watching myself in the mirror, watching my performance and wondering how far I could string Eeles along, and then all of a sudden I remembered that this wasn't hide-and-seek. Eeles was responsible for the death of an innocent man, and by holding my silence I was colluding in the crime. I was an accessory to murder.

'Tell me why you don't want this truck to reach Spain.'

'That's no concern of yours.'

'This is my truck, Eeles. The load's my responsibility.'

'You said you answered to whoever was paying you. Well, you've been paid. Leave it at that. For your own sake.'

'Maybe for my own sake I should turn the truck over to the police.'

'I see,' Eeles said, his voice leached of expression. 'Hold the line one moment.'

I waited.

'How ya doing?' the loss adjuster asked affably.

I regretted my petty bravado instantly. 'Fine.'

'Sure you are. Hey, Rip says you've got an attitude problem. He has you suspicioned for a conniver. Like when you told me –*two times over* – you were gonna not be on that ferry, Rip reckons that was just a pre-tence. He thinks – and I'm not saying he's gauged you fair – he thinks what you were *really* saying was: I'm gonna take this old fool's money and drive up the gangplank and cut out all the way down to Spain.' The voice, which had risen in indignation fell to tones of pained inquiry. 'Tell me you ain't gonna do anything so dick dumb as that.'

'You have my assurance,' I told him. His voice had a hypnotic swing and I pictured him using it as a screen, a distraction to enable him to creep up within range. I found myself inspecting the mirror, even though I was a hundred miles from danger. I hoped I was a hundred miles from danger.

'You use tricky vocabulary, mister, and that makes me kinda nervous, so to ease my mind, you tell me straight out what it is you're saying.'

The long-awaited junction was in sight. 'Don't worry,' I said, lining up for the approach, 'this journey ends right now.'

'It had damn well better, mister, 'cos if you're weaseling me, I swear to high heaven above you ain't gonna have no place else left to turn.'

I didn't catch the full force of the threat because in the last split-second I saw a toppled sign that warned: ROAD CLOSED. FOLLOW DIVERSION TO JUNCTION 19.

In that same small fraction of time I worked out that traffic had ignored the warning and successfully got up the sliproad before me. Committed, I floored the accelerator, but as soon as I was on the slope I knew I was in trouble. The cars had packed the snow so hard that there was no traction and I didn't have their speed to carry me clear. I nearly made it; I was no more than twenty yards short of the roundabout at the top when my momentum ran out and the wheels began to spin. Clumsily I snatched first, making what began as a gentle drift snap into a slide that left me broadside.

'Shit!'

I killed the engine and jumped out.

All around me the city was electrified, but between me

and the commotion of lights lay a divide of dark and hushed air that made me feel like the only person alive for miles. Junction 19 was south, away from the city, away from Eleanor Barry. To have a destiny and to be diverted in the opposite direction was infuriating beyond words. On the roundabout a snowman's black pebble eyes and ear-to-ear grin mocked me.

The truck was slewed across the sliproad, looking out of place and in need of attention. The temptation to turn my back on it and walk on into the centre was sapped by the knowledge that by now the cab would be permeated with my presence. I would never be able to erase it completely: some forensic scientist would find my signature in a strand of hair, construct a genetic profile from a flake of dandruff. Dejected, I walked back, started up, straightened the truck, then half reversed, half slipped back down to the motorway.

Back on the black conveyor, going the wrong way. Soon the city lights became few and far between and then there were no lights at all except for the occasional beams of northbound traffic. My thoughts came and went on the same frequency – appearing far off, approaching slowly and then rushing past too fast to hold on to before falling away like the burnt-out stages of a rocket. 'Ain't no place left to turn.'

Lassitude stole up on me. I was too shattered, too demoralised, to see Eleanor Barry that day. I would phone her to explain that the weather had defeated me. Giving in to fatalism, I decided that I might as well drive all the way to Plymouth. Only going through the motions, I told myself through a yawn. Just making an appearance of effort so that when I called Style, I could tell him quite honestly that I'd missed the boat.

I I

My silent passenger joined me again. Condemnation hung in the air, and I knew that Griffith was angry I had taken the bribe.

'But then you've got something to lose. Pride in your work, a place in society.'

He didn't respond. He was slumped forward, his eyes on the road.

'What was I supposed to do? I've come too far down the wrong road. If I tell the police now, I'm in deep, swirling shit.'

Again Griffith didn't answer, and when I turned I saw that he couldn't speak because he was dead, his eye sockets packed with snow.

Shock wrenched me sideways and the central reservation leapt towards me and the truck hit the barrier a glancing blow that sent it careening back across the carriageway, a chaos of violently opposed forces that cancelled out abruptly, dropping it with a four-square crash that jarred my teeth and toppled some item of cargo so heavily that the truck lurched again.

And then we were pointing straight, the smell of carbonised rubber mingling with the acrid taste of fright.

When my wits had crawled back I considered stopping to check for damage, but the engine sounded fine and the truck still went where I aimed it. The truly frightening thing was not knowing how long I'd been asleep. The road gave no clue. I opened both windows because it was only a matter of time before I drifted off again.

I could still feel the dead driver's reproach pricking at my self-esteem.

By the time I pulled into the next service station, I was chilled to the bone. Arrows directed me to an icy apron occupied by half a dozen juggernauts laid up for the holiday. I parked behind them, away from the sallow overhead lights.

Knowing that if I didn't move right away, fatigue would nail me to the spot, I elbowed open the door and dropped down. My legs buckled under the unexpected weight. The collision had made a mess of the cab's off-side bumper, but nothing vital had fallen off. I stretched and kneaded the back of my neck. Stillness shrouded the herd of trucks. The darkness was thinning at last and I could locate the horizon.

It was a long trudge to the facilities. In the doorway a gorilla was peering this way and that, angrily searching for something. When I tried to pass, it gibbered in front of me. Placing the flat of my hand on its muzzle, I pushed it aside.

Inside, I stepped around an American footballer and a harlequin who were trying to revive a semi-conscious pirate. I didn't find their presence at odds with reality. In the restaurant I drank coffee that tasted like yeast extract. My eyes were pin-points, focused on whatever happened to be right under them.

A waitress clearing my table woke me up. I raised dazed eyes to find that New Year's day had dawned and the fancy dress party had moved on. In less than an hour the ferry would sail without me, so that was one more decision out of my hands. Time was a great sorter, I told my badly sorted reflection in the washroom.

Outside, wintry hills were printed on an oyster-grey sky.

In that cold and commonplace setting the trucks struck a carnival note, suggestive of dawn departures and new beginnings. My truck, which I had thought was big, was the smallest but the brightest, its blue and gold livery shining like a burst of Aegean sunshine. ARGONAUT HAULAGE – the epic message subverted by the miniature Christmas tree above it.

I walked to the rear. There would never be a right time to look behind the doors. Given half a chance, my imagination would always cripple my capacity for action. Now was as good a time as any.

It took ten minutes to crack the set of locks and levers, and only one glance inside to reveal that a thorough search was out of the question. Just as the inventory claimed, the cargo bay was stacked from floor to roof with household effects, all covered in white dust sheets. My gaze roamed the surface layer, noting an upturned table cradling lamp-shades, a wardrobe, a rolled-up carpet, a . . .

I levered myself up and peered deeper into the gloom, making sure that when I locked the doors again I would lock them for good, with no nagging doubts. My mishap on the motorway had apparently added to the chaos, toppling a wardrobe on to a nailed-up container which, I guessed with a wince, recalling the crash of breaking glass, probably held Mrs Hutchinson's best china and treasured knick-knacks.

Some discrepancy in my interpretation of events bothered me – some breakdown in the connection between the men in the Skoda and the people at Style's house. I tried to follow the train of thought but lost it in a tunnel.

'Hey mister – you up there.'

I didn't flinch; I didn't even turn. Only when she began hammering on the floor did I condescend to notice. From ten feet above the ground I looked impassively into a sandy, freckled face framed by curly hair the colour of baked beans. She wore a gauzy gown over a satin jacket and mini-skirt and legwarmers – some kind of fashion statement that was gobbledegook to me. She stood hugging herself and swivelling her body above the hips.

'Hi, I'm Steph,' she said in a predictably northern accent. She had the guileless smile of an infant soliciting friendship in a school playground. There was a green-blue bruise on her temple.

Ignoring her, I jumped down and secured the doors.

'Where you going?'

'South,' I admitted, walking back to the cab.

'South where?'

'Just south.'

'Give us a lift then. Go on.'

'Sorry.'

'Me mam's ill,' Steph pleaded. 'I heard it on the radio – one of them SAS messages.'

'SOS,' I corrected automatically, unlocking the cab.

'Yeah, they said to get home quick. Dead ill, they said she was.'

It was such a ridiculous fabrication that I laughed.

'Hey, it's not funny,' she said, forgetting to dim her own smile.

I climbed up. 'Where does your mother live?'

Steph frowned uncertainly down the broad sweep of motorway. 'Southampton?' she suggested.

'You're on the wrong road.'

'It's a start, in't it? Any road, if that's where you're going, what difference does it make?'

'I never give lifts to strangers,' I told her. I shut the door, settled into my seat and snapped on the belt. Steph hammered for attention. With a sigh, I powered down the window.

She cast a furtive glance behind, as if danger might be

creeping up. 'Yeah, but look. I gorra get out of this place. There's this nutter after me.'

'Sorry,' I said conclusively, and then for good measure, added: 'It's more than my job's worth.'

She cocked her chin. 'It's not worth more than my life, is it?' Her expression turned hopeful. 'I'll pay you.'

I fine-tuned the rake of the infinitely adjustable air-suspended seat. 'If you can pay, take the train.'

'On a motorway? Don't be soft.'

I adjusted the mirrors, paying particular attention to the near-side, which was something of a blind spot.

Steph jumped on the step. 'That bunk looks comfy. Loads of room.'

'Forget it.' Aware that this exchange was about to get out of hand, I reached for the ignition. 'You'd better step off before you get hurt.'

'Please, mister, I'll get hurt worse if you leave me here. Honest.'

I hardened my heart, and under my stare, Steph backed down. She scuffed her foot in the snow. 'I'll toss you off. I don't care.'

'That won't be necessary,' I said, shocked into a bungled start that left the engine flooded. Furiously I worked the starter and the throttle.

'Don't you fancy me then?'

'No,' I shouted over the blessed roar of the engine. 'That's got nothing to do with it.'

Next would come abuse, I guessed, powering the window shut, but after giving me a sad look that struck deeper than expected, she walked away, suddenly increasing her pace as if she had remembered important things to do and regretted wasting her precious time on me.

I passed her on the exit lane. She was writing something in the snow with her foot. HOMELESS AND HARMLESS

I read as I went by. In the mirror I saw her receding, rubbing her arms and looking tiny. 'Sorry, Steph,' I said to her telescoped image, 'but I've got my own set of troubles.'

From out of nowhere the gorilla jumped on her.

It had hold of her by one arm and she was kicking uselessly at it – like Fay whatever-her-name-was in the grip of King Kong. Then the gorilla backhanded her to the ground and it stopped being funny and I stabbed down on the brakes.

'Leave her alone,' I shouted, out of the cab and running before thought had a chance to intervene.

The gorilla looked up and roared, pounding his chest so convincingly that I couldn't help wondering if it was the real thing. I kept on running, making myself heavy, ready to plough through anything. The ape reconsidered its stance. I was ten yards short and unstoppable when it broke and fled, pausing a safe distance away to perform a simian dance of rage. It got smaller, dwindling against the snow until it was no bigger than an irate spider.

Dizzy with exertion, I offered Steph my hand. Stars spiralled across my vision. 'What was all that about?'

'I don't know, do I?' she said crossly, brushing herself off. 'I couldn't make out a word he said.'

I 2

'Don't tell me that's it.'

'It what?'

'Your luggage.'

'Oh,' she said in lofty tones, eyeing her purse, 'my chauffeur will be bringing the rest of my things.'

Feckless, I thought. A feckless and probably drug-ravaged delinquent who hadn't even thanked me for saving her life.

'Where we going then?' Steph demanded when we were up to running speed.

'Plymouth.'

'You catching the ferry?'

'No, I'm dropping a load there and then going back to . . . driving home.'

'Where's that?'

'Bristol.'

'What'ya called?' She was a resilient little creature.

'James.'

'Gorra ciggie, James?'

'I don't smoke.'

'That's a nice jacket. How much did it cost?'

'Er, I can't remember. A couple of hundred, I think.'

'You got a bargain there,' she said wisely. Then she yawned, as if she'd already had this conversation that day, rolled her head to one side and shut her eyes.

I waited a moment. 'I'm the one who should be asleep. If you want to reach your destination in one piece, I suggest you start talking.'

'What about?'

'Anything. Life.'

After a pause she giggled. 'It'll cost you.'

'What?'

'Fifty pee a minute. That's what I charge.'

'Charge for what?'

She sighed and rolled her head towards me as if the rest of her body was too heavy to move. 'I worked on this sex line in Bristol, right? Forty-eight pee a minute, peak-time; thirty-six cheap rate.'

'You – on a sex line?' I blinked. 'How old are you?'

'Old enough.'

I glanced from her to the road and back again. 'Who does the talking?'

'You start the punters off, then . . . ' Steph smiled without mirth ' . . . it's in their hands, in't it? Only you don't, you know, want them to get carried away. Darren says we've got to keep them going for twenty minutes, right? That's his production thingummy wotsit. He used to work for American Express.' She frowned. 'What's that, a computer?'

'Vehicle tracking device. It's switched off. How many girls does Darren employ?'

'Loads. Let's see. There was me, my friend Trace, Moira, Ellen . . . until she got a child-minder job. Eight altogether – two lots of eight working twelve-hour shifts. Round the clock filth.'

I tried to multiply it up.

'Five thousand quid on a good day,' Steph said, reading my mind, 'and Darren paid us two-fifty an hour.'

'That's not a lot.'

'It's bugger-all. So I decided to do a bit of private

enterprise, like Darren was always on about.' Steph made herself more comfortable. 'I had one old wanker, right? A pensioner who called every Sunday morning when his wife was at church. Sundays was always a good day. This bloke always asked for me. I don't know why. Any road, after a few weeks, I said to him: instead of chucking your pension away, why don't you send me a fiver a week and I'll call *you*? And you know what the old sod did?' Steph shook her head at the old sod's inability to spot a bargain. 'He called Darren and said I was trying to put the black on him.'

'What did he do?' I asked, aware that Darren was not the type to refer the matter to an industrial tribunal.

Steph poked at the bruise on her forehead. 'Darren went berserk, that's what happened.'

I was moved to silence for a while. 'That wasn't Darren in the gorilla suit?' The question had to be asked.

'No,' Steph said absently, 'that was someone else.' She smiled at me. 'Anyway, do you fancy it?'

'What, you talking . . . ?'

'I could do with a few quid.'

In no uncertain terms I started to tell her what I thought of the suggestion, but before I'd finished she had fallen asleep.

Clumps of traffic hampered me on the last leg to Plymouth. Steph was still asleep, the strains of her young life ironed out. On balance, I found her dulled presence comforting.

When I next looked, she was awake and watching me with a drowsy stare.

'I'm not a slag, you know.'

I shifted position. 'I never said you were. But if I were you, I'd be more careful what I say to strangers.'

'If I'd known you weren't a proper lorry driver, I wouldn't have told you those things.'

I corrected the reflex swerve. 'What makes you think I'm not a proper driver?'

Steph's gaze was unblinking, like a cat's. 'You don't look like a lorry driver. You don't sound like a lorry driver. You don't even *drive* like a lorry driver.'

'Well I am,' I said weakly.

'Not always you weren't – not with that voice.'

'I was a teacher.'

'You see,' she cried, and then looked at me on the bias. 'What kind of teacher?'

'History.'

'Urgh,' she said, and wriggled as if a slug had dropped on her neck. 'So why'd you give up a decent job for this?'

'It's a long story.'

Fortunately, Steph had the attention span of a bird. She twiddled with the radio, channel-hopping. 'Crap,' she said, passing fair comment on some fruggy-dug-dug music. 'Crap,' she said, dismissing a blip of Mahler and all his works. She overshot a French station, back-tracked and stopped on a wavelength featuring a chanteuse with a voice abraded by black tobacco.

'Like it?'

Steph considered a while. 'What's she on about?'

'Standard issue. Her heart's broken; she'll never love again.'

'Me and all.' She gave me one of her quick glances. 'You married?'

'No.'

'You queer?'

'Life would be easier if I was.'

'So why don't you fancy me then?'

'It's not that.'

'You're not bad-looking, you know. Nice eyes. That's

what I always look at first – a man's eyes. Eyes never lie – that's what me mam says.'

I laughed, feeling sad.

'Well?'

'Well what?'

Steph's voice was patient. 'I gave you a compliment; now you're supposed to give one back.'

I looked at her in a sort of anguish. She had slight, Asian–Celtic features with flecked green eyes that projected a mongrel vitality. A wide, mobile mouth. In fact, if you overlooked the trashy clothes and the mangled syntax, she was quite . . . fetching. But I could hardly tell her that.

She took off her jacket. Her waist was tiny, her breasts fuller than I'd imagined. Quickly I looked away.

'I like your accent.' I did, as a matter of fact. Her r's were dark and rolled, almost a burr.

'Thanks a *lot*.'

'You've got a distinctive face.'

'So's a baboon. Come on, I said a *compliment*.'

'Distinctive *shape*.'

She swivelled the mirror towards her and grimaced. 'What, you mean pointy?'

'Unusual,' I said, floundering. 'Different,' I threw in for good measure. 'Exotic,' I concluded in desperation.

She gave me a narrow look, searching for the lie, but when she turned back to the mirror, I could see she was examining herself in a new light.

On the hour I commandeered the radio for the news. There was no mention of a body by the roadside, but the knowledge that it would be in the next bulletin or the one after put a hole in my spirits. A vision of a spreading stain on the snow covering Griffith made me wince. He wasn't going to go away. He would be my co-passenger for life.

A van overtook and the driver noticed Steph and grinned

suggestively. I nudged her. 'I'd prefer it if you got in the bunk. I don't want anyone thinking I've got a runaway on board.'

She didn't object. In fact when she saw the television she was thrilled to bits. 'Hey, videos. What you got then?'

'I'm not sure.' Plymouth was fifteen miles off and I still hadn't solved the truck disposal problem. It was a trundling millstone and I was a permanent fixture.

'Oo-er!' Steph shrieked. 'Bloody hell!'

'What is it?'

Silence.

I craned round, alarmed that Steph had uncovered evidence of the night's foul deeds, and glimpsed the tiny television screen filled with a tableau of a swarthy man pushing his penis into a blonde woman's gaping mouth while behind him another man . . .

'Turn it off.'

'That's disgusting. Gor, look at that.'

'Just turn the bloody thing off!'

There was a click and a smarting silence.

'It isn't mine,' I said, my voice toneless. 'They belong to the driver who had the truck before me.'

In the mirror Steph was staring at me as if she was seeing me properly for the first time.

'I don't know why you're so shocked,' I blurted. 'You're the one who offered to . . . do all those things.'

'That was before I knew you.'

The ambiguity of my position enraged me. 'You don't know the first thing about me.'

'And I don't want to,' she shouted back.

She vacated the bunk and came and sat down, her hands prim in her lap and her eyes focused a long way down the road. We proceeded in an atmosphere of mutual moral disdain.

'I need to use the little girl's room,' she announced, after a few miles.

'What?'

'I need . . .'

'I know what you said. Why don't you use plain English? Why don't you say you want a piss?'

She looked at me, her eyes small and her flexible mouth crimped in scorn. 'You know what? You're really crude.'

13

Steph had been inside the filling station for over five minutes and I was fuming, convinced that she wasn't coming back and wondering why I was bothering to wait. I edged looks all round. The truck felt oversize and inappropriate on the small forecourt. On the road, traffic went past both ways, slush squirting from their tyres. It was past nine, but the sky was undifferentiated, grey for the duration. Another minute, I decided.

A maroon Cavalier driving north made a sharp U-turn and drove irresponsibly fast into the station, pitching on its suspension as it hit the ramp of the forecourt. It nosed past me and stopped a few yards in front.

By leaning low I could see part of the shop's interior. Steph wasn't in view. She was probably shop-lifting, I decided, or propositioning some hot-hatch owner. What did it matter if she thought I was a sex maniac with gross appetites? The minute was up. To hell with it, I thought, reaching for the key. Another thing less to worry about.

The Cavalier had parked inconsiderately between the office and the nearest line of pumps. Cars occupied all the other pumps, effectively blocking my exit. I glanced at the office, wondering where the Cavalier's driver had got to, then I realised that no one had left the car and my heart hit my ribs with a wallop.

From my perch I couldn't see the occupants, but the

driver's face was reflected in his wing mirror and his avid expression seemed to be directed at me. I didn't recognise the car. It was dark red, dripping slush and streaked with salt, as if it had been driven hard a long way. I turned the ignition as gently as I could and crept into reverse.

Steph showed up all of a sudden, indifferent to the situation. I groaned. She waved, held up a carrier bag and broke into a high-stepping trot, trying to avoid the ridges and remnants of snow. I dropped the clutch, thought better of leaving her and flung open the door. 'Get a move on!'

As she flopped aboard, the Cavalier's doors opened, sickeningly like a replay of the scene with the Skoda. 'Shut your door!'

Two youngish men in casual clothes stepped out with purposeful co-ordination. In a fumble I activated the door locks.

'Who's been a naughty boy then?'

'Get out. Call the police.'

'A bit late for that, in't it?'

The two men acted as if I was invisible. One of them was lean and dark, the other tubby and ginger-haired. The lean one walked up to the front of the cab, while the other one made a survey of the rest of the vehicle. Then the one right under my nose looked up as if noticing me for the first time and held up a badge.

The universe stopped in its tracks. Griffith had been found. This was it. The end.

The policeman with the badge made a winding motion. Eventually I managed to lower my window.

'Good morning, sir,' the policeman said. 'Boss working you hard?'

'Oh, I don't mind.' I made a useless gesture. 'I'm in a hurry. I'm supposed to be on the ferry.'

'We won't detain you long. Just a few questions.'

'Certainly.' The trouble was that I had an innate respect for authority, even when it came dressed in a bomber jacket and trainers and was about to arrest me for murder.

'Would you mind stepping down, sir?'

I did as I was asked and smiled at each officer in turn. My legs felt as if they were made of cardboard. 'What's it about?'

'I'm Detective-Sergeant Acheson,' the lean officer said, 'and this is Detective-Constable Palmer. Plymouth CID. We're investigating the murder of a young woman, Zoe Redman, who was last seen alive at this filling station ten days ago.'

Suddenly the air was full of springtime and roses. 'I don't think I can be of any help. I've been abroad since the twenty-second.'

DC Palmer glanced at Acheson. 'Can you give us precise times, sir?'

It was up to me. Hesitation, fear – all the stigmata of guilt –would sink me. This time I had to throw myself into the part from line one. 'I left the Swansea depot at six-fifteen and caught the midday ferry.'

'And you were driving what kind of vehicle?'

'A Powerliner,' I said, recalling Griffith's pride of ownership. 'Flagship of the fleet.'

'Mercedes would that be? Three-axle artic?'

'I believe so. I mean, yes.'

Acheson looked at me indifferently. 'And you took the M4 –M5 – A38?'

'Naturally.'

'So you would have reached this filling station at what . . . eight forty-five, nine o'clock?'

'Something like that. I didn't check. I had no reason to.'

'Call of nature, pick up fuel, adjust a load? Would those be the kind of reasons you had in mind?'

'If I didn't have any reason to stop, I couldn't have had any . . . ' I trailed into silence, lost in a logical maze. 'None of those things.'

'Is this a regular stop?'

'No.' I took a deep breath. 'No.'

'You're here now.'

'My . . . passenger asked me to drop her for a . . . call of nature.'

Acheson had a very limited range of expressions. 'Do you make a habit of giving lifts to young women?'

'No. Hardly ever. I mean, I found her at the Taunton services. She was freezing.'

'Very gallant, sir.' Acheson stepped around me and looked up at Steph. 'Excuse me, miss, we'd like a word.'

Steph glowered. 'What for? *I'm* not the one who's done anything wrong.'

'Do what he says,' I told her.

Acheson watched Steph commit herself into Palmer's care. When they had removed themselves from earshot, Acheson produced a photo. 'Did you give a lift to this girl on the twenty-second of December?'

She was young and pretty, with a wilful face. 'Definitely not.'

'She was at this filling station at about the time you would have passed.'

But I didn't pass, I wanted to cry. How could I have passed if I'm not the driver? 'You make it sound as if I was the only vehicle on the road. It was rush hour on Monday morning.'

'Tuesday, sir. The twenty-second was a Tuesday.' He looked at me oddly.

'Tuesday then. What does it matter? The motorway was crammed.'

'Not with six-legger trucks.' He waited as if he wanted me

to concede a fair point. 'Right then, where did you go after leaving here?'

'After I drove past this petrol station without stopping, without so much as a glance at it, I drove straight into Plymouth and caught the ferry – the same ferry you're making me miss.'

'Name of the ship?'

I looked away. 'I can't remember.'

'Your memory's not too good, is it? Can you remember your destination?'

'What does it matter where I went? That girl wasn't with me.'

Acheson wrote something down. 'Not much fun spending Christmas away from home, away from family.' He glanced up. 'Married?'

'No.'

'Ah,' Acheson said, and let a silence gestate. 'A bit of a loner are we?'

'What the hell are you implying?'

Acheson shrugged. 'You work holidays. You pick up young women.' He gave me time to see how it looked from his point of view, then said: 'Would you mind showing me your licence?'

I dug into my inside pocket, taking care not to spill the wads of notes. Acheson took my licence over to the car. For the second time in twenty-four hours I heard the tinny percussion of shortwave as my identity was examined. Steph was pointing at me and Palmer was nodding.

Acheson finished his radio check, went over and took Palmer aside. They both looked at me and Acheson shook his head as if vexed about something, then he strolled back, his lips compressed. 'Well, *sir*, appearances do deceive, don't they?'

I swallowed, not sure what he meant. Something about his attitude had changed for the worse.

'You won't mind if I take a look at your tacho.'

It didn't register at first, and then the ground opened. 'Yes I would. You'd better call my gaffer.'

'That won't be necessary. Under Section 99 of the 1968 Transport Act, I can require you to produce your tachographic record on request. I do so require you.'

'This is blatant harassment.'

Acheson hopped on to the step, leaned into the cab, took out the disc, stared at it with a frown, and dropped heavily to the ground as if what he had found had taken all the spring out of his legs. 'It looks to me,' he said quietly, 'as if you've driven all the way from Swansea without recording the journey.'

I squeezed my forehead. 'Look, I've been on the road for nearly two weeks solid. I started this trip at three. I'm supposed to be on my bloody holiday.'

Acheson regarded me with a level stare. 'Then you aren't fit to be behind the wheel.' He stood a little straighter, as if he was about to perform an unpleasant task. 'You'd better show me your log sheet and delivery note. And I think I'll take a quick squint around your cab.'

'That's outside your authority, and you know it. Now look, this is a priority load. If I miss the ferry, my boss will be furious.'

'I know that failure to keep a tachographic record is a serious offence. Now sir, since it's the season of good will on earth, I'm prepared to turn a blind eye in return for your co-operation. Alternatively, I'm going to nick you, which will mean an automatic ban. The state of the economy being what it is, it could be a long while before you land another job.'

I considered the risks. Style's insistence on escorting me

as far as the motorway had prevented me from picking up my own case, so everything in the cab belonged to Griffith. Except for my passport and driving licence. If they found those, I was sunk, but it was clear that they intended to search the cab whatever I said. I turned away. 'Go on then, search the bloody thing.'

Acheson summoned Palmer, who climbed into the cab. 'Lovely driving environment,' he called. The first thing he reached for was the briefcase. 'Would you mind opening it?'

'It *is* open.'

'No it isn't.'

I stared at the three-figure combination. Think! Think! No, don't think. Just visualise. A three . . . a four, no . . . 'Three-five-two.'

The case sprang open and Palmer began going through it.

'Tell me what I'm supposed to have done.'

Acheson glanced at the photo as if refreshing his memory. 'Zoe Redman was a second-year student at the University of Glamorgan. On the twenty-second of December, she and her boyfriend left Cardiff to hitchhike to her parents' home in Saltash. They had an argument and split up in Exeter. Zoe got a lift to this filling station; we traced the driver. At nine-seventeen – we're sure of the time – a motorist saw her over there . . . ' Acheson pointed to the south-bound exit. ' . . . climbing into an articulated lorry described as blue and silver. There was a Christmas tree on the cab.'

It was strange how these circumstantial details made me feel involved, as if I really did have a case to answer. 'If I was going to rape a girl, I wouldn't go about it lit up like Regent's Street.' I risked a glance to see what Palmer was up to.

Acheson studied his toes as if they had assumed a hitherto unnoticed significance. 'You've been abroad, sir, and you say you were unaware of Zoe Redman's death before this morning. I wonder, then, how you know she'd been raped.'

'Oh for heaven's sake!'

'Chief?'

A bomb went off in my chest. Acheson wandered up to the cab, but whatever his partner passed him was hidden from me. It had to be the passport. He came back with his right hand behind his back. 'Well you're right, sir. Zoe Redman was taken to a minor road on Dartmoor and comprehensively raped.' He began to bring his hand round. 'And then she was beaten to death.'

Hooked on a pencil in Acheson's hand was the driver's knuckle duster, uncleaned, still retaining traces of blood.

'Oh my God.'

'You know, when you stepped down, I thought: here's an educated sort of chap – not a violent type, not the sort who carries an offensive weapon.'

'Look, I keep it for continental runs. I don't need to tell you about the trouble we've been having with French farmers.'

'Used it recently, have you?'

'Of course not.'

'Funny,' Acheson said, holding the knuckle duster to the light. 'Looks like bloodstains to me.'

'Nonsense. It's just corroded. Look, I'll show you.'

Acheson removed the weapon from my reach. 'I think I'll hang on to it.' He produced a docket. 'If you'd just sign.'

With shaky hand I wrote my name – Griffith's name, my handwriting, the seal and signature of my guilt. 'Because the driver was seen picking up the girl doesn't mean he killed her. He could have dropped her anywhere.'

'I suppose you could be right, sir.' Acheson turned towards the truck. 'Have you finished in there?'

'Just getting started,' Palmer said, and laughed. A few moments later, he jumped down, holding one of the video cassettes. He handed it to Acheson and they went into a huddle. Acheson strolled back. 'And this?' he demanded. 'What do you call this?'

'It's a pornographic film,' I conceded tiredly. 'It's for a friend.'

'Extreme tastes, his friend has,' Palmer informed Acheson. 'Bloody incredible.'

'I'm not responsible for other people's fantasies.'

'Topical, though,' Palmer told Acheson, grinning. 'There's this motorcycle cop who stops a blonde tart in her Merc and he, you know, gives her an on-the-spot penalty – a bloody big one. Then this bunch of Hell's Angels turn up and . . . '

'I get the picture,' Acheson said. He hefted the cassette as if weighing evidence. 'We may want to clarify a few things. We may ask your office for the relevant log sheets and tacho.' He parodied a smile. 'I take it you filled *those* in.'

'Absolutely.'

'Good. Well, then, you'll want to be pushing on.'

'I'm free to go?'

Acheson spread his hands, half turned away, then frowned. 'Was that the morning ferry you were hoping to catch?'

'Yes.'

Acheson looked at his watch. 'I'd say you've missed it. Looks like you're already in trouble with the governor.'

'Yes.'

He looked around for Steph, but she'd made herself scarce. Acheson shook his head. 'I'd give the scrubbers a miss, if I were you.'

'Thank you,' I found myself saying. 'I will.' Acheson still had the cassette. I hesitated before extending my hand.

Acheson showed he had a sense of fun. He slipped the video into his pocket and gave me a wink. 'Like you, sir, I know someone who could do with putting a little sparkle back into their romantic life.'

14

Steph dived in from nowhere, dumped herself firmly and locked her arms tight.

'Out!'

'No bloody fear.'

To evict her bodily would have required an effort infinitely greater than I could have mustered. Besides, the damage was done. All I wanted to do was get out of there. I got the wheels turning. From the way Acheson and Palmer watched our departure, I knew that they hadn't finished with me.

My thoughts were in pandemonium. The other traffic seemed to scatter before them. It wasn't fair. It just wasn't fair!

'I got us a burger each,' Steph said, holding up the carrier.

Her nonchalance made me lash out. 'You silly fool. Didn't the police tell you what kind of man you're riding with?'

Steph composed her words with care. 'Yeah, they said you were violent and I should give you a miss.'

'And you ignored them. Haven't you got *any* instinct for survival?'

Steph shrugged. 'I told them if it wasn't for you I'd be in casualty.'

'Oh well, with such an impeccable character reference, no wonder they let me go.'

'I don't know why you're so stroppy. I could've said something different. I could've said you molested me.' She eyed me darkly. 'I know a few people would've.'

The truth of it quenched my anger. None of this was her fault. The Cavalier was following, as I knew it would be. I watched it settle in the mirror.

Steph held her burger in both hands and prepared to take a bite. 'What they reckon you done this time?'

I could see the patient outlines of the detectives. 'Rape,' I said, 'and murder. A student of about your age who hitched a lift with a truck driver ten days ago.' I let it sink in. 'Still want a ride?'

Steph spent a long time reconsidering her burger. Finally she took a bite. 'If you *were* planning to have a go at me, I reckon you aren't in the mood no more.'

But she kept glancing at me through mouthfuls – short nervous takes, looking for the psychotic. 'You didn't, did you?'

'Suppose I said yes?'

Her chewing slowed and stopped.

'As it happens, I have never seen that poor girl in my life. Not only did I not rape and murder her, but I have a perfect alibi. The trouble is . . . '

My perfect alibi rang cracked to the core. Wouldn't it be ironic, wouldn't it be the ultimate bloody twist, if the man I was impersonating was a homicidal rapist?

'I don't reckon it was you,' Steph said, half to herself. 'Because if you'd done what they said, you wouldn't have asked me to call the cops.' She frowned at me over her meal. 'Why did you do that?'

'I thought they were someone else. I thought . . . ' My explanation withered under its own impossible weight. The Cavalier was still behind us. At some murky level of consciousness fresh alarm bells sounded. I shot Steph a glance. 'You asked me what I'd done "this time". What other crimes am I supposed to have committed?'

'Come off it.'

Pressure built up under my chestbone. 'Humour me. You mentioned violence.'

'This burger's crap,' she said, and stuffed it back in the bag, half-eaten. 'Yeah, they told me about that man you beat up. The man they sent you to prison for.'

All the air in the cab seemed to have been squeezed out. The driver had a police record. I had shoved the knuckle-duster into the glove compartment with my prints still on it. My prints weren't known to the police, but Griffith's were, and when they were identified, the police would know that the driver they had stopped was an impostor. Enquiries would be instigated, my description would be circulated, and when the body was found, I would be the prime suspect. I groaned aloud. I had gone round five circles of hell only to find myself back in the middle. I thumped the steering wheel. It wasn't fair. It just wasn't fair!

'Bloody funny teacher you must have been,' Steph said, and gave the door an idle kick. 'I believe you, you know. About you being a teacher and everything – even about them dirty videos not being yours.'

'Now you'll know better than to judge a man by his eyes.'

Steph's sigh came from deep down. 'Yeah, my mam got it wrong with my dad, an'all.' She gave a wasted smile, as if criminality was part of some sad but inescapable process and she was embarrassed because she'd been stupid enough to think any different.

'If you want me to drop you, you only have to say so.'

'Doesn't bother me,' she said. 'I'd only meet some other nutter.'

Acheson and Palmer were still right behind when I reached

118

the outskirts of Plymouth. Steph was scratching at the vinyl trim on the dash, building up to some statement.

I felt a little cooler. In a way, the knuckle duster was the main exhibit for the defence. The blood on it belonged to one of the killers in the Skoda, not to me nor Zoe Redman. The killer's blood was probably on the driver, too. If only I had thought of it sooner. If only I had used my *brain*. Even now it wasn't too late to present my case to a solicitor.

'You said you weren't going abroad.'

I stared down the road, my predicament stretching to infinity. 'Steph, I don't know where I'm going.'

'Take us with you. Go on.'

'The boat's gone. It sailed an hour ago.'

Steph sulked, picking at the trim. 'Why do you want to go and miss it?'

'I don't want to miss it.'

'Then why did you waste all that time back at the services?'

'The only time I wasted was over you.'

Steph began fidgeting with the switched-off radio. 'I saw you in the caff,' she said. 'You must have been asleep for an hour. And then afterwards you were hanging around in the back of the lorry.' She gave me an oddly mature stare. 'You didn't look like you had to get anywhere fast.'

'I was checking the load. I had an accident on the motorway.'

Steph's eyes held a queer gravity. 'Dead worried you looked.'

I dragged my forearm across my forehead. 'Steph, I'm in a rather ticklish situation, and if you don't mind, I need some peace and quiet to think my way out.'

'That's why you were so frightened when the cops turned up. Someone's after you.'

'Everyone's after me. They're queueing up.'

'What for?'

I'd almost lost track. 'An act of moral dereliction.'

'What's that when it's at home?'

'Drop it.' I felt so weary, so unable to cope.

'Go on,' Steph said, touching my arm with gentle solicitude. 'You can tell me. I wouldn't let on. Honest.'

Guilt made me vindictive. '*You*? What do you know about moral anything? Look at you – dressed like a tart, offering sex for a ride to the next filling station. I mean, talk about *asking* for it!'

She snatched her hand away and made a furious pretence of watching the road going by. Tears magnified her eyes.

At some point in this sordid exchange, the Cavalier had dropped out of sight. That didn't signify I was out of mind. The police would have handed over the surveillance to colleagues in another unmarked car. Having seen how edgy I was, they would follow me to the dock to increase the pressure, or even to make sure I didn't make a bolt for it. Well, they were going to be disappointed. I would drive to the port, be told the ferry had left, and turn round in an orderly manner.

A sign with a ferry symbol pointed me towards the port. I was supposed to call Style, I remembered, but I simply didn't possess the necessary reserves of deceit. He'd find out soon enough.

'Look, the sea!' Steph called, excitement overriding her dejection.

Two frigates rode at anchor on a choppy wedge of water. I searched for the ferry or a dwindling wake, but it must have already dropped below the horizon. The road began to descend past the port compound.

Ahead, the public highway ended at a barrier manned by security men. Beyond that there was no going on.

I halted fifty yards short and turned off the engine. A

silence filled the space between me and Steph. The end of the road, I thought, and remembered what Lisa had said about reaching the sea and all life's troubles catching up. Though I didn't really understand what it meant, it left a morose aftertaste. Steph stared moodily at the uninviting cityscape.

'You should have asked to get out earlier,' I told her. 'Now you'll have to walk back to the centre.'

'Doesn't matter.'

'What will you do?'

She shrugged and scored a line across the dash. Then she slid towards the door.

'Here,' I said, catching her wrist.

She eyed the money as if it was forged. 'What's that in aid of?'

'To keep you out of trouble.' I sounded like a hearty uncle or guilty client.

'I'm not a trucker's tart,' she shouted. 'I'm none of those things you said. If I was a tart, do you think I'd be bumming lifts off an old tosspot like you?'

I winced under her attack. 'You have my unreserved apology. Take the money. I want you to have it.'

Slowly she riffled the notes, her bottom lip stuck out as if I'd given her a Christmas present she hadn't wanted. 'Cheers.' She slipped to the ground. 'Remember,' she said invisibly, '*you're* the one who's in the shit.'

I left her standing forlorn, her breath clouding around her face. But if she was still waiting when I came back, I was going to ignore her. I had saved her from grievous bodily harm and given her more money than she could have earned in a week on the sex line. I regretted taking out my bitterness on her, but apart from that, Steph was about the only person who wasn't on my conscience.

I idled up to the gates. A security officer leaned out.

'Santander?'

'Meant to be.'

'Well what are you fucking waiting for?'

'But . . .'

'Ten minutes,' he bellowed, holding up both sets of fingers.

Only one thing to do. I banged the truck into reverse. 'I've left my passenger behind.'

'Too late, mate.'

'I can't,' I called, backing up.

And then I saw the red Cavalier squatting in the mirror, about a hundred yards back. I hit the brake.

'Make your mind up!'

But my mind wasn't mine to command. Once again, circumstances had hijacked me and I was rolling across the tarmac apron, following the signals of a dock-hand in a day-glo waistcoat. I came round a building and there was the quay and there, berthed alongside it, lay the gleaming white ferry with its bow doors open and a car driving up the gangway.

More men in fluorescent orange were waving bats at me, shepherding me towards a bay on the quayside. The ghastliness of my miscalculation hit me. I had no plans for dealing with this contingency. I couldn't board the ferry even if I wanted to. I had no idea of the procedures involved. Griffith's passport didn't match my face, and my passport didn't match anything.

One of the dock-hands made a two-handed cutting gesture. GO NO FURTHER. 'He strolled to my door.

'Why hasn't the ferry gone?'

'Delayed, mate – same as you. Better get a hurry up.'

I stared around with shallow eyes. 'I'm only a relief driver. Never done a foreign run. I don't know the ropes.'

'Christ,' he said, rolling his eyes. 'Got your T2?'

'T2?' I stroked my case. 'I've got a lot of forms in here.'

'Get over to Customs. Now.'

'Where's that?'

'Christ, mate. In *there*. Shift it.'

Half walking, half running, I made my way to the Customs and Excise post. Behind the windows uniformed officers bent over their computers. One of them looked up, saw me and nudged a colleague. Look at this poor sod, he seemed to be saying.

A shout from the man by the truck impelled me across the threshold. Everybody else had been processed. Only one officer was in the room, sitting behind his desk with his hands neatly placed on top. There was just him and me, separated by a no-man's land of white light. He beckoned me forward.

Somehow I was walking, my legs feeling as if they were borrowed from someone else, my face rigid with the effort of appearing unconcerned. The officer sat up alertly and folded his hands into a different position. The light cast no shadows.

I dropped the case on his desk. 'I . . . I shouldn't be here,' I stammered. 'But everyone else had flu and I . . . '

'Let's see what we've got. Ah, Argonaut.' He gave me a quick upward look. 'I didn't think your face was familiar.' He bent to his work again. 'Yes, we see quite a lot of you boys. Let's see now. Griffith. Griffith J.V.' He made a fluent pass over his keyboard and print jumped up on his screen. 'There you are. Shouldn't take long.' He began to hum.

One of the neon tubes was faulty and made an itchy buzzing. The officer worked at a bureaucrat's pace, occasionally feeding information into his computer. He punched the keyboard and frowned, punched it again and frowned harder, as if a sinister pattern was beginning to take shape. He didn't say anything. Everything he needed to know was available at a touch of the button. I was drenched in sweat.

The ship's siren wailed.

'Time gentleman, please.'

'Am I going to miss it?' I asked, trying to concoct tactics for all eventualities.

'Very possibly.' The officer gave me a grave look. 'But whose fault is that, Mr Griffith?'

He commenced humming again. I began to pace, peering out at the ship, praying for it to move.

'Sign here.'

I signed. The officer did a half-turn on his revolving chair, held the paper to the light, then swivelled and thrust it at me.

I stared at it like a hungry dog eyeing a suspect bait. As I took hold I felt a slight resistance.

'Griffith?' the officer mused, his eyebrows fidgeting. 'Griffith, Griffith, Griffith.' He frowned. 'Got anyone else by that name at Argonaut?'

'Gri*ffiths*,' I said huskily. 'John Griffiths. He's on holiday.'

'That'll be the fellow. Came through before Christmas, did he?'

'Two weeks ago.'

The officer beamed in tribute to his memory.' Thought so. On you go then, Taff.'

I went out trying to look like a man desperate to catch a ship. The ferry was still docked, its doors gaping, and the hand guarding my truck waved furiously when he saw me. It seemed that the entire workforce was determined I shouldn't miss the boat. I ran over, trying to think on the move, trying to plot all the repercussions of the action I had to decide on in the next two seconds.

Nobody could stop me leaving the port, but desertion

now would look bizarre in the extreme and would inevitably start an investigation. For a start, the Customs officer had only to press a couple of keys to find that James Vernon Griffith, the novice driver who didn't know a T2 from a . . . Half a second's review of the ensuing sequence of events put that option out of the running. I was following the arrows pointing towards the ship, towards the passport check. I had no choice.

In some precinct of my mind the loss adjuster's warning lay coiled, but he wasn't an immediate menace, whereas the immigration official beckoning me to a halt threatened instant disaster. Did I use Griffith's passport or my own? I didn't look like Griffith, but if I showed my own passport, the name wouldn't tally with the ship's passenger list. Griffith or Reason? Reason or Griffith? While there was the faintest chance that the police wouldn't connect me to the dead driver, it had to be Griffith.

The immigration official didn't even glance at the passport.

I was through, the last hurdle cleared, bumping into the ferry's jaws. Daylight was eclipsed and the beat of the engine vibrated in the hull. Hands directed me to my place in a nearly empty section of the vehicle deck. With a flourish a crewman signalled stop. He gave me the thumb's-up and then puffed out his cheeks and shook his hand as if he'd burned it – Gallic for 'you lucky bastard'.

I lowered my head on to the boss of the steering wheel. Behind me the doors closed with an iron clang. Seconds later the gentle throbbing underfoot coarsened to a judder as the ship backed away from its berth. I remained slumped in the dark and clamorous womb until a tranquil rocking told me that we had put to sea.

15

Drifting at the edge of consciousness, I reviewed the charge-sheet to date. In the space of twenty-four hours, I had committed acts of criminal deception, fraud, various perversions of justice. That was me, Matthew Reason, who had done those things, yet somehow I couldn't come to terms with the fact. Lying there in the dark, I felt a stranger to myself. It was as if by taking on the driver's identity, I had absolved myself of responsibility – as if I had become the spectator of someone else's actions.

Try telling that to the judge.

I groaned and fumbled for my watch. It took a while to make sense of the dial and work out that I'd slept right round the clock. I tensed, thinking of all the moves that might have been made against me while I slept, then fell back slack on the pillow. If anything bad was going to happen to me, it would have happened by now.

Gradually I became aware of a discrepancy in sensations. Although I was cocooned in warm dark silence, the boat was pitching steeply, rising and falling on a violent surge. We must be heading into a Biscay storm. Insulated from the turbulence outside, my mind grew quiet. I was in transit. The storm was a calm interlude between landfalls, a time to take bearings.

Danger threatened from four different quarters. I'd called Style to tell him I'd made it, so until I reached Spain, he was the least of my worries. The police were a serious concern, but unless Griffith's body had been found, all they had to go on was the knuckle duster, and I doubted whether they would be able to get a fingerprint identification before tomorrow at the earliest.

By then James Griffith would be in Spain, lost and gone. Assuming I cleared the port, that is. Spanish Immigration and Customs might not be as casual as the officials at Plymouth. It might be wise to leave the truck on the ferry and walk off under my own name. I had about eleven hours before we docked. No point fretting over a decision now.

That left the loss adjuster, the last threat and the deadliest. I had no doubt that when he found out I'd boarded the ferry, he'd come after me. The voyage to Santander took twenty-four hours, and even during the New Year slowdown, he could do a lot of catching up in that time. Suppose he'd left Style's place by car before midday and taken four hours to reach Heathrow for a Paris or Madrid flight. Say three hours flying time, maximum, then an hour's hop to Bilbao, which couldn't be more than thirty miles from Santander.

Panic fluttered in my throat. Even allowing five or six hours waiting for connections, the loss adjuster could be in Spain already, pointing his hire car towards Santander in time for a good night's sleep before he ambled down to the quayside to greet me.

There was no remission from fear. Fear had goaded me into this predicament; fear made mincemeat of the mental process. My intelligence had counted for nothing. I would have managed better with a room-temperature IQ and a half-ounce of unthinking bravado.

Maybe I should have squared things with Style. Not completely, of course, not to the point of admitting the driver's death and my own deception. But I should have told him about the attempted hijack and warned him that his associates were behind it. I could still do it; I could pick up the phone and give chapter and verse on Eeles' treachery and Axnoller's subversion. Style had come up the hard way, and I imagined that his treatment of disloyal colleagues would be old-fashioned.

But the picture of Eeles being stepped on was precious poor consolation for the image of the loss adjuster's off-centre smile beaming up at me from the dock.

Hold it, I told myself. There was something about my plight I kept distorting. I kept slipping into the delusion that Axnoller & Co. knew I was a witness to murder, whereas so far as they were concerned, the driver was alive and I was him – an ordinary working man, give or take a streak of common or garden greed. Although the loss adjuster would be affronted by my breach of contract, it was inconceivable that he'd kill me for it. The real driver had indeed been murdered, but somehow I couldn't see the American's steady hand in the deed, nor from the messy nature of the killing could I believe that the two thugs had set out with murder in their hearts. They were local boys, probably recruited by Eeles to hijack the truck, and they had killed in panic when the driver started beating the shit out of them.

Ergo, there was nothing personal in this. What Axnoller and the rest were after was the truck. The driver was irrelevant except as the motivating agent of the vehicle. Which meant that all I had to do was walk away from the bloody thing and let them claim it.

The ship rose on a crest. Suspended on the wave of fortune, I thought, and in spite of all the risks and uncertainties, I experienced an odd thrill of excitement. Custom was the only guide to humanity, it was said, but I'd broken the shackles of convention and for the first time in years I felt free, the master of my fate.

In Spain I could be anyone I wanted to be. I could go to Madrid and resurrect my teaching career. I saw myself pale and studious, strolling down one of Madrid's austere avenues under winter sun. This solitary image pierced me with a dart of loneliness, so by a seamless shift of imagination, I found myself transported to a bar, an intellectual dive, in the company of one of my female students. When I took a second look, I found that it was Eleanor Barry.

My failure to meet her stirred bitter disappointment. I tried to console myself with the thought that nothing would have come from it.

'Hello, Eleanor. Do you remember me?'

And how did I expect her to respond? 'Oh, Matthew. What a pleasant surprise!'

No I didn't. Her eyes would go round and her mouth would make a huge O and I would have about half a millisecond before she screamed the place down.

Slipping into a half-doze, I began to construct a different combination of circumstances. If I'd been travelling to Spain on legitimate purposes, maybe I could have persuaded Eleanor Barry to meet me there. Perhaps the prospect of a tryst between strangers in a foreign capital would have struck a romantic chord. The fantasy enlarged itself to accommodate a vision of Eleanor Barry waiting on the steps of the Prado in a Goyaesque twilight.

My heart stood still and then began to race. I switched on the light. Maybe the dream wasn't dead after all. It was a quarter to midnight. Bubbling with excitement, I struggled into my clothes and let myself out.

The corridor was blank. Bracing myself against the heaving floor, I mounted the companionway to the assembly deck. The duty-free boutique dazzled with redundant brightness. My resolve wavered.

No woman appreciated being stood up. Pleading loss of nerve wouldn't persuade Eleanor that an overseas rendez-vous was a realistic proposition. I walked up and down, trying to come up with a convincing excuse and an irresistible invitation. Pressing business covered every eventuality, I decided.

Even so, it was midnight by the time I had cranked up the courage to call. And then I got through with such shocking swiftness that in the first instant I could only assume that she'd been waiting by the phone.

'Eleanor, this is . . . '

She cut straight in and spoke without drawing breath, without admitting a word in edgeways. 'I'm sorry about this afternoon but I've been thinking about your proposal and I'm afraid I really don't think it would have worked out. I hope you weren't too disappointed but today's been rather hectic. I'm sure you'll find someone more suitable. Goodbye.'

'Eleanor!'

'Sorry, but there's no point in . . . '

'Please!'

'Look, it's gone midnight. We were just on our way to bed.'

The air stilled. 'We?'

'That's right. So if you don't mind . . . '

Two facts clattered from the chaos. She had stood *me* up. And she was speaking for someone else's benefit. I tried to climb out of the wreckage. 'I know this is an awkward . . . '

'Yes it is. Extremely.'

In a moment she would hang up. 'I must see you. I have to go abroad. To Spain.'

'What a pity. Well, thank you for letting me know.'

'I want you to meet me there.'

'Me? It's out of the question.'

'Don't put the phone down. Give me one minute. Please.'
My mind galloped to catch up with the revised situation.
Maybe the man – it had to be a man – was just a casual friend
who had dropped in for a seasonal drink. 'The person with
you – is he listening?'

'Oh yes,' she said airily.

'On an extension?'

She hesitated. 'No.'

'Does he know about me?'

'No. That wouldn't be a good idea. In fact, I must . . .'

'Just tell me one thing. Is he the reason you didn't turn up
for lunch?'

This time her paused ended in a bleak laugh. 'Nothing
ever works out as I hope. My life seems fated.'

'Let me change it, Eleanor. Think about it. A week in a
beautiful city. We could go south, to the coast. We can go
anywhere you want.'

'It's not realistic.'

'You don't have to worry about money. I'll pay your air
fare and hotel bills.'

'It's not that.'

'Then what?'

'Everything.' Suddenly she was angry. 'Surely you can
understand the situation.'

'I can understand your doubts about meeting me abroad,
but you don't have to tell me where you'll be staying. I'll
give you my hotel number and you can call me when you
arrive in Madrid. We'll arrange to meet at the place of your
choice and take it from there.'

'I can't. I have other commitments.'

'Your guest?'

'Yes,' she said, the admission squeezed out.

I wasn't going to give up now. 'But if he wasn't there,
you'd at least consider it.'

Her voice broke. 'I'm not in a position to consider anything. Why can't you . . . ?'

I snatched inspiration in passing. 'Tell him it's business. Tell him I work in television. Tell him I've asked you to come to Spain as a researcher.'

She went so quiet that I thought I'd lost contact.

'Give me your number,' she said at last, 'I'll call you back first thing tomorrow.'

I couldn't tell her I was on the high seas. 'I'm catching a plane to Madrid at six. I have to know tonight.'

'Then the answer's "no". I'm sorry. In other circumstances I might have been . . . '

'Eleanor, we have to make our own circumstances. What was it you said in your letter? Your dreams have failed you. Maybe you failed them. Maybe you weren't prepared to turn them into reality. That's the chance I'm offering.'

Her laugh was bemused. 'Excuse me a moment. My friend is rather curious about what's going on.'

In the dragging silence I re-examined his status. She had said that they were on their way to bed. He had to be a boyfriend, but not someone she'd been expecting. And his presence couldn't be wholly welcome, or else she would have hung up on me straight away. But why couldn't she just tell him that I was a new man in her life? Perhaps she was too embarrassed to admit that a computer had brought . . .

'Mr Reason?' Her tone was businesslike. 'You'll have to tell me more about your project. All I know is that it's got something to do with maps.'

There was no time to shower blessings. 'A documentary on the history of cartography. Madrid has some stunning Arabic charts and the world's finest collection of sixteenth-century New World maps. Say I'm a producer for an independent company.'

'Leave that to me.'

'You're wonderful.'

'How long will you need me for?'

'The research should take a week. I was hoping you could get to Madrid by the fifth. Will that be possible?'

'London on the fifth. Right, I should be able to manage that.'

'That's marvellous. Oh, Eleanor . . . '

'And you say expenses are payable in advance.'

'I'll put five hundred in the post immediately, along with my address.'

'Send it to Llanarchgoch. That's double "l" . . . '

'Who is he, Eleanor?' I asked, scribbling the details.

'Right then,' she declared with brisk formality, 'we'll talk about that on the fifth. I'll be coming up by train and I'll call you on arrival.'

'Eleanor, I can't tell you what this means to me.'

Her voice was cool, her act perfect. 'I look forward to it, too.'

I reeled from the phone and slumped down the wall, numbstruck and grinning like an idiot.

'You all right, sir?'

An English seaman was peering at me with some concern.

'Just my wildest dreams come true.' I felt in my pocket and produced a tenner. 'I wonder if you could find me some writing paper and envelopes. Blank, no ship's letterhead. Oh, and I need a list of Madrid hotels.'

'No trouble,' he said, magicking the note into his hand.

When he'd gone, I looked at the scrawled address, thrilled by the outcome but also slightly alarmed at the erratic way fate was cutting the cards.

16

Intoxicated by my success, I staggered aft, lurching from wall to wall at each shift in the seas. I emerged into the saloon deck, a glassed-in lounge deserted except for a single passenger curled asleep under a ship's blanket. Up here, even the air inside the ship trembled with the storm's ferocity. Access to the stern area had been closed. Through the streaming glass, the horizon and the sky were merged invisibly.

I found the weather appropriately operatic. I made myself comfortable, took out my writing materials and began to pen a letter.

Dear Eleanor . . .

My head was whirling with things I wanted to say, but I was checked by thoughts of the man who had been listening in to our conversation.

His identity was a vexation. In her letter, Eleanor had referred to the painful break-up of a long-standing relationship. I suspected that her guest was the man in question – one of her failed dreams.

Something about his presence rankled. She must have been expecting me to call and had positioned herself to answer before he could get to the phone. 'That wouldn't be a good idea,' she had said when I asked if she'd told him about me. Her tone had been dark, warning of unpleasant consequences if he found out. A jealous former lover, then – a man who couldn't accept a rival, even though he himself was no longer in the reckoning. That's why she hadn't gone to the restaurant; that's why she was pretending to meet me in London. She was *frightened* to tell him there was a new man in her life.

I tried to picture him, this man I had never met. All I could bring to mind were the fringe dwellers who had made up Eleanor Barry's social circle at university – malcontents, sloganisers, the architects of my downfall.

Tendrils of anger had twined around my heart. I wrenched them away. Whoever he was, Eleanor Barry had slipped his hold. Pleasure darted through me at the way she had so smoothly slipped into the role I had offered. Duplicity was second nature to lovers. The word arrested me, but I let it stand. Yes, lovers is what we were. Eleanor wanted to escape. She needed rescuing.

My adieu was tender.

It was nearly two o'clock. I yawned and decided to return to my cabin. The truck disposal problem and the complication of Spanish Immigration still had to be tackled.

On the way out I felt mild indignation on behalf of the sleeping passenger. You'd think that with the ferry three-quarters empty, the crew would have given the wretch a decent berth.

I was at the doorway when a neurotic impulse made me look back. Just nocturnal whimsy, I told myself. The passenger was probably a Spanish waiter taking the cheap passage home. I exited the saloon and had reached the head of the companionway when I halted again, unable to shake off the stupid delusion. Like the ghost in the cab, the huddled shape in the saloon wouldn't stop haunting me.

Feeling a complete fool, I traipsed back. The figure was wrapped up except for one feminine hand dangling to the floor. The evidence was inconclusive. I cleared my throat and moved a step closer. 'Excuse me.'

The bundle mumbled resentment. Drunk, I thought, and gave it a tentative prod.

'Shove off you old tosser.'

I stepped back so smartly that I fell into the opposite seat. 'What the hell are you doing here?'

Steph's curly red head emerged from the blanket. She blinked sleep-doped eyes.

'What,' I enunciated, 'are you doing aboard this ship?'

Her eyes cleared in recognition and she grinned in triumph. 'On me hols,' she said. 'In't I?'

I shut my own eyes tight. 'Did you smuggle yourself on board?'

She burrowed in her nest and flourished a ticket and a passport.

'Oh shit.'

'Ta very much.'

I pinched my forehead between fingers and thumb.

'I been looking for you,' Steph said, 'but I didn't know your last name.'

'Get one thing clear, Steph. You are not coming with me. When we said goodbye at the docks, that was it. Understand?'

'Oh, don't go on,' she said vaguely, as if some internal thought had captured her attention. An expression of alarm moved slowly over her face and she put her hand to her mouth and went very still. 'Ooh,' she said, 'I'm going to chuck.' Abruptly she threw off her blanket and set off doorwards in a semi crouch.

I flopped down. Her possessions were scattered on the seat. I picked at them with listless hands – a can of Tango and a half-bottle of vodka, a packet of cigarettes and a copy of *Cosmopolitan*, some new clothes still in their wrappings, a bottle of perfume and some expensive aftershave. She had left her passport. Stephanie Geraldine Canaway she was called in full – a name too big for her. She was five feet three inches tall, twenty years old and every page in her passport was blank.

Master of my fate, I thought, watching her grope her way back.

'Here I am,' she said unsteadily. 'Sort of.'

She looked awful. 'Let me help you,' I said, taking her elbow.

She plopped into her seat, her face waxy and huge-eyed. I arranged the blanket round her shoulders. She managed a wan smile. 'Are we going to sink?'

Spray lashed against the saloon from all directions. 'Not at all.'

'Pity,' she said, and let her head droop to her knees. She took a shuddering breath. Her teeth began to chatter. Her face had gone the colour of tin.

I couldn't leave her in this state. I looked round for assistance and saw the seaman who had supplied my stationery. 'Excuse me,' I called. 'This young lady's extremely seasick.'

The sailor hove to with an obliging smile. 'That's all right sir. I'll escort her to a cabin and get her some pills.'

'Keep off of me,' Steph cried, rallying in a flash. 'He's been after me all night – him and his mates.'

'Now then,' the sailor said, reaching down for her. 'Let's get you into a warm bed.'

Stephs hands balled into tiny fists. 'Put your poxy mitts on me and I'll puke on your boots.'

The seaman engaged me with a rubbery smile. 'If I were you, sir, I'd go below before she starts on you.'

Steph glowered at me. 'Don't let him get his maulers on me.'

'All right,' I told him. 'Just fetch her some seasick pills.'

The sailor's mouth made a tube. 'Oh,' he said softly, 'I didn't realise you were making arrangements of your own.'

'Just get the pills.'

He unpursed his lips and wheeled away. 'She can spew her guts out for all I care.'

'Get them,' I barked. 'Or I'll report you to the duty officer.'

His mouth moved in and out some more, then he moved off, his mutterings unintelligible but the gist clear.

'And fuck *you*,' Steph jeered.

I rounded on her. 'No need for that.'

'Yeah?' Steph cried, transferring her anger to me. 'I suppose you think I was asking for it.'

'I don't think any such thing.'

'If I was what you said I was, I'd have enough dosh to travel first class.'

'I dare say.'

'I dare say,' Steph scoffed. 'At least you know where you are with scuzzies like that.'

'What's that supposed to mean?'

'It means don't *you* start getting any pervy ideas.'

'Steph,' I said, riled into retaliation, 'astonishing as it might seem, not a single carnal thought involving you has crossed my mind.'

Suspicion narrowed Steph's eyes. 'What's carnal?'

'From the Latin meaning "flesh", specifically relating to bodily pleasures and appetites. Sex in other words – or not in our case. My sexual appetite for you is roughly zero.'

'And that's more than I feel about you, you poncy bugger.'

'Then perhaps you'll tell me why you followed me.'

'Didn't follow you, did I?' Her expression became elusive and she did some complicated fiddling. 'Fancied a bit of sunshine.'

I sat down opposite and placed my palms on my knees. 'And where in this world will you find that?'

She leaned forward until we were nose to nose and eye to eye. 'Mind your own business.'

Quite out of the blue and against the run of play, I realised how lovely her eyes were – an unsullied green like pale jade, flecked with amber. I passed my hand over my brow. 'This is ridiculous.'

'You started it.'

'No I didn't.'

'Yes you did.'

'For heaven's sake.'

'Asking for it, you said.'

I jumped up. 'I'm not wasting my time in a juvenile wrangle. I'm going to bed. Good night.'

'Sod off then.'

'I will.' Fuming and cross-grained, I marched off.

'All right,' she said when I was at the door, 'I'll tell you why I followed you.'

'I'm not interested.'

'That money you gave me. It was shut-up money.'

'If it was, I'd be within my rights to demand its return.'

'It's all right,' she said complacently. 'I won't open my mouth to anyone. I stick by my mates.'

The notion of us being 'mates' was flooded out by genuine grievance. 'That money was to help you on your way, and if I'd known you'd take such a churlish attitude, I wouldn't have bothered.'

Steph wasn't impressed. 'My dad used to say no one wasted honest money.'

'I'm glad you agree it's wasted.'

'Not money they'd worked for. And he should know. He never had a job all the time I knew him, but you should have seen the dosh he chucked away on gee-gees.'

'Are you suggesting I stole that money?' I had stopped my exit. In fact I was making my way back.

Steph gave one of her irritating, non-committal shrugs.

'That money,' I said, 'was a bonus for giving up my holiday to do this trip.'

Steph smiled up with evil intent. 'Lucky the boat was late, else you'd have to give it back. Wouldn't you?'

A response was there somewhere, but not to hand.

She held up the bottle of vodka. 'Fancy a drink?'

I was so rattled that I did what I hadn't done since I was a teenager; I drank straight from the neck. As the liquor burned down, it occurred to me that if Eeles had shown half the wit of this delinquent, he would have unmasked me in a trice.

She took the bottle back and squirrelled it away with her other duty-free purchases. Seeing me studying the evidence of her solitary binge, she became defensive. 'I was celebrating.'

I felt a twinge of . . . not exactly affection. Well, all right, affection, but of the paternal kind – concern that someone so unprepared should be so adrift. Poor Steph, catching a boat with no idea where she was going.

And then, of course, it struck me that my own destination was even more uncertain. I gave a rueful laugh. 'We're a desperate pair, right enough.'

Her eyes met mine and she pulled the blanket closer. 'Is someone else after the money?'

I shook my head. 'You can spend what I gave you with a clear conscience.'

More than you can do, a weasel voice said.

She cocked her head. 'You said someone was after you. You said *everyone* was.'

'Anyone who's been questioned about a rape and murder is entitled to feel just a little bit paranoid.'

Steph's mouth composed itself in patient lines. 'You thought the police were someone else. You said so yourself.'

I'd forgotten exactly what I'd babbled after my grilling by the CID. 'Someone was following me. I expect it was the police, but I didn't realise that at the time.'

'Chasing you,' Steph said, 'for an act of moral who-jamaflip.' She looked at me without blinking. 'Are they after you now?'

'Steph, the only person who won't leave me alone is *you*!'

She shut her eyes as if she was meditating. 'I'm going to be sick again.'

Her complexion had drained to corpse-grey. I raked my hands through my hair. I couldn't abandon her to the ship's personnel. For this one night only I was stuck with her. This time tomorrow she would be a memory, along with the truck, along with everything.

I offered my hand. 'You'd better use my cabin.'

Steph regarded me with woozy suspicion. 'What for?'

'There's a spare bunk, and a bathroom.'

'I'll try not to make a mess.'

'One more won't make much difference.'

At the door we met the seaman returning with the pills. I took them in one hand, holding Steph's lolling form in the other. His face found it hard to contain all the emotions he felt – just about the whole range available to man, and a few more besides.

17

For the next two hours I ran a shuttle service between Steph's sickbed and the bathroom. To be honest, I didn't find my duties too repugnant. It was like looking after a child. Besides, Steph's wretched state staved off my own problems.

Eventually she sank into sleep. I remained in my chair and tried to read a *Cosmopolitan* feature titled 'Sado-masochism *Can* be Fun'. After ploughing through a couple of paragraphs the words blurred beneath my eyes.

It was four in the morning. The hours had flashed by. Now the minutes dragged. The silence bore down on me. The cabin had become suffocating, and although the sea had moderated, I began to feel giddy.

It wasn't the onset of seasickness. Fears of the approaching landfall were beginning to oppress me. If the loss adjuster had reached Santander, there was nothing I could do except explain how my intentions had been thwarted by the delayed sailing. The port was a public place. He couldn't harm me there.

Maybe he wouldn't be given the chance. Spanish Immigration officials would have first claim on me. My best chance of clearing them would be to disembark on foot under my own name, but then the unlisted passenger Matthew Reason would be irrevocably linked to the abandoned truck. So far, all the police had was a description; with a name they would have me cold.

The balance of risks tipped in favour of me driving off the ferry as Griffith.

Quietly, not wanting to disturb Steph, I fetched the two passports and compared photos. The dissimilarity made me wince. No one with the slightest acquaintance of me or Griffith could have mistaken one for the other. I tried to look on the bright side. We were roughly the same age, both of us tall and dark. There comparisons ended, but it could have been a lot worse. Unless I crossed a particularly suspicious Immigration official, I reckoned that the physical discrepancies would fall within tolerable limits. I mean, if travellers were only allowed across frontiers on condition that their faces exactly matched their passport portraits, a lot of us would never get beyond our country of birth.

Only partly reassured, I placed Griffith's passport in my jacket and locked my own in his briefcase.

Spanish Customs would be the next obstacle. My spirits sagged at the prospect of cutting my way through God knows what bureaucratic thickets. After a minute or two of glum contemplation, I decided there was no point worrying about it. I would meet the inevitable forms and declarations with polite and monolingual ignorance, explaining that I was a relief driver pressed into service when the original driver . . . etc, etc.

A search of the truck was the other worry. Spanish checks might be stringent, and a trained eye might spot in a second whatever Axnoller and his friends were after.

Again I racked my brain for some clue to what it might be. Style's business was on the skids, which suggested a desperate money-making venture. Drugs seemed the most likely possibility, but somehow I couldn't make it stick. If I'd been carrying something valuable or illicit, the loss adjuster wouldn't have risked alerting me to the possibility. Also, the trip had been ordered at the last moment, which suggested it was the outcome of hasty arrangements rather than meticulous criminal planning.

An intuition that had been hovering on the margins pinned itself at the centre of my thoughts. The murderers hadn't planned to rob the truck; they had intended to prevent it from reaching Style's house. It was there that something had been put into the truck. That's why Style had delayed me for five hours, despite the risk of missing the ferry.

Five hours? In that time the entire load could have been changed. Alternatively, the time might have been used to construct a secure hiding place. I checked the time. Five hours for Style to hide something and five hours for me to find it. I reached for the cargo manifest.

After I had committed the major items to memory, I rose, took the briefcase and documents and crossed to the door. Steph lay with one arm thrown up, undefended.

Down in the belly of the ship there wasn't another soul to be seen. In fact, the entire ship seemed to be manned by a skeleton crew. Above the door to the vehicle deck a red illuminated sign said: NO ADMITTANCE EXCEPT TO AUTHORISED PERSONNEL.

With a backward glance, I pushed open the door and stepped on to a metal catwalk. I had exchanged the zone of carpets and piped air and soft lighting for grey riveted walls, clammy diesel fumes and meagre fluorescence. The light was like a mould, covering everything. The ship's mechanical systems throbbed close by.

The few commercial vehicles stood nose to tail, like a slumbering herd, with my truck at the end. I peered both ways, trying to penetrate the shadows, and when I was certain I was alone, I crept out.

First I collected the torch from the cab, then I went to

the rear doors. Fighting the urge to rush, I got them open.

Somehow I had thought that my subconscious had been working on the mystery, and that when I confronted it afresh the answer would leap out of the muddle. But everything was as before, only more impenetrable. The spectral light on the drapes gave the load a creepy air, like the attic of a mad aunt.

I stared until I no longer knew what I was staring at. The beat of the engines and pumps seemed to get louder and I felt as if I was looking right into the heart of things without being any the wiser. I pulled off a dust cover. Underneath was a coffee table. I yanked away another shroud to reveal a small chest. I went through the drawers. They were empty except for an air freshener. I examined it carefully before putting it back, aware that even if I found what I was looking for, I might not recognise it. I attacked another piece of furniture. I was beginning to pant.

'Oi, what's your game? Get out of there.'

I almost welcomed the disembodied challenge. 'It's quite all right,' I called. 'I'm the driver.'

'Stay where you are.'

Out of the defective light waddled a portly sailor, fingering a two-way radio. 'You're not allowed in here,' he said, glancing at the cargo to gauge the extent of my interference.

I waved a hand to indicate the frontal damage. 'Had a bit of an incident on the way down and upset the load. Thought I'd better check it before I get back on the road.'

He shook his head, not softening. 'No way, mate. Security regs. You'll have to wait till we dock.'

'It's my truck,' I pointed out, fanning documents. 'If I wanted to steal anything, your regulations wouldn't stop me.'

'They will on my watch,' he said, and lifted his chin,

pointing out the security cameras I'd failed to notice. 'If one of the officers sees you, it's not you who gets the blame.' He poked himself in the chest for emphasis.

I smothered my exasperation under a smile. 'I've got a problem,' I confessed. 'This load's an express delivery for an important client. I'm on a bonus if I reach Zaragoza by this evening.' I unbelted another tenner. 'I can't afford to waste travelling time.'

The sailor ignored the inducement. He peered into the truck and sniffed. 'Looks like a load of second-hand furniture to me.'

'I know,' I sighed, 'but the owner wants it delivered today. His wife is arriving tomorrow. You know what wives are like.'

'Not my problem,' the sailor said gratuitously, then squinted in suspicion. 'Anyway, there's not much wrong with that load. Not that I can see.'

'Far end. That wardrobe. It's filled with her best china. You should have heard the crash when it went over. I mean, I ought to find out the size of the damage before handing it over.'

For a few more seconds he hesitated, then he plucked the bribe out of my hand and stuffed it away. 'Ten minutes,' he said, 'and I'll have to keep an eye on you.'

I decided to risk his supervision. I couldn't reach the wardrobe from this end, but there were side doors. I chose the nearside access to find the entrance blocked by a large crate. CHINA I read on the side. FRAGILE.

''Ere,' the sailor cried. 'I thought you said . . . '

'Best porcelain,' I emphasised, hauling myself up. 'Spode, Limoges, Delft.' I began my ascent on the crate, but as I elbowed my way over, my sleeve snagged on a nail, pulling me off balance. Grabbing for a hold I dropped the torch. It clattered to the deck and went out.

'I'm going to get a right bollocking for this,' the sailor grumbled.

Lying flat on the crate, I could make out some kind of cavity beyond, but without the torch I couldn't distinguish anything within. I reached down to arm's length and felt about. My hand contacted something upholstered, soft. I leaned down as far as I could and groped deeper.

'Here is a message for James Griffith. Will James Griffith of Argonaut Haulage please report to telephone five on C Deck?'

The air froze around me.

'Griffith,' the seaman said. 'Hey, that's you, isn't it?'

'Here is a message for James Griffith . . .'

'Ship to shore. Must be urgent.' The sailor activated his radio. 'I've got Griffith here with me. He's on his way up.'

I dropped from the cargo bay like a dead weight and trance-walked out. If the police had found the driver or the contradictory fingerprints, they wouldn't have phoned for an explanation. They would have alerted the ship's captain or asked the Spanish police to detain me at the other end. There was no reason for Style to phone.

That meant the call was from the loss adjuster.

Phone five hung limp off the hook. No one else was around. I picked it up.

'Hidey,' he said, and whistled a ditty. After a few bars, I recognised the banal little number that goes, *You say tomato, I say tomato / You say potato and I say potato . . .*

I gnawed my lip.

'Is that it?' the loss adjuster asked amiably. 'You figured you'd call the whole thing off?'

'Things aren't what they seem,' I said, my voice a croak.

'Bet on it. You thought you could make an out-wit of me, ain't that the way?' He sighed. 'I got a low tolerance for deception, mister. You got yourself some strife coming.'

'I had no intention of catching the ferry. I turned up four hours late and the damn thing was waiting for me.'

'Where there's a will,' the loss adjuster pointed out, 'there's a way.'

'You're right. I want you to have the truck. I can't wait to get rid of the thing.'

'You been poking around in there, mister?'

'No.'

The loss adjuster mulled it over. 'Here's how it works. You get to Santander and you find a quiet place and set there until I come along. Now where do you pro-pose we meet up?'

'I don't intend meeting you.'

'I ain't negotiating, mister. Remember you said down's only a state of mind? Let me tell you, it's one hell of a long ways lower than that.'

'You can have the truck,' I told him, 'but I'm staying out of it.'

The loss adjuster chuckled. 'You're a treat.' He whistled a variation on a theme while he considered the position. He broke off with a sniff. 'Shoot, I can always catch up with you someplace down the road.'

I breathed a fervent sigh. 'There's a Mercedes centre in Santander. I'll drop the truck there. I'll tell them you're a relief driver.' I hesitated. 'And you are?'

'Lock the truck with the paperwork inside. And I expect you'll want to re-fund all that money you took off me.'

'Will that put us all square?'

'I ain't offering any deal but one,' the loss adjuster said, and whistled another sweet tune. 'Know it?'

'Magic Flute,' I said dully.

'You're a man of culture and intelligence, mister, and as big a fool as I could meet between here and sundown. So let me lay it out straight. Act contrary on me one more time, and when you hear that tune again, I ain't gonna be but one heartbeat behind.'

With that folksy threat ringing in my ears, I was already glancing over my shoulder before he'd replaced the phone. But even as I hurried back to my cabin, I knew I was safe, and I experienced the sense of triumph that comes from baiting a vicious animal and getting away with it. The loss adjuster wouldn't have called me if there'd been any prospect of him meeting me off the boat.

Cock-a-hoop at this guarantee, I barged into the cabin. Steph was still asleep, her bedclothes in disarray, one naked leg sprawled over the cover. I covered her up and she moaned. I touched her brow and was struck by its velvety smoothness, a natural refinement that wasn't just the gift of youth. Despite her lack of social adornments, I could understand why other men found her attractive.

I sat in a chair and watched her slumber. 'I stick by my mates,' she had said, with that fierce little intonation she used when she wanted to get across some basic claim. I wriggled as if my skin had grown a size too small. If I was so certain that I was doing the right thing, why did I feel myself fall in my own estimation?

18

The dawn of creation, I marvelled, watching the light seam open over the mountains. The crack of doom.

It had gone seven, time to call Style, but I didn't have the gall to keep his hopes alive when whatever scheme he had cobbled together would run aground in about forty minutes.

The sea was running in a long swell and the air was washed blue and noisy with gulls. I stayed on deck, watching the coast draw nearer. Light crept down the mountains and to my surprise I saw that they were snow-covered from crown to foot.

In my hands dangled the keys to the truck. The shoreline approached at an excruciatingly slow rate. One hour was all I needed. In one hour, given luck, the whole continent would lie open before me.

Only one thing flawed this vision. Looking at the keys, I realised that the moment I tossed them away, my involvement in the mystery would be at an end. I suppose that in a part of my mind I had harboured a fantasy of myself as the player who unmasks the villains in the final act, and it came as a letdown to admit that nothing whatsoever hinged on my performance. Style's plans – whatever they were – would come to nothing. Axnoller and his accomplice would get their way – whatever that was. The driver would receive no justice, certainly not from me. All my actions had been irrelevant.

Too bad. This wasn't make-believe. Whatever my own role might have been, I had no doubt what part the loss adjuster played, and I was just as certain that at some point between me and any resolution of the mystery I would find him waiting. Better to write myself out of the script on my own terms than let the loss adjuster kill me off on his.

But a dissatisfaction still rubbed, and even the consolation of my rendezvous with Eleanor couldn't smooth it away. Last night I had envisaged golden opportunities, but in daylight I saw how futile my imaginings had been. Even the mediocre prospect of a renewed teaching career looked absurdly out of reach. I was a fugitive. Without references, without a past, no half-decent academic institution would employ me. At best I would end up teaching the rudiments of commercial English to Madrileño businessmen.

Now the coast was close enough for individual houses to be distinguished. A decision had to be made soon and I didn't know what hung on it. All I knew was that I didn't feel *ready* to return to being Matthew Reason. For all the dangers I'd experienced, my role had liberated me from myself. These last three days I had lived at the limits of my nerves, and though I hadn't exactly covered myself with glory, things had happened – not all of them bad – that could never have happened to Matthew Reason.

Even if I could find my way back to normality, did I want to return? I took stock of normal; I laid it out before me. Normal was a Chiswick bedsit on a landing between an anorexic Australian chiropodist and a HIV-positive bicycle courier. Normal was finding myself glued to cut-price early afternoon quiz shows. Normal was cloud-cuckoo fantasies about Eleanor Barry. Normal was a dyslexic job-centre functionary telling me I was setting my sights too high because I turned down a job as spare parts co-ordinator in a Toyota franchise. Normal was . . . a silent scream in the abyss.

With a thrilling blast the foghorn announced our imminent arrival. Until that moment, I hadn't known my mind for certain. I still didn't in any sure or logical sense, but I knew that if I aborted my journey now, I would spend the rest of my life regretting it.

The mountains stood in full light under a sky of barely remembered blue. After all the days and weeks of gloom, I found the sunshine quite alienating. I decided to go below, grab something to eat and call Style after all. A certain fatality was in control, and it would almost be an act of sacrilege to buck it.

He spoke without frills. 'I've just seen the forecast for northern Spain. You've got trouble.'

'I know. There's snow down to sea level. How's the weather with you?'

'It's been snowing all night. The motorway's closed. You were lucky to get away.'

In my mind's eye I could no longer see the driver – only a frozen hummock.

'You probably won't make Zaragoza today. That's okay, provided the wagon reaches the depot no later than tomorrow night. Got that?'

I spoke with formality. 'Mr Style, the weather isn't the only thing I'm worrying about.'

'Axnoller,' he said at last, pronouncing the name as if it were a blight.

'It goes back further than that. The accident that held me up. The two thugs who were killed had tried to break into the truck an hour earlier.'

'Why didn't you . . ?' Style began, and then changed aim, his tone flat. 'Did you tell Rip?'

'The men knew I was there. They knew where to find me.

I understand that the locating device was fitted on Mr Eeles' instructions.'

'Rip's no longer with me,' Style said after a moment, and swallowed his loss. 'Why tell me now?'

'You're right about the Americans. The young one, the one who calls himself the loss adjuster – he offered me money to miss the ferry. I took it.'

'But you're on the ferry.'

'That was a mistake.'

'A very bad mistake.'

'I know. He called me last night. He offered one last chance. Leave the truck in Santander or face the consequences.'

'And?'

'In the circumstances, I thought it best to accept.'

Style was cautiously nonplussed. 'I'm not sure what you're saying, Griffith.'

I found myself flushing. 'Mr Style, I don't like the position I've been forced into. The least I can do is let you know what's going on behind your back.'

'My back is taken care of. Double deal with me and you'd better start worrying about your own.'

'That's more or less what the loss adjuster told me.'

'That's your lookout.'

'But you can see my difficulty.'

'How much did he pay you?'

'Twelve hundred.'

'I'm not going to offer you more. Get the wagon to Zaragoza no later than tomorrow night and I'll forget about your dishonesty. Those who know me will tell you that's an extremely generous offer.'

'I've heard the stories, Mr Style. Unfortunately, I bet there's a tale or two to be told about the loss adjuster.'

'Change your route. Stay off the main roads as much as

153

you can. I'm going to book you into another depot. Call me this evening before seven. I'm catching a plane at nine.'

'At least you acknowledge the risk.'

'The American's a temporary inconvenience, Griffith. Once you've delivered the load, he'll forget about you.'

'I doubt it.'

'You have a job and a home here. I can destroy both.'

An impulse seized me. 'I'm not coming back.'

A note of desperation sounded in Style's voice. 'Go where you like. Just finish the job first.'

'Mr Style, this job is more likely to finish me.'

With a lengthy sigh, Style altered his negotiating position. 'All right, Griffith. Five hundred on top.'

It was money I could never claim. 'I'm sorry.'

'A thousand.'

'Mr Style, I'm not auctioning my services.'

Style had begun to breathe hard. 'Then what the hell *are* you after?'

My finger doodled a question mark on the glass booth. 'I'll consider completing my journey on condition that you give me full details of my cargo.'

'You have the list.'

'It's junk. The whole lot wouldn't fetch more than three thousand.'

'You're right. There's nothing on the wagon that's worth a penny to you or the Americans or Eeles. Nothing at all, you hear.'

'Mr Style, I'm not going to risk my life for nothing.'

Style was struck by a thought. 'Have you spoken to anyone at Argonaut?'

'Not a word.'

Style was bewildered. 'You go against the Americans, you go against me, and you go against your employers. They said you were *reliable*.'

'I know my motives must seem less than clear. I'm hoping you could clarify them.'

'I asked for a fucking *driver*,' Style shouted, 'not a halfwit lawyer.'

'Tell me what I'm carrying that I shouldn't be.'

Style kept a stubborn silence.

'Mr Style, in less than an hour I'll be going through Customs.'

Style pitched his response low. 'Mr Griffith, if you take your imagination elsewhere, my cargo will be delayed and I will hold you personally responsible. You might think you'll be safe in Spain. You'd be wrong.'

'Look, I'm not in a position to tell anyone else. You're not the only person with problems. Why do you think I'm not coming back? Why do you think I haven't called Argonaut?'

Style thought it over for a long time. When he spoke again, he sounded weary. 'Tell me what you think I'm hiding.'

'I heard the way Axnoller talked about you. Your . . . ' I got a halter on my tongue before it let slip that on the night in question I had met his estranged wife. For some reason, her image set my thinking cock-eyed.

'My what?' Style snapped.

'Your business,' I said, 'would appear to be in difficulties.'

'Not if you deliver the goods to Zaragoza.'

'Then it seems to me, that if you want to protect your investment, you should recognise the strength of my bargaining position.'

'If you knew anything about business, you wouldn't be driving a wagon. Never bargain for something unless you know what it's worth.'

'I'm prepared to take a chance.'

Style composed himself for a small moment, and then he

spoke in the lilt of his native valleys. 'When I was a little boy – no more than four – my dada sent me and a younger lad, Cliff, to steal some coal from the pit. As we were climbing over the fence on to an old slag heap, a man came by and said: "You shouldn't go in there, boys. There's dragons live there." And he showed us a sign, and though I couldn't read, that's what it seemed to say. DRAGONS. There was even a picture of flames. But we knew there wasn't any such thing as dragons, you see, so we told the *gorgio* to bugger off and over we went, on to that slag heap. It was full of interesting places, so because we were young we forgot about the coal and began to play, me and Cliff, hide-and-seek and cowboys and indians. I was on one side of the top and Cliff was on the other when I heard him scream. "Vic," he screamed, "the dragon's got me." '

Style paused. 'You know what had happened?'

I shook my head, but only because I could guess what was coming.

'Cliff had fallen through the ground up to his waist, and under the ground where he'd fallen the coal was burning – hot as a furnace it was. I tried to pull him out but I couldn't, and anyway he was as good as dead, though he kept on screaming for a long time. I could smell him cooking, Griffith.'

My jaws had parted in a snarl, as if I, too, was smelling roasting flesh.

'A man of your education,' Style said, 'should know the word DANGER however it's spelt.'

His voice returned to its commanding brusqueness. 'Unlike you, Griffith, I *am* a man of his word. There'll be a thousand pounds waiting for you in Zaragoza, payable on confirmation of safe arrival. Disappoint me and you'll live to be sorry.'

Just as long as I live, I thought. I could have told him to

keep his money. I could have told him that he would be chasing a ghost. I considered saying all those things, but for better or worse I had made my decision and was duty-bound. I ran my tongue over my lips. 'Make that two thousand, Mr Style. I don't want to be buried in a pauper's grave.'

'A deal.'

'I'd better go up now. We're nearly there.'

'And stay the right side of the door, Griffith. For your sake, not mine.'

I emerged on deck to find the shoreline drawn in around us. Cars were crawling along the coast road, and the possibility that the loss adjuster was in one of them made me turn sternwards, seeking a line of retreat. Dark cloud massed on the horizon. We had run ahead of the storm, but it was no more than a league behind.

Setting my face to the shore, I tried to ease my anxiety by thinking of the extra two thousand waiting in Zaragoza. I mean, if I was going to stick my neck out, it was only right that I do it for the highest bidder. Wasn't it?

'It's not like in the brochures.'

'Steph! I hardly recognised you.'

She had changed into her new clothes. They were nothing fancy, just jeans and a sweater, but she was transformed – a clean, fresh, strikingly pretty young woman on holiday.

'You look terrific.'

She made her little cat face. 'About a billion times better than last night.' She tossed her curls. They were newly washed and the sun caught in them. 'Thanks for looking after us and everything.' Her attitude was composed, grown-up.

'Not at all.' My own manner was awkward. I sensed that we were about to have one of those stop-start conversations that mark the parting of strangers.

A passing Spanish gentleman gave a courtly smile of approval. Steph met his eye with studied coolness then directed a mischievous look at me from under her lashes. 'Think I'm in with a chance?'

'You're a very attractive woman.'

'Not last night I wasn't. I was *revolting*.'

'You were no trouble, Steph. Honest.' I cleared my throat and gestured at the Spanish snowscape. 'Not what you expected, I imagine.'

Steph squinted at Santander. 'What part of Spain is that then?'

'Cantabria.'

'Is that near Málaga?'

Her ignorance alarmed me. 'I'm afraid you'll have to go a lot further south to catch up with summer.'

We were entering the pincers of the harbour and I could see people lined up on the pier. Suddenly I felt starved of oxygen. 'What will you do?' I asked Steph, my voice pitched louder than necessary.

'Bar work. Maybe I'll find work as a dancer. I'm a brilliant dancer.'

'I'm sure you are.' My response was vague. I was straining to pick out the loss adjuster's smile.

'You expected?'

'What? Oh, no. I hope not.'

'Where are you off to now?'

I couldn't make out the loss adjuster, and unless he was waiting, my destination was decided. Contrary, he'd called me, and I had to concede that I'd spun like a weathercock at each shift of circumstance. But there would be no more detours, no more backtracking. A shiver of anticipation ran down my back. 'All the way.'

'Where's that?'

'Zaragoza.' The word had an appropriately grave ring, the sound of a destination rather than a place.

'Can I come too?'

I'd been expecting it and had a gentle but inflexible smile in place. 'Not this time, Steph.'

The corners of her mouth drooped. 'I've never been abroad before. Not properly abroad. I don't speak Spanish.'

'They'll make allowances.'

'And I'm nearly skint.'

'Don't tell me you've gone through two hundred pounds?'

She itemised her expenses. 'Ticket, ninety quid. Clothes, eighty. You can't expect me to go abroad looking like *that*. I've only got a tenner left.'

Even if I stayed alive to collect my bonus, I would need to husband my resources. 'I'm staying on for a week's holiday after this run. I can let you have . . . '

'I'm not after your money. I want a lift, that's all.'

The ship's siren blared and there was a general move below as the passengers went to the cars. A woman waved excitedly at a group of relatives. When I looked back at Steph, her eyes held an appeal I wasn't willing to acknowledge.

'I'm really sorry, Steph.'

'I thought we were friends.'

I took her arm. 'We are,' I said, and gazed at her with all the eloquence at my command. 'Which is why I can't take you with me. I'm bad news, Steph. You've been round me long enough to know that.'

She was first to look away. She went to the rail, rested her elbows on it and spoke with her hands cradling her chin. 'I suppose I can always stick a card in a telephone box.' She eyed me at a tangent. 'What's the Spanish for Lancashire hotpot?'

'Oh Steph,' I laughed. I pulled out my wallet and pressed another hundred into her limp hand. 'Use it for train fare. Forget hitchhiking. Believe me, it's not safe.'

Her fingers curled over the notes. 'I'll pay you back,' she said at last.

'Any time.' We stood for a moment, off-balance with the knowledge that there was no more to be said and that our brief convergence was over. I held out my hand. 'You take good care of yourself.'

She ignored my hand. Instead she pulled my head down and planted a clumsy kiss on my mouth. 'Yeah, you too.' She strode away, but stopped a few yards off. 'I forgot,' she said, dipping into her duty-free bag. 'I got you this.'

It was the aftershave, bottled in homoerotic crystal substitute. 'It's very kind of you,' I told her, touched. I wished I could have taken her with me. I didn't like the idea of her fending for herself.

Steph misinterpreted my hesitation. 'I didn't nick it, if that's what you're thinking.'

19

A gentle collision announced our arrival in Spain. Seconds later the bow hinged apart and my pulse quickened at the sight of figures stark in the sun. They were only ferrymen, but against the light they were like a premonition of ill fate. I groped for the ignition and the engine clattered obediently. The trucks ahead were already warming up. Soon the view was fouled with exhaust vapours.

Last on, last off. I spent the time studying a map. Style's advice to avoid the main roads was superfluous, but there were only two ways out of Santander, and both of them were major highways. If I took the logical route, east to Bilbao and San Sebastian, there was a risk of meeting the loss adjuster head on. The alternative route, via the Burgos – Madrid highway, climbed to a high pass less than twenty miles from Santander and might be blocked.

It was the same with all the minor roads; every one of them ran through sierra and cordillera.

A rap by my ear startled me out of this quandary. A sailor was walking away rotating his hand. The truck ahead was pulling out. I took hold of the wheel as if there was a rocket strapped to my back, fed in the clutch and inched forward.

Outside, my exposure was total – acres of blinding asphalt fenced by chain-link. I rolled towards Immigration – a uniformed arm outstretched from a glass and concrete booth. In front of me the driver of a refrigerated rig from

Pontefract offered his passport and was sent through on the nod. A formality, I told myself, moving into place, holding the truck on the clutch.

I spread Griffith's passport open. The inexpressive hand reached for it. For a moment we both had hold of it. The official glanced up at me.

'*Momentito.*'

My heart jumped to the level of my adam's apple. I rested my elbow on the window in a display of professional nonchalance and stared ahead. Ten seconds went by and I knew I was dished. The official was frowning at the photo as if it affronted him. Slowly he looked up and his eyes dead-panned across my face, trying to fit the unconformable image to the features it was supposed to represent.

I dredged up a smile. 'Everything okay?'

He indicated that I switch off the motor.

'I'm in a hell of a hurry.'

'Please,' he said, 'get out of your truck.'

I slid out on legs that seemed to have been severed at the anklebone. The official side-stepped, getting me in profile, then circled about as if I was a newly-discovered object that he was classifying for science.

I was rooted to the spot. My eyes followed him round until he was behind me and couldn't see me swallow. 'What's the problem?'

For answer, Griffith's portrait was waved under my nose. 'This photograph does not look like you.'

From a blurred six inches I contemplated the snapshot. I raised a sickish laugh. 'It's a terrible likeness,' I agreed. 'I ought to sue.'

He examined me full frontal. My own stare was determinedly blind – the look of a man avoiding the eyes of his firing squad. With judicial deliberation, the official pronounced his verdict. 'I think,' he said, flicking the passport with his thumbnail, 'this man is not you.'

I unstuck my tongue from my palate. 'Of course it is.'

'The eyes. Look at them. Do not tell me they belong to you. And the mouth.'

I glanced at the pathetic deception. 'Appearances can deceive.'

He tripped an on-off smile. 'I think they do not deceive me – eh, Mr Griffith?'

'If it isn't me, who else could it be?'

'We shall see,' he said, then looked up. We both did. Clouds had snuffed out the sun. Around us the light dimmed and turned ashen, and suddenly the air was filled with soft, coin-sized flakes.

I seized on nature's intervention. 'Hurry it up, will you? This rig's got to be in Zaragoza tonight and I'm already three hours late.'

'I would like to see additional proof of identification. You have another document with your photograph on it?'

I ran a finger down my jawline. 'I don't believe I have.'

The telephone rang in the booth. The official ignored it. 'What are you carrying?'

'Furniture.' I hoisted my case. 'It's all in here. Go ahead, look.'

The phone was still bleeping. Keeping his eyes fixed on me, the official backed off and picked it up. He held it about six inches from his mouth and watched me like a hawk. It was snowing hard enough to curtain off the perimeter. A sailor ran for shelter, drawing the official's gaze. I stamped my feet in a show of furious boredom. 'Hey,' I shouted, 'how long are you going to keep me here?'

The official made a down-playing gesture. His eyes had begun to glaze and now he was cradling the phone with one hand and scribbling with the other. Whoever was on the other end was pulling his concentration out of shape.

'What happened to the Single Market?' I demanded.

The official rolled his eyes, inviting solidarity between workers.

Scowling, I turned my back on him. 'Take your time. Don't mind me. I've got all fucking day.' I reached for the cab door. 'Let me know when you're ready.'

'Señor!'

I expected to see a drawn pistol or something equally compelling, but he was beckoning me forward with the passport. As I reached for it, he took another glance at the photo, gave me a bewildered look, then slapped it into my hand and turned away before his judgement could get the better of him.

Customs was an open-plan office sunk in post-holiday torpor. Men and women in white shirts stared at screens, occasionally rising to confer with a colleague before planting their arses back in their seats with a sedentary little wriggle. At first the lethargic atmosphere provided a soothing respite. The officer assigned to me was friendly and conversational, but as his thumb-licking deliberations went on and the minutes ticked by, my answers grew shorter and my face began to stiffen as if a mud mask was drying on it.

'Excuse me,' I asked eventually. 'How much longer is this going to take? I gestured at the falling snow to emphasise my concern. 'I have to be in Zaragoza tonight.'

He riffled the stack of documents. 'Forty minutes?'

Forty minutes! I tugged at my open collar and went to stare out of the window.

Snow was still falling, though not so heavily. Cars drifted through yellow haloes. I watched them in an anguish of impatience, grudging each wasted second, and suddenly my stomach muscles went taut and I knew that the loss adjuster had arrived and was out there now, patiently waiting for the system to spit me out.

Ultimately it did. My papers were in order. The officers had no desire to search the truck. Apparently the consignee or his agent was supposed to deliver it for inspection at a bonded depot within one week. I could have been carrying ten tons of narcotics and no one would have been any the wiser.

By the time I emerged, the park was empty. The city sounds were padded. Nearly half the day had gone, and the dismal half-light made it seem even later. I surveyed the perimeter. At one point, a muffled figure loitered. I climbed aboard in the knowledge that the loss adjuster had got the drop on me.

At the exit a policeman stepped in front of the barrier, one mitted hand upraised, the other resting on his machine gun.

'Where you driving?'

'Zaragoza. By the Madrid road.'

'Closed. You drive Bilbao. After that, maybe Pamplona. The snow is very bad.'

'Isn't there any other route? I don't mind how long it takes.'

Shaking his head, he retreated into his shelter. 'One way only, señor.' The barrier began to rise.

My eyes scouted the street. Pedestrians were few and far between and apparently going about legitimate business. Down the far side cars were parked, their windows plastered with snow. My eyes came to rest on a blue saloon. On the screen in front of the driver's seat a peep-hole had been scraped clear. Steam clouded up from the car's exhaust.

'Excuse me,' I called, 'a friend arranged to meet me here. A tall, blond man. American.'

The policeman shrugged. The barrier was vertical.

ALL ROUTES, a sign opposite the gate said, pointing right. One way only. Overcoming massive inertia, I nosed into the street and followed the arrow, driving right past the idling car. It was a Seat with a registration number ending in 6-4 and what looked like a hire firm sticker. I didn't see it pull away from the kerb.

Christmas lights were strung across the town centre, but down at street-level the atmosphere was crabbed and frantic – like a refugee bottleneck on the road out of a disaster area. On the pavements gnomish figures hurried lop-sided against the falling snow.

At a major junction I was trapped in honking gridlock, everyone jockeying to get home before the snow cut them off. I kept seeing the loss adjuster from the corner of my eye, but whenever I turned it was someone else. Policemen in capes hurried between the files of traffic, trying to sort out the chaos. It was every man for himself, and with more urgent motives than anyone else, I used the truck's bulk to open up a passage. Even so, it took ten minutes to intimidate my way clear. I scraped through on an amber light. Nobody followed.

I sat a little straighter and held the wheel more lightly. It seemed that I'd made it. My reflection appeared to agree.

My cautious high took a dive at the next crossroads. Again I squeezed through on the amber, only this time I wasn't last across. About six or seven vehicles behind me a car jumped the signals so late that it was nearly crushed under the wheels of the opposing traffic. 'Bloody idiot,' I murmured. My reflection looked sober.

I never took my eyes off the mirror. The car swerved out, looking for a way through. There wasn't one. It tried again a minute later, dodging oncoming destruction to leapfrog past three or four vehicles. Now it was only two cars behind me. In the filthy conditions I couldn't identify make or colour. Sweat had gathered on my upper lip.

Maybe he thought he was following me to our agreed rendezvous. Stupidly, I hadn't even bothered to find out where it was. I reached for the town plan, then stopped, my belated hope knocked cold by the knowledge that the time for concessions was past. I had lied to the American not once, not twice, but three times, and by any reckoning that put me in the dead loss column.

He was a killer. I had never articulated the fact in so many words, but there it was, plain and simple. Not a murderer, nothing so emotionally complex as that. The loss adjuster killed for a living and he whistled as he worked. My skin swarmed. I avoided my eye in the mirror.

At the next junction he was still behind me, despite a couple of chances to get alongside. He must be holding back until we were beyond the town limits. Already the pavements had the unpopulated look of the urban outer circle. I thought about leaping out and making a bolt for it. I peered down the road to the right. It converged into snow and distance and didn't encourage flight. In any case the lights had switched to green and the traffic was surging away, carrying me with it.

What a compulsive activity driving is. Back in town I could have jumped out and vanished into the crowd with minimal risk, but a more urgent dynamic had kept me in my seat, going forward. My reluctance to take to my feet was an extreme version of the mass dementia that makes otherwise sane men and women drive blind in fog at eighty miles an hour. Don't stop; keep up; get on; stay ahead; pray the bastard in front doesn't jam on the brakes – the herd instinct on wheels.

Bilbao 110 kilometres, said the sign at the next round-about. The road beyond opened into freeway where he could pick his spot. Out on the open road I wouldn't have a chance. I thought of Griffith in his unmarked grave and that put a harder edge on me. My brain performed calculations – speed, velocity, mass.

On the approach to the roundabout I cut into the outside lane. An anxious little toot greeted this manouevre. I watched the mirror, waiting for him to come up on my blind side, ready to force him into the barrier. Adrenalin fizzled.

He made his move as I straightened on to the freeway, still in the overtaking lane. He hooted for me to give way. I held my space. For a few seconds more he stayed under my tailgate, then his lights appeared full beam. He was cautious, though, aware that I'd identified him and ready to take evasive action. Slowly his blazing reflection moved up. I stared into the dazzle, unblinking, knowing I would have only one chance. His lights slid abreast and we were cab to cab, seat to seat, only feet apart. Half-blinded, I glimpsed the pointed gun and veered hard over, not trying to fend him off but to ram, to crush, to annihilate.

In the instant before impact, my brain caught up with the message sent by my eye and I sheered away. The car dropped out of sight, horn baying. I looked for it in the mirror and caught sight of myself, teeth bared. 'Oh dear,' I said.

The car I had nearly wiped out was overtaking again, keeping maximum lateral space between us. My neck went hot. I didn't want to look. I wanted to skim over this unfortunate episode. But the jammed horn told me that she wasn't going to let me off. Yes, it wasn't the loss adjuster and no, that wasn't a gun. It was a middle-aged woman driver jabbing her middle finger up at me, projecting a fury that shrivelled my insides to little black coals.

I think I must have driven a couple of miles before I came sufficiently to my senses to do something about the doltish smile I found hanging off my face.

20

On the run to Bilbao the snow turned to sleet. I fought to stay alert for pursuit, but inevitably a degree of slackness crept in. What vigilance I possessed was needed for driving. The road was a deathtrap, the traffic throwing up gouts of salt-slurry that dried on the glass, reducing my field of view to the quadrant swept clear by the wipers. A forty-tonner was right up my arse, shoving me along at an insane speed.

Rape. It was the most uncompromising word in the language. It allowed no leeway; it gave no quarter. I hadn't raped Eleanor, but after all these years she might have persuaded herself that I had. Even if she was prepared to admit the lie, what about my own barefaced deceptions? How could I ever hope to talk my way out of the mare's nest I'd created? In her letter, she'd made it clear that she wasn't after a romantic fling. She wanted stability, loving kindness, a brand new start. She thought she was meeting a prosperous businessman. Ha! Look at me – thundering down death alley in a stolen truck with the law on my heels and a hired killer somewhere up ahead.

This train of thought fizzled out in a tortured squeaking. The sleet had stopped and the night was suddenly as clear as glass. I reached to switch the wipers off and saw something that nearly jolted me into the windscreen.

Steph was marooned on the verge, clutching her carrier to

her chest, using it to shield her from the motorway rush and spray. She didn't see me, but I got a good look at her as I went past. I expected to see her pathetic and waif-like, but she was glaring truculently through the traffic, like a martyr facing down some ritual humiliation.

I pulled in as soon as I was able and ran back. She didn't look at me even when I was right in front of her, and she didn't speak when I took her arm and helped her back to the truck. Her skin as far as I could tell was blue. Her teeth chattered. I set the heater to maximum.

I waited until she'd thawed. 'I thought you'd be halfway to Barcelona by now.'

She didn't answer. Her arms were like ramrods, her hands balled into fists.

'I thought I told you to stay off the road. Why didn't you take the train like I said?'

'I was going to, but then I met this man who said he'd give me a lift to Pamplona – wherever bloody Pamplona is.'

My concern expressed itself as anger. 'Steph, it's time you became a little wiser in the ways of the world.'

She gave me a whipped look and studied the dark passing by.

'What happened?'

'What do you think happened? He had a go at me – that's what. All right?'

Sensing that if I pried any deeper, it would be me who ended up mortified, I gave my attention to the road. One of those inexplicable gaps had opened up ahead, and all the traffic seemed to be using me as a pathfinder. The loss adjuster could be freewheeling behind any of the lights in my wake. The screen was misting up with the damp from Steph's clothes. I could smell the musk of her perfume. To hell with it.

'I'll take you to Zaragoza.'

'How far's that?'

'We're going the long way round.' I wiped the screen with the back of my hand. 'We won't make it tonight.'

She sneaked a look as if wondering where that put her in relation to me.

'I don't see it,' Steph announced.

I gave my eyes a furious rub and sat up. I got the impression that Steph had been watching me for some time, compiling doubts.

'See what?' I asked, reviewing the available memory for cues.

'You being in prison – for an act of violence.'

My wince was genuine. 'A criminal record isn't something you invent.'

'What else have you done apart from beating up that bloke?'

'Isn't that enough for you?'

'Not really, no.'

From Steph's opaque scrutiny, I gathered that she had detected a basic flaw in my story.

'Anyone would think you found criminals attractive.'

'Depends. Like this bloke you done over. What did he do to get on the wrong side of you?'

I tried to come up with a convincing felony that wasn't too injurious to my self-image. 'We had a fight.'

'You don't say.'

'Over a woman.'

'You? Give over.'

I found myself resenting the cold fish implication. I shrugged, man of the world.

'What – like a crime of passion?' Steph squiggled with interest. 'Who was she? Come on, what was her name?'

This was only conversation, I thought. It didn't matter

what I told her. 'Eleanor Barry.' The sound of her name made me flinch.

'Were you in love with her?'

I could see the slope getting steeper. 'Yes.'

'Do you still love her?'

'I . . . still have strong feelings about her.'

Steph patted her knees. 'Tell us what happened.'

Retailing the past in this frivolous way made me feel as if I was tampering with some delicate mechanism that could blow up in my face. 'You don't want to know.'

'I bloody well do.'

I side-tracked as best I could. 'So far the confessions have been one-way. I don't even know how you came to be in that service station.'

Steph slumped back, bored. 'I was meant to be going to a rave in Bristol.'

'The chap in the gorilla suit – why did he attack you?'

She shrugged. 'He was trying to get something off of me.'

I gave her a quick look, not sure if this was another of her euphemisms.

She laughed. 'His wallet.'

'You stole his . . . ?'

She held up her nails for casual inspection. 'He sold me some dud whizz. You know, speed.' She met my scandal-ised stare with frank indifference – and then she burst into laughter.

'What's so funny?' I demanded, throttling my indig-nation.

She stopped laughing. 'That's the difference between us. When *I* lie, I make it convincing.' She gave me a kindly smile. 'Watch the road. Else you'll have an accident.'

Whether or not Steph was a thief and drug abuser, she'd come out of this exchange a clear point ahead. I looked for an advantage to gain, but she had consolidated her superiority with an aloof silence. I let the road take up the slack. The traffic had thinned out and settled into some sort of rhythm.

I tuned the radio. 'You might as well get some sleep. It'll be another three hours before we stop.'

'My jeans are soaking. Is it all right if I take them off?'

'Er . . . sure.'

She arched up in her seat and began to peel off the wet denim.

'Not here! In the bunk.'

'It'll make me seasick again.'

'Not as sick as I'll be if I'm stopped with a naked woman in my truck.'

'It's a free country, in't it?'

'Is it?'

'Oh, don't be such a big blouse.'

That effectively stifled conversation. I glared down the beam of lights and thought of all the things I could say if I wasn't so sensitive to other people's feelings.

Steph stripped efficiently. She reached to pull a blanket down from the bunk and though my attention to driving was a hundred per cent, I couldn't avoid a flash of thigh as white as candlewax, the curved line of her underwear. The warmth in my groin took me by surprise.

She laid her cheek on her hands and closed her eyes. I found Chopin on the radio, the piano concerto in E. I listened and the music drew me in. By the time the last chord had died away, day had merged into night and Steph was asleep.

The dark was solacing. The radio was off and the cab was insulated by a thick, vascular silence. I had the sensation of being transported by a dream – floating, locationless, filling perfectly my allotted space in the universe. Watching my fellow travellers gliding past, imagining their commonplace lives and routine destinations, I knew that even if I'd been offered the chance, I wouldn't have changed places. I was uplifted by the sheer uncertainty of my situation.

One thought led to another. Steph was still asleep, her mouth slightly open. I chose my starting point at random.

'You're right about one thing? I am on the run.'

One eye glimmered. 'Who from?'

'An American. A criminal.'

'You're bonkers,' she said, and yawned and blinked out at the night. 'Where are we?'

'Approaching Bilbao. He's after something I'm carrying. I don't know what. That's what I was looking for when we met. That's why I panicked when I saw the cops.' I intercepted Steph's rearward glance. 'House contents.' Her sceptical expression made me laugh. 'Honestly, Steph, I haven't got a clue.'

'All right,' she said, sitting up, 'tell me about this American.'

'Late twenties, a little shorter than me. He has fair wavy hair parted in the middle, protruding ears, big hands and feet. Oh, and he whistles extremely well.'

'He sounds gormless.'

'Not when you get to know him.'

'Where did you meet him?'

'He tried to rob my truck near Bridgend. I got a good look at him then.'

'How do you know he's American?'

'Er . . . I heard him speaking to someone.'

'And whistling, too. What do we do if we run into him?'

'We won't. He's had his chance.'

Two commas dimpled Steph's forehead. 'You tried to miss the ferry. That means you thought he'd follow you to Spain.' Her eyes held the astute look that generally meant trouble. 'That's who you were looking out for when we landed.'

'You don't need to worry about that.'

'I'm not.'

I realised that I'd lost my narrative line. 'The ridiculous thing is, he's chasing the wrong man. Remember you said I wasn't a truck driver? Well, you're right. This is the first time I've ever driven one. You see . . .'

'Yeah?'

Under Steph's close supervision, I surveyed the morass of explanation ahead – Eleanor Barry, Griffith, Eeles, Style, Axnoller, the loss adjuster. I couldn't place them in any meaningful relationship. It was so much simpler, so much more convincing to be Griffith, even to myself.

'Nothing.'

'Are you kidding?'

The traffic was clotting, merging into the Bilbao rush hour, and I was just another driver trying to stay out of trouble and reach journey's end. 'You'd better get dressed.'

Steph's breasts under the blanket rose in a long-suffering sigh. 'Sometimes,' she said, 'I think you must have escaped from the bin.'

21

By the time we broke out of the Bilbao orbit, I was more than tired. I'd been on the go since before midnight and I hadn't eaten since dawn. My head was muzzy and my empty stomach burned from the acid secreted by the sudden frights and near misses. My spine felt short by a couple of inches. I rolled my head to ease the strain.

Steph's caress sent a current through me. 'Here,' she murmured. 'Let me.'

My hand closed over hers and gently set it aside. 'Not now.'

She remained close, her shoulder lightly brushing mine. I was glad of her company. She made me feel protective.

'Steph, you mustn't take people at face value.'

'I don't. I always give people the benefit. That's my philosophy.'

Since I was a beneficiary of her good nature, it would have been churlish to point out the trouble it had got her into.

'When are we going to stop?'

I'd decided that the best strategy would be to lie low in a cheap hotel in Logrono, then strike out in a different direction before first light.

'About an hour.'

'Brilliant,' she cried, then looked at me expectantly. 'Will you take us out?'

'What?'

'It's not late. I thought we could like go out.' Her tone became wheedling. 'Go on, it's my first night abroad.'

The thought of catering to Steph's low cultural tastes filled me with alarm. 'What kind of thing did you have in mind?'

She raised her hands and fluttered her fingers in imitation of flamenco. 'Dancing,' she said, her voice dropping into a sultry register.

Fortunately I had the perfect let-out. 'I can't dance.'

'Course you can. It's not as if you're fat or anything.'

I gave her a sour glance. 'Thanks.'

'I'll teach you.'

My headache took a turn for the worse.

Steph settled in her seat, starry-eyed, her plans already in place. 'How old are you, anyway?'

I hesitated, but only for an instant. After all, I wasn't old in absolute terms. 'Twenty-eight.'

'Six years older than me,' she lied.

It was the first time I'd thought of myself as old in relation to any woman I'd been involved with. Not that I was involved with Steph. But still . . .

'What do you reckon?'

'About painting the town red?' I shook my head. 'Not this evening. Not until I've discharged my duty.'

She did her down-in-the-dumps routine.

'Tomorrow,' I told her, relenting. 'In Zaragoza. Once I've dropped off the load, we'll celebrate.'

Steph wasn't conciliated. She plucked at the hem of her blanket. 'So what are we supposed to do tonight?'

'You go out if you want to. My plans are limited to a meal and a good night's sleep.'

Her maddening silence worked right into me.

'Have a heart, Steph.'

We drove on. A smiling roadside bull invited us to break

177

our journey at a service station coming up in six kilometres.

'Let's stop there,' Steph declared.

'We're nearly at Logrono.'

'I need a piss,' she said, and nudged me hard. 'There, that satisfy you?'

'Call it what you like. I'm not stopping on the main road.'

'Only for a bit.'

'No.'

'Honest, I'm bursting.'

If Steph's strained bladder had been the only consideration, I would have ignored it, but other factors undermined my decision. The fuel gauge had sunk to below the quarter mark and I didn't want to be caught empty in the shut-up hours before dawn. Also, it was approaching six, and by the time I found a telephone in town I would be cutting Style's deadline fine.

'All right,' I told Steph, 'but let's make it quick.'

It was a big motel complex festooned with seasonal electrics. The car park was surprisingly full; the truck park next to it was half-empty. I backed into the front row facing the right way for rapid exit. The sky had cleared and a frost had fallen, laying a treacherous sparkle on the tarmac. Steph clung to my arm as we walked over and I found I didn't mind. Unease struck when we entered the lobby. It was teeming with people and baldly lit. Before going our separate ways, I gave Steph a stern reminder. 'Ten minutes, not a second more.'

She walked away at an eager shimmy, then turned and caught me out in the act of smiling. Her eyes narrowed.

'If you do a bunk, I'll come back and haunt you.'

In fact I'd been smiling at the picture of myself dancing the night away with her. Why not? Another country, different rules.

My smile was wiped out by the discovery that there were queues at all five telephones. I decided to clean myself up while the logjam cleared.

Motorway washrooms have always struck me as sinister in a crummy, B-movie way – a downmarket place of assignation with the less glamorous forms of death. That ominous gurgle of water. The threatening hiss of the cisterns. The insistent mortuary lighting. When I walk down a row of cubicles I expect to find the legs of murdered junkie or low-grade informer sticking out from under a door. Standing at the urinal, my back felt chilled and I kept one eye cocked towards the door.

When I had completed my business, I glanced in the mirror to check how I was standing up to events. A sharper face had emerged through the familiar mask. My hand rasped over my stubbled cheeks. Jekyll, I thought, and Hyde.

All the telephones remained occupied. I took my place in the shortest queue. Inevitably I picked the one with the windbag who was detailing his social diary for the forthcoming year. The ten minutes were up and Steph still hadn't appeared. I searched out the eye of the blabbering dago and glowered. He smiled imperviously and pointed to the next floor.

Upstairs there was a restaurant, quite a classy one, hosting a function for a party in evening dress. Outside the booth I nearly collided with a young woman in a pearlescent gown. I performed a clumsy waltz to let her get past. The timidity of her smile made me realise that my appearance might appear threatening to the tender of spirit.

Communications with the UK were poor that night. Waiting for Style to answer, I found that the encounter with the girl had brought back to mind one of the most hideous experiences of my life. An Oxford friend had invited me to a hunt ball in Gloucestershire. When the time came to change, I discovered that I didn't have dress shoes. Too embarrassed to say anything to my host, I improvised. I found a tin of black shoe polish and painted my suede casuals with it. I used the whole tin, and very glossy they looked, with a shine the equal of patent leather. And so, rather pleased at avoiding a nasty little gaffe, I went dancing. The night was going swimmingly. My partner, a pure-bred gel studying estate management at Cirencester, had clung close during the smoochy numbers, giving me hopes that the night would end with me pretending not to look as she slipped out of her pale magnolia satin gown.

At midnight we retired to the lounge for a bumper of champagne. Her mother was there. She spread her arms at the sight of her ravishing daughter, and even worked up an approving nod for me. And then her face crumpled and dropped, leading our eyes down to her daughter's swart and lampblacked hem, and then slowly across to my own blotched and culpable Hush Puppies.

A definitive episode in my life. Oddly enough, remembering it now gave my spirits a boost. There were unlikely compensations to be found on the dark side.

'You're cutting it fine.'

Style's voice bundled everything else out of mind. 'I wanted to cover as much ground as possible. I'm about halfway.'

'The American's left you alone?'

I didn't relish the implication that the loss adjuster had any choice in the matter. 'So far. Do you know where he is?'

Style seemed reluctant to admit his ignorance. 'No. Spain, I imagine.'

Putting the loss adjuster in any kind of geographical proximity made me itchy. 'Unless you have anything important to tell me, I'll be pressing on.'

'Nothing's changed this end. I've made the arrangements. By-pass Zaragoza and take the Lérida Road. About eight kilometres out of town you'll see an unfinished industrial estate on the left. There's a scrapyard next to it. That's where you leave the wagon. You can't miss it.'

On the basis of that vaguely ominous description, the scrapyard sounded well worth a miss. 'Lérida Road,' I repeated. 'Scrapyard on the left.'

'When can we expect you?'

We? All of a sudden I saw myself as a small wheel in a complex system of gears and pulleys and cams, all turning in phase to activate some instrument whose function remained known only to Style. 'Tomorrow,' I said. 'About midday.'

'If I were you,' he said, 'I'd try and make it tonight.'

I had an intimation of a net closing around me and a voice told me to quit pronto and bugger the two thousand. 'If my life depends on it, I will. Otherwise I plan to catch a few hours' sleep.'

'Hold on,' Style ordered.

His presence grew faint, and then I heard his footsteps returning.

'My car's arrived. I have to go.' He sounded careworn. 'Stop off if you must, but make sure you don't pick anywhere obvious.'

As if I needed telling. 'And the money?'

'It's taken care of. Someone will be waiting.'

'You?'

'You won't see me again,' Style said. 'If you have any problems, leave a message on this number.' He hesitated, composing his valediction. 'You're riding your luck, Griffith. In any other circumstances I would have punished you for the trouble you've put me to. Punished you severely.'

'We're both riding our luck,' I told him, and hung up.

22

Steph stood on tiptoe and gave a little wave. Still absorbed in Style's news, I returned an automatic smile. This precarious lifestyle wasn't for me. I'd had enough hairbreadth escapes. My constitution wasn't designed to take such punishment.

Below me in the lobby Steph waved again and I saw that her expression was over-bright, anxious even. I hastened down the stairs.

'I've seen him,' she squeaked, her eyes lit up like green glass. 'The bloke what's after you.' She was as excited as if she'd spotted a media star.

The news staggered me. 'That's impossible.'

'Curly fair hair. Big feet. Sticky-out ears. American.'

I grasped the straw. 'How do you know he was American.'

'You know – like American.'

I stared at her in a frenzy of not knowing. 'Did you hear him whistle?'

'Don't be soft. It's *him*!' She jabbed her finger floorwards. 'Right here. I came out of the caff and there he was.' She hunched her head into her shoulders and peered around, milking the melodramatic moment. 'You know – looking.'

My eyes bolted from side to side. I hurried Steph behind a fibreglass Santa Claus. 'Where is he now?'

'Back in his car.'

'How do you know?'

She grinned. 'I followed him, didn't I?'

I boggled. 'Tell me where.'

She seized my wrist and began to pull me doorwards.

'Stay out of sight,' I hissed, yanking her back. A passing couple turned their noses up at such ungallant treatment.

Steph rubbed her arm. 'He's opposite your truck. One row back.'

I made a mental sketch. My truck was facing the car park across the main exit lane. 'Is his car pointed towards the cab?'

'Yeah. I think so.'

Her vagueness brought a veil of blood down across my eyes. I waited for it to lift. I eyed the lobby entrance, plotting a path towards the truck. 'Would he see me if I left through there?'

'Yeah, he would, 'cos I looked in case you came out.'

'Did he see you?'

'Dunno. Don't think so. Doesn't matter if he did. He doesn't know who I am.'

An awful thought collided with all the others. I couldn't believe that he'd stumbled on me by chance. He must have been following me. The image of the blue Seat with the peep-hole and the burbling exhaust turned like a knife. He must have followed me all the way from Santander. I stared at Steph. If he'd been behind us, he would have seen me stop for her.

The implications went down my throat in one un-digestible lump. 'Steph, I want you to get right away from me. Forget about going anywhere tonight. Book yourself into a room here and stay in it. In the morning take a taxi to the station and catch a train to Zaragoza. Here,' I said, diving for my wallet. 'You'll need this.'

She ignored the money. 'What about you?'

'Don't you worry about me.'

'Bugger-lugs's got you shit-scared, hasn't he?'

My answer came as a dry sucking of air.

'What happens if he gets you?'

'Don't even think about it.'

She chewed it over for a moment. 'Wait here.'

'Steph!'

But she was gone, the door swinging behind her. I groaned. When I didn't come out, he would hunt me down, room by room. My eye fell on the phone. Call the police. There's a man after me. I think he intends to kill me. I squeezed my temples. Stupid, stupid, stupid. One stupid fucking lapse had finished me.

Steph came back after three or four minutes, her expression sober. 'He's still there.'

Out of the blackness emerged a thin ray of light. 'Listen, I'm going to call a cab. I'll tell it to pick me up at the door. If I'm quick he won't see me get into it. Even if he does, he wouldn't dare . . . ' The scrawny hope died. He'd follow me.

Steph was eyeing me with the detached sympathy of a spectator watching a chess player come to terms with a hopeless losing position. 'You can't stand around here all night,' she pointed out.

'You go,' I told her.

She frowned and pulled down her bottom lip with her finger. 'He wouldn't see you,' she said, 'if you got through my door. If you sort of crept up.'

My response was apathetic. 'Are you sure?'

'Dead sure. He's not parked right opposite. He's a bit to one side. He's expecting you to get in the same way you got out.'

'He'd see me drive away.'

Steph shrugged. 'It's worth a crack.'

Whatever I did, I couldn't stay here. At any second the

loss adjuster might walk through the swing doors. My eyes fastened on the sign marked SALIDA DE EMERGENCIA. There were a lot of people about.

'Oh, don't be such a scaredy-cat. No one's looking. Come on.' She began to march away, turned to see if I was following, and lowered her head like a mother calling a dilatory child. 'Come *on*!'

I sidled up to the escape door with my back to it and pulled down on the handle. It wouldn't give. I turned and exerted all my force. It was locked.

'That's not allowed, that isn't,' Steph said, offended by the breach of safety regulations. Her eyes cast about. I was humbly aware that her crisis-management skills were better than mine. 'This way,' she commanded, taking my wrist. She led me into the café. A few customers looked up with interest at the sight of a mature man being dragged along by a young woman. Some residue of bourgeois embarrassment made me grin sheepishly.

Steph marched right round the counter, past a mildly alarmed check-out girl. We stopped before rubber doors. 'Right,' she said, and barged through.

We were inside the kitchens, strolling between stainless steel work-stations. We had only got a few yards when an indignant shout struck between my shoulder blades.

'Scarper!' Steph cried.

Time speeded up. Our exit was freeze-frame slapstick. Chefs with cleavers. A waiter pirouetting with a tray of seafood. The slack face of a bemused washer-up.

And then we were outside, among the garbage bins and under stars. We kept running. Behind us the hue and cry expended itself on air. I experienced the lung-bursting relief of a drowning diver bursting through the ocean surface. I laughed and grabbed Steph in a hug.

'I love you.'

She went still. Stiffly she levered herself out of my embrace. She gave me a level stare. 'I'll remember that.'

We continued round the complex until we came to a corner that offered a view across the vehicle park. My truck was hidden somewhere on the diagonal, slap in the middle. The car park was a sea of glistening reflections. Brake lights pooled blood-red on the tarmac.

'You say he's to the right of the truck.'

'His right or ours?'

I gritted my teeth. 'Ours.'

'Yeah, he's on the right.'

'How close?'

'I'm no good at distances.'

'Steph, it's important.'

'Close enough.'

Steph's plan was no longer so persuasive. I was conscious that the night had turned very cold. 'He might have got out of his car. He might have changed his position.'

'Hang on, I'll take another look.'

This time I grabbed her before she could get away. I held her at arm's length, by both shoulders. 'You don't understand how serious this is. He's a professional. He may not have seen you the first time, but a thousand to one he spotted you when you went back.'

'I've not done nothing to him.'

'Steph, I don't think that's how his mind works.'

She must have absorbed the threat because she stopped resisting. 'I know,' she said, brightening. 'we'll nick a car.'

'Try to be constructive,' I snapped, then blinked, the simplicity of the suggestion blossoming like a flower. I looked at her with trembling hope. 'Do you know how?'

She wrinkled her nose. 'Not really. I thought you would. All the blokes where I come from know how.'

'I'm not like the blokes you know.'

Steph stamped her foot. 'Didn't they teach you anything in prison?'

A new idea struck me. 'He's not going to stay in his car forever. He's bound to come searching for me. That's the time to clear out.'

'If bugger-lugs's as clever as you say, he'll make sure you can't start the truck before he starts looking.'

On to the scrap heap went another idea. Stalemate. My feet were cold, my brain numb. I was a university lecturer, for God's sake. I was supposed to be able to analyse, deduce, solve.

Occam's Razor. When considering a problem, eliminate all unnecessary facts. I drew myself up. 'I'll try to sneak in through the passenger door.'

'That's what I said.'

I considered the best approach. There were gaps in the lines of trucks. I would have to work my way down the shadowy edge of the park and come up broadside.

'Where's that supposed to leave me?' Steph complained.

'Take the train to Zaragoza. Leave a message at the station telling me where you are and I'll come and meet you tomorrow night.'

She prodded the ground with the point of one shoe.

I felt for her hand. 'Steph, we'll go dancing. I promise.'

She shook my hand off. 'You're always trying to get rid of me, you are.'

It was a long and exposed walk, and when I was in my starting position I was extremely reluctant to commit myself. Halfway to the rear line of trucks I looked back. Steph was outlined under the lights. I gave a small wave but she didn't respond. By the time I reached the shelter of the rearmost truck she had disappeared.

I zig-zagged between the big wheels, always keeping at

least one vehicle between myself and my truck. At last I saw it, its livery fouled by road muck. Praying that Steph had got the relative positions right, I dashed for the tailgate.

For the moment my nerves could take me no further. I rested, panting, looking up at the stars. Sounds from the service station carried on the sharp air and I could see a coming and going under the lights of the fuel station.

I edged down the left side of the truck to the cab. When my heart had settled back on its mountings I reached up to unlock the door. At the last moment I pulled it away. What if the loss adjuster was waiting for me inside?

I stood there for five freezing minutes, straining for the slightest sound from within.

A soft whistling fell on my ear. I nearly died. A cardiograph would have registered a complete cessation of heart activity. My heart stopped. I nearly *died*. There was no time to move, even if I'd been capable of movement.

Down the exit lane came a man – another driver, juggling his keys. He stopped whistling when he saw me and smiled in slight surprise. I grimaced back. When he had gone I rested my forehead on the cold door.

At last I reached for the lock. In the nick of time I remembered to deactivate the alarm. Teeth clamped into my bottom lip, I opened the passenger door just wide enough for me to squeeze in. I dragged myself up on my belly until I was lying flat across both seats.

A hand caught my ankle and I kicked out.

'Leave off, you daft bugger.'

'Steph,' I hissed, 'fuck off will you. Please.'

'I'm used to this,' she whispered, sliding in on top of me.

Her weight tipped off my legs as she deposited herself in the passenger footwell. In my cramped position there was nothing I could do to eject her. I was going to have to start the truck lying down. I guided my key to the ignition and saw the note stuck under the wiper. From my prone position I was able to read it.

Some people, it said, *you can't do anything with.*

'It *is* him,' I said in a lifeless voice.

''Course it bloody is.'

Still lying flat I inserted the key. In ordinary circumstances, starting was guaranteed – foot half down, one turn of the key. With my left hand I primed the throttle. I hadn't realised how much force was required and I had to pump twice to lever the pedal through the required arc. Grimacing against the anticipated detonation, I turned the key.

The starter turned lustily, but the engine didn't catch. The racket had been so appalling that I was certain the loss adjuster must have heard it. I had to make sure. Awkwardly I raised my eyes to a level just above the door line. Second row back, Steph had said, to the right, but the overhead lights sucked all colour from the vehicles and made them all the same.

'How may cars to the right?' I whispered.

'Dunno. About four.'

After a while I thought I saw the suggestion of a face, a predatory whiteness. If I could see him, he could see me. My head ducked down. I tried the ignition a second time, with the same negative result. There was no way of knowing whether the fuel injectors were oiled and wet or dry and starved.

'Hurry up,' Steph muttered. 'Me foot's gone to sleep.'

Another try, another failure. At this rate I would drain the battery of its juices. I was oiled with sweat. In my contortions I'd pulled a muscle in my neck.

One more try. Please God, I prayed, this time.

The engine uttered a cough and then a furious backfire. My head bobbed up.

'Now you've done it.'

The cab illuminated.

'Run for it!' I shouted, heaving myself upright.

As Steph jumped into her seat, my eye snapped the scene of the loss adjuster spilling from his car in a sort of astonished crouch. I held the throttle down and spun the starter. One, two, three. The loss adjuster was gliding through the front row of cars. The engine burst into a full-blooded roar that wrapped the tacho needle round its stop. Twenty yards away the loss adjuster halted and spread his feet, finding his balance. I was moving, closing the range.

Both arms pivoted smoothly up and I saw the gun.

'Get down!'

His head turned as if he'd heard an interesting sound. His features were etched clear in the lights of an approaching car. He glanced at it, one hand shielding his eyes, then turned back towards us, calculating margins to the finest degree. We both realised that in a very short time two vehicles would be trying to occupy the same space. His response was to lower his gun and step back. Mine was to spin the wheel counter-clockwise and keep going.

'Lights!' Steph shouted.

I flicked them on. Vaguely I was aware of the screech of rubber as the car nose-dived to a halt a foot or so from my front wheel. At the blurred frame of vision I saw the loss adjuster jogging towards his car.

'Keep your eye on him. Tell me what he's doing.'

Steph sprawled across me to get a view.

'Can you see him?'

'No.'

'Get off. I can't drive with you on top of me.'

Steph flopped back in her seat. 'He's behind us. He's catching up. No, he's slowing down. He's nipped between a couple of trucks. He's dodging between them. Hey, he's a dead nifty driver.'

'I don't want a fucking race commentary.'

'Sorree!' Steph said, and crossed her arms.

'All right,' I said, fighting for calm. 'I've got him.'

He was slaloming across the park towards the exit. I had to go round two sides of a square to reach the same point. There was no chance of beating him.

Steph arrived at the same conclusion. 'He's going to block the road.'

I imagined the effect of ten tons of truck meeting a flimsy Eurobox. My foot went hard down. 'No he isn't.'

We rounded the corner at a perilous tilt.

'Where's he got to?' Steph cried.

He'd vanished. The corner of the park nearest the exit was empty. GIVE WAY, the sign said. Like hell I would. Next to it was a portable cabin of the type used on building sites.

'He must be behind the hut,' I said. 'He's going to . . .'

But I didn't complete my insight because I'd seen another car converging on the junction of my lane and the access to the filling station. One glance was enough to see that it was packed with people and that the driver was confident of his right of way.

So was Steph. She screwed tight back in her seat. 'I don't think he's . . .'

I swerved off the lane on to the park.

Steph clung to the door. 'Is there another way out?' For the first time, she sounded anxious.

'Who cares?' I said, and spun the wheel opposite lock. The back of the truck threatened to come round like a pendulum.

'There he is!'

I'd already spotted him, wheel-spinning backwards from the lee of the cabin. I straightened on to a collision course, my foot still hard down.

'Hold tight,' I said, gripping the wheel and leaning forward as if I was pushing the truck.

The loss adjuster had unscrambled my intention. His brakes locked. He still had time to get out of my path. Even before he'd stopped he'd thrown the car into forward. His wheels couldn't grip. I could hear the squeal of tyres. Exaltation filled my soul and for the last few yards we were flying.

Faster than was humanly possible the loss adjuster ejected. I wasn't doing more than forty when I hit his car, but the kinetic energy packed into the loaded truck crumpled the nearside front like Bacofoil and flung it aside with a delicious crunch and splinter. I hardly felt the impact. I went straight on through the exit.

Steph stuck her head out. 'Gor,' she said reverently, 'you haven't half made a mess of him.' She gave me a wondering look, as if I had revealed a side of my character neither of us had suspected.

23

'He had a gun,' Steph cried, bouncing up and down. She still had the fever of violence in her blood. 'He was going to kill the both of us. You should have run him over. Squashed him flat.'

'Pack it in. This isn't a joyride.' My own hot excitement had already congealed. The gun had raised the ante to vertiginous heights.

Steph went off the boil so quickly that I realised she was as shocked as I was. She subsided warily. 'What are we going to do?'

'I'm dropping you at the Logrono turning. It's me he's interested in.'

She grabbed hold of her door handle. 'Like hell you are. I'm not going out there on my own.'

I couldn't force the issue now. I had to get us off the main road. I shoved the map at Steph. 'We're giving Logrono a miss. Look for a turning to Soria on the right.'

In Steph's untutored hands the folds got away from her. 'You'd better tell me who bugger-lugs is,' she said. 'Who he *really* is.'

Various strands had come together. Whatever kicks the loss adjuster derived from his vocation, he killed to order. A contract killer isn't someone you can pick from the Yellow Pages. Presumably he was part of the same corporate structure that included Axnoller. But when he'd told the waste contractor that, with or without his say-so, he was going ahead with his job, he'd sounded like a man who answered to a higher authority. Like the papal inquisitor, he was an agent of last resort, with powers to match.

'He calls himself a loss adjuster,' I told Steph. 'That's someone who checks insurance claims to see if they're genuine. You're not meant to take it literally.' I glanced at her. 'I think he works for the Mafia.'

The ambiguity of her silence made me think she didn't believe me. 'Maybe not the Mafia, but definitely organised crime. He's serious business, Steph. That gun was real. If it hadn't been for you, I'd be dead.'

'I know,' she said. 'I was *there*.' She squinted across the screen. 'What did he say in his note?'

Some people you can't do anything with. The message was still stuck under the wiper. He'd meant me to see it. He wanted to watch me read it before killing me. I switched on the wipers. The message arced back and forth and then blew into the slipstream.

'It sounds,' Steph said, 'like he's really got it in for you.'

'Yes, I think we can safely say I've set the seal on his disapproval.'

'But why?'

At the very least I owed Steph an abridged version. 'What I told you about him trying to rob the truck wasn't strictly true. I met him at the home of the client who ordered this job. This client is called Style and he made his money in the American property market. He's got financial problems and in some way I can't work out, this load is his way of putting things right. But the loss adjuster and the people he works for don't want him to succeed. He offered me money to miss the ferry. I took the money and then I took the ferry. He's very cross.'

'Gosh.'

194

Thinking of the loss adjuster's crossness, we both fell silent. Our speed was governed to fifty, and on the wide carriageway it felt like a dawdle. With each mile I sensed the margins of safety narrowing. My fingers drummed on the wheel. 'Have you found the turning?'

'I've got it,' Steph said. She was staring at me in a rapt way. 'You're smuggling drugs.'

'I've considered that possibility.' I really didn't want to go through all this. It was going to be a long night, and I was starting it whacked.

'I mean you, *personally*, are.'

'If there are drugs on board, they're not mine.' I scratched my eyelids.

'But you're not a driver. You said so yourself.'

Now wasn't the time for explanations. 'Whoever I am doesn't make the slightest difference. If the loss adjuster catches me, I'm dead.'

'If you've not done nothing wrong, why haven't you gone to the police?'

Speaking was like drawing stones out of thick mud. 'Because I'm in a deeper hole than you can possibly imagine.'

She gave her reflection a tight smile. 'I'm in it too, now.'

I bit my lip. Alone, I could still escape at the switch of a passport, but I couldn't cut Steph loose while there was the slightest chance of the loss adjuster picking her up. The tyres hummed a monotonous note. I looked in the mirror. 'Hurry up with that map, will you?'

'I can't read it. It's in Spanish.'

'Here,' I said, taking it off her. None of this was Steph's fault. Quite the reverse. If she hadn't spotted him . . .

Trying to decipher the small print in the haphazard lights caused a certain loss of directional stability that spread alarm among other road users. Eventually I found the turning. It was further than I'd hoped. I marked the spot with my thumb and passed the map back to Steph. 'The distance is marked in kilometres.'

There was another huge delay. The tyres played their complacent song.

'A hundred and twelve,' she said at last.

About seventy miles – more than an hour's driving. The loss adjuster's car was a write-off, certainly undriveable, but he wouldn't be put out of action for long. Probably he had contacts in Spain. The van Damm woman had said that she and Rip were planning to be in Madrid. 'Tentacles' – that was an overdone word often used by journalists writing about the Mafia. 'Their tentacles reach everywhere.' The road slipped by in slow motion. I thought of tentacles. My fear was systemic now.

After ten miles or so the headlights picked up a signpost pointing west. Steph's eyes locked with mine.

'That'll do.'

We passed through one small town and discovered that the road was no more than a loop that returned to the main road. I turned round and drove back into town. I'd seen another junction, a minor road. *Ruta Turística*, the sign said. Logic told me it was a cul-de-sac, but we'd wasted half an hour and the impulse to flight had its way.

Soon the road began to climb. Below us the town appeared as an electrified grid that was abruptly switched into darkness. We met no other vehicles, coming or going. Through the top of the screen I could see a horde of stars. Steph switched on the radio for company. Fir trees hemmed us in. Snow was piled high on both verges. I could feel it getting colder.

Four or five twisted miles went by. We were grinding up rutted hairpins and I could see the frozen glint of peaks. The fuel needle had sunk close to the baseline. The atmosphere in the cab grew fraught, neither of us wanting to be the first to admit a mistake.

Steph gave in first. 'We're in the country. Maybe we should go back.'

'This road's got to lead somewhere.'

'I reckon we should go back,' Steph intoned mournfully.

Our lights picked up the eyes of a deer. It bounded away through the forest, sinking belly deep in the snow at each leap. I switched on the fan to maintain the temperature. The fuel gauge showed empty and exerted a dreadful fascination.

'*There's* somewhere,' Steph cried, pointing at a house set back in a clearing. It was shingled in the Basque manner. Cosy lights shone in a downstairs window. 'Look, it's a hotel.'

I drove past.

'Hey, what's the idea?'

I had shied from the prospect of explaining why I was driving a commercial vehicle up a snowbound mountain backroad. When I tried to explain this to Steph, she straitjacketed herself with her arms to keep from flying apart.

'A bloke tried to kill us, and you're worrying about what people *think*.'

I licked my lips. 'Let's see if we can reach a town.'

The incline got steeper. As we turned into a tight bend, the fuel warning light flickered orange. I picked my teeth with my thumbnail.

'My mistake. We'll go back.'

We crawled another kilometre, but there wasn't space to turn and the road was too tricky to permit reversing. I felt the climb relenting and then we were on the level. I sensed the presence of a giddy drop to the left. On the next bend the headlights probed out deep across the dark.

Ahead of us the road mysteriously vanished. In its place was a bed of snow. I slowed, saw the road begin again thirty yards further on, and accelerated. I kept my foot pressed down and the truck fishtailed through the drift. We were nearly to the other side when the truck dragged to a stop. The engine note rose and the truck crabbed left. Just in time I lifted my foot. I switched off the engine.

Silence fell like a stone. I could sense the recriminations choking Steph's mouth.

I jumped out. The front of the truck was bogged up to the sump. My collision with the loss adjuster hadn't done the cab much good. The rear wheel had swung to within five feet of the drop. When I looked over I saw the quicksilver signature of a river down in the forest. I floundered back and paddled at the snow around the front wheels. Within seconds, my hands and feet were blocks of ice.

'You'd better get out,' I told Steph.

I stationed her well clear, climbed back in and started the engine. Picturing the drop, I shifted into reverse, let the revs build and raised the clutch as delicately as I could. The truck trembled and one of the rear wheels whined.

All of a sudden the snow let go. My foot dived for the brake but the truck continued its swing left. I grabbed for the door, knowing it was too late. The truck stopped. I spread my elbows on the wheel and rested my head.

Steph opened her door and held her arms to half span. Back in the cab, she stared through the screen. 'Now what?'

'We'll have to spend the night here.'

It was only nine-twenty. I no longer felt sleepy. The contracting engine clicked and pinged. The bitter air sucked out the warmth from the cabin. I took blankets from the bunk and handed one to Steph. She snatched it with a mean look.

'Go ahead,' I told her, 'I deserve it.'

She preferred to nurse her wrath. Her stomach growled with hunger. She switched on the radio.

After five minutes of head-thudding Euro-rock, I'd had enough. I reached for the radio and Steph grabbed my wrist. For a moment we pitted strength, Steph's face very close to mine, then suddenly her anger was snuffed out and in its place was a wary stillness. I let go as if I'd been burnt.

'Go watch your dirty pictures,' she muttered, and flung herself back in her seat.

We waited at a standstill. An owl screeched overhead and Steph tensed and followed its imaginary flight. Her eyes continued to prowl. The empty landscape gave her the willies. Her survival talents had been honed in the urban underbelly, not in the wilderness backwoods.

'This is the safest place to be,' I told her. 'He'll never look for us up here.'

'You'll feel a real prat when bugger-lugs taps on your door.'

Over the next few minutes, the image worked its way down to the core. 'Wait here,' I told her. 'I'm going to borrow a shovel.'

Steph sprang up. 'Not without me, you're not.'

On the icy downslope we had to cling together. A pale wash of stars filled the skies and the moon stood high in a giant ring. A dog barked down the valley. Steph tightened her clutch.

'Do you think it was a wolf?'

I smiled. On this matter I couldn't go wrong. 'There aren't any wolves here.'

Her eyes narrowed. 'Yes there are. I saw a film about wolves in Spain.'

'Not this part. Besides, wolves don't attack people. Believe it or not, most of their diet is made up of mice.'

All the spite Steph harboured was distilled into synthetic sweetness. 'I'd be dead worried if I were you.'

24

Resinous smoke drifted from the chimney. Three vehicles, all four-wheel drive, occupied the yard. A slain deer hung on a scaffold and antlers were nailed above the door. A cautious knock raised a chorus of barks.

A young man with the build of a tree stump opened up. He took one look and stepped aside. A fire glowed in a room full of men. The first person I saw was a policeman, corpulent, unbuttoned, off-duty. The other two were hunters wearing *gilets* and boots laced to the knee. A couple of German wire-hairs sniffed us, their hackles stiff. Everyone was equally silent.

I stepped forward. 'I'm awfully sorry to disturb you. We got stuck in a snowdrift. We were looking for a short-cut. My friend misread the map.'

'Bloody liar,' Steph said, not at all quietly.

All eyes turned to her. I detected a wry softening of expression.

'I was wondering if I might borrow a shovel. Also, I'm afraid to say that I'm rather low on fuel.' As I delivered this request, I saw myself as the quintessence of English incompetence.

The man who had let us in asserted proprietorial authority. 'Where you stuck?'

I pointed uphill. 'About two kilometres, at the *mirador*.'

Our host laughed grimly and everyone made a meal of

wagging their heads and clicking their tongues.

'You were lucky,' the policeman said. His hand described a falling arc. His cheeks ballooned in a soft explosion.

'Better stay here,' our host said. 'We'll get your car out tomorrow.'

'Actually,' I said, and it cost me a lot of pain, 'it's a truck.'

Everyone exchanged more astonished looks. A faint caution entered the policeman's eyes. He tugged down his tunic, a little the worse for drink, but recalled to duty.

'You're driving to Soria?'

'Zaragoza,' Steph said, while I was still vacillating.

'But this is the wrong direction.'

Steph slipped her hand into my palm and smiled demurely. 'We were looking for somewhere to spend the night.' She trapped my hand against her thigh. 'Somewhere quiet like.'

One of the hunters grinned behind his hand and murmured something to his companion, who half-hooded his eyes and nodded with a connoisseur's deliberation. The policeman eyed Steph with a lugubrious hunger, like a hound ogling its master's dinner. Our host spoke to him in Basque, then turned to me. 'My neighbour has a tractor. He'll come up tomorrow, but not before eleven.'

A woman entered, cradling a sleepy child. Our host explained the situation to her. She smiled at us, her smile aimed mainly at Steph. 'Would you like something to eat?'

'*Gracias*,' Steph said, digging her nails into the back of my hand. 'That would be lovely, wouldn't it, sweetheart?'

'*Sí*,' I said, '*muchas gracias*.'

One by one the other guests left. Relief at the policeman's departure was offset by anxiety that a witness might have reported our break-out from the service station. There was also the possibility that the woman I had nearly run off the road had lodged a complaint. Even the damaged truck might raise awkward questions. Looking back, it seemed that the entire journey had been a mad rampage designed to attract maximum attention.

While I fortified myself with wine, Steph cuddled the baby and exchanged talk with the mother. At last the mother withdrew, leaving us alone at the table. Shadows slid on the walls. One of the dogs by the fire whined in its sleep. Gradually the wine and warmth unravelled my nerves.

'It's hot in here, in't it?' Steph said. She took off her sweater. Underneath, her breasts were perfectly delineated.

'It's not exactly the nightclub you hoped for.'

Steph inspected the room like a prospective house purchaser. 'I like it,' she said. 'It's foreign.'

Watching her tackle the Basque cuisine, I couldn't help contrasting her enterprising spirit with my own soggy will. She saw me studying her, popped back her forkful of food with a bravura gesture, and in that moment my heart flooded with fondness.

'Why you looking at me like that?'

'Because I can't help it.'

She cast down her eyes, shy for the first time since we'd met. I was a little drunk, I realised, and gave myself a reprimand. I was on my way to Eleanor. Trifling with Steph just wasn't on. I put my hand to my mouth and coughed.

'Your family,' I said. 'Won't they be worried about you?'

She choked on her food. 'My lot? Not them.'

'Don't you stay in touch?'

'Not for yonks. Well, I phone me mam at Christmas. I got out when I was sixteen. Me dad's an addict – gambling addict. Horses is what he's hooked on. He's not too awful when he's winning, but when he's losing, he's right nasty.' She made a fist of her hand. 'He loses loads.'

'Your mother?'

'She's all right. She has a hard life. Well she would, wouldn't she, being married to a little nose-bleed who knocks her about every time one of his horses gets beat?' Steph picked at her plateful. 'If you must know, she's on the game.' She looked at me angrily. 'I don't know why I'm telling you this. You'll only chuck it back in my face.'

'Any brothers or sisters?'

'Sean. He's a nutter. Possession of a deadly weapon – that's what they done him for last time. I've got a sister, too. She's got a baby. She's only sixteen. I ran away; she got pregnant.' Steph's shrug implied that they were different means to the same end.

Our hostess brought dessert – a lemon flan more to Steph's taste. The flush of alcohol brought out the slightly oriental cast of her features.

'I hope you don't mind, but I can't help wondering where you get your marvellous looks.' The words were clumsy and off the mark, but I couldn't find the right expression.

She balanced the point of her chin on the tip of one finger. 'Dad's Manchester-Chinese. It's the Chinese that makes him gamble. Me mam's Irish from Glasgow, but with a bit of Nigerian thrown in.' She looked up. 'Does that put you off?'

'It makes me feel inbred.'

'I thought you might be French when I saw you.'

I shook my head. 'I'm very ordinary.'

'You're family's posh, in't it?'

'Far from it. My father's an electrician. My mother's a nurse. But they had aspirations.'

'Why are you looking so down in the mouth?'

'I was supposed to be the aspirations realised, the generation that made it, the sacrifices made worthwhile. Big disappointment.'

'Like a black sheep.'

'Grey would be more accurate. Present circumstances notwithstanding, I'm conventional to the point of dreariness. I really was a teacher.'

Steph smiled faintly at her plate.

'Don't you believe me?'

Steph laid down her fork. 'Teachers don't get sent to prison –not for a first offence.' She looked me in the eye. 'Not unless you hurt that bloke bad. Not unless you half-*killed* him.'

I saw a diversion that would take me part way to the truth. 'He was a student of mine. Naturally, that was taken into consideration.'

Steph's mouth opened. She pulled her chair closer. 'Was this Eleanor Barry woman a student, too?'

Again, hearing Eleanor's name in someone else's mouth caused a superstitious twinge. 'She was.'

Steph's eyes were round. 'You mean, like under-age?'

I laughed. 'I'm not that depraved. She was a university student. Both of them were.'

Steph's face shone in the light of my revelations. 'Interestinger and interestinger.' She banged her fists down. 'I want to know *everything*. What she looks like, how you met, who the bloke was. This time, I'm not going to stop until I know everything about you.'

In fact, with the initial scruples overcome, I found I could take the facts in my stride. After all, my confession wasn't too wide of the mark. Truth and truthfulness aren't the same thing.

'She was one of my students. I fell in love with her. Her boyfriend found out and threatened to expose me unless I stopped the affair. He said he'd tell my wife.'

A contented smile gathered at one side of Steph's mouth. 'I thought you were married. I can always tell. So then what?'

'One night I confronted him. I lost control. We came to blows.' I shrugged.

'That it?'

'Serious blows.'

Doubt clouded Steph's face. 'How long did you get?'

'Six months. They took previous good character into consideration.'

'Did she wait for you? Did you get her in the end?'

That was a question beyond answering. 'No.'

'What – she was in love with the other bloke?'

'That was the way of it. So it seems.'

'What about your wife?'

'Divorced, remarried. People have certain expectations, and if they're disappointed they find it hard to make the necessary adjustments.'

Steph wasn't buying any of this waffle. 'Adjustments? How's a wife supposed to adjust to a husband who goes round screwing his students and beating them up?'

'Well, yes, but we were never in love. We'd married too young, before we knew what paths we wanted to take. We would have separated eventually.'

Steph mused a second. 'What did your family make of you going to prison?'

'They took it badly – my father especially. He's a lay preacher, very rigid on the sanctity of marriage.'

'Do you never go home?'

I saw the house and the river, all the places I'd never see again. 'Never.'

Steph was comically forlorn. 'So after all that, you ended up with nothing.'

'Not quite. I live in hope, Steph. And in the meantime . . . ' I raised my glass to her ' . . . here's to vagabonds.'

Our host came in and poked the fire. The dog lumbered

to its feet and followed him out. There was a period of stillness.

'Well,' Steph said, 'you wouldn't have to make any adjustments for me. Bloke-wise, my expectations aren't exactly high.'

'Raise them, Steph. You have remarkable qualities. You deserve the best.'

'Like a university teacher sort of thing?'

'You can do a lot better than that.'

Our host came in and drew the bolts on the door.

'I think he wants us to go to bed,' Steph said, and raised her eyes to mine. They were quiet, full of unspoken thoughts.

Our room was tiny and freezing, with ice on the inside of window panes. A bleeding Christ hung between the beds.

'You choose,' I said.

'Eeny-meeny-miney . . . That one.'

The bathroom was down the hall. Steph went first and returned scented and enigmatic, as if she had gained access to some privileged knowledge. I came back to find she'd changed her mind about which bed she wanted to sleep in. Her privilege. Turning my back, doubled over by cold and modesty, I began to undress. I reached for the bedclothes and prepared to dive in.

'My expectations aren't that low, stupid.'

Steph was lying naked, her cover thrown back. Her gaze was serene.

'Steph.'

'What's the point of going abroad if you don't try something different?'

I raised my hand and prepared to deliver the relevant objections.

She sighed and turned on her back. Her breasts shifted

heavily. She caressed them, lingering on the hard nipples, then she spread her hands on her ribcage. They glided down into a waist so tiny that the splayed fingers of each hand almost touched, down to her lap and beyond, meeting and stopping with a silky rasp on some locus of sensation that made her stiffen and close her eyes giddily. She opened them and looked at me, as if she was out of control and only I could save her.

I stood in anguish, seeing all my intentions going up in smoke. 'Steph, I can't.'

'Then what's that doing halfway up to your chin?'

I crept in beside her and she enfolded herself around me.

'I'm ever so wet,' she whispered, guiding my hand.

'Please, Steph,' I said, trying to mount a last-ditch defence, 'I'm enormously flattered.'

'I can feel that.'

'Can't we just hold each other?'

'We are. It's lovely.'

'I meant . . . '

'Sshh.'

Our love-making was avid, uninhibited. Neither of us spoke. We communicated with sudden intakes of breath and tiny cries that might have been taken for pain. Her head arched back, her white throat straining to release the helpless mews that inflamed me to my own shuddering climax.

When the last spasm had died into floating stillness, I looked down at her bruised wet mouth, her distant dreamy eyes, her remote face so strange and different.

She touched me lightly on the nose. 'I came three times.'

I sank my face into the crook of her neck. 'I hope I had something to do with it.'

Her hand probed my vertebrae, 'Sometimes I come five or six times.' She half pushed me away. 'But only with blokes I like.'

Gently I bit the vein in her neck. 'Does that mean you haven't made up your mind about me?'

Her hand extinguished the light. 'You were done for the moment I clapped eyes on you.'

In the dark I smiled. Not bad, I congratulated myself, for someone so out of practice. Not at all bad.

Steph stroked my hair in an abstracted maternal gesture. 'You said you had a week's holiday after you finished.'

A negative charge collected on my skin. 'After today, I think I'd better cancel my holiday plans.'

She drew back as if she could see my face. 'Aren't you scared bugger-lugs will be waiting back in England?'

I would have to tread extremely carefully and take nothing for granted. 'I thought I'd spend a few days in Madrid while I decide what to do.'

Her breath feathered my ear. 'I'll help you make up your mind.'

A dissident voice told me to say yes, to forget Eleanor Barry, to install a shred of certainty in my life. Steph and I were incompatible at every level above the sexual, but that was a sounder basis than I'd stood on for years, and a lot sounder than I deserved.

'I'd love to, Steph, but I'm meeting someone. An old university friend.'

'He won't mind.'

A crisis was in the offing and I could see no way of skirting it. 'It might prove awkward,' I said, and hated the depth of betrayal plumbed by those words.

'Oi,' she said, shoving me, trying to be boisterous but unable to hide her consternation. 'Don't tell me you're bi.'

'It's a woman.'

'You're having me on.'

'It's true, Steph.'

'Who?' she demanded, her voice grim.

'An old girlfriend.'

'Oh yes? I suppose you're going to tell me it's this Eleanor Barry they sent you to jail for.'

Her shrewd guess or intuition triggered the capitulation. 'We'd planned to get together in Swansea, but then this trip came up and . . .'

'Liar,' she said, striking me hard. 'Liar, liar, liar!' raising her voice with each blow. 'You said she didn't give a shit about you. You said you didn't know you were coming to Spain.'

I smothered her flailing hands. 'I arranged it last night. I called her from the ferry.'

Steph gasped.

'I didn't know you were going to be on the boat. I didn't know we were going to end up in bed together. Look, Steph, I'm only human.'

She lay slack. 'Why do I believe the things I don't care about and know you're talking bollocks about the things that matter?'

'Steph, it doesn't make any difference to how I feel about you.'

She pummelled me again. 'Oh, great! Oh, terrific! That really makes everything right.'

'Steph, I didn't mean that. I meant . . . oh, hell, lay off, will you?'

She threw herself down as far away as possible. Cautiously, braced for the next punch, I reached for her arm. I could feel the tension in her, the heartache and the anger.

'I had to tell you, Steph.'

'No you didn't. Why don't you know when to lie and when to tell the truth?'

Grey misery washed over me. 'I'm not sure I know the difference any more.'

Steph flung herself for the light and sat up. Tears splashed on her breast. 'Well I lied too,' she shouted, loud enough to wake the house. 'I didn't come, not once. I faked it. You're bloody useless, so bloody there.' Using the headboard for leverage, she kicked me out.

Picking myself off the floor, I skulked away into the other bed. The bedclothes were icy winding sheets. Gradually the sound of Steph's breathing grew less ragged, but I could sense her eyes blazing into the dark.

The moon shone its haggard light through the window. I tossed and turned, chasing justification up every blind alley.

25

A crash shattered sleep into splinters. A mug of coffee had been banged down, half its contents sloshed on the bedside table.

'Get that down, then get dressed.'

Hands raised against the inescapable light, I saw Steph planted at the foot of the bed. She was dressed for a day in the woods – boots, parka, mittens. Her cheeks glowed as if she'd already taken bracing exercise. She moved with the steamroller efficiency of a chambermaid evicting a guest who'd overstayed his departure time. From the brightness in her eyes I knew that forgiveness wasn't on the cards.

'Is the tractor here?' I mumbled, foraging for my watch. 'I thought it wasn't due until eleven.'

I found my trousers tangled around my head. Steph was shying my clothes at me with a fast overhand. 'We're going to look in your truck.'

Scorpions under my spine couldn't have raised me quicker. My jack-knife blacked out vision and robbed me of speech. I fluttered my hand like a man drowning. At last my vocal cords cleared. 'Leave it alone. Whatever's in the truck was put there by the client. He warned me not to look and he isn't the type whose warning you ignore.'

'Oh I see. I've put a stash of drugs in your truck, so if you don't mind, I'd rather you left well alone.'

I thumped the blanket. 'It isn't drugs. He didn't mean that.'

'Then what?'

I struggled for the modulated tone that carries its own conviction. 'I don't know. He meant that what I'm carrying is dangerous.'

'Oh,' Steph cried in mock amazement, 'now he tells me.' She lowered her head as if she was about to charge and articulated her words as if she was addressing an idiot. 'I *know* it's dangerous. I was there when bugger-lugs tried to kill you.'

'Then why, Steph, are you so keen on a repeat performance?'

'Because if someone tried to kill me – which they probably will now – I'd want to know why.' Her brisk tone returned. 'Now get dressed. We're going to turn that truck inside out.'

'I forbid it.'

She snatched the keys of the truck from the table, ran to the door and dangled them aloft.

I swung out of bed and hopped up and down after my pants. Steph surveyed me in one theatrically disgusted sweep. 'Not so high and mighty this morning, lover boy. I told you my expectations were small, but not that teeney-weeny.'

'For crying out loud, Steph. Grow up.'

'You've got three seconds. One and two and . . .'

'Right,' I shouted. 'Stick your head out. Don't blame me when it gets cut off.'

Downstairs, breakfast had been laid out for me. The rolls stuck in my throat like chaff. Chewing on them, I watched Steph dandle the baby and practise Spanish phrases with its mother. If I'd been in her place, I would have been sulking with an intensity that would have registered on a barometric chart. But women took their revenge differently – maintaining a sunny patina of everything's all right while making it bloody clear that they were going to make you pay right down to the very last drop.

At the appropriate moment, I told our host that we were going up the hill to fetch something from the truck. He lent me a flashlight and suggested we take one of the dogs with us.

Freezing mist had settled in the night, lacing the firs in a fantasy of white. Our breath steamed from our exertions. Steph, keeping up her infuriating pretence that she was out for a constitutional, threw sticks for the German pointer. Being a hunting dog, it had no interest in such suburban games. The fatuous cries of 'Fetch' and 'Good boy' only emphasised the gulf between us. I ached for reconciliation.

'About last night.'

'Don't want to hear.'

'Listen, I can't undo my past to suit you, but . . . '

She clamped her hands over her ears.

Anger rose like liquor in a sight-glass. I seized her elbow. 'That's why you end up assaulted by some low-life druggie in a car park. That's why you end up thrown out on to the hard shoulder by a pervert.'

'You think I'm better off with *you*?'

'No I don't. Why do you think I refused to take you with me? I never invited you along. I've got enough on my plate without worrying about you as well.'

'Yeah. Like Eleanor so-called bloody Barry.'

'She's nothing to do with this.' My words appalled me. I ploughed on. 'I might not win any medals in the hero stakes, but I'm alive, Steph. I'm alive because I know when to draw back from the edge.'

'Oh yes? The only reason you're alive is because I was there to warn you. Well, I don't reckon shit of you any more. Go and meet your clever student tart. See if *she'll* stand up for you when bugger-lugs turns up.'

She stomped away and the sight of her retreating back rent me.

'Steph! Look, I'm sorry, right? I think you're great. In any other circumstances I wouldn't think twice about . . . Oh shit!'

I toiled after her. A small wind brushed the firs and the mist parted on a backdrop of plunging forest and icy niches. Over the shoulder of a mountain the sun struck crystals from the rocks. Down the valley, vultures floated out of the smoking mist, looking like a vision of life from a time before man.

An unspoken truce declared itself when we stood before the truck.

'I've already tried the back,' I said stiffly. 'We'll concentrate on the front section.' I held out my hand for the keys.

She dropped them into my palm as if she suspected trickery, then retreated to a watchful distance. At that moment, I think I could have talked her out of going ahead, but having been marched up the hill, I could see no point in marching back down again without making at least a token effort. I had already trapped myself by my own fear, and nothing I found in the truck could make things any worse.

With a rumble the side door slid open and crashed into its stop.

Steph approached a couple of paces. 'Who's this lot for?'

'Hutchinson's the name on the documents. I don't think we need worry about him. My guess is he's an invention of Style's.' My gesture encompassed the load. 'Take your pick.'

Confronted by the tightly packed disorder, Steph faltered.

'I've had two cracks at it,' I told her. 'Both times I was interrupted, but the last time – on the ferry – I did notice something slightly odd about the area around the wardrobe. I got the impression that a space had been left clear.'

Steph's glance slid past me.

'What's *he* doing?'

Behind us the dog was frozen on point, jaws slightly apart, flanks trembling with the intensity of its stance. Its muzzle was aimed at the packing case.

'Maybe it's a drug sniffer dog,' Steph whispered.

I didn't laugh. 'Its owner runs a hunting lodge. These dogs are trained to scent game.'

'What kind of game?'

'Live game.' My shaky hand patted the crate. 'Get on,' I ordered. 'Seek. Find.'

With one fluid movement the dog leapt up to the lip of the cargo bay, gathered itself again and sprang on to the crate. It cast around, vacuuming scents, then put its head over the far edge. Its docked tail quivered. Then it disappeared, hitting the floor with a muffled thump. I heard a questing snuffle, followed by the sound of jaws working.

'It's eating something,' Steph said, huge-eyed.

After a while the sounds of mastication stopped. Down the valley a chain saw started up. We stood for an age in the black enchantment of the moment.

'Keep watch,' I ordered.

'Be careful.'

I scaled the crate and shone the torch into the recess I'd sensed on the ferry. The flashlight penetrated only a couple of feet before meeting furniture, but the cavity had to go deeper because the dog wasn't visible. At my soft call, it whined as if it might be stuck. 'Leave it,' I ordered. 'Leave it.'

Without warning, its whiskery head appeared below me, its tongue lolling and its yellow eyes glowing like the orbs of Lucifer.

'What have you found, boy?'

'What's he got?'

'Can't see. The gap's too small. I'm going to try moving the wardrobe.'

First I pulled the dog out. The wardrobe was wedged at an awkward angle and didn't offer a proper grip. The only solution would be to unload some of the surrounding furniture. 'I can't shift it.'

'Let me look,' Steph said. She scrambled up and eyed the hole. 'I could get in there.'

My misgivings were consumed in the fires of curiosity. 'Only if you're sure.'

'Keep an eye out.'

She wriggled in and disappeared. A terrible excitement was hatching. The mist had rolled away right down to the town and I saw that we were perched on a viewpoint visible for miles.

'There's like a little . . . ' Steph began, and then fell silent. I glanced over my shoulder before hurrying forward. I put my ear to the case.

'Steph?'

Above me her face popped up white and staring. 'There's a bloke down here. He's dead.'

He was sitting in an armchair under the toppled wardrobe. His head was skewed to one side and he was stone cold. Bracing myself like Hercules, I heaved the wardrobe upright. It was a Victorian hardwood item and heavy.

In the diffused light I examined the corpse. Here was my ghost, the presence which had haunted me during the lonely night shifts. He was scruffy with the self-elected scruffiness of someone who has no need or regard for decent clothes. At the same time, he was conventionally and old-fashionedly dressed – shabby chain-store jacket; synthetic shirt, not clean and not dirty; shiny trousers without creases; and scuffed and dull shoes with virtually no wear left in them.

Even allowing for the shrinking effects of death, he was small – about five-six I estimated, with the physique of a whippet. I guessed that he was in his mid-forties. His hands were tattooed with the name Mona and a couple of designs that meant nothing to me. Around his neck he wore a weighty gold chain. Blood from a head wound had run down his face and congealed. I parted the hair. The blood was slightly tacky.

'He's been murdered,' Steph said.

My own reflex verdict, quickly overturned. 'Style wouldn't go to all this risk and complication and expense to dispose of a body.'

'He would if he wanted to get him out of the country.'

'Style's house is near some old mine workings. He knows every inch of the place. If he'd wanted to lose a corpse, all he'd have to do is drop it down a pit shaft.'

'Maybe he was sending it to someone.'

Bizarre as this notion was, I tried to make it stand up. It wouldn't. 'I can't see the loss adjuster chasing after us to recover a dead man.'

There was blood on the man's hands and blood on the chair. I was no expert, but it seemed unlikely that he'd died from that single blow to the head. I shone the torch on him. He'd been sick. Dried mucous streaked his chin and there was vomit in his lap and on the arm of the chair. Its foetid sweetness flooded my own mouth with sickness.

My hand probed around the corpse. It encountered crumbs and then a metal cylinder which I identified at first touch. I pulled out the vacuum flask and showed it to Steph. Then I unscrewed the top and poured a little of the liquid into my palm. The faintest residual warmth made itself felt. Nauseous suspicion grew to full-fledged certainty.

'Unless Style buries his enemies with grave goods for the afterlife, this man was put on the truck alive.'

'Maybe bugger-lugs did him in when we were in the services.'

'It wasn't him.'

'Who then?'

'Remember the night we met? Remember I told you I'd nearly crashed? I hit the central reservation. That's when the wardrobe fell over. It must have concussed him, knocked him cold and then . . . ' My voice petered out, drowned in the heaving darkness of the storm. What an awful way to go. I raised my eyes. 'It was me, Steph.'

'Let's get out.'

'Not just yet.'

Teeth strained in distaste, I felt in his pockets. They were empty. I extended my search to the furniture immediately around him. All I came up with was a dry cleaner's ticket in the bottom drawer of the wardrobe.

'What you got?'

I shook my head. 'There's nothing on him. No identification of any kind, no money.' My gaze roamed the cargo. 'There must be a thousand places he could have hidden them.'

'Right,' Steph said, as if that was the cue she'd been waiting for, 'I'm off.'

Inside me another intuition was taking form, blood-dimmed and thick. 'Steph,' I said, 'if you can bear it, I'd like you to take a close look at him.'

The torchlight shining full on his face spared nothing. His lips were drawn back in rigor, exposing yellow sharp teeth. A thin stubble covered his chin and I remembered that the beard goes on growing after death.

Steph bit her knuckles. 'He's horrible – like a dead rat.'

'Death's unkind,' I told her. 'Try to imagine him alive. Think where you might have seen someone like that before.'

Steph sawed her knuckle between her teeth. 'He looks like some of the Spanish men.'

He did indeed resemble a work-hardened and down-at-heel peasant. Superficially, he could have passed for a native in any part of Spain or Mediterranean Europe.

'You're right, but he isn't Spanish. His clothes are English. Tell me where you might have seen someone like that back home.'

Despite Steph's horror, the corpse exerted a dreadful magnetism. 'In the bookies with me dad. Or down the boozer. Or down the DHSS office. Manky places like that.'

'Not a man gainfully employed.' I needed to hear her own judgement. I wanted independent corroboration.

'How do you mean?'

'Not a man with a nine-to-five job.'

'You must be joking.'

'A waster?'

Steph regarded the corpse with disgust. 'A thiever and a dosser and a nasty little toe-rag. And now can we go?'

Confirmation of my suspicions made my head spin. 'Yes, now that we've identified him, I think we can go.'

Already scrambling for the light, Steph froze and turned wide eyes. 'You know who he is?'

'Not who. What.'

'You've seen him before?'

'I'm sure that I've been very close to him. He was at Style's house the night I picked up the load. He was in a darkened room watching television.'

Steph snagged her bottom lip between her teeth. 'What are we going to do?'

I knew only what my next step would be. When I had taken it, I would know the next. And so on, step by step. It was the only way I could proceed. I held out my hand to Steph. When we were outside, I drank in the mountain air. The world sparkled and I had never been so glad to be alive. Up from the hazy blue distance drifted the faint sounds of the ordinary world going about its vast business. Inexplicably I felt part of it again. In some way, I felt that I had been restored to the body of mankind.

'Maybe we ought to go to the police,' Steph muttered, without force.

'With my record? No, I'm going to have to get rid of him.'

Steph's fearful glance switched from me to the lip of the cliff. She eyed the drop as if I'd suggested that she make an unassisted leap.

'Not here,' I told her. 'The dog may lead them to the spot. He'd certainly be found eventually, and they'd remember us.'

Meeting death face to face had sapped Steph. Her stance was round-shouldered and submissive. 'I've never seen anyone dead before.' She looked up at me and she shook. 'I'm scared. I'm really scared.'

I wasn't. This was my second corpse. The killings, the deadly scrapes had hardened me. What I felt above all was relief that a central part of the mystery had been dragged into the light. In some way that I couldn't define, it made all my evasions and lies worthwhile. It gave my assumed role a new stature and significance. It brought me centre stage.

'Where can we put him where he won't be found?'

'It's my problem, Steph. I'm not dragging you any deeper.'

Steph's response was wrung out against her will. 'I'm worried about you, too.' She glared at me. 'Even if you are a rotten, lying bastard who ought to rot in hell.'

I wanted to make it right between us, but this wasn't the time or place. 'Provided no one connects him with the truck, I have a feeling it doesn't matter whether he's found or not.'

'They'll trace him. They always do. They'll find out who he is from his fingerprints or his teeth.'

'I think it's a good few years since he went to a dentist and I'd bet that he has no police record. That's why Style chose him, you see.'

'See what?'

'He's a gypsy, Steph. Officially, he doesn't exist.'

26

Driving back down to the main road, we maintained a harrowed silence. Our departure had been engineered smoothly, involving no more than a couple of routine lies about the damage done to the truck. Back at the lodge, our host had sold us ten litres of diesel, enough to get us to the filling station in the town down the valley.

I was glad of the silence. Freed from distractions, I rewound the spool of memory, stopping it on the picture of Style standing at his window. He was a hard man, a man tempered by poverty who had risen from nothing, asked for no favours and gave none. Such men didn't have the flexibility to bend in a crisis. Their hardness was of the brittle kind. If the pressure got too great, they shattered. That's the image he had presented – a man shattered, a man contemplating not the heights to which he had risen, but the depths into which he must fall.

Pressure had certainly been piled on Style. His polo injury had crippled him in mind as well as body and led to the desertion of his wife. His virility was gone and his wife now found her gratification elsewhere. That was enough to turn a proud man like Style murderous – so murderous that I wondered again what pressing decision could have induced Lisa to call on him that night. She knew that he was impotent not only sexually, but also in the stab and push of business. Axnoller knew, too, and Eeles and God knows who else. No wonder Style had snapped.

I turned forward to the man in the video. He was the antithesis of Style – tall and cultivated, with the boardroom poise of a man who claims membership of an executive elite. But whatever directorates he held and whatever clubs he belonged to, he must have played foul with Style. I remembered Style's treatment of the unscrupulous rival who had burnt his betting shop. Style had scarred him for life. I suspected that Style had something worse in mind for the man in the video. The gypsy had been familiarising himself with a target.

Yet there still remained more questions than answers. If Axnoller had a common business cause with Style, I would have expected him to be an ally in any attempt to recoup losses or take revenge. The only plausible explanation was that the Americans had decided Style was out of control. The loss adjuster had been commissioned to prevent a crime that might jeopardise their own interests.

My foray down this avenue was halted by our arrival at the filling station. I pumped in enough fuel to get to Zaragoza, with plenty to spare. There was a café attached to the station, a greasy-spoon diner. My glance crept towards Steph. She was young. She would heal.

'We'd better get you something to eat.'

'I'm not hungry.'

'It'll be four or five hours before we reach Zaragoza.'

For the first time since we'd left, she looked at me properly. We hadn't discussed what we would do when we reached the city. I saw something I never wanted to see in a woman's eyes –the subjugation of dignity by injured hope.

'I didn't mean them things I said.'

My hand covered hers. 'I deserved them.'

'Are we still friends then?'

My hand squeezed hers. 'The best of friends.'

In the café I ordered coffee and a pastry, though it was all I could do to get the food down without gagging. Steph's expression suggested that I'd turned cannibal. She pushed back her chair and went to play electronic pinball. Some of the workmen eyed her – not with overt intent, but with the speculative interest with which most men observe a young and pretty woman who descends unexpectedly into their midst. I couldn't help imagining what their reaction would be if I wasn't present. The furtive exchanges, the tongue pushing out the cheek as the brashest one rose from his seat with studied casualness.

Steph left the machines and headed for the toilets. I was ready. I had written a note in a stolen couple of minutes back at the lodge.

Dear Steph, this can't repay the debt I owe you. I wish that one day I could tell you the whole story, but you will be happier and safer if you never see me again.

Smug garbage. I longed to say more, but neither time nor words were on my side.

Best of luck, I had written underneath. *And love*, I added, but no signature.

Hastily I folded the note around fifteen hundred pounds and stuffed the wad into one of the envelopes I'd bought on the ferry. I left the envelope on the table, calmly walked out and climbed into the truck. The engine started. The wheels turned. I didn't look back. I don't know what I'd have done if I'd seen Steph standing in the door, but I knew that what I was doing was in her best interests.

I drove with a sliver of ice in my heart.

Afternoon brought sweeping rain and wind that made the high-sided truck weave. From a place called Cortes, I headed into the Sierra de Moncayo. I took a minor junction at random, and then another. At last I found a spot that met my requirements – a lay-by above a wooded river canyon. Dusk was falling. The rain had stopped and a gangrenous stain spread through the sky. I pulled in on the dirt, angling the truck so that no one could see the nearside from the road. I had only a vague idea of my location and deliberately didn't take in my surroundings so that I wouldn't know the place again.

I ran back, opened up and heaved the unobliging corpse on to the crate.

Only a moment. That's all it would take. And yet I hesitated, filling the forest with eyes. Down the gorge the wind moved with a hushed roar, covering all other sounds. But only fairy-tale ogres lived in forests, and there was no need to create fears out of nothing when I had real monsters on my back.

The gypsy flopped to the ground. I leapt down and like a disfigurement of nature I hauled him feet first through the leaf mould and into the undergrowth. Burial was out of the question; the best I could manage was a scrape in the forest litter and a few branches for camouflage. Five or six hours was all I needed. By then, Griffith, too, would have been finally laid to rest.

The gold chain leached a last glimmer from the failing day. It occurred to me that the gypsy was carrying it as convertible property – contingency funds. It must have been worth several hundred pounds and was probably untraceable, but I hadn't yet sunk to grave-robbing. Even if I'd been down to my last penny, I wouldn't have taken that necklace. I'm not ordinarily superstitious, but gypsies are. They believe in magic, in omens, in the supernatural qualities of things. Everything is invested with symbolic value, and I reckoned that if ever a piece of jewellery was unlucky, that one was.

27

STOP! – CAUTION – GIVE WAY. The motorway signs were flash-cards telling me what I already knew. If I went all the way, I was going to crash. All I had to do was take a turning – this turning, the next turning, any turning. With the truck ditched and Matthew Reason's passport in my pocket, I wouldn't have an enemy in the world. End of story.

Zaragoza 69 kilometres. If I drove to the depot, I could play it two ways. I could tell Style that the gypsy was dead and that his plans were irretrievably screwed up, or I could act dumb and hope to get away before they opened up the truck and found out for themselves. The first option virtually guaranteed my death, the second merely postponed it.

So why didn't I take the turning?

Zaragoza 63 kilometres. Because I had come too far down the wrong road. I had to find out where it led. I had to go the final mile.

My approach was slinky. It took me three hours to circle Zaragoza and pick up the Lérida road.

I think I could have found the place in my sleep. The road was a causeway across the blight zone between town and city, past sidewalks with no walkers, down an avenue of suspended lights that wasted their vapour on the air. It was all super-familiar – the plots scraped of soil with the surveyor's flags hanging like prayer flags, the advertising boards displaying universal families at table, the arbitrarily scattered industrial units.

There, replicated from my imagination, was the derelict building site, a property developer's failed dream, interred in corrugated iron. And there, beyond it, was the breaker's yard, with its temples and ziggurats of mangled cars.

The gate was open and a light had been lit within. Not ready to face the moment, I continued past for about a mile, turned and came back. A watchman at the gate rose from his brazier and saluted me through. I bumped over flooded potholes between the mountains of scrap. The light came from a prefabricated office. Beside it was a new Mercedes.

I revved the engine and left it to die. I wound down the window and listened. At first, nothing, and then the far-off murmur of the city. My eyes patrolled the canyons between the heaps of scrap. It was a perfect place to kill someone.

A man had framed himself in the doorway. My hands shook so much that I could hardly pick up my belongings. Climbing down, I barked my shins on the step and splashed into a puddle.

'You have removed everything from the truck?'

'*Si.*'

He wasn't looking at me. First he studied the buckled cab, then he ran his eyes along the cargo hold. 'An accident?'

Now was the time to tell him about the gypsy.

'Nothing serious.'

His eyes searched mine. 'Your boss says a man is looking for you.'

'He didn't find me.'

'Police? They have stopped you for the accident?'

'There was no need. The only damage done was to myself.'

His eyes reserved judgement. 'It is important to speak the truth.'

I was up to my neck now. 'No one else was involved.'

'*Bueno*,' he said, and took my hand in a warm clasp before turning to lead me into his office. 'There have been many accidents because of the storms. I was worried. I was told you would be arriving earlier.'

He made for his desk – a middle-aged businessman with a sedentary paunch and bags like marshmallows under fine, lustrous eyes. He was flashily dressed and I got the impression that he had once been poor and liked to throw money around. When he picked up the phone, gold shone on his wrist and on his fingers.

After dialling, he waited with raised chin, breathing in through his nose. '*Sí*, he has arrived. No, it is as expected.' His eyelids drooped as Style said something at length. His gaze wavered in my direction. 'No.' He drew himself up and looked directly at me, a little smile frozen on his face. 'No. I will. No, no problem.' His manner as he replaced the phone was thoughtful.

'What did Mr Style have to say?'

Apparently, a judgement had been made. The scrapyard king drew himself up as if a ceremony was about to begin. 'The keys, please.'

He was going to search the truck. Bluff was my only defence. 'Passenger? What passenger? You mean to tell me I've been carrying a stowaway?'

He hung the keys on a pegboard. They swung slightly, then stopped. The uncertainty of the situation was like being weightless in space and not knowing up from down. He reached into his desk and I hitched myself up to full height, waiting for the gun to be produced, for the invitation to accompany him out into the yard.

Into my palm he slapped a fat envelope. 'He pays you

well, your boss.' He slid his finger along his nose. 'But maybe he will make you pay for the damage.' His own face mirrored my alarm. 'No, is joke.'

I tried to display a sense of humour.

'Where are you staying tonight?' he asked, shrugging himself into his jacket. 'Zaragoza?'

'If that's possible.'

He pondered a moment, then reached for the phone again. Every move he made was fraught with grisly possibilities. 'I'll call a taxi. I'd take you myself, but I live out of town and I want to be home by eight.' He hesitated, wanting to get a confession off his chest. 'Tonight is Zaragoza versus Atlético Bilbao.' He twinkled. 'That's like your Manchester United against Liverpool. Do you love football, Mr Griffith?'

Nothing was going to expectation. It took so long for me to express an opinion that he took my answer for granted.

'You are English, so I am hoping you will understand and forgive me if I leave you here alone until the taxi comes.' The decision appeared to vex him. 'Unfortunately, I must lock up this office.' He hesitated, then plucked the keys from the board. 'I think it is best if you wait in the truck. Before you leave, put the keys on the front wheel.'

He ushered me outside, switched out the lights and locked up. I wasn't fooled by the rigmarole. He was softening me up for whoever came next.

'So then, goodbye Señor Griffith. Enjoy Zaragoza. It is my city.' He made another off-the-cuff gesture, producing two cards. 'Here,' he said, 'this one has the best food in town, and this one has the best girls. Tell them Paco sent you.' He winked. 'I promise you will leave my city with beautiful memories.'

Still smiling, he backed into his car and beeped *adios*. His tail lights blink-blinked as he slowed for the potholes, then they were gone.

I was left dangling on my nerves, not knowing if a sentence had been passed, suspended, postponed or revoked. If they knew the gypsy wasn't in the truck, why had they handed over the money?

Ten minutes went by without anything happening, and then lights undulated across the cinder surface. Shielding my eyes, I saw the illuminated taxi sign. The man who got out had a hack's badge and moved around his car with swift precision. He reached to take my case.

I held on to it. 'Before we leave, I want to speak to Mr Style.'

'*Qué?*'

'I need to speak to Mr Style.'

'*No hablo inglés.*'

His radio crackled. He leaned in and a woman's laconic voice said something beyond my grasp. Turning to me, the driver raised an eyebrow. 'Which hotel, please?'

'Somewhere in the centre. Anywhere will do.'

'*Centro,*' he told the woman, and consulted his watch. '*Aproximadamente treinta minutos.*' He listened, nodding. 'Okay,' he said, and signed off with a smacking kiss. '*Mi mujer,*' he explained, opening my door.

He was genuine. They were letting me go. He switched on the radio. I heard horns and firecrackers and a wall of chanting. The soccer match had begun. The cab started to move.

'Stop!'

He swivelled, one arm straddling the passenger seat.

'There's something I forgot to do. It'll take me some time. Don't wait. How much do I owe you? *Cuanto cuesta?*'

When he'd gone, I wandered the maze of lanes, between precarious triple-decker sandwiches of iron. No one was coming for the gypsy because he wasn't expected here. Style must have told him to let himself out of the truck as soon as we cleared Santander. I'd been a decoy, the false hare. I came to the fence. Sunk low on the horizon were the lights of a fairground. At intervals the wind carried the faint shrieks of dizzy passengers on the illuminated ferris wheel.

At the gate, the old watchman sat looking into his fire. '*Buenas tardes*,' he said without raising his eyes.

The black road ran away under the lights. Nothing stood between me and the floating highway. I could walk away and no one would follow. My job was done and I'd been paid off.

I took out Griffith's passport and dropped it on to the coals. It curled and charred but didn't burn. The watchman looked on, impassive. For good measure I added Griffith's credit cards and licence and other documents. When they were disposed of, the watchman picked up a poker and looked at me as if seeking permission. Upon my nod, he stirred the blackened card and plastic into ashes.

Curtain, exit walking. But first I had to deposit the keys. That done, I stood looking at the truck. I slapped its flank and turned my back on it for the last time.

Over the domed glow of the city rose brighter lights – pagan reds and brimstone yellows and chromium blues. A firework display had begun. The pyrotechnics held me. Ribbons and trailers slid down the sky; anemones blossomed and nebulae spiralled into extinction. A battery of rockets skittered up and exploded with soft splutterings and fierce screeches.

When I turned, two men were approaching, black as Indian ink against the residual flare. Hands in pockets, they picked their way around the puddles, leaning sideways as if they were competing in a pedestrian slalom. I knew who they were and I knew I was done for.

The *Gitanos* stood in front of me, straddle-legged and loose-wristed, matching their toughness against my height.

Both of them wore black leather jackets and jeans that were probably black too. One of them looked down at his gleaming shoe and went 'Tsk.' The other led my eye towards the truck and held out his hand. I dropped the keys into it. He unlatched the side door, vaulted up and peered in.

I'd had my chance and blown it. 'There's no one there.'

'*Qué*?'

'Gone,' I told him. '*El va. Vacio.*'

He laughed and jumped down. They nodded to each other, then indicated that they would like me to go with them.

Their car was parked by the gate. It was slung low, with lots of after-market add-ons. White wool cushioned the seats and furry dice and devils dangled at the screens. One of the gypsies opened a rear door and watched me take my place before getting in beside me. He was heavily scented. We turned in the direction of the city.

A cassette played, very softly. The driver drove hunched over the wheel, as if his competence or restraint was newly learnt and he could only exercise it by conscious effort. His eyes found me in the mirror. My escort was examining me, too. He gave me a diffident nudge. I turned to see an open pack of cigarettes in his hand. I shook my head and faced to the front, trying to work out his intentions from his expression. It wasn't friendly – it was more than that. It was respectful.

I sought my reflection in the side window: black leather jacket, lean unshaven cheeks, exhausted eyes. Beside it I placed the image of my escort, a smaller, darker, more elemental version of myself. Christ, I thought. They think I'm one of them. They think *I'm* the gypsy.

So fiercely did the realisation hit that I was sure it must have communicated to my escorts. I didn't dare move. I cramped myself in the corner like a game bird squatting under a setter's nose. My mind began to run ahead. They must be taking me somewhere to discuss my mission, but that was a role I couldn't play, no matter how much rehearsing I did. As soon as I opened my mouth I would be exposed. I had visions of my bin-linered body jettisoned from a speeding car, pulped in the jaws of a vehicle crusher.

I grunted and changed position. We were in the city, sliding along channels of light and dark. Faces floated past, bland and animated, happy and glum, all of them so close, separated only by a sheet of glass. Their unconscious individuality was almost comical. How remote are other people's lives.

The music stole into my senses. It was melancholy and erotic and made me aware of how much more to life there was than I knew, or would ever know. A lump formed in my throat. I didn't want to die.

Then you must play the killer, a voice said distinctly in my head. They know you can't speak Spanish. They expect you to be taciturn. It's the assassin's mantle. Simply do what they say.

A bead of sweat dripped from my armpit and ran cold across my ribs.

Around us the lights had merged into one vibrant dazzle. We were in the city centre. The pavements teemed with people – youngsters linked elbow to elbow in laughing chains so wide that they spilled out into our path. There must be a fiesta. My escort leaned forward and spoke in a sibilant whisper. The driver nodded and turned right.

It was the approach to the railway station. Two policemen stood outside the entrance. My escort placed a cautionary hand on my arm as we drew up under their noses. One of them flicked his hand, indicating that we had stopped in a no-waiting zone.

The driver kept his engine running. My escort spoke in laboured English. 'You have your ticket?'

All I could think of was being out of there. 'Sure,' I said, and patted my pocket.

With a nod, he leaned across me and released the door catch. By the time I got out they were already pulling away, merging into the shoal of lights. To enter the station I had to pass both policemen. They looked straight through me as if I was invisible.

28

After the wild relief, the comedown. I felt as though I'd charged through a door and found myself in a desert without a single reference. I couldn't go back. The door was slammed shut behind me. I couldn't return to the scrapyard. There was no point calling Style.

A fiasco, that's what it was, but not without its farcical side. Style had been reassured that everything was going to plan. The driver had been paid off, the gypsy had been received and delivered safely to the station. The loss adjuster was still hunting for him high and low. None of the directors knew that the drama was being played out without the key player. To have caused such an upset was almost embarrassing.

And the irony was that I was still a target. The loss adjuster didn't know that the gypsy was dead, and even if he did, it wouldn't make any difference. He knew that the gypsy had been heading for Zaragoza, which made the railway station a very dangerous place in which to linger.

Madrid was where I wanted to be, the sooner the better. I checked the departure board. The next train to the capital left ten minutes after eleven. I made my way to the ticket office and bought a second-class single. There was nearly an hour to kill. I skulked on a trolley at the extreme end of the concourse.

My eye fell on three women who were hustling a tourist

couple. The women looked like they might be three generations of the same family, and they were *Gitanos*. The tourists were trying to preserve an aloof countenance, but they were finding it hard to keep it up, and eventually the man's poise snapped and he dipped into his pocket to pay them off. Still hunting, the women stood in a group facing out, like a coven. The youngest spotted me and all three turned my way. The oldest one stared for a moment, then said something. They moved off in the opposite direction.

Two propositions presented themselves. Either I wasn't a sufficiently tempting mark or else they'd been warned off me. There seemed to be a number of men standing around with no obvious purpose. They might have been *Gitanos*; in the grimy light everyone looked suspect. My position, I now saw, might be more delicate than I'd allowed. Style would know that the gypsy would be at his most vulnerable while he was in Zaragoza. He might have set someone to watch over him.

I inspected the departure board again, wondering if I should take the first train to come along. At this time of night there were few through services and the Madrid express was the first before midnight. Another possibility rose up like a hand from a swamp. Odds-on, the capital had been the gypsy's destination, which meant that he would have caught the same train as me. Style, it seemed, could tap into a network of gypsy connections. He might have arranged an escort. Worse, there might be someone waiting to take me in hand the other end.

Every changed situation had its own peculiar hazards; the only constant was fear. When I started out down this road, fear was something I couldn't handle. Like a strong drug, it scrambled my senses. But I was getting used to it; it had become part of my metabolism and I could take larger doses without losing my head.

My head told me that if someone challenged me when I got off the train, all I had to do was claim mistaken identity. For reassurance, I looked at my passport. There I was, with my photo to prove it. Matthew Reason – quick-change artist.

Anxiety subsided into lethargy. That was the other side of fear – the dull low succeeding the galvanic high. The digital clock blinked away the time in a way that reduced every second to insignificance. I still had my Russian map. I unrolled it and looked at the railway line cutting with such certainty through the desert before it reached its meaningless terminus.

Well, I still wasn't there. I still had Eleanor Barry to look forward to. The prospect bucked me up, but not as much as I might have expected.

An announcer broadcast the message that the Madrid express would be arriving in five minutes. I stretched my legs and one of my shoes scuffed across a laundry ticket. My hand started for my jacket before I realised that it wasn't the ticket I'd found in the wardrobe. It took another moment to digest the fact that it wasn't a laundry receipt and that my *Gitano* escort hadn't been inquiring if I'd purchased my railway ticket.

Both hands flew to my jacket. I clutched my pockets like an aviator suddenly aware that he'd forgotten his parachute. My face flushed hot and then cold. I didn't know what I'd done with the bloody thing. I couldn't remember whether I'd ignored it, picked it up or thrown it away.

Nothing in my trousers, nothing in my outside pockets. My hand burrowed into my inside pocket – and closed on the crumpled cardboard scrap. I straightened it out and saw that it was indeed an exact match for the ticket on the ground. Only the number was different – 73. With hindsight, I saw what an idiot I'd been to overlook its significance. I hadn't found any documents or money in the truck because there hadn't been any to find. Style had organised the gypsy's journey so that there would be no record of him coming or going, but he'd need funds and papers when he got to Spain. And where better to pick them up than a railway left-luggage office?

Passengers were already moving on to the platform, but that ticket was like a winning lottery number, and though I didn't know what the prize was, I couldn't resist claiming it. For all I knew, there were *Gitano* eyes on me, wondering why I hadn't already redeemed my deposit. I walked as fast as I dared to the left-luggage office. No one was at the counter. I called and at last a bored attendant wandered out. I forced my features into calm. God knows what I was picking up. I didn't want to look like a demented bomber. The attendant accepted the ticket and mooched along the meagre stacks of luggage. A tic started in my cheek. The announcement of the train's arrival was drowned out by the iron clanging and electric hum of the thing itself. The attendant turned, a cheap red sports bag in his hand. I grabbed it, already running.

Dashing through the barrier, I waved the bag in the air as if it was a diplomatic pouch containing treaties that could save the world from war. The guard had his flag raised, his whistle in his mouth. The whistle blew and the flag fell and the train began to move. I sprinted for the nearest door. The guard shouted. I fell inside. A wild elation filled me. Braced against the sway of the train, I watched the scrap merchant's city of beautiful memories slipping back in a blur of speed.

Despite the lateness of the hour, the express was crowded. The only vacant seat was in a section occupied by a sleepy extended family and a nun. A boy levelled a toy gun and took a few potshots at me. I smiled thoughtfully down the barrel, thinking of what might be in the bag.

I nursed it for an hour before making for a lavatory. All of them were occupied, and it was another forty minutes before I gained admittance and locked the door behind me.

The bag was exactly the kind of tacky item the gypsy would carry – a pirate version of a designer name. The zip was faulty and took some undoing. Cautiously I dug my hand inside. There was no weapon and I hadn't really expected one, having seen the security notices on the wall of the left-luggage office. Most of the space was taken up by a change of clothes, as shabby as the ones the gypsy had died in. My hand closed on a notecase. The money compartment was stuffed with about fourteen hundred pound's worth of pesetas, an oddly precise sum in either currency. There was also a plastic credit card issued by a organisation calling itself AutoRest.

The passport I left until last. I held it, wanting to spice the moment. I opened it. The face of the dead gypsy stared back dead centre. The name that went with the photograph was Stringer Vane.

My vigilance slipped away into a blankness punctuated by a peculiarly unpleasant dream involving Steph and half a dozen faceless assailants. I opened my eyes to find the passengers opposite smiling drowsily and the kid with the toy gun grinning fit to burst. As consciousness caught up, my first thought was that I must have committed a solecism in the unzipped fly category, but it turned out that I'd dozed off on the nun's shoulder. She accepted my apologies charitably.

We were within an hour of Madrid and the countdown made me twitchy. I went back to the lavatory, took out Griffith's washbag and shaved myself clean. I experimented with various hairstyles before choosing one that least resembled my usual look. Getting rid of the red bag was a headache. I didn't dare leave it in the lavatory and I couldn't abandon it elsewhere on the train. I still had Griffith's briefcase and I shelved the problem by shoving it inside.

Back in my seat, I kept my fear on stand-by until the steady rhythm of the wheels broke into counterpoint on the junctions and switches of the station approaches. I positioned myself by a door. I didn't want to be first off and I didn't want to be a straggler. I wanted to be part of the main rush. The leading coaches were smoothly rounding the final bend. I gripped the briefcase tight. My fingernails dug into my palm.

Nothing was to be gained by adopting a low profile. My stride and demeanour as I alighted were decisive – a man in no doubt as to where he was going. No one checked me through the barrier. I paused and under cover of an expectant smile surveyed the concourse. Again it seemed to me that there were too many small men who should have had better things to do than stand about in a railway station at four in the morning. Twenty yards ahead a woman was making for the exit. 'Eleanor,' I called, so loudly that several people turned. I waved at the woman and she glanced behind her. Beaming, I closed on her.

'Good lord,' I brayed. 'I'm frightfully sorry. I mistook you for my wife.'

She smiled feebly and continued on her way.

'You look awfully like her,' I blathered, matching my pace to hers. 'Same hair, same colouring. You could be her double.'

Her eyes switched in both directions.

All through my drivel, I kept my concentration on the other passengers. We came out of the station into a thin winter rain. I saw the taxi rank, measured the distance and broke into a run. Only two cabs were waiting and they were spoken for, but I was next in line. Passengers queued up behind me. My back felt about ten feet wide and made of glass. A taxi drew up and I threw myself in. The driver turned.

'Anywhere. Just drive.'

It was the short interval of slack in the Madrid night. The boulevards had emptied of people and seemed ridiculously wide. What traffic there was seemed to be cruising for no other purpose than to kill time. When I was reasonably satisfied that no one was following, I leaned forward and presented the AutoRest card for the driver's inspection.

He muttered and did a bad-tempered U-turn.

'I don't want to go there. I want to know what it is.'

He took both hands off the wheel to express his impatience. 'You want hotel? Which one?'

In the lavish upsurge generated by my persuading Eleanor Barry to meet me in Madrid, I had booked a room at the Ritz from the fifth, the day she was due to arrive. I frowned.

'*Qué día es hoy?*'

The driver gave me an oblique look. '*Martes.*'

Tuesday? An extra day seemed to have been slipped into my life. That meant the fifth was still two days off. The loss adjuster might know that Madrid was the gypsy's destination. Until Eleanor Barry arrived, it would be wise to stay in an establishment off the tourist track.

'Can you recommend somewhere quiet,' I asked, 'not too near the centre?'

I was still leaning forward, the card held in my hand. The driver flicked it shirtily. 'Is not in centre.'

I frowned at the card. I'd assumed it gave access to car hire facilities. 'It's a motel?'

'Not motel. Is hotel. By *aeropuerto*.'

My imagination constructed a tower block peopled by conventioneers with name tags on their breast pockets. It didn't conform to my expectation of the gypsy's likely lodgings.

'I'd prefer somewhere less busy.'

The driver gave a phlegmy chuckle. 'Is peaceful like grave.'

I explored a few variations on this image. '*No comprendo.*'

The driver struggled to bridge the linguistic gap. His eyes scanned the sidewalks as if he might find the explanation there. Suddenly he stopped in the middle of the road, pointing at a bank. Narrowing my aim, I saw that he was indicating a cash dispenser.

'An automatic hotel?'

'*Sí, automático.* Is factory for sleep. You want me to take?'

My mind's eye framed a picture of guests laid out in air-conditioned cabinets, like bodies in a mortuary. I opened my mouth to say no, then backpedalled. Looking couldn't do any harm. 'I'd like to check it.'

We left town and sped solitarily along the periférico, under confusing flyovers and down tunnels of curving lights. The driver kept half an eye on me as if he suspected I might spring some other vexatious change of mind on him. The wheels hissed; the wipers clicked away; the meter counted off the miles. I wasn't used to being a passenger and the random architecture of the city limits made my eyes heavy. I began to wish that I'd left this venture for another day.

We siphoned off the motorway on to the airport road and then diverted into a commercial estate regimented like a military complex. The glistening alloy tail fin of an airliner stuck up above a cargo terminal. On the low cloud cover, runway lights glowed like a fitful chemical reaction.

'Hotel AutoRest.'

Even though the frontage carried the inscription in lights, I might have missed it. Located between an air-freight company and a film processory, the hotel was a poured-concrete cube that any competent architect could have draughted between teabreaks.

'Go past,' I ordered.

The lobby was empty, with lights left burning.

'There's no one on the desk.'

'Of course, is *automático*.' To underline his point, the driver placed a cassette in the machine. The tape began to play. He punched a button and the cassette ejected with a whirr and a clack. '*Comprende?*'

'Go back.'

The driver made another run-past. The lobby was still deserted. I noticed the electronic box at the doorway.

'What kind of people stay there?'

The driver shrugged. 'Is not expensive. Is close to *aeropuerto*. Is for peoples who want to sleep, not enjoy.' His look invited me to state my classification.

'Stop a moment.'

The air was static and smelt of kerosene. The windows in the hotel gleamed blackly, as if they might be opaque or made of one-way glass. A plane passed low overhead, its jets rumbling on one note for a long time then quickly dying away with the sound of a cistern filling. No one entered or left the hotel AutoRest. The place was dead, yet its lifelessness was mesmerising. There was something absolute in its stillness – like the consummate silence of space.

I touched the driver on the shoulder. 'Wait.'

I got out and crossed the street. The empty lobby made me think of a display cabinet from which the exhibits had been removed. Feeding the card into the electronic entry device produced the room number 214 and a five-figure pass-code. Then the machine disgorged the card and the door jerked open.

'Welcome to AutoRest,' a pre-recorded message said, 'a new concept in international hospitality. Every possible care has been . . . '

I couldn't cross the threshold. Nothing could induce me to take that final step. I retreated to the cab.

'You don't like?'

'Take me back to the centre.'

29

Next day, after getting up, I festered in my hotel room. I mean *that* day, Tuesday – the same day I had arrived in Madrid. I was operating on a different clock to the world outside and everything was out of kilter.

Keeping to my room was a trial. The strident décor was designed to hurry tourists down to a continental breakfast and out sightseeing. But I shunned the daylight. I imagined turning a corner and seeing the loss adjuster's pathological smile tighten in greeting. I sat slumped on the end of my bed. Unplugged – that's how I felt, disconnected. I needed a fix.

In a little more than twenty-four hours, Eleanor Barry would be touching down in Madrid. The prospect didn't resonate as it should have. I couldn't concentrate on her. My priorities had been subverted. Every waking moment was obsessed with the gypsy's mission. Finding his things had been a landmark discovery, but it didn't lead anywhere except to the anonymous sleep factory. I wanted to move things along, but not by that route.

Drastic action would be necessary, though. I opened my wallet and took out Style's telephone number. I toyed with the notion of telling him how things stood. That was an all-or-nothing approach – nothing being the most likely outcome. I wrapped the possibility away for the time being.

Putting his number back in my wallet, I noticed the piece

of notepaper which Camille van Damm had given me. For the first time, I wondered about her part in this affair. Her presence at Style's house had struck me as decorative rather than functional, and from her provocative attitude to me, I guessed that she couldn't have known much of what was going on. Of course, Eeles might have brought her up to date since then.

Now Eeles himself was another matter. Although he was a party to murder, I suspected that he'd been embroiled by special circumstances. He might be susceptible to pressure. Threaten to call in the law unless he spills the beans? I was thinking purely hypothetically, but the possibility stuck. All manner of foul play seemed to be ripening within me.

Also, I didn't like him and I wanted to pay him back. The loss adjuster I respected out of unabashed fear. Style was a man driven by passion, and passion was a mitigating factor, as was the two thousand pounds I carried in my pocket. Eeles, though, was just a little shit who had betrayed the man who paid his wages.

A man on my level, I thought. An even match.

Blackmail. The word smouldered away while the short day drew in. I couldn't make things any worse for myself. I looked at the phone. There was no risk. I could be calling from anywhere. After dark, I vowed.

Night came down early. By four o'clock the lights were on in the streets. When I could no longer see myself in the mirror, I switched on the bedside lamp. Its bulb illuminated only my hands. I watched them dial the number.

Van Damm answered. My disappointment was brief. I could leave a message, let Eeles stew a little.

'I'd like to speak to Richard Eeles.'

'Who is that, please?'

I couldn't decide if the peremptory tone was her standard telephone manner or nervousness.

'James Griffith.'

In a blink her manner altered. 'The driver,' she crooned, in a tone that raised goose-pimples. 'I thought I recognised that gorgeous voice. How are you? How delightful of you to call.'

Out of the mental scrimmage emerged the extraordinary fact that she seemed genuinely pleased to hear from me.

My preamble was halting. 'I found your number and, er, I remembered that you'd, er, suggested that when I was in Spain . . .'

'Sure. Great. Are you in Madrid?'

I glanced at the window. I was one man in a metropolis of millions, but even with those odds on my side. I wouldn't have given away my whereabouts except for the fact that I was Matthew Reason, not James Griffith. My security was ironclad.

'For one night only. I'm leaving for Barcelona tomorrow.'

'Oh shame! I was going to suggest you join us for a drink, but Rip and I have something planned for this evening. I mean, *I* have something planned. It's his birthday and I've organised a small surprise party.' She hesitated. 'But hey, maybe you could be part of the surprise. Oh gosh, yes. Fantastic idea.'

The thought of being a birthday treat for Rip took a lot of getting used to. 'I'm not sure that Rip would appreciate my company. I gained the impression that he doesn't like me.'

'He hates you,' she said, surprised that I might entertain the slightest doubt. 'He looks cyanide at me whenever I mention your name.' Her tone became suggestive. 'I've mentioned your name a couple of times as a matter of fact. I use it to get a rise out of him. Rip,' she added crossly, 'has not been a lot of fun these last few weeks.'

'Did he say why?'

'Work. He's been all tied-up working.'

'I meant why he hates me.'

'James, don't tell me you didn't notice. He hates you because he thinks you want to fuck me, and he hates you even more because he thinks I like the idea.'

I scratched my scalp and resisted saying 'I see'. 'In that case,' I said, my voice not quite hitting the intended note, 'I don't see how my presence could contribute to his happiness.'

'Contribute to his happiness,' she repeated and gave a tinkly laugh. 'I love it.' Her voice fell into coyness. 'Rip is an uptight kind of guy, wouldn't you say?'

'He must have a lot on his mind.'

'Well, it might surprise you to know, James, that on the interpersonal level, Rip is more liberated than any guy I know.'

'That does surprise me,' I said. I wondered if van Damm was insane.

'In one respect, Rip is the most sharing adult I have ever met.' She paused, her silence multi-layered. 'How about you? Do you like sharing?'

'Secrets?'

Soft laughter pealed. 'Sure, secrets. Your most intimate desires.'

My heart had instigated a peculiar beat. Mind-boggling though it was, the only possible interpretation was that she was suggesting a threesome, a *ménage á trois*, troilism. I tried to summon some pretence of savoir-faire. 'I think he might make an exception in my case.'

Again, van Damm laughed. 'He won't know who it is. You'll be incognito. That's what makes it so perfect.'

'Perfect,' I said, speaking very slowly, 'how?'

'It'll be dark and you'll be wearing a mask and you won't speak. He won't know who you are. Not until afterwards. Do you like role-play, James?'

Role-play is what I excelled at. 'Exactly what do you have in mind?' I asked, still sounding like a remedial patient in deep speech therapy.

'James, I want it to be a surprise for you, too.' Her voice became matter of fact. 'Okay, what it is, I've arranged to take Rip to a masked cabaret.'

My mind flashed a memory of a painting that had hung on the landing of my parents' house. It was a cheap reproduction, school of Longhi, and showed a Venetian harlequinade – black and gold and silver, but mostly black. The people in it were very still and clustered like insects, and the shadows all around the hall were so dense that I imagined that anyone entering them would never get out. As a child it had given me nightmares.

Van Damm was explaining the timetable. 'He's scheduled back about seven and we're dining at nine. The show starts at midnight, so we'd pick you up about eleven-thirty.'

It sounded as if more than three people might be involved. 'Excuse me,' I said, 'but I'd like to get it clear. Are you suggesting an orgy?'

'God, no – nothing so unsophisticated. After the show we come back to the apartment, and then the three of us – you, me and Rip – can give our fantasies a work-out.'

'Still in fancy dress?'

'No, you'll be wearing the mask, that's all. Say you'll come, James.'

'What do I wear – I mean, apart from the mask?'

'Come as you are – the rougher the better. That's what Rip likes.'

'I don't know, Camille. It sounds risky.'

'For me,' van Damm said, 'it's the risk that makes it worthwhile. For Rip too. But especially for me.'

'Where do you want to meet?'

'Let me think. Oh yes, the perfect place. There's a *taberna* near Las Ventas called Los Pelégrinos, which is where the bullring workers hang out. We'll pick you up there. Oh, and James, I want you to do one small thing for me. When I come into the bar, I want you to pretend I don't know you. Act like I just picked you out of the crowd. Will you do that for me?'

It didn't matter what I said. Moral sensibilities aside, I wasn't going. 'Of course.'

'Does it excite you?'

'Yes.' There was a sob in my voice that might easily have passed for arousal.

'Hey, control yourself.' Her voice hardened. 'I'll make sure you stay under control, James. I set the rules, okay? Rule one, you don't speak. Rule two, you do what I tell you. Rule three, afterwards, you leave when I say. Understand?'

'Yes,' I answered. I didn't give a damn about her rules. She was definitely deranged. 'There was an American with you when we met. Will he be going to the show?'

'Carl?' Her voice cooled off. 'No, that's who Rip is with now. They're at the Hilton.'

'I meant the young one. I don't know his name.'

'Neither do I. And truth to tell, James, I don't want to. There are risks, and then there are risks.'

'I know what you mean. Have you seen him recently?'

'Rip has, I think. He called up a couple of nights ago and Rip was *very* depressed afterwards. That's why I want to cheer the darling up. Say you'll be there. The chance is much too exquisite to waste. Oh, yes! It's so neat, even thinking about it makes me hot.'

30

Common sense told me I'd be insane to go, but I'd been flying in the face of logic for so long that instinct wouldn't get in step with thought. Pacing my room, I kept going back over van Damm's performance and I couldn't fault it. She couldn't have known that I'd call. If she'd been primed to set me up, she wouldn't have gone to such bizarre extremes.

By nine-thirty I had walked myself into deadlock. At ten I called a taxi and asked the driver to drop me at a cheap outfitters. I bought jeans and jacket and then found a barber's shop. On the wall was a poster of a punk who reminded me of my gypsy escort. I asked for a hair cut in similar style. Gelled and scented, I took a cab to Los Pelégrinos.

The bar was a smoky dive of leathery, hard-faced men with a sprinkling of louche arty types attracted, I guessed, by the slight edge of threat in the atmosphere. It was a way-station of the night, with a lot of coming and going and prolonged handshakes and long-distance body-language. Unwatched in the corner, a television gameshow dispensed frenetic moonshine.

The one drink I'd allowed myself disappeared without my noticing how. I ordered another and vowed to make it last, but it was gone the next time I looked. I kept checking my watch. Time seemed to be on the point of running backwards.

I was wound like a spring. Every time the door opened I jumped another cog. The uncertainty was making me physically sick. At eleven-forty the door opened and I tensed again and every sound shut down except for the hysterical applause of the TV audience.

Van Damm knew how to make an entrance. Her face was concealed by a Venetian domino mask and she stood tall in spiked heels and an ankle-length black gown laced tightly across a snow-white décolletage. In her hand she carried an executioner's mask. She took one imperious step into the room and gazed around. Her eyes behind the slits stopped on me a moment. I began to rise and then remembered that I wasn't supposed to recognise her. The eyes swept on. A man by the door peered behind her, looking for the film cameras and production crew. Her gaze touched on a saturnine individual who could have been an aspiring matador or an actor resting between perfume commercials. She indicated that she would like him to stand up. He did so, spilling his drink.

But her eyes were already panning back towards me. They settled and she raised her hand. I climbed to my feet almost as awkwardly as the first man, for despite the contrivance, she was a terrific performer. She moved closer, sizing each of us up. The other man's grin had gone fixed and his gullet bobbed. She put the varnished tip of her finger to her mouth, unable to make up her mind. My rival smirked. Her eyes drifted back to me.

She crooked her finger and I went to her. She placed the executioner's mask over my face, whisked on her heels and sashayed out. I followed submissively. Behind us, the silence lasted a moment longer, then dissipated in a furious babble.

Her taxi was in an alley around the corner. My nerves wobbled and I hung back, looking for bushwhackers. In the rear seat was the shape of a man. The driver opened the door for van Damm.

'Get in the front.'

Role-play or no role-play, I decided that she was a thorough pain. But with Eeles' eyes boring into the back of my neck, that was only a side-thought. I tried to shape my posture into something unrecognisable.

'That didn't take long.' His voice behind the mask was gruff.

'An easy choice. I guarantee you won't be disappointed.'

He grunted, out of sorts.

Fifteen minutes' driving brought us into an old district of patrician houses gone to seed. On the corner of one run-down terrace, a gang of youths eyed the passing car like a tribe of cats. If risk was what gave van Damm her kicks, that's where she should be recruiting.

Our cab stopped at a palatial house built in a grim ceremonial style. A glass *porte cochère* extended from the street to a grand double door overlooked by a security camera. At the jangling of a bell, a man like a haughty stick in a dinner jacket opened up a discreet distance. There was a murmured exchange between himself and van Damm before we were granted access.

Faded plush, masquerading as *fin-de-siècle* splendour, greeted my staring eye. The air was distinctly mousy. Conspicuously hovering in the shadows were two very large men and a woman, masked. At a click of the gaunt man's finger, the woman led us up a double staircase and along a corridor lit by lamps pretending to be candles. The general effect was of an early cinema, or a film-maker's concept of a Victorian brothel.

Our usher opened a door to a draped box lit so unobtrusively that anyone entering unwarily could have precipitated themselves into the well of blackness below.

We took our places on balding velvet. There was a smell of dust and mustiness. Around us I could hear the faint crepitation of other guests. A bottle of champagne stood in an ice bucket. There were even opera glasses to hand.

Van Damm poured me champagne. It might have been decent stuff, but on my tongue it tasted sweet and left a coating like glycol. While we waited, van Damm whispered with Eeles. I relaxed a notch. It was so dark that he couldn't have recognised me even without the mask.

Light beamed down. The rustling hushed. The curtain went up.

Top of the bill was a two-hander starring a nun and a psychiatrist. From there on, it was downhill. Bestiality and buggery apart, there was something for every taste – a hardcore assortment of dwarfs, fat ladies, schoolgirls, priests, satyrs, bacchantes, flagellants. All the turns were performed in committed, amateur style by dire and mostly unattractive actors wearing masks. Often, the acts didn't seem to have been rehearsed.

Under the lights the cheesey locker-room smell grew more intense. Between routines, there was no applause. Audience involvement was furtive. I did hear a few strange sounds from round about. Eeles and van Damm sat as still as mummies.

Maybe I'd have got more into the pantomime spirit if I hadn't been so worried about my own upcoming performance. Van Damm had said we were returning to her apartment, but I still hadn't worked out how to play things when we got there. Blackmail no longer looked like the key that would unlock Eeles' tongue. He'd parted company with Style, so there was no pressure to be exerted there, and I couldn't use the driver's murder as a lever because Griffith wasn't dead.

Meanwhile, the show went on. On stage, a sadomasochistic romp was coming to its predictable conclusion. Unmasking myself would have shock value, of course, but once that wore off, my only recourse would be physical threat – an area unfamiliar to me. Frankly, I didn't have the stomach for rough stuff.

During the next number, a Southern belle broke out of the tender embrace of a black man and ran sobbing off stage.

Van Damm put her mouth close to my ear. 'Aren't they sweet?'

'What!'

'Ssh. She's shy. It must be her first night.'

As criticism, that seemed over-generous. 'A few rehearsals wouldn't go amiss.'

'I know,' van Damm whispered. 'They're awful.'

'I expect the management can't pick and choose.'

'Oh, there's no shortage of volunteers.'

'Then they ought to shoot the director.'

'You still haven't got it, have you?'

'Got what?'

Van Damm's laughter feathered my cheek. 'They're not professional actors – not most of them. Why do you think they're wearing masks?'

I was flabbergasted. We were watching the lewd theatrics of amateurs – secretaries, postmen, bank managers, school-teachers. Hence the cellulite and clod-hopping direction and attacks of stage fright. I didn't know whether to be indignant or beguiled.

A terrible thought impaled me. 'I hope you're not expecting me to . . . '

Van Damm gave my hand a reassuring pat.

In my relief the next couple of acts went by quite quickly.

Once more the stage dimmed. A spot grew bright and into it strutted a woman in dominatrix leather leading three men on a chain with their hands tied behind their backs.

The men wore rags and animal masks – a bull, a donkey and a dog. They stopped in a row and the woman slipped the chain but left their hands bound. She ripped their clothes off. Naked, they were markedly different figures – a smooth, musclebound teutonic type (donkey); a swarthy ectomorph with a pelt of body hair (dog); a squat, pugnacious-looking fellow (bull).

'These guys are pros,' Van Damm murmured.

Another spotlight brightened. Out of the wings ran a woman in virginal white.

'But she's not.'

Her mask covered only her eyes. Anyone acquainted with her would surely have been able to penetrate the disguise.

Van Damm put her hand on my thigh. 'I bet her husband's watching.'

Seeing the three men, the young woman stopped and her hand flew to her mouth. I folded my arms and suppressed a growl at the banality. Timidly she approached the men. There was a lot of choreographed circling on tiptoe before she made contact. This was supposed to be the show-stopper, the class act. She reached out and touched each man as if she had no idea what they were for. Growing bolder, she began to caress them, insinuating herself between them, brushing past, the silence now so deep that the whisper of her clothes against their flesh was loudly audible. I found myself leaning closer.

One by one and to greater and lesser degree, the men began to stiffen. The girl was startled by the effect she had raised and looked up at the invisible audience as if for enlightenment. Her expression grew thoughtful and then cunning. There was a subdued shifting from the dark circle. I had an urge to cough.

The woman began to work on the men, turn and turn about, gliding from one to the other. They bore her balletic attentions stoically, staring straight ahead like men in an identity parade trying not to notice their accuser. Van Damm raised her opera glasses. Eeles was breathing as if he had a pain.

Her interventions grew bolder and more inventive. The veins on the dog's neck congested as if he was trying to lift an impossibly heavy weight. She seemed puzzled by the effect she was creating. He buckled at the knees and glycerine streaks shot into the light. A collective sigh rose and an unguarded soul yelped. Someone's going to have to clean that up, I thought. The girl clapped with delight. She was getting the point. Van Damm's hand stole into my lap to gauge my own response.

Next, the girl went to work on the blond body builder. He was made of more enduring stuff and his resistance only ended when the girl found what her lips and tongue were for. Afterwards she turned her glistening mouth to the audience. The lights faded down. There was only the bull to come and a certain dramatic tension was inevitable.

'This guy,' van Damm murmured. 'is incredible.'

What a trouper! What a stand-up artist! No matter how lasciviously she caressed and straddled him, he bore it all like a very steady horse. She began to show signs of frustration and appealed to the audience for inspiration. It was a moment of vaudeville, light relief before the climax. She struck him punily. She twined herself about him. Finally, she took his sturdy cock in both hands and pushed herself on to it.

But no, not finally. Still she couldn't make him soften. In pique she stalked away and mimed her need for assistance. Out from the wings came the leather-clad Amazon cracking her whip. For the first time, the bull showed response, squirming under the lash with outward signs of arousal. Still there was no resolution.

She fell to her knees, not in some inspired erotic kink, but in mute supplication. Contemptuously he looked down at her. She clawed at him. He raised his bound hands. She shook her head. He shook his. She gave in and slipped his bonds. He still wasn't happy. He pointed towards his fellow-captives. The light pinned them. Both of them were erect again.

Consternation showed on the girl's face. Her captive was adamant. No release until his fellow prisoners were liberated. All for one and one for all. Finally, timidly, as scripted, she gave way. As the last of the men was released, the lights began to dim blood-red. Realising what was to come, the girl turned to run.

Of course they caught her. As they closed on her, as they fell on her and she disappeared in a sprawl, her legs splayed white, she screamed. What happened after that can be reconstructed from the pornographer's catalogue in any-body's stackroom of musty fantasies. I wish I could say that the rites I witnessed in that filthy fleapit left me cold, that I found the couplings and triplings as uninvolving as the copulatory antics in a nature documentary. But I can't.

Black-out fell eventually. Van Damm touched Eeles' arm. 'I think that's enough, don't you, honey?'

31

On the way out, my hosts gave the impression of having been impressed by the drama beyond words, transported to a higher plane of feeling. In silence we took our places in the waiting cab, and we were back in the centre before van Damm spoke.

'Still worried about the meeting with Carl?'

Clearly, the extravaganza hadn't done much to raise Eeles' spirits. 'It's a nightmare. The way things are going, I'll be looking in the Situations Vacant as of tomorrow.'

'I don't see how Carl can blame you for Victor's foul-ups.'

I craned my head as far as I dared.

'They don't need reasons.'

'I wish you'd tell me what's going on.'

'Drop it, darling. Lets not spoil the evening.'

She squeezed his hand. 'I've got you the perfect *antidepresivo*.'

Back at their apartment block, they walked ahead, with me tagging along at a servile distance. In the lift, though, we were crammed at brushing distance, and if Eeles had looked at me properly he must surely have seen who I was. But he didn't. My presence, fundamental though it was to his gratification, apparently made him deeply uncomfortable.

He entered the apartment first. Van Damm hung back a moment to remind me of the rules of play.

'Remember,' she concluded, 'this is Rip's night.'

'Let's make it one to remember.'

She gave me a thin-lipped look. 'Don't get any weirdo ideas, lover. I've got good security here.'

Her apartment was modern and unmemorable, consisting of a large sitting room communicating with a bedroom. Eeles was already going inside. Van Damm explained that some scene-setting was necessary and that I should wait outside.

'Help yourself to a drink. Try not to steal anything.'

As soon as the door closed behind her I made for the kitchen. A rack of chef's knives hung on the wall. Resisting the temptation, I went back to the sitting room. Several minutes passed.

'Come in,' van Damm called.

My palms were silty. I clenched and unclenched them. The bedroom seemed to come towards me. With my fingertips I pushed open the door.

I couldn't have stage-managed it better myself.

Eeles was sitting on the floor unmasked, in a paisley dressing gown, gagged and manacled to a vanity unit by handcuffs. Van Damm, still wearing her evening dress, lay artfully lit on the bed. She was staring at the ceiling. Eeles' eyes followed me across the room. Van Damm never stirred. I loomed over her. My hand reached out, and faltered.

'What are you waiting for? Permission?'

In some dark vault of my consciousness I wanted to go through with the debauched charade. I touched her ankle and felt her tense. Behind me Eeles gave an uninterpretable whimper. My hand caressed the soft flesh inside her leg, parting the skirts to the naked triangle.

'Call me names,' she whispered. 'Anything you like.'

The air had gone sluggish. 'Bitch,' I said thickly.

'Nnng,' went Eeles.

'Don't be bashful.'

'Slut.'

She gripped a pillow with one up-thrown hand and moaned.

'Mmm,' Eeles said, swinging his head back and forth.

My desire was unavowable. Like van Damm had said, risk was a powerful aphrodisiac. And there was another thing that pumped me hard. I wanted Eeles shocked out of his wits. And what could be more shocking than finding out that the man who'd just fucked his mistress before his very eyes was the same man he'd tried to murder? I loosened my belt. I felt colossal.

The phone bleated.

Van Damm's smudged stare hardened. 'Shit!' she blurted, and threw her forearm over her eyes as if she'd been exposed to a brilliant burst of light. We waited in stilted silence, like actors riding out a disturbance in the auditorium. The phone kept on ringing, and as its peevish note drilled deeper, lust wilted and shamefaced awareness spread over me like a post-coital flush.

From Eeles came a series of farmyard sounds. He was striving at his bonds and eventually it became apparent that he wanted van Damm to answer the phone. 'Shit to fuck,' she snarled, scrambling for the instrument.

My hand swooped. 'Leave it.'

Anger fissured her glossy lips. 'Playtime later. Go get yourself another drink.'

My grip tightened. 'I said leave it.'

She winced, her fury poised to go nuclear. 'Get your fucking . . .'

But my hand cut her off. I grabbed her bodily and ran her kicking and gouging into the bathroom. Behind me, Eeles tried to drag the vanity unit across the carpet. Van Damm got one hand free and scored fingernails down my face. I pushed her back against the mirror. Her heel stamped down on my instep with a force that made flashbulbs go off in my head.

'Pack it in,' I panted, eyes watering.

'My ass.'

There was a great flurry of hands and feet with me at the centre. 'Camille, I'm warning you.' I could see no way of subduing her this side of a strong right hook.

All at once she stopped resisting. I could smell her fragrance and my own ferment. 'Hey,' she murmured, working herself against me, 'you like to play rough.' From the bedroom came muffled howls. 'Why don't we let Rip in on your big secret?'

I shook my head, using the standoff to breathe in big gulps.

Her lower lip vibrated in an attempt to smile. 'It's only part of the game, isn't it?'

'The show's over, Camille. The production's cancelled.'

Her swing missed me by a whisker and carried her off-balance. I pinioned her arms and bundled her into the shower stall. With one hand I turned the cold tap on full. I stepped back as the jets hit and held the door shut.

'Cool off,' I shouted over the spray. 'I'm not going to hurt you. I don't want to hurt Rip either. You said he liked to share secrets. That's all I'm after – his secrets.'

The shower stopped and for a moment everything went quiet, then the door slid open and Camille stood there, like a fire that had been put out.

'Promise you won't hurt him,' she said in a miniature voice. One of her contact lenses must have been knocked out. One of her eyes was aquamarine, the other an everyday grey.

'All you have to do is stay quiet. Raise the alarm, and I can't guarantee what will happen.'

The phone had been ringing throughout, and when it stopped there was a clear, shocking silence. As I turned the key on van Damm, it started again.

Eeles was pop-eyed and purple. When he saw me, he stopped struggling and went still. I ignored him. Awash with adrenalin and disgust, I went through into the kitchen and ripped off the mask. I ran water and cleaned up my face. There was a bottle of cooking brandy on the counter. With spastic hands I poured a slug and threw it back. My reflection ambushed me. For a moment I looked at myself in dull loathing, then downed another drink, donned the executioner's mask and went in.

Eeles made a thin, high sound and pulled his knees up to his chin. However I handled him, it was going to be unedifying. I put my finger to my lips and held it there until his eyes signalled acquiescence. Then I slipped his gag and moved back as if he was a source of contagion.

Give him credit, his first thought was for Camille. His eyes went to the door. '*La señora*. What have you done with her?'

'*Nada.*'

The skin under his eyes was soft and moist. 'You want money – *dinero*? There's about a thousand in my jacket. Take it.'

'I'm not after money.'

At the sound of my voice, his face drained into whiteness and his mouth opened.

Crouched in front of him, I raised my mask. 'Happy birthday, Rip.'

I think he fainted. Only the whites of his eyes showed for a moment. They flickered back into an unfocused goggle.

'Camille did warn you to consider the unexpected.'

Eeles strained at his anchorage, then fell back with a gasp.

'So here we are, Rip. Together in the lower depths.'

He looked up in weak hatred. 'You're dead.'

I laughed – a shallow snort. 'No, Rip, you screwed up. It's the two men you sent to kill me who are dead. Think about it.'

Sweat budded on his forehead. 'I swear to God. They were told to stop the truck. Nothing else.'

'That's not how it looked from the driver's seat.'

'It was a mistake.' He licked his lips, very quickly, as if any motion on his part might give offence and tip me into violence. 'Look, I don't know what Style's told you, but you're working for the wrong man. It's not too late to change sides.'

'I'm working for myself, Rip. There's no appeal. You can't go over my head.'

'We can work this out. How much do you want?'

'Everything.'

'Everything?'

I squatted on my heels. 'I know about the gypsy, Rip. I know what he came to do and who sent him. I've even seen the man he's supposed to kill. I want to know who that man is, what he's done, and why Axnoller and the psycho are so much against the idea.'

'I can't. I don't know about any gypsy.'

'You're off to a bad start, Rip. Two nights ago the loss adjuster tried to kill me. Whose side did you say you're on?'

Eeles fought his bonds. 'Listen, I'm only an accountant.'

'Don't make it any worse for yourself.'

His dressing gown had fallen open. I averted my eyes from the pot belly, the timorous mollusc beneath. I didn't possess what it takes to be a torturer. I was too ready to see myself in the victim's shoes. But some instrument of compulsion would be necessary. On the bedside table was a set of telephone directories.

'What are you doing?'

'Looking up a number.' I flicked through the pages. 'Rip, how do you think I know about the gypsy and the man he's after?'

A new unease entered Eeles' eyes. 'Style must have told you.'

My finger marked the page. 'Style's told me nothing. I've picked up the bits and pieces on the way, but all this fuss and bother started because the two apes you hired cocked up a highway robbery and made the driver wonder what manner of cargo he was carrying.' I began to dial. 'Even then, I wouldn't have made the connection if you hadn't installed the Location Device.' The number was ringing. I wedged the phone under my chin. 'Right now, Axnoller still thinks I'm nothing more than a reckless driver, but when he finds out how loose a cannon you started rolling, I think it's safe to say your career prospects will take a steep dive.'

'Please. Wait.'

The number answered. 'Carl Axnoller.' I put my hand over the mouthpiece. 'It's up to you, Rip.'

'Stop! Put it down.'

'Mr Axnoller? It's the driver here – Griffith. Listen. No, listen. I thought I'd better bring you up to date on my progress.'

'I'll tell you,' Eeles squeaked. 'For fuck's sake, I'll . . . '

I put down the phone on some irate woman dragged from sleep. 'Start with the man Style wants dead.'

Tears had welled in Eeles' eyes.

'The name of the man.'

Eeles' mouth worked soundlessly for a moment.

'Rip,' I said, 'you're in a terribly vulnerable situation. I can't retrieve your dignity, but I can spare you a great deal of pain.'

'Holloway. Gilbert Holloway.'

That workaday name blunted the atmosphere. 'And Holloway is or was?'

'Style's chief executive.'

'What's he done to deserve a death sentence?'

Eeles' voice had ebbed almost right away. 'He embezzled a large sum of money from one of Style's companies.'

'Money belonging to Style?'

'Yes,' Eeles said, and his eyes flicked fractionally. I sensed that he was searching for a level where he could balance his fear of me against the other threats.

'Another whopper, Rip. Consider your predicament.' I gave him a moment to consider his predicament. 'You were about to say . . . ?'

'From . . . from funds invested with Style.'

'By Axnoller?'

'An American consortium.'

'Headed by Axnoller?'

A germ of puzzlement crept into Eeles' expression. He was wondering where my involvement ended and my ignorance began. 'Axnoller has a stake.'

'Give me his background.'

'He's a businessman with international interests.'

'Give me a run-down.'

Anger sparked in Eeles' eyes. 'You've no idea who you're dealing with, do you?'

'The Mafia. Axnoller's a racketeer and the loss adjuster's a hit-man.' I shrugged. 'See what you've got me into, Rip.'

The effect on Eeles was profound. He screwed up his eyes as if I had uttered terrible blasphemies. 'They'll kill me. They'll kill us both.'

'Then you'd better keep our chat a secret. Tell me about the money invested by Axnoller. What was it for – drugs?'

If Eeles' hands had been free, he would have been wringing them. 'I don't know.'

'You're testing my tolerance.'

'To . . . to . . . to buy some land.'

'What kind of land?'

'A development site.'

'For a dump.'

'I don't know.'

I skipped the lie. 'But Gilbert Holloway, former chief executive, stole the money.'

Eeles nodded.

'Foolhardy of him, I'd say. This happened when?'

'Last week.'

The timing made sense. 'And Style commissioned the gypsy to get it back?'

'Yes.'

'Perfectly reasonable. So why is Axnoller against it?'

Eeles' fear had stabilised. His eyes were calculating what he could get away with. He found a more collected voice. 'Style said he'd take personal responsibility for the recovery of the money. He's a gypsy. He's like that. He tracked Holloway down in Spain and arranged to send the gypsy after him. Axnoller insisted that his own people be used. He doesn't trust Style to do it right.'

There it was – the answer to the question that had plagued me across Europe. And yet I sensed if not a lie, some clouded version of the truth. My legs had gone dead from crouching. I stood up and crossed to the window. Rain had started and trickles were converging on the glass. Street neon was mirrored on the pavements.

A phrase from formal logic came into my head – 'the undistributed middle'. I knew how the affair had begun and how it was supposed to conclude, but between these two points sagged a vast bag of loose ends. I turned and the sight of Eeles made me wince. It was going to be another long night and I was damned if I was going to spend it with a semi-naked homunculus.

'Where's the key to those contraptions?'

Eeles' eyes rolled towards the table.

I unlocked the cuffs from the unit but kept one wrist secured. 'Make yourself decent,' I told him.

'Where are you taking me?'

'Next door. No reason why we shouldn't continue this conversation like civilised beings.'

In the sitting room I locked him by one wrist to a sofa leg. As I walked towards the kitchen, I could feel the weight of his stare on my back. 'I'm going to make some coffee. Want some?'

Eeles seemed to have withdrawn into himself.

I shrugged. 'Suit yourself.'

'Who are you?'

I was at the door and his voice barely carried. I became aware of the silence of the moment.

'You know who I am. I'm the driver. I'm James Griffith.'

'I made enquiries at Argonaut. They told me that Griffith . . . that his . . . '

'Yes?'

His humid gaze raised itself to mine. 'The description didn't match . . . '

'Good for you,' I said, and suddenly felt deflated, wondering how much this changed my own situation and whether it was time to bale out. 'Does Axnoller know?'

'I didn't dare tell him.'

'Wise. What about Style?'

Eeles shook his head. 'I haven't seen him since New Year's Eve.'

'Of course,' I said, 'if I'm not the driver, you must be wondering what happened to the real James Griffith?'

Eeles' eyes made me think of something that lived in a cave.

'He's dead, Rip. How does that make you feel? More secure or less?'

Eeles punched the sofa. 'Why don't you just tell me what you want?'

'I'm driving in the dark, Rip. Until I've heard the whole story, I'm not sure.'

Eeles sagged back. 'It's blackmail. You're looking for Holloway yourself.'

'Anything's possible.'

'I swear I don't know where he is. Only Style knows that.'

'And the gypsy,' I reminded him. 'I know *his* whereabouts, Rip. I drove him there myself.'

Eeles swallowed and a dim hope lit his eyes. 'It could be worth a lot of money. A lot more than you imagine.'

'You're negotiating very tricky ground. For all you know, *I* could be the gypsy. I could be the man Style has sent to kill Holloway.'

Tears began to ooze. Qualified pity mingled with my contempt. Poor podgy, thin-shanked Eeles who couldn't get it up unless he watched someone fucking van Damm. The perverse emotional formula required clarification. 'Eeles,' I said, 'what exactly is your relationship with that woman?'

He was more startled than at any other point in my interrogation. His lips tightened and he looked away. 'I don't expect you to understand.'

They loved each other. That's what he meant, and in his silence he clung to some small shard of dignity. Secretly I was thwarted. Eeles and van Damm – made for each other. What a world it was out there. Nothing remained of normality. Anger washed over me. It was people like Eeles and Style and Axnoller who led the dance, and it was me who was out of step. Fuck it, I thought, if Eeles tells one more lie, I'll sock him in the mouth.

I went into the kitchen. 'Tell me how much money is involved,' I called. I found an espresso machine and looked for the coffee. 'More than I could imagine, you said.'

After a while I realised that Eeles hadn't answered. 'The money,' I repeated. 'How much?'

When I looked through the door, his eyes were swivelled full-lock. My own stuck wide. Around me the air had electrified, charged by the perfect pitch of the loss adjuster's whistle. I even recognised the tune – the 'Entry of the Queen of Sheba' from Handel's *Solomon*. I grabbed a knife from the rack and charged back into the sitting room, but before I had time to pull up Eeles' gag the doorbell buzzed.

The loss adjuster broke off in mid vibrato. 'Open up, Rip.'

I shook my head at Eeles and put the knife to my lips. 'It's you or me,' I mouthed. 'And you don't have a vote.'

The loss adjuster leaned on the bell.

'He knows I'm here,' Eeles whimpered. 'That must have been him phoning.'

I struggled to undo his wrist. 'Is there an entryphone in the bedroom?'

'Yes. Oh God, he'll kill us. You've met him. You know what he's capable of.'

'Shut up,' I hissed, frog-marching him back into the bedroom. Fear had bound us in babbling complicity. 'Ask him what he wants. Tell him you're ill – anything.' I pushed the phone into his hand.

'That you, Rip?'

'What's the problem?' Eeles piped. 'You got me out of bed.'

I was nodding along, willing him to say the right thing in the right tone.

'We found the truck. The gypsy's done got clean away. He's gotta be in town. That sonofabitch driver, too. We ain't found where he's at, but we got a lead and it ain't but twenty-four hours before we pick him up. Carl's brought in some help. He wants us back at the hotel.'

A cord drew tight in my stomach. The scrap merchant must have told him that I'd taken the Madrid train. My terror feasted on the thought of what it must have taken to extract that information.

Eeles eyes begged for instructions.

'Shoot, Eeles, what's holding you? Git your drawers on and open this goddam door, godammit.'

'Tell him you have a guest.'

'We're entertaining. We have someone with us.'

'Tell someone the entertainment is kindly over and kick their ass out whoever it is.' He paused. 'Who you got in there anyways?'

'A client, a friend – someone Camille brought home. Look, it's a bit embarrassing. We've been to a fancy dress party. We're in the bedroom, changing. Would you mind waiting in the lobby? I'll join you in five minutes.'

The loss adjuster flat-handed the door. 'By God, you degenerate little fuck. The gypsy fella is running around loose in town and you and that bitch are kindly humping trash dragged in from the street.' His voice fell away into a terrible murmur. 'I'd hate for you to keep me waiting 'cos your bitch is in heat. I can cool her off if you cain't . . . '

'Five minutes,' Eeles cried.

'By God,' the loss adjuster shouted, 'are you in-citing me?'

One more prevarication would be one too many. My eyes skidded hither and thither, but we were six or seven floors up and the only way out was by the door.

Eeles' eyes rose in pleading. 'If he finds you, it'll go just as badly for me. Hide here until we leave. I swear I won't tell him.'

I considered the suggestion only to reject it. Precedent told me that Eeles untied would not be the same as Eeles bound. I put my mask back on.

'Tell him your guest will let him in on his way out. Tell him you're just finishing dressing.'

I could see the words rising in Eeles' gullet and then slipping back. A jab with the knife forced them loose.

'He's going. I'll be with you as soon as I've put my clothes on.'

I slipped the gag on and clipped him back to the vanity table. From the bathroom there was silence. I tapped on the door. 'Camille,' I said, looking at Eeles, 'the loss adjuster's arrived. At the moment, Rip is still in one functioning piece. If you want to keep him that way, you'd better tell the American that I'm just a piece of Spanish street theatre.'

I tiptoed to the door. I could hear the loss adjuster's controlled breathing. My hand touched the knife in my waistband. I drew the bolts and chains, but even as I turned the handle he barged in. His face, set in tetanic hardness, swung on me then aimed into the empty room. He shoved me aside and took one step forward. His eyes held the blank look of an unintelligent predator.

'*Perdóneme*,' I said, cringeing past.

'Hold it, freak,' he said, his hand shooting out. He sniffed, his nostrils flared, and then he looked straight at me. His coyote eyes were no more than a foot from mine. He saw the scratches on my face. 'What you guys doing in there? Where's Rip?'

Timidly I raised my wrists as if they were bound and turned my face towards the bedroom door. I mimed a spit.

'Jesus,' the loss adjuster said, and flung my arm away.

He looked at me again, but the only thing registering was profound revulsion for all weakness of the flesh.

32

I took the stairs in breakneck multiples and spilled out on to the street. At four in the morning the city was still swarming. I scanned the barrage of neon for a cab, then set off running. The crowds balked me. It was like trying to make a full-throttle getaway on a slipping clutch. Rock music blared from the cafés. I made it back to the hotel, checked out, and didn't slacken pace until I'd left the lights behind. I tramped the city grid, and only when I was completely lost did I feel I'd won a breathing space. If *I* didn't know where I was, then even the loss adjuster would have difficulty finding me.

At last, soaked and footsore, I took refuge in a bar. Sitting there in the wan company of other vagrants, I saw how much my initiative had cost me. No place was safe now. Axnoller had brought in extra hands and they would be scouring the city for a face, not a name. But it wasn't just my life I'd put at hazard. Today was the fifth. This evening, Eleanor Barry was arriving in Madrid. Tonight she was supposed to call me. Tonight was supposed to bring the fulfilment of my dreams.

There was only one place to go. Sodden dawn was breaking by the time I found a cab. '*Aeropuerto*,' I told the driver.

The rush hour had started and everyone seemed to have a plane to catch. Well short of the airport, the traffic jammed into a bottleneck. We stop-started like a piece in one of those vastly complicated puzzles which has only one possible solution, and where only one unit can move at a time. A car drew abreast in the next lane. Inside were two men, both wearing dark glasses and grim expressions. I turned and made myself small, and when the car had inched well ahead, I leaned forward.

'Drop me here.'

'Is two kilometres.'

'It'll be quicker on foot.'

Under the dead drizzle of cloud, I trudged towards the airport buildings, then turned left into the commercial hinterland, following the route I'd taken by taxi the day before. I was trapped in the inexorable process of a nightmare, but it wasn't dream logic that led me back to the sleep factory. It was my only bolthole. No one would see me enter; no one would see me leave. Stringer Vane was a solitary agent whose movements were known only to Style.

Nothing had changed in my absence. The lobby was empty, hermetically sealed. Once again I posted my card and the door sighed open. With the cowed tread of a barbarian entering a cathedral, I went in.

'Welcome to AutoRest, a new concept in international hospitality. Every possible care has been taken to make your stay comfortable and pleasant. In your room you will find a brochure and a video showing full details of the amenities available. In emergency, please call extension 900. This number should be used only in the event of emergency. Enjoy your stay. Have a nice day.'

I screwed down my will and padded down the corridor, past rooms that declared no signs of occupation. The recycled atmosphere was hot and dry, furred with static electricity. Breathing in, I could feel the friction of the air. I came to door 214. A cramp was inserted between my ribs.

With robot fingers I keyed in the entry code. The handle turned. The door swung slick on its hinges.

Modular functionalism had been the designer's brief – how to make a ten-foot box minimally inhabitable. For decorative relief, the pastel walls were hung with prints of bodegas, flamencos, costas and sierras that were probably all that AutoRest guests were likely to see of Spain.

The television had switched itself on and a screened message invited me to state how long I would be staying. Ignoring it, I searched the room for signs of present or previous occupation. The green light over the miniature bathroom showed that it was safe to enter. A red light would have meant that automatic sluices were in action. I checked the telephone for an answering machine. There wasn't one. I picked up the receiver and got the disengaged tone.

I held my breath, listening. The curtains were made of pale crêpe material and against the winter light they looked like dirty bandages. I opened them an inch and put my eye to the gap. The sky had sagged right down. A man went past on the other side, hurrying as if he was crossing a line of fire. Other people passed. None of them looked my way.

But someone was expecting the room to be occupied. I sat on the edge of the bed and called extension 900.

'Good morning, Mr Vane. How can I help?' The accent was unclassifiable, delivered with the fruitiness of an English butler.

'Oh . . . yes. I was wondering if there were any messages for me.'

'A gentleman called last night. I told him you'd checked in yesterday morning. He didn't leave a message.'

Yesterday morning? But I'd only just got here. 'Did he give his name?'

'No, sir.'

Understanding hit. On the night I'd arrived in Madrid, I

had inserted my card in the lock. The computer had recorded my entry, checked me in. So far as Style was aware, the gypsy was alive and in place.

'Was the caller English?'

'Spanish, I believe.'

My eyes moved to the door. 'I don't suppose anyone's called in person.'

'No, sir.'

'Could a visitor come to my room without you knowing?'

'No sir – not unless they were a card-holder.'

'So if someone wanted to see me?'

'They would have to speak to me, and I would pass on the request to you. As you will have seen from the information pack, visitors are not allowed in guests' rooms.'

'If someone should want to see me, tell me.'

'Is that all?'

'Yes. Oh, are there many other guests?'

'We're nearly full. So if I could remind you that this number should only be used for emergencies.'

'Sorry to trouble you.'

'My pleasure.'

Someone besides Style knew I was here. The caller would be wondering why the gypsy hadn't made contact. Maybe Vane was supposed to have done his job by now. Or perhaps the caller had been phoning to give final instructions. None of these possibilities offered reassurance, but it was a matter of balancing risks. On the street I'd have no warning of danger, whereas here there would be at least a minute's notice.

Wondering what kind of guest ever pressed the 'Indefinitely' key, I booked Stringer Vane in for 'One Night'.

For the moment, that was as far as my initiative could take me. One night was all I needed, but I wasn't going to spend it here. Meeting Eleanor Barry was surely worth the risk.

And perhaps the risk wasn't as great as I'd imagined. The loss adjuster knew I wasn't James Griffith, but that wouldn't get him far; a physical description was all he had to go on. I blessed the extravagant gesture that had made me book into the Ritz. It was the last place he'd expect to find a truck driver. I'd lie low here until seven. I checked my watch. There were about ten hours to kill.

Back at the window, I stood guard over the wet street. My gaze kept moving between the door and the telephone. A ringing bell was the last thing I wanted to hear, yet every nerve and fibre was tensed for the moment when the silence shattered. It didn't. The minutes passed and the silence tightened around me until I could hardly breathe. I did sentry-go, back and forth, back and forth, making shorter and shorter turns until I found myself stalled, unable either to come or to go.

I was nearly toppling with exhaustion. I tried to compute how much sleep I'd had since my odyssey began. None last night, a few hours at the hotel the previous day, a hectic doze on the train in Madrid. Before that, a racked night with Steph, a round-the-clock top-up on the ferry, three hours at Style's place . . .

My energy account was heavily overdrawn. The light seemed to sift down like spores. My sinuses ached. I fell fully clothed on the bed and rolled to face the phone. It squatted impassively, a plastic buddha. I fell unconscious contemplating it.

Reluctant to disturb the atmosphere, I lay in limbo with my eyes fixed on a point where images of Eleanor Barry drifted. The silence wasn't flawless. Occasionally its surface was scratched by a ghostly telephone, a door shutting.

I hoped Steph was all right. The recollection of her came out of nowhere and perked me up. Eleanor Barry I envisaged as cinema, whereas Steph was preserved in an album of holiday snapshots. Even our love-making had the wanton simplicity of an end-of-pier romance. Recalling how I'd deserted her, I suffered a wrench of regret.

Winter dark was falling. I sat up and massaged my throat. Swallowing had become uncomfortable. Other symptoms – tingling joints, crawly skin, stinging eyes – made themselves felt. No doubt about it, I was coming down with something.

Groaning at this malign fluke, I rose and went to the window. A great weight of cloud was pressing the last glow of day into the city. Now and then a vehicle swished past. The few pedestrians seemed intangible, figures from an internal landscape. I stood there for perhaps an hour – or maybe it was no longer than a minute. Time glided emptily by. This, I thought, is what it must be like to be a ghost.

A man was going to be killed and there was nothing I could do to prevent it. If Style didn't get him, Axnoller would. Holloway must know that they were after him. Somewhere he, too, would be waiting in suspended animation, braced for the ringing bell or the knock on the door. I turned and looked at the wall. He might be in this very hotel.

An airliner warbled overhead and my face lifted, tracking its descent. I checked my watch and was startled to see that I'd overrun my deadline. I began to throw my things into my bag, hurrying to make up the wasted time. I squeezed the bag shut and decamped, banging the door behind me. Rejecting the lift, I sped down the stairs and was halfway to the ground floor when I remembered my passport. My passport! In a pathetic nod at security, I'd hidden my own passport under the bed. Gutsick at the almost suicidal oversight, I galloped back. Panting, I lined up the card in the lock, then froze, doubled over in an animal crouch.

Inside, the telephone was ringing.

There wasn't any choice. I couldn't leave my passport. I barged in, fell on all fours and swept my hands across the carpet. By my ear the phone kept up a polite chirrup. Not now. Not *now*! My fingers closed round the passport. I sped back to the door, started to draw it shut, and was reaching for the light when another thought struck like a lash. It might be the manager calling to say that I had a visitor downstairs. I could have blundered straight into him. My mind raced over the other possibilities. It didn't matter if it was Style calling long-distance. I could be clear in seconds.

Praying that the caller wouldn't ring off, I dashed for the phone.

'*Señor* Vane?' a voice said in a breathy whisper.

'*Sí.*'

'Why haven't you answered?'

'I was taking a shower.' Instead of the reedy gasp I had expected, my response came out solid, matter-of-fact.

'You did not answer yesterday when I called.'

'I had to go out for some air. Staying here is like being walled-up alive.'

'Is not wise to go out,' the soft voice said.

I let that seep in. 'What's happening?'

'Okay, is tonight. Is tonight.'

I lowered myself on to the bed. In the mirror my face was a zinc-white smear. 'What time?'

'The car is outside now.'

My stomach contracted. '*Uno minuto.*' I parted the curtains. Outside the entrance, where my imagination had parked a funereal black limo, stood an innocent city cab.

More money than you can imagine, Eeles had said. But it wasn't the money that dictated my response, nor was it the near certainty that my gypsy caller was taking me to

Holloway. Rational thought didn't come into it. I took a deep breath, like a man going underwater.

'I'm ready.'

'Bring money.'

'I have it.'

'You ask the driver for Angel's.'

'Angel's.'

'Okay. See you about one hour.'

With slow deliberation I cradled the phone. My lungs filled and emptied, filled and emptied. I could feel my body working away – the purposeful engine with its pumps and valves and switches. Life had been resuscitated.

Calmness marked my exit. There was no need to hurry. Events waited on me now.

33

I'd assumed we would be heading into the centre, to some inner-city pit of low light and criminality, but our route was cross-grained, through neglected outer suburbs. On the way the heavens opened and fat pellets burst on the roof. The driver had a bronchial cough which he stoked up with unfiltered tobacco. Ever since he'd picked me up, his mirrored eye had been too attentive for comfort.

'So what kind of place is Angel's?'

His eye stopped still. 'You not know?'

'All I know,' I said, 'is that someone's arranged to meet me there.'

He turned right round, then returned his attention to the road. 'Is a club,' he said in a throwaway voice.

'A *Gitano* club?'

'*Sí.*'

'Popular with tourists?'

Caution slid over him. 'You *turista*?'

'Businessman.'

The driver's lips pinched.

'Is it dangerous?' I asked. '*Peligroso*?'

He slipped eye contact. 'That depends on your business,' he said, and then made me none of *his* by filling the cab with easy listening.

Rain was still bucketing down. I had no idea where we were, and from the way the driver slowed and scouted about, his own bearings were hazy. For several minutes we patrolled a dead-end district on the edge of open flatlands.

Finally we stopped outside a degraded shopping mall under the lofted hulk of a housing development. I sat in the slap-slap of wipers, the rain falling plumb and spraying back from the road. Racist slogans and counter-slogans had been aerosoled on the steel shutters protecting the shops. Litter swilled down the gutter. The living here was marginal.

'Are we there?'

The driver pointed to a sign etched in argon italics. The letters bled arterial red in the rain beaded on the screen. Fear squatted in my stomach like a tumour. Even now it wasn't too late to pull out.

'*Dos mil*,' the driver said.

I found myself counting out the notes. The driver twitched them out of my hand then, with the heavy grunt of the spectacularly unfit, he leaned back and unlatched my door.

I turned my collar up, took a breath to last the rest of my life and plunged across the road into the shelter of the next doorway up from the club. The taxi was slipping away. I gave the driver a half-wave. He didn't wave back. The cancer in my abdomen had spread.

A man came out of the club and walked away in the opposite direction. Either they had Vane's description or they hadn't. Either I was dead or I wasn't. Either or, win or lose, heads or tails.

One dash brought me to the door. Getting through it required infinitely more effort. I wiped the rain from my eyes. Two men blocked the dingy entrance hall. One was young, sprawled with his feet on a table, reading a magazine about the domestic arrangements of the rich and famous. The other was middle-aged and watching television with drop-jawed concentration. The younger one unslung his feet, stood up and rolled his shoulders.

'Vane,' I said.

The older man had taken only half an eye off the television antics. He said something sideways and the youth stepped back, giving me more room than I needed, exposing a door shaped like a Moorish arch. The air held a dense peppery fragrance more oriental than European.

The ambience wasn't as I expected. The room was cheap and tired, more like a neighbourhood drop-in centre than a den of villains. About a dozen dark-skinned men were grouped among the plastic tables, playing cards and dominoes or frowning at the sports pages and lottery results. Beside the bar was a little stage, and around the walls hung framed and autographed posters of bullfighters and flamenco artists and football heroes. My entrance killed off what little sound there was. Eyes sloped towards a corner where a man and a very obese woman were thumbing through a stack of receipts. Neither of them made any apparent gesture; in fact they didn't even look up. The customers slowly resumed their activities, but they weren't taking me for granted.

My face had gone numb. By another supreme effort I walked towards an isolated corner. I had the grimly comic dread that my show of tough nonchalance would end with me tripping over a chair or walking smack into a wall. I made it to the table without upsets. Immediately I sat down, a skinny waiter shuffled up. I ordered coffee. With it he brought a shot of brandy and a plateful of chorizo.

My posture was supposed to be an insouciant slouch – a killer's devil-may-care slump – but it quickly degenerated into a paraplegic huddle. I didn't dare move and I regretted not bringing along an improving book or some other occupational aid. With nothing to focus on, I seemed to be floating out of myself. I hunched over my cup of coffee, both hands wrapped around it.

From the corner of my eyes I became aware that everyone was studying me without making a point of it, but one man looked at me and didn't look away. Maybe he was just more noticeable than the rest. He had bootblack hair and a checked jacket that stood out in the sour light like a TV test card.

Between him and me a pair of feet came strolling. They were shod in snakeskin and had a lordly tread. My perspective enlarged as the man approached, so that by the time he stopped, my eyes were at the level of his midriff, focused on a hand tricked out with thousands of pounds worth of jewellery, a cigarette dangling, the smoke going straight up in a thin line.

My stare rose. He wore a puce suit with flared lapels, an avocado-green silk shirt and a hothouse tie. My eyes rose and went rigid.

Presiding over the motley costume was a face burnt beyond expression, a face that had been melted like plastic and then cold-quenched into total statis. Nothing he was thinking registered on the surface, and that frightened me more than the terrible disfigurement. It was like looking into the face of a heathen god. His lidless gaze absorbed the contents of my brain.

'Angel,' his lipless mouth said, or seemed to say.

Erratic pulses beat under my own puny mask. 'Vane,' I said huskily.

With a barely perceptible lift of his chin, Angel intimated that he wanted me to rise and follow him. I lumbered to my feet and stumbled; he had the grace not to notice. He led me behind the bar into a domestic corridor. Deeper in the house a baby was having a tantrum.

We stopped outside a door. Always there was another door. His arm came out and settled on my shoulder.

'The Americans got Paco,' he murmured. 'They cut his fucking ears off.'

I gave an infinitesimal shrug. '*Lo siento*.'

His eyes filmed over and he gave a carefully calibrated nod of what I took to be sorrow. Standing back, he pushed open the door. A television was on, the sound turned right down, its flickery luminescence brighter than the light from the coil of a single naked bulb. One corner of the room was stacked with boxes of electrical goods. On the table rested an old-fashioned telephone, the receiver off the hook.

'Is Señor Style,' Angel said, and ever so softly pulled the door to behind me.

The room tilted slightly. Before moving to the phone, I turned up the sound on the television. 'Bravo!' cried a gameshow host with a pumpkin-coloured face split by a manic grin. My hands were all thumbs. I flexed my fingers like a cardsharp. As I picked up the phone, my eyes squeezed comets out of the blackness.

'Did Angel tell you?' Style asked. His voice was filtered by distance, relayed by satellites that put it slightly out of phase and gave it a metallic timbre.

'Yeah, tonight.'

He was too lit-up to identify my voice. 'I'm talking about what that animal did to Paco.'

'Yeah,' I muttered, 'his ears.'

'They're looking for you – for the fucking driver, too. Don't go back to the hotel. Angel will take care of you until it's safe to come home.'

'Right.'

'What's that? The line's terrible.'

Terrible or not, the moment I launched a coherent sentence my masquerade would be over. Shock was my only means of pinning him.

'There's been a change of plans. Don't hang up. If you do

I'll leave immediately. You won't find me and you'll never know what happened and all your efforts will be forfeit.'

Across the electronic wastes, Style's breathing was audible. On the television one of the female contestants was taking off her bra to whipped-up applause. In her bemused way, she looked like it was the proudest moment of her life. The host was bent double with laughter.

When Style spoke again, his words issued from mists of longing. 'Wear black,' he whispered. 'No one else will.'

I relaxed to weather the threats. Threats were something I was getting acclimatised to. 'I've served you better than you know. Beyond all reasonable expectation.'

'Where's the passenger?' he said, his voice a tremolo of hate.

'He didn't reach journey's end.'

Style cursed in what I took to be Romany.

'It wasn't the loss adjuster and it wasn't me. It was an accident. He suffocated on the ferry.'

Style's curses rang like an incantation, pagan cadences from out of time. Abruptly, he switched to English. 'There are no accidents. You'll find that out soon enough.'

'Join the queue.' There was no point labouring my innocence. 'How he died doesn't matter. What's important is that no one but you and I know.'

'I don't believe you,' Style said, but slower, more perplexed.

'It's the truth.' At this rate, we would be at cross-purposes all night.

Style got a lock on his anger. His bewilderment was drawing him in. 'How did you find the . . . hotel?'

'The ticket. There was a mix-up at the scrapyard. The two men you sent mistook me for the passenger.'

Style made a sound of deep disgust. 'What kind of a mug do you take me for?'

'How else did I end up in that dump?'

'Why did you go there?'

'I needed somewhere to hide. I was on my way out when your friends called. I decided you deserved an explanation at least, and then I thought, maybe I can offer more.'

'You think you can squeeze more money out of me?' Style laughed richly. 'You don't know when to quit.'

'I want only what the job's worth.'

'You've been paid ten times the rate for a job you . . . '

'I'm talking about the job the passenger was sent to do.'

'Job? I don't know what you're talking about.'

'I saw him watching the video at your house. You have a business problem which needs ironing out.' I considered amplifying this with information extracted from Eeles, but there were enough worms crawling without adding him to the pile. 'I'm offering to step into the passenger's shoes.'

Enlightenment gentled Style's voice. 'The Americans found you. Or you went to them.'

'Then why are they still looking for me?'

An explosion of hilarity from the TV audience filled out the silence. A hostess was sticking a rosette on the lucky finalist's naked breast.

'Why?' Style demanded.

'Money, what else?' I framed my words with care. 'When we last spoke, I told you I wasn't returning to England. I can't go back. I'm under suspicion for a crime that could put me away for life. On top of that I've got the loss adjuster after me. I need to buy a new identity.'

Style humoured me. 'Suppose I did have a job that needed doing? What guarantee can you give me?'

'The deed will be its own guarantee.'

'The deed?'

'You want total severance from a former employee.'

'You're crazy.'

'My services are offered strictly on results.'

'If I wanted someone to do a job – any job – you're the last person I'd hire.' His voice trembled with the frustration of being unable to get his hands on me. 'There are half a dozen people where you are who could tidy up for me. One phone call is all it will take.'

My eyes were stationed on the doorknob. 'Then why did you send the passenger?'

There was a dead spot in the dialogue.

'I know that you can call on other resources,' I continued, 'but for your own reasons you'd prefer not to be under obligation to the locals. This way, no one at this end is involved.'

For a long time it hung in the balance.

'I need to think,' Style said quickly. 'I'll call you back.'

'Put the phone down and the deal's off. My offer is limited and unrepeatable.' I looked at my watch. There were seven minutes to go before eight. 'Time's passing. You said you never worried about things outside your control. I think you'd better start worrying.'

'No.'

'To quit now would be as dangerous as going on.'

Style seemed to go off air for a long time – so long that I wondered if I should cut and run.

'On confirmation, you said.'

His manner had become expansive and he sounded a lot closer, almost as if he could be speaking from the next room. I descried his threat reshaping itself in a different, subtler and therefore more dangerous form.

'That's correct.' Mentally I toned myself up for every nuance.

'The job's worth ten thousand,' he said in a take-it-or-leave-it tone.

Frankly, I was shocked. 'Life's cheap, but not bargain basement.'

'It's what the passenger would have got. There are people where you are who would do it for half.'

'I bet there are people where I am who would do it for the price of a drink. Twenty-five.'

'Twelve.'

'For twelve,' I told him, 'you don't get much of an identity. Twelve doesn't put you out of the loss adjuster's reach.'

'Fifteen.'

'Think in round numbers.'

'Split the difference.'

'Twenty?'

'The job's yours.'

I held the phone away from me and stared at it. 'You won't be disappointed.'

'Tonight,' he said. 'It must be settled tonight.'

'That's cutting it fine.' Suddenly my head was rowdy with misgivings.

'The time isn't negotiable. After eleven tonight and before six in the morning. No later.'

Behind the TV's silicon glaze a newscaster had taken the place of the gameshow host. Somewhere in Asia there had been a devastating flood. Style was setting me up.

'Let me confirm your instructions. You want me to close the account of an unsatisfactory associate.'

'Permanently.'

'For ever. Is that all?'

'What do you mean – is that *all*?'

'I was wondering,' I said, 'whether you wanted to claim financial redress.'

'Forget it.'

'You sure?'

'I have another rule: know when to cut your losses. With bad debts, the best thing is to wipe them out.'

'You'd better tell me the name of the debtor.'

'A name isn't necessary.'

'The place?'

Style's misgivings jostled for position, then came tumbling out in a rush. 'I can't tell you that over the fucking phone. Christ, this isn't going to work.'

'Without directions,' I pointed out. 'it won't.'

Style breathed harsh and fast. 'Take the Toledo road. About an hour's drive south, you'll come to the Griñon turning. Go straight past. After fourteen kilometres, you'll see a sign marked Los Pinchones to the right. That's it. It's a farmhouse set back about four kilometres from the road, down its own track. You'll come to a small wood about halfway down the track. Leave the car and walk the rest. There are no other houses nearby.'

Calmly I noted the details. 'It sounds,' I said, 'ideal.'

'There'll be only one occupant. No one else is involved and no one else must be harmed. Is that absolutely clear?'

'I'm not throwing in any extras.'

'To reach the house you have to go through a gateway. By the right-hand pillar there's a large stone. Under it you'll find a key to the back door.'

I stored the implication that someone else had prepared the ground. 'That only leaves the arrangement for payment.'

'Go back to the hotel. Someone will call on you.'

'That's not satisfactory. I'm sure you understand.'

'All right, fix something up through Angel,' Style said, as if he couldn't be bothered with trivial financial details or because –and this was a million times more likely – the issue of cash settlement wouldn't arise.

'Twenty thousand is a lot to take on trust.'

'So is your word. Look, in business, both parties have to profit. Any other strategy is short-sighted. Do the job and you'll be paid in full.'

I filed away the double-edged guarantee. 'That's what I'll do. When it's done, I'll call Angel.'

'Tonight,' he said again. 'After tonight the account will be transferred. Have you got that?'

'I'll need transport – and means.'

'Angel has them.'

'Then I'd better get on with it.'

His voice shook. 'If you let me down . . . '

My response was authoritative. 'Stay calm. It's as good as done.'

He hung on for a second or two. 'It was you who . . . '

'Killed the passenger? What difference does it make?'

My fingers were cramped around the phone and it took an effort to release them. I pressed the rest to break the connection and then replaced the receiver askew, blocking further calls. I flexed my fingers to get the tension out of them. I felt as if I'd wobbled across a tightrope suspended over a chasm and stood looking back at a tiny figure left behind on the far side.

34

Angel was waiting outside with the man in the strident jacket. 'Everything is good?' he inquired, his face a caul.

'Everything is good,' I assured him. 'But now I must go. I have a busy night.'

The man in the jacket bared teeth that made me think of rocks at low tide. 'You have the money?'

'Naturally.' In fact I was carrying on me every pound and peseta of my ill-gotten gains. My inner pockets were bulging.

Without softening the demand with unnecessary politeness, Angel held out his hand.

'I wasn't told how much.'

For a moment, my professional credibility was under strain, but then their glances met and dissolved in venal rapport.

'*Cuatrôcientos mil*,' Angel said, his inflated quote bracketed by the faintest suggestion of question marks.

I raised a token eyebrow. 'The arrangements had better be sound.'

It was Angel who took the money and unabashedly counted it twice before folding it away. But it was the man in the jacket who led me out of the club and down the street. He had stacked heels and the busy gait of a man just starting a night's round of satisfying work.

The rain had stopped and the air was saturated. I was

slightly out of breath when the man in the jacket bustled around a corner and presented me to a slab-sided and scabrous Volvo.

I backed off a step. 'No good,' I told him. '*Malo*. Too conspicuous. Too . . . '

He laughed merrily and wagged his fingers. 'Is my *coche*,' he said, and opened the rear door. I got in.

We splashed through the *barrio* to a backstreet lock-up. The man in the suit went in and drove out a few seconds later in a newish and forgettable Seat.

'Is stolen yesterday,' he said, opening the passenger door. He patted the seat and looked up with a leer. 'The *aparejo* is under here.'

I felt under the seat to ascertain the nature of the *aparejo*. The touch of cold metal burned my skin.

'Then I may as well get started.'

He passed me a scrawled telephone number. 'My name is Lucio. You tell me where you leave the car. Somewhere else. Not here.'

'Sure,' I told him, sliding behind the wheel.

He rapped on the glass by my ear. When I opened up, he displayed all his bad teeth. 'The hombre who hurt Paco?' He pinched thumb and forefinger together and rubbed at a smear on the windscreen.

'If there's any killing to be done, I'll do it myself.'

He stepped back as if I had given him an answer he admired. The digital clock showed less than three hours to midnight. I sat for a moment, then slotted the car into gear. Only the fact that I drove without lights for half a mile betrayed the insurrection taking place down in what remained of myself.

Style would kill me whether or not I carried out my side of the contract. It wasn't just that he couldn't risk letting me go loose. He believed I'd murdered the gypsy and I was sure that by the code of Romany honour, he was bound to avenge the death. The question was whether he'd already sent someone after me, or whether he'd wait until the job was done and I surfaced to claim my fee.

The first possibility kept my foot pressed hard down, even though the atmosphere had condensed into fog that hung heavy in the hollows. I wasn't just racing the clock. I had the idea that if only I didn't slow down, if only I could keep up the momentum, I could get there before the whole pack of doubts caught up.

One of the measures of human ingenuity is that a man armed with only a couple of co-ordinates can target a particular spot anywhere on earth, a place unique not only on this planet, but in the whole wide universe. Style's instructions were accurate to the letter. A few minutes short of the hour, the Griñon turning flicked by. Fourteen kilometres beyond that my lights picked out the sign on the right.

I had time to suppress one last surge of misgivings before swinging across the road on to the dirt surface. I was driving on reflex, barrelling into the dark, no lights to be seen anywhere. Drive right up to the house, I thought, rush in, grab Holloway, slam the door behind us and be gone.

Trees in twisted shapes stretched out of the dark. I flailed to a halt. The wood described by Style was a cork oak plantation and the regular spacing made it look watchful. Strands of mist hung across the track like becalmed ghosts. The apprehension that I'd been trying to outrun caught up in a rush.

Someone working for Style had driven this route before me. Someone had tracked Gilbert Holloway to the middle of this empty plain. That someone had procured a key to the back door. The implications pushed me back from the steering wheel. Why hadn't that someone already killed

Holloway? Divisions of labour, I told myself, the right man for the job. Using a local might be cheaper, but I could imagine that it might involve all sorts of hidden extras.

I backed into the trees and doused the lights. Without them I couldn't see my hand in front of my face. I felt for the *aparejo* and pulled on the leather gloves that came with it. At first the weapon and the darkness made me feel a little more secure. I let myself out and felt my way back on to the track. I began to shuffle towards the house.

Even when my pupils fully enlarged, I couldn't distinguish the line between earth and sky. Only the feel of the gravel underfoot kept me on the right path. The scale of the pitch-black night raised the hairs on my neck. It made me feel diffuse and puny, as if I was inside something that would suddenly snap shut. This is how primitive man must have felt, I thought, benighted and stalked by monsters.

Something the driver had said came back. 'It's not as if I'm sending you to the ends of the earth.' That's the direction I was headed. Somewhere over the invisible horizon lay Estremadura, the Spanish province renowned for its explorer sons who left their poor native pastures to search out the limits of the wider world.

I ducked down as I came over an unseen brow and saw the houselights anchored dead ahead. No other light showed. A shot would carry for miles, but there would be no one around to hear it. I sneaked forward.

It was so dark that I sensed the gateway rather than saw it. My hands groped down the right-hand post and located the rock below. Blood throbbed in my temples. My fingers closed round the key.

The lights shone from rooms at the front and side of the farmhouse. Gravel grated beneath my shoes. The light from the front was shuttered; the light from the side came from an uncurtained kitchen.

My heart bumped the wall of my ribs. Holloway was standing at the window, staring out. He must have seen me or heard a sound. I teetered in mid-step and then I realised that his stare was directed inwards, and that the invisible curtain separating light from dark made me impossible to see even if he'd been looking. He was definitely the man in the video, but the assurance he'd displayed on film had been eaten away. Holloway was a man overborne by events, a man stressed for the worst.

Nobody else was in the house. I could tell that from the vacancy of his expression. It was then that I realised Style did trust me to complete my assignment. No one was coming after me. Afterwards, yes, but for now I had time to spare. Studying Holloway's big, undefended face, I felt the power I had over him. This, I thought, is how psychos get their kicks, standing in the darkened wings, looking in to the spotlit stage, judging their entrance.

After a while, Holloway glanced down and seemed to remember why he was there. He picked up a plate, towelled it dry and placed it in a rack. Wafts of piano music reached me. I watched for a minute longer before withdrawing my presence.

I slipped to the back door and fitted the key. I seemed to float forward, towards the source of the music. It came from a tiled sitting room restfully furnished and lit with rosy accents. I established myself on a couch facing the door and laid the shotgun alongside my thigh. It was an ugly, sawn-off, utilitarian object loaded in both barrels. I yawned. My heart was beating hard and fast, but inside was a dreamy vacancy. I felt like a stable atom in a vortex.

Sitting there, listening to the sonata, it came to me that I wasn't absolutely certain that I wouldn't do it: kill Holloway. I had lost touch with my own self, and with everything so different, comparisons ceased and anything seemed possible – even murder.

I pulled the shotgun closer and everything around me seemed to dwindle.

35

Holloway was still wearing an apron when he entered the room. He appeared so quietly that I think he saw me first. If he'd had his wits about him he could have turned and run and got away before I could have reacted. His stupefied eyes took in the gun, then me, then the gun again. I placed it across my knees so that there could be no illusions about our relationship.

My face was as expressionless as stone. 'Mr Holloway?'

He didn't say yes and he didn't say no. He didn't say anything. His eyes began to crane round, getting ahead of him.

'Sit down,' I told him, before he could do anything impetuous. 'Over there, by the window.'

He made a sound in his throat.

'Yes?'

His hand fluttered at his apron strings. 'Do you mind if I take this off?'

I could understand why a man wouldn't want to suffer the terminal indignity of being shot in a pinny, and since there were no practical objections, I told him he could. Then I told him again to sit down.

He dropped square and clenched his hands on his knees. The sonata had reached a transcendent moment.

'Who else knows you're here?'

'Only me.'

I sensed a fractional hesitation. 'And?'

'No one.' His eyes were fixed on the gun. Tiny drops of perspiration beaded his upper lip. 'Who sent you?' His accent was provincial, Black Country.

'Style.'

Holloway gulped. 'Nothing's changed. I still have the documents. I still want an equitable arrangement.' He looked at me, hardly daring to put his hope into words. 'Have you been sent to negotiate a settlement?'

My first thought that this was some lame ploy dreamt up on the spur of gunpoint. 'Mr Holloway,' I said, making no attempt to soften the blow, 'I was told nothing of documents. In my line of work, as in yours, I imagine, employees are told only what they need to know. In your case, all I know is that Style wants me to kill you.'

His face crumpled like wet tissue, but furious red lesions appeared on his cheekbones. 'Style isn't so fucking crazy.'

'Apparently he is.'

Holloway's voice changed pitch. 'If I go, he goes too. He knows that. He knows it all comes out if anything happens to me.'

I felt an all-too-familiar chill factor. 'Take it easy, Mr Holloway. If *what* comes out?'

He appeared not to have heard. He began blinking as if a fly had flown into his eye.

I sat to attention, a classroom gesture long unused. 'I'll give you a push start. You're Gilbert Holloway and until recently you were chief executive to Vincent Style, property magnate.' I rotated my hand.

His head drooped. 'What's the point?'

'Remember Scheherezade?'

His attention drifted sluggishly back. 'No. Is it a nightclub?'

Under the handsome exterior, I discerned a suburban

soul. 'The point is, I'm holding a gun at your head.'

He stared at it. 'What do you want to know?'

'How long have you been Style's chief executive?'

'Two years.'

'You work for him before?'

'No, it was a leap into the dark.'

His glance led my own eye towards the window, but there was nothing to see. 'How's that?'

'I was head-hunted. I was a senior manager for a national supermarket chain. Style had just finalised his plans for his out-of-town shopping centre. The projections were good, but he was starting from scratch and needed someone with retail experience at the highest level.' Holloway scratched his knees. 'I'm one of the country's leading experts on one-stop shopping.'

'With respect,' I said, 'you don't strike me as a man who would take a leap into the dark.'

'Career-wise, I'd hit a crisis point.'

'Oh?'

'I don't see how this is relevant.' One of Holloway's feet had begun to twitch. His restlessness bothered me. It didn't seem wholly connected with his current predicament.

'Let me be the judge.'

Holloway made an effort to concentrate. 'My wife and I had divorced. The promotion I'd expected had gone to a younger man from outside the organisation. I'd been with the same company for seventeen years and I realised that I'd become part of the furniture.' He hesitated. 'It had always been my dream to start an independent retail organisation from scratch – to take on the big boys.'

'Well, that's one ambition achieved.' I crossed my legs. 'When did the dream go wrong.'

'I became aware of the financial discrepancies about six months ago.'

I frowned. 'For a leading light in the high street, you seem rather slow on the uptake.'

Holloway's eyes engaged me properly for the first time. 'Do you have any idea what starting up a hypermarket involves? Six hundred staff to train, more than fifteen thousand product lines, over . . .'

'I'll take your word.'

'I was working a sixteen-hour day. Style handled the financial side. I signed whatever was put in front of me.'

'You're implying that his accounting methods were chaotic.'

'To the point of criminality.'

'In what way?'

'Many of the financial irregularities involved large transfers through fly-by-night banks and investment trusts in the Bahamas and Virgin Islands. I asked a journalist friend to investigate.'

'And he came up with Carl Magnus Axnoller.'

Again, Holloway glanced at the window. 'You know this already.'

His edginess was catching. The sooner we were out of here, the better. I jogged the gun. 'What did your informant have to tell you about Axnoller?'

'That he was a criminal who'd made his fortune through marine insurance scams.' Holloway paused to gauge my level of interest.

'I'm listening.'

'He'd buy or lease an old and barely seaworthy freighter, load it with a valuable and highly portable cargo – cigarettes was a favourite. On the high seas, the merchandise would be transferred to another ship, the old scow would be scuttled, and Axnoller would claim for both the ship and the cargo – which by then would be on sale in Peru or Venezuela or

Manila. Have you any idea how many cigarettes can be carried in one freight container?'

'I thought,' I said, 'that Axnoller was in waste disposal.'

'That was a variation on the insurance fraud. He started marine dumping of toxic waste that no one else would touch – or only at a prohibitive price. Waste was wealth without risk. With it he set up chemical reprocessing plants in the States and other concerns in Third World countries.'

'Does Wales come into that category?'

'I wouldn't have thought so. I mean, controls are too tight.' His eyes slid towards the door.

I couldn't restrain a sigh. 'Mr Holloway, are you sure you're not expecting someone?'

His attention moved smartly back. 'If I'd been expecting someone, I wouldn't be here.'

It was an irritant I couldn't scratch. I tried to ignore it. 'Maritime swindles and waste dumping are a long way from supermarket trolleys and check-out girls.'

'Axnoller invested his profits in the Florida property market during the boom. That's where he and Style came together. Style needed financial backing for a big property development. Axnoller supplied it.'

'He used Style to launder the proceeds of crime.'

'Parts of Florida are built on dirty money. The development was very successful. When Style tried to repeat the success over here, Axnoller was a major investor.'

'He put money into Style's businesses?'

'About thirty million pounds, so far as I've been able to work out.'

I whistled. 'What's he getting in return?'

Holloway raised a bleak laugh. 'Nothing. Less than nothing.'

'What's gone wrong?'

'The timing. Style ran into the recession at the worst

possible moment. I thought we could ride it out until I did my own bottom-line calculations.' Holloway's jaw squared with anger. 'Style's been hiding the extent of his losses by transferring funds from one business to another, but by my estimate he's in hock to the tune of two hundred million.'

All those noughts seemed to float through the room. 'Axnoller can't be too pleased.'

'He doesn't know. Like everyone else, he's been fed false figures.'

'He knows now – or is about to.'

Holloway nodded. 'He must have realised something was fishy. Just before Christmas, a man called Eeles was sent in to go over the books.'

'I've met him. A very tortured individual.'

'That's when I knew everything was going to blow up.'

'Why didn't you resign? I imagine you must have negotiated a handsome compensation package.'

'What I stood to lose was beyond compensation. It was only a matter of days before everything came out, and where would that have left me? Ten years ago I might have been able to climb back, but not now, not with my current profile. My signature was on key documents. I hadn't done anything knowingly dishonest, but at my level, you can't afford the slightest taint of suspicion.'

'Don't gild the lily. You could have reported what you knew to the police or the Serious Fraud Office.'

'I confronted Style. He told me that what I'd found out about Axnoller was only the tip of the iceberg – that his connections reached right up into government. He warned me that if I made my suspicions known, I'd be dead inside a week.'

'You panicked.'

'My career was finished. I was being threatened with murder. What else could I have done?'

'Few jobs are for life. You could have looked for an alternative career.'

Holloway was contemptuous. 'Do you think Style was going to let me walk away with what I knew? Do you think Axnoller would have?'

I had to concede the point. 'So you took the money as severance.'

He batted his eyes. 'Took?'

I pulled on an earlobe. Getting the facts was like caging rainbows. 'My instructions were to kill you for having embezzled a large sum of money.'

'Style said that?'

'Eeles, actually.'

Holloway looked away. 'I didn't steal any money. All I took were documents linking Style to Axnoller.'

'Blackmail?' I regarded Holloway with a measure of awe. 'Given the nature of the people you're dealing with, don't you think that was a trifle rash?'

Holloway chewed on his lip.

I leaned back and briefly closed my eyes. 'How much are we talking about?'

He made a restless motion. 'Let me call him. Please, there's been a misunderstanding. I know there has.'

And I was part of it. 'There's no error. My instructions were to drive out here and kill you no later than six tomorrow morning. At six, I assume, you planned to be somewhere else.'

Holloway didn't disagree.

'With how much?'

'Seven million.'

The jolt was seismic. 'Seven million *pounds!*'

'Look, a man with my earning power. With bonuses, a share of the equity, my lifetime remuneration would have been at least double that.'

'Spare me your projections.' Seven *million*? That wasn't a sum Style would write off. And why had no one mentioned blackmail before? He'd bamboozled me, but the why and wherefore eluded me. He must know that Holloway would spill the blackmail story, and that there was little to stop me taking the documents myself and carrying on where Holloway had left off. I inflated my lungs to give my new fears breathing space and rose to my feet. Holloway misconstrued my movement and worked himself back in his chair to cushion the anticipated impact. Big patches of sweat ringed his ribs.

'All right,' he said. 'Tell Vic I'm prepared to compromise. Five million in return for all the paper.'

'On your feet.'

'I don't know how much Style is paying you, but I'll double it – treble it. Name a price. We're talking about seven million.'

'Time's short,' I said, glancing out of the window, 'so why don't you shut up and do what you're told.'

Holloway stood up as if he expected to be shot in the attempt.

'These incriminating documents. I don't suppose you have them here.'

Holloway wet his lips. 'No.'

'Where?'

Holloway gave a sickly smile. 'They're my pension scheme. Without them I won't stay alive to collect.'

I was really angry with him then. He was like the greedy monkey which, having put its fist into a bottle to grab the candy, won't let go to withdraw its hand. I assumed my grimmest manner. 'You're skating on very thin ice, Holloway.'

His eyes turned moist. 'They're in Madrid.'

'Right, where's your car?'

'Around the back. Look, what do I get out of it?'

'Your life if you're lucky. Let's go.'

'It's not as simple as that. The arrangements I've made mean . . . '

'Shut up.' The last notes of the sonata had strained into silence. I moved to the window. 'Turn the light off.'

It seemed to me that the night wasn't as quiet as it had been on arrival – nor as dark. I couldn't see any traces of a moon. All the play in my ligaments was taken up. 'I'll ask you again. Who else knows you're here?'

He twitched in the dark. 'I told you.'

'I found you, didn't I? Who does the house belong to?'

'A friend. He's in Brunei. It couldn't have been him. Come on, we still have time.'

No we didn't. A wash of light was spreading up from the horizon. I looked at my watch. It was quarter past eleven. 'You've got another visitor. I take it you won't object if I blow their brains out.'

Holloway was a big man, but something inside seemed to collapse. 'It's Lisa,' he said.

36

'Lisa,' I said again, and laughed. It had been so obvious that I simply hadn't seen it and still couldn't take it in. Each time the thought rounded the corner, it took me by surprise and made me laugh.

'We were survivors clinging to wreckage,' Holloway droned in the dark. 'My divorce had left me an emotional burn-out and the rift between Lisa and Victor was irreconcilable. He abused her, you know. He'd had an accident that impaired his manhood and he took it out on her. Lisa's a beautiful and healthy woman. We met through tennis and then . . . '

I paid scant attention to Holloway's tale of hearts twinning over the tennis net. The sound of an approaching vehicle was unmistakeable now. Thoughts rocketed past, all kinds of shooting stars that disappeared into a black hole.

'How long have you known she was coming?'

'Since this morning. I called her from Madrid.'

It was becoming more complicated with every passing second. 'Mr Holloway, it might not be her, but whoever it is, they mean to kill you. Is there any other way back to the main road?'

'It *is* her,' Holloway insisted. 'And I'm not going to desert her. I love her, and she loves me. It's as simple as that.'

'Give or take seven million pounds.'

'Half is hers by right. If Lisa had waited for the divorce,

there'd have been nothing left to collect. The receivers will take it all. Everything's going to go – the businesses, the property, the cars, the whole damn lot.'

As a student, I'd had a recurring dream of turning up at the examination hall and realising that I hadn't done a moment's revision, hadn't prepared for a single question. The same sensation of utter helplessness filled me now. I shook Holloway's elbow. 'Whose idea was the scam?'

'It was a mutual decision,' he said, making it sound like they'd consulted professional opinion before taking the plunge.

'Taken when?'

'After Eeles showed up, last month.'

'Did Lisa ever see Victor after the bust-up?'

Holloway was emphatic. 'He would have killed her. His attitude to women is primitive. To a gypsy, a wife going off with another man isn't just a betrayal, its . . . polluting.'

My suspicions set in a block. 'Gilbert,' I said, 'the love of your life visited her husband on New Year's Eve.'

Holloway snorted. 'She was in Florida on New Year's Eve. I spoke to her.'

'Gilbert, you're a certifiable fool. Style sent me here to murder you. Not Lisa. *You*.'

'Because he doesn't know Lisa's coming. She hasn't been here for a week.'

'Then ask yourself what brings her back tonight of all nights.'

'She's spoken to Vic. She told me there'd been a breakthrough.'

'Lisa's taking you for a ride,' I said, but some of my assurance had leaked away. 'You're the fall-guy. You're the idiot who . . . ' I broke off. 'Who's got the documents? You or her?'

Holloway was impregnable in his emotional bunker. 'I

know what game you're playing. Next you'll be telling me that Lisa plans to take the money for herself.'

'Nothing would surprise me.'

'A man like you knows nothing about love or loyalty.'

Halogen beams fingered the sky, then dipped back. I made my hold on Holloway more secure. 'I'm about to find out. We both are.'

We waited, our breathing unrhythmic. A wedge of light floated across the ceiling, carrying our shadows with it and pouring them into a corner. Tyres scraped to a hurried halt. A door slammed and heels crunched on gravel. From my viewpoint I couldn't see the vehicle or the driver. A pulse ticked in my side, but I wasn't sure if it was Holloway's or mine. The front door opened. Heels counted off a few steps, then stopped. The memory of Lisa's perfume reached me first.

'Gilbert? You home?'

Under my hand, Gilbert's well-exercised forearm strengthened considerably. 'Not a word,' I whispered, tightening my grip.

'Gilbert?' she called again, her voice fainter and more nervous.

Maybe there was an entirely innocent construction. Maybe Lisa's arrival *was* coincidental. For a man like Style, being cuckolded might be so humiliating that he was prepared to kill Holloway and to hell with the documents – particularly since the cupboard was bare and he was finished anyway.

'In here,' I called softly. 'It's done.'

Her steps moved tentatively towards the door. Not away from me, but towards me. My heart crowded my throat. Payment in full, Style had said, and that's what I had coming unless I killed her first.

'Lisa, don't!' Holloway yelled, twisting in my arm.

'Bloody idiot!' I shouted, and felt him tear loose. The dark in front of me was activated by a blur that connected with my head in a sheet of white light. My legs liquefied and I had the foolish sensation of falling that lasted until I hit the floor and temporarily stopped feeling anything.

Light flashed on. My splintered vision took in Lisa Style, née Hope, standing gloved and coated and apparently unarmed, eyes stretched wide to view the spectacle. Holloway was diving for the gun, and though there seemed to be plenty of time for me to get to it first, my body wouldn't obey my will and I had the agitating experience of watching incapacitated as he scrambled it up.

'Gilbert!' she cried. 'Are you okay?'

Holloway had the shotgun in hand and was gibbering. Around me the floor was splattered with blood. Slivers of glass sprouted from my gloved hand. Stars danced in front of my eyes, bright lights that turned grey and then black.

'What the fuck are you doing here?' Lisa demanded. Not pausing for an answer, she rounded on Holloway and her hand flew to her mouth. 'My God! Victor!'

'He sent him to kill me,' Holloway shouted. 'To kill both of us.'

My left eye was slightly misaligned, and although I could formulate speech in my head, my tongue couldn't get in touch with it. 'That's not true,' I tried to shout back.

Lisa made a firm entry, determined to impose control on the situation. 'Easy, Gilbert. Get a hold of yourself.'

My hand dabbed at my face. It came away daubed with blood.

'What are we going to do?' Holloway demanded.

'Get the hell out. Right now.'

'And leave *him*?' Holloway cried, jabbing the shotgun at me as if it was a pitchfork.

Lisa's glance was lacerating. 'Forget him. He's nothing.'

312

'Nothing? He tried to kill me!'

Lisa made a wry mouth. 'He couldn't have been trying very hard, and he's trying even less now.'

Spittle had gathered in the corners of Holloway's mouth. 'Because he was waiting for *you*.' He advanced towards me, his eyes glittering with menacing fixity.

'Leave him,' Lisa shouted. She ran to him. 'Oh, sweetheart, what's this punk against seven million?'

Holloway's frame of mind was too volatile to hold an argument. 'Vic's never going to pay up. He'd die first.'

'You're wrong! I've spoken to him. He's prepared to concede.'

Holloway brandished the shotgun with a flourish I was sure must end in detonation and death. 'You call this a concession?'

'It was his last shot,' Lisa cried. 'You're right. He tried to get the two of us, but he's failed, and now we're going to make him pay.'

My tongue found itself in spontaneous motion. 'She's lying, Gilbert. She's the one who set you up. How else do you think I found this place?' I wriggled for my pocket and came within an ace of getting shot. 'The key was left by the gate. Who else could have put it there?'

His eyes darted between her and me. 'You really think Victor will pay up?'

'He's got no options besides.'

'Don't believe her, Gilbert. The money's for her and Victor. They're going to ditch you.'

She didn't even trouble to look at me. She stamped her foot. 'Gilbert, come away now. It's time to ship out.'

Everything in the room was on a fulcrum. Holloway began to shake with sobs. She ran the back of her gloved hand down his tears. 'Oh honey, what you've been through.' She reached out. 'Give me the gun before there's a nasty accident.'

Paralysed, like a dreamer unable to combat the dream, I spectated while she disengaged the shotgun from Holloway's amateur grasp.

'Oh baby,' she laughed, 'you had the safety on.' And she fluttered her fingers down his cheek as if his ignorance of firearms was one of his endearing qualities.

They folded into each other, united at every joint and crook. She laid her head against his shoulder and when she opened her eyes, they were replete with a declaration that nothing could come between their devotion. I saw how infallibly wrong I'd been. They were true lovers, and their love made me feel soiled.

'I wasn't going to harm him,' I mumbled through numb lips. 'I was trying to get him away.'

She looked at me around his shoulder. Her eyes were contemptuous.

'Then I'll have to do it myself.'

The explosions were simultaneous, hideously loud, and Holloway shot back as if he was on a spring-loaded tether and hit the wall with a force that shivered the room. He hung there for a moment, pinned by the blast, then slid down in a big red smear.

When Lisa spun, she had another gun in her hand, a dainty silver pistol. 'Take your gloves off.'

The double blast had atomised my senses.

'Here,' she said, lobbing the shotgun at me.

I caught it in stunned reflex.

'Break it open.'

I did so. Both chambers were empty.

'Now lay it on the table.'

Still pointing the little pistol, she grabbed the shotgun and pushed it blunt barrel first into her pocket. The nub of the stock stuck out from her coat like a grotesque fashion accessory. She held the pistol impressively steady. 'You weren't kidding, were you? You never had any intention of killing Gilbert?'

I shook my head, torn up inside.

'Or me?'

'No.'

'What about the poor gypsy?'

'It was an accident.'

My responses relaxed her. 'That's what I told Victor. Victor thought it had to be you, but I knew better.' She spoke as if we were long-time intimates, and she peered at me as if she really was interested in what made me tick. 'What was it all for? A quick buck?'

'I don't know.'

'You wanted to find out, right?'

'Something like that.'

'Oh boy,' Lisa said, and liberated a pack of cigarettes with one hand. 'Knowledge makes man free,' she observed. 'A hippy philosopher said that. I read it at college.' She frowned, about to tap a cigarette loose. 'How did it go? "A man of knowledge has no honour, no dignity, no home, no country, but only life to be lived." '

My head had begun to hurt like hell. ' "He that increaseth knowledge, increaseth sorrow." I can't remember who said it.'

'Yeah?' Lisa shook her head. 'I still don't know why a cultured guy like you is driving a truck.' She flicked her lighter and concentrated on the first draw.

Watching her, I had a sensation of vacuity. 'You said you were giving up.'

Lisa admired her cigarette. 'I'm an addict. I can't.'

'It didn't take long for you to break all your resolutions.'

'Not the important one. This year is still going to be the year of hope.'

'Is that what Holloway believed? Your hope, his faith.'

Her eyes sharpened. 'Can you imagine me running off with Gilbert?' His body was lying only feet away, his blood sprayed on the wall, but she spoke as if he was living his life somewhere else. 'You should have seen him in his supermarket, marching down the aisles like a general inspecting the troops. "Good morning, ladies. How are we today, girls?" Patting the cereal packets like they were babies. Eyes right at the cans of beans; eyes left at the freezer bags. Ajusting a display here, removing a date-impaired item there.' Lisa frowned at her cigarette as if she suspected she'd been sold the wrong brand. 'Gilbert,' she said, 'had the soul of a grocer and the charisma of a spreadsheet.'

Anger broke through. 'There are worse crimes.'

'Try blackmailer.'

'I bet I know who hatched that idea.'

Her gaze was clear. 'You'd lose. Gilbert floated it one night after we'd made love. He'd found out that Axnoller had transferred twelve million dollars to one of Vic's companies.' Her mouth widened mischievously. 'Yeah, it's Axnoller's dough. Makes it feel a lot righter, doesn't it?' She exhaled smoke. 'The money was for a land acquisition, but because of who Axnoller is, he used Victor to front the transaction. Gilbert knew Vic's businesses were going bust and he figured we were entitled to the liquid assets before they all went down the plug.'

'Did Victor know about your affair?'

'Not until I told him.' Lisa sucked on her cigarette hard enough to make it fizzle. 'My fling with Gilbert started months before any of this came up. It was purely a physical thing for me, but he was too vain to see it.'

'You didn't love him?'

'The only man I love is my husband. Like I said, love isn't something you can reinvent.' Lisa shrugged. 'So when Gilbert came up with the blackmail idea, I told Victor.'

There was a persistent ringing in my skull, like a distant burglar alarm. 'He forgave you?'

Her smile was crooked. 'I'm still alive.'

'Holloway isn't.'

She looked about for an ashtray. 'Victor has only one way of dealing with people like Gilbert. Come down hard. I told him snap actions wouldn't get him anywhere except jail. We were hemmed in on all sides – Gilbert, Axnoller, your fraud police, the banks. Gilbert was right, I told him, but we should take the money ourselves. So Vic emptied out the account and told Axnoller that he'd used it to pay off Gilbert.'

'Axnoller isn't fooled.'

'Maybe not, but he was diverted. And you know why? Because I'd gone off with Gilbert, and Axnoller knew – thought he knew – that Victor was too proud a man to go along with that.' Lisa slanted a smile at me. 'You following this? You still sure who's using who?'

My mind was jumping tracks.

Lisa tapped ash. 'So while Axnoller's been chasing after Gilbert, I've been getting on with organising a new life for Vic and me.' Her mouth lifted in a winsome smile. 'At heart,' she said, 'I'm a home-maker.'

I made myself look at Holloway – a lifetime complex of sensations and memories snuffed out for no other motive than to buy Style and his wife a few days' grace.

'A distraction? Is that all he was?'

'It was my ass, too. It still is.'

'But you're alive and he's dead. Why kill him? Why in the name of God did you have to do that?'

'Because,' Lisa said, her patience thinning, 'you didn't have the guts.'

I tore my gaze away from hers. 'Gilbert was the price you paid for Victor's forgiveness.'

'You think I should have paid it instead? You think I

deserve to die because a guy gave me a few orgasms and a couple of candlelit dinners.' Her tone became beseeching. 'Look, Gilbert was double-crossing Victor, and anything I think or you think wouldn't have made a spit of difference to how he ended up.' She strode towards the ashtray. 'If you wanted to get to the bottom, I guess you just scraped it.' She ground out her cigarette. 'I've got to go,' she said, as if I'd been holding her against her will.

The blood on my face had started to crust and itch. 'To the ends of the earth?'

'Sure,' she said, her thoughts wandering elsewhere. 'With seven million, why not?'

I sat there observing her beauty. She had just killed her lover without hesitation or scruple, and I knew that before she left she would do the same to me. I hadn't seen intent in her face then, and I couldn't see it now, and I realised how pathetic all my own dissembling had been.

'They'll come after you.'

She eyed me calmly. 'At least this way, Axnoller will have to work for it.'

'I wasn't thinking of him. Remember what you told me about reaching the ocean and finally coming to a stop and all your troubles catching you up.'

She gave me an interested look, but didn't speak.

'Gilbert will be coming after you, and me, and all the other baggage you dropped off on the way.'

Her mouth turned mean. 'Let's not keep you waiting,' she said, and took a quick step towards me, her fingers tightening on the pistol. 'You made a bad call,' she said, bringing the pistol in line with my face. 'Victor's an honourable man. He always pays his dues.'

I closed my eyes. There was a *thwack* and then the sound of her heels walking on the tiles. I opened my eyes to see notes packaged on the table.

'Your pay-off,' Lisa said from the door. 'You killed him. You struggled, he hit you with that vase, and you shot him.' She saw my incomprehension. 'It had to be you who did it. If Victor knew his wife was a murderer, it might keep him awake nights.'

'I don't want your filthy money.'

'You're going to need it. From what I hear, that unpleasant American boy they call the loss adjuster is real mad at you.' She looked at me with a smile that seemed left over from the night we first met. 'Too bad,' she said, and soundlessly closed the door.

I sat there, clock stopped, mainspring broken. At last I moved to the phone. I picked it up and dialled the emergency number.

'Police,' I said from the ruins of consciousness.

It took for ever to get through, and while I waited the switchboard girls chatted about holiday destinations for the coming year. Blood was spreading in a huge pool on the tiles.

'*Policia.*'

'There's been a murder.'

'Murder? No espik English. You wait. You wait okay?'

There was a faint hubbub as the officer sought a translator.

'What number are you calling from?' a voice asked.

Number? The phone was unmarked. 'I don't know.'

'Your address, please.'

Somewhere in the house a clock struck the hour. Midnight. Eleanor would be in Madrid. She would have called and been told I hadn't checked in. She would be thinking it had all been a cruel hoax.

'Please, your address and your name.'

Why should I be the one to pay for Lisa's crimes? Why should I be the scapegoat?

Suddenly I was racing against the clock, bursting out of the door, pounding into the dark. Legions of phantoms seemed to cavort about me, laughing and laughing. I staggered blind over the *meseta*. Branches whipped my face. I tripped over a root and sprawled headlong. I forced myself up and thrashed on – on and on until my heart was splitting. I fell against a tree. Gripping the rough bark I leaned and spewed out everything – coffee and greasy sausages and . . . oh, everything. Tears scalded my eyes. Three deaths. Everyone I came in contact with ended up dead.

37

Eleanor Barry had called the Ritz twice and been informed that I'd confirmed my reservation but hadn't yet arrived. The second time, she left her own number and the message to call her any time. The night clerk had underlined 'any'. Midnight was three hours past by the time I was in any state to get back to her. My wound had bled profusely and my head felt twice its right size.

'I'm sorry to call at such a late hour.'

Her voice was lazy with sleep. 'No, I'm relieved. I was beginning to think that business had summoned you to the other side of the world. Imagine coming all this way and then failing to connect.'

I was in the wrong frame of mind for this conversation. 'I'm here now.'

'Are you okay? You sound odd.'

'It's been a tiring day, and I'm afraid I have a cold.'

Her voice was studiedly polite. 'Poor you. Does that mean we'll have to postpone the great event?'

'Only until tomorrow night.'

'Well,' she said, 'what do you suggest?'

I'd made no plans. All my investment had gone into the anticipation, not the fulfilment. 'You choose,' I said, 'it's a woman's privilege.'

She was disappointed. 'I don't know anywhere. I've only just arrived.'

Close to the hotel I'd seen a restaurant and remembered its name. It would do.

After we'd fixed the time and place, Eleanor went quiet.

'I'm in a state,' she said.

'There's no need.'

'Matthew?' she said, as if uttering my name might start a chain reaction that she wouldn't be able to control. 'Remember when you phoned, I had someone with me? I have a serious confession to make. I couldn't tell you then because he was standing right over me.'

I was too washed out for confessions. 'It's late. Save it until we meet.'

After that, I sat on the edge of the bed, my mouth hung open with exhaustion. Another hour went by before I had harnessed suffecent willpower to make the next move. Squinting with effort, I pushed each digit of the phone number down to its stop. With the connection made, I fell back, eyes turned blank to the ceiling.

'Vane,' I said.

'*Cómo le va?*'

'You suggested I call you if I needed extra help.'

'Is big problem?'

'Pretty big.'

'*Es urgente?*'

'*Sí.*'

'Los Gatos. Is bar on Gran Vía.'

'I'll find it. *A qué hora?*'

'*Las ocho y media. Hasta mañana.*'

And that was all it took. How wonderful it was to let a professional take the strain. Relieved of my murderous responsibility, I lay back and let it all go.

But it wouldn't let go of *me*. A cloud of dreams smothered me, images clawing out of the fog, squirming and bloodied and calling for me to join them, down there in the mire with Holloway and Eeles and Angel and Vane and Griffith and, presiding over the infernal cabaret, Lisa, stealing out of the room, one eye watching through the narrowing crack as, taking exquisite care not to let the door click, she locked me in.

Too bad.

I woke in weak delirium, my soft tissues inflamed and my head stuffed full of hot wool. I tried to sit up but the cords tied to the back of my eyeballs yanked me back. I groaned. At last I had entered the disease pool.

All morning I shivered bed-ridden, slipping in and out of reality. At noon I called the hotel doctor. I had mild concussion and influenza, he confirmed, and should stay in bed or, this being the Ritz, he could arrange my transfer to a private hospital. I told him that I had an appointment I couldn't miss and he gave me a shot of antibiotics, another of vitamins, plus pain killers and decongestants and a couple of pills that he said would keep me soldiering on.

At six, overriding the dizziness and shooting pains, I dragged myself up and prepared with scrupulous care before taking a cab to Los Gatos. The night, clear and cold as anaesthetic, energised me. On the dot of half-past, Lucio framed himself in the door and went out again with me following. His scrofulous Volvo was parked down the street. I got in beside him.

As I explained the nature of my problem, Lucio's jowls drooped. 'Is difficult. You kill a foreigner, the police are biting – *pic, pic*.'

'I know all that.'

He wheezed a sigh. 'How much do you want this person dead?'

With all due gravity, I laid out Lisa's twenty thousand pounds in two halves.

Steering with one hand, Lucio used the other to gauge the extent of my blood-enmity. He whistled like a falling bomb. 'For this, I get you the best.'

'The worst will do,' I said, handing Lucio one half. 'The worse the better.'

Cheeks bunched in pleasure, Lucio tapped the down-payment into a neat wad, first cross-wise, then longways. He stopped smiling and looked efficient. 'When?'

'How soon can it be arranged?'

'Tonight?'

'So soon?' I said, my pulse speeding up to meet the schedule.

'We try.' He squinted forward, his mouth a concentrated gape. 'Here is the place?'

The restaurant was in an arcade of smart shops and galleries under a brutal-looking office block. From the absence of strollers, I guessed that it catered to the luncheon trade. 'This is it.'

He evaluated the location with a scavenging eye. 'Okay, I will take care for you.'

After he'd left, I stood for a while on the pavement, merging into myself. Until this moment, my thoughts had led in one direction, my deeds in another, but at last thought and action were as one. Walking to the door, I felt in command of myself and perfectly balanced.

As a venue for a romantic liaison, the restaurant was an awful choice. Panelled oak and haughty portraits contributed to a courtroom atmosphere. It was only nine, early for Madrileños to dine, but that alone couldn't have accounted for the empty tables in the main dining room. A wizened *camarero* led me towards an annexe where, he murmured, the lady was waiting. I followed on a surge of nervous expectation.

Eleanor was reading a newspaper and for a moment I had

her to myself. There she sat, just as I had envisaged, so familiar and so strange. Studying her downcast face, I felt an emotional stoppage in my chest, a sensation like heartburn. And then sadness came over me as she began to raise her eyes. All those years wasted. All that time lost.

Exactly as I'd expected, she looked up and smiled the over-energetic smile of someone impressing a stranger, then, when I had closed the distance by half, her smile became a gawk and she gained two inches in height. Her eyes shot from side to side, but by then I was right up to her and she decided, more or less decided, that her eyes were playing tricks.

'Hello, Eleanor.'

'I'm sorry,' she said, brushing a hand across her brow, 'for a moment I thought you were . . . you remind me of someone I once knew.'

'Oh, who's my doppelgänger?'

'A man called Hugh. Hugh . . . ' She raked her memory but it wasn't there. 'It's gone.' She smiled. 'Not important.'

A dart of pain pierced me. 'Travers.'

Her jaw dropped. She shook her head. She rubbed her eyes. She bit her fingers. And then she laughed – an hysterical yelp followed by utter silence. She covered her face with her hand, staring at me through splayed fingers.

'It's not.'

'It is.'

With antiquated formality, the waiter pulled back my chair. In silence I took my seat. Eleanor was still gaping through her fingers as the waiter placed leather-bound and tasselled menus before us.

'God, I can see it now.'

'I expect I've changed quite a bit.'

She shook her head, still wondering if she was dreaming. 'I don't know what to call you.'

'Hugh or Matthew, it's all the same to me.'

Another gust of laughter escaped. 'I can't believe this is happening. How did we end up . . . Did you . . . ?'

'Rig the computer? No. It was blind luck.' I smiled. 'But I like to think destiny took a hand.'

'That sounds like Travers.'

Our laughter died at the same moment, but we remained smiling at each other, our smiles camouflage for our mutual reappraisal. She hadn't changed much – the same dark wavy hair, the neat triangle of her face – but some of the zest and expressiveness that I'd wanted to be part of had drained away. Thinking of the toll that time had taken of us both, my heart dilated with tenderness.

'You look wonderful,' I told her. 'Just as I remember you.'

'You don't – obviously. You look better.' She pushed back in her chair to take another sighting. 'You've lost weight. It suits you. You make quite an impression.'

'Not enough to jog your memory.'

Her eyes grew guarded. 'What do you want? Why did you bring me here?'

My smile was intended to allay fears. 'Don't blame me. It was the computer.'

'You know what I mean.'

Five years of pain and longing escaped in a sigh. 'I'm here because a computer reunited me with the woman I once loved.'

She grimaced. 'Don't.'

Between us was the unhealed wound, and it would have to be tended. 'Eleanor, I know it's going to be difficult, but I have to know why you accused me of rape.'

'You know why.'

'In all honesty, I don't. Maybe I've turned things round in my head, justified actions that can't be justified. I need you to tell me what happened that night.'

'You know what happened. You raped me.'

'The police thought differently.'

'Oh, the police!' she cried, as if bringing them into it clinched her case. She began to speak in jerks, the sentences like uneven stepping stones. 'That evening. I came to your office to discuss an essay, right? Nothing else. I hardly knew you. I mean, you were my tutor, right? I didn't know you lusted after me. If I had, I wouldn't have come. I never said you could touch me.'

'Not in words.'

She scrambled for her bag. 'I think I'd better go.'

I reached for her hand. 'I'm not here to harm you. I loved you then. I still do.'

She twisted her hand free. 'You're scaring me.'

'I need to know, Eleanor, and then we can put it behind us.'

Her gaze wandered the room. 'What do you expect – a grovelling apology?'

'Apologies always make me uneasy. They remind me of all the crimes I *have* committed. All I want is an explanation.'

She gave a phoney laugh. 'You certainly picked a dreary spot.' She studied each wall in succession and then, as if the gaze of the grandees was too heavy to bear, her eyes lowered themselves to her plate. Half a minute went by without either of us speaking. The blood beating in my face was only my immune system doing battle with the virus.

Eleanor made a tiny adjustment to her place setting. 'I had a boyfriend call Glyn – Glyn Evans. You may remember him. Tall, thin, very . . . un-establishment.'

I shook my head. 'There were a few like that.'

'He didn't show up at the university much after the first year.' She scored the linen cloth with a fingernail. 'That night you . . . we . . . ' She winced as if her finger had snagged on a splinter. 'I'd arranged to meet some friends in a pub. I wasn't expecting to see Glyn, but he turned up as I was leaving.' She looked up, though not at me. 'He knew. I didn't have to tell him. He just knew.'

'It was him who beat you up.'

She slid her glass around. 'I had to say you raped me. I had to.'

'To save your relationship.'

She banged the glass down and it shattered. 'To save my fucking life.'

The waiter came hurrying up. While he cleared up the fragments, Eleanor and I faced in different directions. Inside me, nothing moved. My heart lay in my chest like a stone.

'You know what attracted me to you? Your vivacity, the sheer certainty you took in living. I used to envy you and I used to think how different my life would be if some of the radiance you shed fell on me.' Bewilderment and indignation massed in my throat. 'Why the hell did someone like you choose a shit like Glyn?'

Eleanor's mouth set in lines of resentment. 'Why did you marry your wife? Why did she marry you?'

The question threw me off-balance. 'We thought we were suited. We were wrong.'

'Well, Glyn and I thought we were suited, too. And in some ways we were – badly suited, horribly bad, but suited. It took therapy to find out why.'

In the interior dialogues which I'd held in my imagination, the conversation always went my way, but now it struck me that the script was about to go badly awry. 'You don't have to tell me.'

I don't think she heard me. 'My dad used to beat me. He started beating me from as long ago as I can remember, and he didn't stop beating me until the day I left to go to university. He beat me drunk and he beat me sober, and when he was drunk, beating's not all he did to me. You know where I live, the village where I grew up? More than half of all households had incestuous relationships.' Her voice became a parody of Welsh. 'So, boyo, being fucked by someone who beats the shit out of you is normal where I come from.'

My gaze crawled about the table. 'I'm truly sorry, Eleanor.'

Before she could turn the screw any tighter, the waiter arrived with our first course. His spectral presence subdued me even more. I couldn't think of anything to say and that was crazy.

'I looked up your wife,' Eleanor said all of a sudden. 'You wouldn't recognise her. She quit teaching and now she's running an executive employment agency in Guildford. She lives with an actor called Robin. They seem very fulfilled.'

I tried to imagine Angela's lifestyle in Guildford. 'I'm pleased that she's happy.'

'She told me you never see each other.'

'No point in digging up what's dead.'

Eleanor seemed to consider taking issue with this statement, then suddenly relaxed. 'We had a good laugh, actually.'

'Over me?'

Eleanor smiled. 'She said you had a very unrealistic view of things – that you were hopelessly out of touch. She'll be surprised at how much you've changed.'

Acrimony trickled over me. 'Did you tell her that the rape was a lie?'

Eleanor gave me a dismal look. 'You're going to keep dragging that up, aren't you?'

'It's fairly central.'

Eleanor looked at her plate. 'I'm not hungry.'

'Why her?' I asked, striving for a light touch. 'Not me? Didn't you ever wonder what had become of me?'

'You seem to have done pretty well for yourself.'

'It hasn't been the happiest . . . ' I stopped, alarmed by the emotion building on Eleanor's face.

It burst out in a flood. 'You're not the one who's suffered. So you lost your job for screwing one of your students. Big deal. Look at you now – successful businessman, swanning around Europe, staying in five-star hotels. What have I got? Out of work, renting a ratty farm cottage, frightened out of my wits.'

'Frightened?'

She went motionless and put a hand to her throat. 'There's something I have to get off my chest.'

My expectations for the evening, already revised downwards, took a plunge. 'Glyn?'

She straightened up, her manner possessed. 'After I graduated, we moved to London. I got a job in television and for a while things were good. Then Glyn started doing drugs in a big way and completely freaked out. I left him, he found me and that was the pattern set. I'd leave or he'd walk out, but he always came back. It was because of him that I lost my job.' Her eyes swam. She snatched her hand away from mine. 'No! Wait until I've finished.'

What she was saying was of the utmost importance, but my medical cocktail was starting to do strange things to my perception. Points of light had begun to play around the room and there was a buzzing in my head that obliterated sections of what Eleanor was telling me. I caught her frown of irritation.

'I'm sorry,' I said, forcing a smile. 'I missed that.'

'I hadn't seen him for six months. After he got out of prison, he found out where I lived. He turned up on my doorstep the day I was supposed to meet you in Swansea.'

She made a bitter face. 'Happy fucking New Year.'

'Did he find out about us?'

'Ha! You can't keep secrets from Glyn. He's a total paranoid.'

'He knows you're here on a blind date?'

'Are you kidding? He'd have murdered me – literally. No, I stuck to the story about you being a television producer. He's waiting back at the hotel for the thrilling news.'

'Hotel? You mean he's here in Madrid?' I could hardly make Eleanor out and her voice seemed to be coming from the opposite side of the room.

'I couldn't stop him. He smelt money and he wants some of it. He says I owe him.'

Some annexe of my throbbing brain disclosed something she'd said earlier. 'Eleanor, are you married to Glyn?'

There was a brief silence. 'We've been separated for over a year.'

'But not divorced?'

'It's only a formality. I've got enough grounds to divorce him a dozen times over.'

'But you've never done it.'

Eleanor didn't answer.

'You didn't say you were married in your letters.'

'You didn't tell me you were the man who . . . oh, forget all that. The point, is what are we going to do?'

I couldn't think for the hurly-burly in my head. 'What do you suggest? You know Glyn better than I do.'

'We've got to get away.'

'With me? You mean you'll leave Glyn and run away with me?'

'I always liked you. With someone like you I can make something of myself again.'

In an image of shocking lucidity, I saw the blood-spattered trail that had led me here. The loss adjuster would still be on it. I had never seen him blink, I realised. I had never seen him hurry. 'Eleanor.'

She locked her fingers in mine. 'The computer's never wrong.'

All at once there was no longer enough air to breathe. I placed my hand on my chest. A flush scalded me behind my ears and an unpleasant taste flooded my mouth. I pushed back in my chair, pressing down on the table with both hands as if gravity had been reversed. 'Excuse me,' I said, 'we'll sort it out when I get back. I'll only be a minute.'

By careful consideration of each limb, I managed to stand up. I fixed my woozy eyes on the door and set off.

'Hugh?' she said. It was the first time she'd used the name.

I turned, glassy-eyed, all my concentration devoted to staying standing.

A tear hung from her eye like a pearl. 'You won't walk away, will you?'

'I've come too far for that.'

The lavatory was through the main dining room. The lighting was coarse-grained and hurtful to the eye. I sluiced water over my face to douse the fever. Hands propped on the basin, I raised my head, presenting myself for inspection. Eleanor was either kind or short-sighted. I looked ghastly – wide-eyed and staring and drained of blood, like an experiment in germ warfare, like a soldier who had seen too much service on the front line. I considered taking more pills but calculated that my system had sustained enough damage. I had to make the most important decision of my life and I could barely stand.

The reflection separated. Two heads were sprouting from my shoulders. A chill reached to my bones. My lips scrolled back from my teeth.

'Lookee here,' the loss adjuster said affably. 'The dope on a rope.'

38

'What's the lady doing?' the loss adjuster said, kicking my legs apart.

'She's called Eleanor Barry. She knows nothing. I've only just met her. She's a blind date.'

The loss adjuster laughed. 'You do all your thinking with your dick?' He delved my pockets with brusque expertise. 'You toting?'

'A weapon? I wouldn't know how to use one.'

He found Lucio's final payment and pocketed it in passing. Satisfied that I was unarmed, he stepped back, got himself waylaid by his own eye in the mirror, and gave his hair a congratulatory primp. 'I guess you've run up against the end of your luck.'

I felt like something small in a fable – a mouse ambushed by a wolf. 'You said you'd whistle.'

The loss adjuster pursed his mouth. 'Too cold. My lips are all froze.'

He marched me to the door and through it. The waiter stood aloof, as if had known all along that the evening would not turn out well. I cast a despairing glance towards the alcove where Eleanor sat hidden.

'At least let me tell her that I've been called away.'

'She'll only be storing up disappointment for when you don't come back.' The loss adjuster peeled money off the wad he'd taken and slapped it on the cash desk. 'Can't let the lady pick up the tab.'

The waiter bowed us out. The loss adjuster steered me like a fast automaton down the arcade, heading in a direction that was unfamiliar. The air was a dense substance parting on each side of me. I had one hope and one hope alone.

'How did you know I'd be there?'

'That pretty kid you threw overboard.'

Momentarily I was lost, then my legs caved. 'Steph? What have you done to her?'

The loss adjuster bore the strain and swung me to arm's length. 'Hellfire,' he said, 'what kind of guy do you think I am? That Steph reminds me of my kid sister, who was taken from this life in an automobile wreck one week short of her nineteenth birthday.' He shook his head, discounting any possibility of his sentimental streak accommodating me. 'No sir, I've lavished too much attention on you. This time you go down for the count.'

He marched me on, puffing little clouds of steam into the frosty air.

'That Eleanor lady – she ain't no blind date. Steph says it's some woman you've been carrying a torch for since you were at college.'

'Yes.'

'You know she's got her old man installed with her? Some geek.'

'She was just telling me about it when you came along.'

'You're a carnival,' the loss adjuster said, 'the damnedest business I ever had to attend to.' My lax private life seemed to put warmth into his lips and he began to whistle – a rockabilly number – to his customary brilliant standard.

In the fables, mice always smooth-talked their way out of the jaws of the cat. 'You have a remarkable talent and repertoire. You should be a professional.'

'There ain't no money in whistling.' The loss adjuster paused to make a serious point. 'What happened to the real James Griffith?'

'He was killed by the men Eeles sent.'

'That man is not destined to go far in this life.' The loss adjuster frowned. 'So where did you spring out from?'

'Nowhere. I was just hitch-hiking.'

'And you took Griffith's place behind the wheel? Why'd you go and do a damn-fool thing like that?'

'It's complicated. It seemed like a good idea at the time.'

'Well, shitfire, ain't you somethin'? Come from nowhere and played us all for a bunch of fools.' He looked at me admiringly. 'Eeles said you know about the gypsy. You got a name for him?'

'Vane. Stringer Vane.'

'Where did he get to? I cain't find him anywhere.'

'He pulled out. The going got too rough for him.'

'Shoot, you know more about this than I do. You know about Holloway and all that?'

'Oh yes.'

'Well you kindly tell me where Holloway's at.'

'Will it make any difference?'

'Come up with the twelve million and it might.'

I knew the loss adjuster was going to kill me whatever I told him. 'He's dead. Lisa shot him last night. She and her husband dreamt up the blackmail. They've got the money.'

The loss adjuster allowed himself a tight smile. 'You ain't telling me anything I ain't suspicioned for myself. Know where they've run off to?'

'The ends of the earth.'

He breathed as if warming up for exercise. 'Makes no difference, I'll find him. See, folks like you and Style, they do something bad, they run until they think they're safe. Then they relax and set there, maybe with another name, but just setting. But me, I never stop coming on after them, 'cos that's my job. They just go on setting there and I'm getting closer every day. May take two days, like with you, or may take two years. Makes no difference.'

His arm directed me across the road towards a park. The street lights were few and far between and the sky was hoary with stars. At the park entrance, I dug my heels in.

'Easy, boy. You cain't say I didn't give you due and proper warning.'

Bits of cardboard and glass scuffed beneath my feet. At first I thought the wilderness was unpeopled, but gradually I became aware of leery glances in the darkness, illicit faces frozen in the night. A faint repeated cry – oh! oh! – came from somewhere over to the right. The soil had a fusty odour.

'Ain't no one going to save your ass,' the loss adjuster said. 'Just a heap of faggots and junkies fixing to die.'

He dumped me down on a park bench. Crouched over, furtive, he busied himself with something in his lap. I saw the lustre of surgical steel. They say that the eye of someone about to die dwells on irrelevant details, but I saw only the needle. I had become mute with the certainty of dying.

'This ain't gonna hurt,' he said, taking my left arm.

I was in thrall to some infinitely superior force and I couldn't move to save my life. I gritted my teeth and looked away through prisms of tears.

'Hold still, cain't you?'

I'd flinched because someone was approaching, edging out of the night as if he was sidling through a half-closed door.

The loss adjuster looked up at the junkie, his breath misting, the syringe still poised. 'Git,' he said indifferently.

'*Cómo le va?*' the junkie said, judging how close he could get without giving offence.

337

'Jes' fine, thank you,' the loss adjuster said. His beaming smile plunged into a thunder cloud and a gun appeared in his hand. 'Now beat it.'

'No offence.'

'None taken.'

Fingers waggling, the junkie retreated into the dark.

I laughed.

The loss adjuster doled me a melancholy smile. 'Share the joke?'

I passed a hand across my eyes. 'Only my life flashing by.'

The loss adjuster focused on the point of his needle. 'You're an aggravation to me, mister. You cloud the issue.' He began measuring up, tongue slightly protruding. 'Guaranteed finest quality, for my special customers.'

Behind him another junkie had emanated from the dark. The junkie paused, calculating chances. I filched a look at the loss adjuster. He was whistling under his breath, watching the liquid rising the glass. The shadow had drifted closer, its face an uninhabited planet, deaf and blind to any appeal.

'Give me your arm,' the loss adjuster said. 'It won't take but a second.' He uncovered a grin. 'You'll be fast asleep before you hit bottom.'

I offered up my hand as limply as a patient under the care of his family doctor. The shadow had drawn closer and I still couldn't make out its features.

'What do they call you?' the loss adjuster asked.

'Reason.'

'Reason goes,' the loss adjuster said, and laughed.

'What's your name?' I asked.

'That's for me to know,' the loss adjuster said, 'and you to find out.'

My heart vaulted into my throat. I couldn't see the interloper's face because he didn't have one.

The loss adjuster pulled my arm towards him. 'Happy dreams,' he said, 'whoever in hell you are.'

There was a swishing in the air and then a smaller sound, like gristle parting, and the loss adjuster leaned towards me, smiling, as if he had changed his mind and was about to divulge his identity after all. 'Rockling,' he seemed to say, and at the same time something black crept from his mouth and he sagged sideways, slowly at first, then with increasing and unstoppable force until he pitched. Once down, he didn't move again except for one hand, which went on opening and shutting, clinging for a hold on something vital.

'He's got the money in his pocket.'

Angel stooped over him and emptied his pockets. From his own he took two coins and tossed them at the loss adjuster's eyes. 'For Paco,' he said, then looked at me. '*Finito?*'

'*Finito.*'

Angel gave me something that looked like a smile but wasn't, and backed away until he merged into the grain of the dark.

Bit by bit the night reconstituted itself. Sounds formed – the wail of a police siren, the grumble of traffic, the wow and flutter of the human hive. I waited for arrest, knowing I wouldn't get Eleanor Barry after all, thinking with dreary resignation of the marathon confession that awaited me.

A man walked towards me, saw the body and hastily diverted to a different path. The wail of the siren was fading out in another direction. The loss adjuster had stopped moving his hand. He lay at my feet in the starlight, his eyes staring into eternity. No one was coming. I stood up and walked with slurred feet through the frozen grass, one more light gone out in my heart.

EPILOGUE

Finding her again took me seven weeks and all my money. I hired a private detective to trace her and that marked my return to normality, because Ramon was a supercilious, manicured Castilian with an agenda that apparently didn't include client satisfaction. That's one of the things about ordinary living: you entrust your most tender affairs to idle incompetents who charge forty thousand pesetas a day, plus expenses.

During those seven weeks, nothing out of the ordinary happened. No one arrested me. No one threatened me. I monitored the news from Britain and learnt that Griffith's body had been found ten days after he was murdered. Two motorists came forward to say that they'd seen him fighting with two men in a Skoda who had been killed minutes later in a motorway smash. Both men had a series of convictions for violent assault. There was some speculation about the identity of the man who had driven Griffith's truck to Spain, but the truck hadn't been recovered, and most of the column inches were devoted to the rise and fall of Victor Style, the gypsy entrepreneur who had vanished days before his 'empire' had gone into receivership owing hundreds of millions. The police wished to interview Style about some of his business dealings and the brutal murder of his chief executive, Gilbert Holloway. Style's American connections were dusted off, and the name of Carl

Axnoller – the subject of an FBI investigation – was mentioned.

Mine wasn't, and no one answering to my description appeared in the reports. Nor did Stringer Vane's name make it into print.

After a couple of weeks, when the stories dried up, I stopped looking and started to get on with my life. At first it was strange to be rubbing shoulders with people who weren't out to kill me, but I soon grew accustomed to it. I visited galleries and bookshops. I found a map dealer and exchanged professional pleasantries with the owner.

My money was dwindling at an alarming rate. Sinking my pride I answered an advert for English language teachers and was engaged for three half-day sessions a week. It was a low-grade position, but I enjoyed the contact with my students.

One day in late-February, Ramon called me into his office. He'd found her. She was waitressing in a bar-restaurant called Nicky's on the coast outside Marbella. By then I was down to less than a week's living. Without hesitation, I took my tsarist map to the dealer, who offered me about half what it was worth. I didn't haggle. As I looked at it for the last time, I found myself wondering where Lisa had got to and my heart gave a little wobble. The heart has its own moral imperatives; it turns on an axis all its own and everything else – truth, morality, even the instinct for survival – is subject to its gravitational pull.

To save money, I made the trip to Marbella by bus. A gypsy woman outside the station sold me a bunch of flowers – anemones. To save even more money, I walked the three miles out of town to Nicky's. A strong offshore wind was blowing and the sky was yellow, making everything seem low-spirited and out of season.

Nicky's was a gimcrack glass-walled palace offering

English beer and chips and karaoke evenings and satellite coverage of English league matches. Lager signs creaked in the wind and palms rattled over moulded plastic tables. I entered high on anticipation, but it was late afternoon and at this time of year no one was about.

'Hello?' I called.

A man with a conk like a plum tomato in a string bag issued out of the back. 'What you after?'

'I'm looking for a girl called Stephanie Canaway. I was told she worked here.'

His mouth shaped itself into a dismal trumpet. 'Not here, mate. Must be some other Nicky's.' He looked at me to reinforce the lie. 'There are hundreds.'

'In Marbella?'

'All over.'

'I think I've come to the right place.'

'What's this Steph done then?'

I noted the diminutive. 'Nothing. She's a friend.'

He stuck out his lip gloomily. 'Well, you may as well have a drink. Whisky do?'

When he'd handed me my glass, he lay back in a low-slung seat as if his drinker's gut was his most attractive feature and he didn't want me to miss it. 'Been in Spain long?'

'Since the beginning of the year.' I glanced around at the posters and sombreros and guitars and all the other ethnic bric-a-brac so dear to the vacationing Brit. 'You?'

'Three years,' he said, and closed his eyes under the burden of time. 'Justify my exile,' he said. 'Tell me how fucking awful it is back home. Go on – the weather, the contraflows, the spin doctors, the social security scroungers, the single mothers, the state of English cricket, ditto football, the poofs and lezzies, the dog-shit, the collapsing bloody infrastructure, the, the . . . ' He opened his eyes in startlement. 'I miss all that. Know what I mean? Bred in the bone. Heritage and such.'

'Why don't you go back?' I said, knowing he couldn't.

His sour smile acknowledged the low blow. 'Why don't you?'

'I might. I haven't made any plans.'

'Come off it, pal. You're in free-fall, same as I was.' He struggled more or less upright in order to pour himself another huge Scotch. 'I was something in the City.' He pointed the bottle at me. 'Not *anything*. *Something*. And then, because of certain misguided attempts at financial preferment which I won't go into, I was nothing. People like us, the rug gets pulled out from under the feet, and down we go. Can't make the adjustment, see. Free-fall until we crash-land at some level unforeseen.' His face twisted as if acid was burning his insides. 'Stuck,' he said, still in contention with his digestive tract. 'Property's unshiftable in today's climate.' He gave a suppressed belch and that seemed to ease the internal pressure, because he looked out to sea as if settled in a state of grace, following the silvered wake of a speedboat. 'Got any objections to drug trafficking?'

'Thanks for the drink,' I said, planting a note on the table. 'If you should see Steph, give her that.'

I had reached the door when he spoke again. 'It's her day off. She's probably riding.'

'Riding?'

'Onna horse, mate, a horse. That's what she does on her day off.'

'Is she well?'

'Steph? In the pink. It's her who stops this place falling apart.'

'If you could give me her number.'

'Not on the phone, and I'm not giving out her address. I

343

don't know you, do I? You could be something iffy from her past. No offence, but that's life. Innit? Tell you what. I'll get someone to stroll round with a message.'

I realised that I was expected to supply some pithy appeal.

'Just that I'd like to see her.'

'And if she doesn't want to know?'

'I won't pester her.'

He nodded at the flowers. 'You want me to give her those?'

They'd been tired to begin with, and they were now beyond reviving. 'I'll hang on to them, thanks.'

I dawdled along the beach, postponing the moment when I would have to return and face the future. Eventually, I came to a muddy creek and couldn't go any further. The buildings on the seafront looked small and far away. All was quiet. Above an offshore sewage outlet, seagulls rose and fell on weak elastic wings.

So it ends here, I thought, by the sea, just like Lisa said, when you've gone as far as you can and there's no escaping who you are. But you can't complain. Everything that happens, happens as it should, and that's life. Innit? Quite instructive really, though I was unsure what lessons I was supposed to draw.

No country, no dignity, no honour. Only life to be lived. I dropped the flowers on to the tide. As they floated away, Eleanor Barry came quietly into my thoughts. For years she'd occupied most of my reality, and it was chastening to realise how far she'd receded from the centre. Sometimes though – even now – I found myself wondering what might have been if the loss adjuster hadn't brought the curtain down on our reunion.

Ah well.

The flowers had drifted from sight. I took a deep breath and opened my mouth to let it out, allowing emptiness to fill me, before turning round and retracing my own steps in the sand.

It's extraordinary how discriminating the human eye can be – how from a distance far too great for features to be seen, it can pick out some trick of posture, some unique cock of the head, some infinitesimally small signature that can't be isolated by itself, but which identifies one particular person from among billions.

Steph was waiting on the beach, and from a mile away I could see she was braced for censure. Walking towards her, I felt like a dog returning to its mistress after running off on a spree, timidly wagging its tail, unsure if it's in for a thrashing or a hug. I tried to compose my features into a smile that wasn't a simper.

'What are you after?'

'I wanted to see how you were.'

'I'm fine, and you've seen, and now you can bugger off.'

That's my girl, I thought, and smiled loopily. 'You haven't changed.'

'That shows how much you know. I'm learning Spanish. I'm taking riding lessons. I'm teaching English. I've got friends here.'

'I'm glad,' I said. Mentally I had already accepted failure and was tiptoeing away. I can't compete, I thought. I just can't compete at the level that matters. 'I just wanted to be sure.'

She didn't soften. 'How did you find me?'

'A private detective. Not a very good one. It's taken him more than a month to track you down.'

'Sorry you wasted your money,' she said, not looking in the slightest bit penitent.

'Oh, I wouldn't say that.' My smile was only just holding up. 'Now I can draw a line under things.'

Her slight tan accentuated her cat's eyes. 'Did bugger-lugs get you?'

'As a matter of fact, he did.'

'That was me, wasn't it? I dropped you in it.'

I hastened to reassure her. 'You did what was right. I'm only glad that you got out of it in one piece.'

'What about you?'

'A third party sorted out our differences. Fortunately, the decision went in my favour.'

She examined me intently, then turned away and stared out to sea. 'I don't want to know. I read things in the paper –about that man Style and some bloke called Holloway who got murdered.' She studied me as if I was a problem she didn't quite know how to deal with. 'Anyway, here you are.'

'Here I am.'

Curiosity softened her stance. 'Does that mean you finally met up with the Eleanor woman?'

'Finally and briefly.' I had no wish to talk about it. 'It didn't lead anywhere.'

'I could have told you that.'

I had an awful feeling that if I stood here much longer, I was going to blub, which wouldn't do at all. I made a show of looking at my watch. 'Well then, I'd better be off. I have to get back to Madrid.'

'What to do?'

'Live my life. What else? Goodbye, Steph.'

She ignored my hand. 'Nicky said you brought me some flowers.'

I made an apologetic gesture. 'They didn't last.'

'I'm not bothered.'

'Well,' I said, and began to walk away, each step taking an age.

'Oi! You owe me.'

My feet seemed to be shod with lead. 'I know.'

'So what are you going to do about it?'

'Look,' I said with a grimace, 'I'm rather pushed for . . . '

She poked me firmly in the ribs. 'I'm talking about the dance you promised.'

When I turned, the haze seemed to be rolling off the sea, leaving it an invigorating blue. My voice shook. 'I don't want to talk myself out of it, but for your own sake, it might be better if you didn't keep me to my word.'

She gave me her mature stare. 'You really got shot of the lot who were after you?'

It wasn't a question I could answer with certainty. 'As clear as I can be.'

'Well, you must be pretty light on your toes then.'

'There was a large element of luck.'

'Luck counts.'

'Does that mean . . . ?'

She shook her head. 'You're going to have to work a lot harder. For a start, you can tell me why you really came chasing after me.'

'As I told you,' I began, and then I looked into her face and saw the prompt in her eyes and realised there was only one answer, only one chance, even though it wasn't one I could swear on oath. 'Because I love you, Steph.'

'Don't be soft. You hardly know me.'

'But what I know, I love.'

She took it very calmly, merely nodding as if she was weighing my declaration against a lot of other factors, some plus, some minus. 'You looked after me,' she said. 'Well, most of the time you did. No one's done that before.' Her shrewd green eyes made a final evaluation. 'I reckon I'll take a chance.'

She consented to let me take her in my arms and for a long time I didn't have to put anything into words.

'I was dead worried about you,' she said, her voice muffled against my chest.

'Me too. I thought I'd lost you for good.'

'Well,' she said, her voice muffled against my chest, 'what goes round, comes round.' Her face turned up in inquiry. 'Is that silly?'

'No,' I said, and squeezed Steph as if I was holding on to luck itself. 'Just don't go betting your life on it.'